Order of the Green Rose

by George F. Vohs

PublishAmerica
Baltimore

First printing

This is a work of fiction set in a background of history. Public personages both living and dead may appear in the story under their right names. Scenes and dialogue involving them with fictitious characters are of course invented. Any other usage of real people's names is coincidental. Any resemblance of the imaginary characters to actual persons, living or dead, is entirely coincidental.

ISBN: 1-4241-3506-0
PUBLISHED BY PUBLISHAMERICA, LLLP
www.publishamerica.com
Baltimore

Printed in the United States of America

Table of Contents

I. Background

Ever since the creation, the world has been in a constant turmoil between church and state, with both sides claiming victories and experiencing defeats down through the centuries. Often these conflicts end up in violent wars which claim the lives of both the innocent and guilty.

From a political perspective, war is often the culmination of political policies which fail or which are so adverse that they cannot be accepted by one side or the other. And, throughout our history, the church has often played either an active or a sub-rosa role in such events. And, so it continues even to this day.

This tale takes place just prior to what was termed the ***Wars of the Roses*** which happened in England during the glory days of the Middle Ages—about 1450-1490—although its beginnings date far earlier than that. I suppose one could push the beginnings of this story as far back as Peter and the formation of the church itself, based upon a perusal of early church history.

The church was involved in its long struggle for supremacy over the dictates of the various Kings or Emperors when one of the greatest of the Roman pontiffs was elevated to the office of Pope in 1073. His name was Hildebrand (Hellebrand) signifying either "a bright flame" or a "brand of hell," depending upon whether he was loved or hated. He was known as Pope St. Gregory VII. **(1)**

It is important for the reader to understand how Gregory VII ascended to the highest office in the church. It is this experience and background that led directly to the formation of the ***Order of the Green Rose***—the subject of this publication.

Hildebrand was born between 1020 and 1025 and his early years are quite obscure. It is said his father was a carpenter or a peasant depending upon whom you would believe. His mother is unknown. He was sent to Rome at a young age to be educated in the monastery of Santa Maria on the Aventine Hill where his maternal uncle, Laurentius, presided as abbot. He subsequently became a Benedictine monk at Rome. He soon entered the service of John Gratian, Archpriest of San Giovanni by the Latin Gate. On Gratian's elevation to the papacy as Gregory VI, he became his chaplain. **(1)**

When Gregory VI was deposed as pope, Hildebrand went into exile with him in Cologne and remained there until Gregory's death in 1047. He was created a cardinal-subdeacon by Pope Leo IX and appointed administrator of the Patrimony of St. Peter's where he restored to the church property which had been diverted into the hands of Roman nobility and the Normans and rebuilt the revenues of the Holy See whose treasury had been depleted. **(1)**

In 1054 he was sent to France as papal legate. It was there he learned of the death of Leo IX and spent the next 11 months in securing the appointment of Gebhard, Bishop of Eichstadt, as Pope Victor II.

During the reign of this pope, Hildebrand was sent on several negotiating missions of importance to the church where he was called on to use both his skills and guile to defeat schemes, one of which secured the election of Gerard, Bishop of Florence, to the papacy as Nicholas II. **(1)**

The two most important transactions of this pontificate—Nicholas II—were a celebrated decree of election by which the power of choosing the pope was vested in the college of cardinals and an alliance with the Normans secured by the Treaty of Meifi in 1059. Both were in a large measure achievements of Hildebrand. By this time Nicholas II had raised him to the office of Archdeacon of the Holy Roman Church. The succeeding pope, Alexander II, made him Chancellor of the Apostolic See. **(1)**

Thus, when Alexander II died, Hildebrand, who had been the most prominent figure in the church for some twenty years, chiefly instrumental in the selection of her rulers, who had inspired and given purpose to her policies, and who had been steadily developing her sovereignty and purity, was elected pope and took the name Gregory VII in 1073. He sought and received the approval of King Henry IV of Germany for his appointment despite announcement of the reforms he sought to install. **(1)**

There is little doubt that Gregory VII fully appreciated the problems of the church and the office to which he ascended. The Christian world was in a deplorable condition and undergoing a period when society in Europe and all existing institutions seemed doomed to utter destruction and ruin. In writing to his friend, Abbot Hugh of Cluny, Gregory lamented the unhappy state of the Church in the following terms:

"The Eastern Church has fallen away from the Faith and is now assailed on every side by infidels. Wherever I turn my eyes—to the west, to the north, or to the south—I find everywhere bishops who have obtained their office in an irregular way, whose lives and conversation are strangely at variance with their sacred calling; who go through their duties not for the love of Christ but from motives of worldly gain. There are no longer princes who set God's honor before their own selfish ends, or who allow justice to stand in the way of their ambition....And those among whom I live—Romans, Lombards, and Normans—are, as I have often told them, worse than Jews or Pagans." (Greg. VII, Registr., 1.II, ep. Xlix). **(1)**

Gregory VII made every effort to stamp out of the Church the problems he faced. He traveled extensively and concluded treaties to defend the pope and property of the Holy See and was determined to deliver the Oriental Christians from the oppression of the Seljuk Turks via a crusade. To this end he tried to rally the support of the faithful to rescue their Eastern brethren, but the project met with indifference. As a result he set about a reformation of the clergy and followed up his decrees by sending legates into all quarters, fully empowered to depose immoral and simoniacal ecclesiastics. **(1)**

King Henry IV continued to oppose or ignore the papal decrees and even attempted to dispose Gregory VII. In turn the pope excommunicated Henry and all his ecclesiastical supporters, and released his subjects from their oath of allegiance in accordance with the usual political procedures of the age. **(1)**

Thus, the power struggle between the church and the royalty continued.

Somewhere in the vast archives of the Vatican probably lies an unnoticed paper, signed by Pope Gregory VII, and properly witnessed, but without the usual leaden seal, which establishes the **Order of the Green Rose**. There is evidence that during the Middle Ages there was an abundance of forgeries, of all kinds, exercised over the authenticity of papal Bulls, royal charters, and other instruments. It is known that Gregory VII refrained from attaching the leaden seal to a Bull for fear it should fall into unscrupulous hands and be used for fraudulent purposes. **(2)**

There is also the problem of secrecy. There can be little doubt that the **Order of the Green Rose** was created in complete secrecy. And, that it was actually created, stands witness to the fact that it received papal funding then—and may still be receiving it even now. It is thought that such funding may even have come out of the private funds available to the pope, himself, and didn't go through the ordinary channels of the Holy See. But there is no evidence to confirm that procedure.

That the pope would carry such power as to create the **Order of the Green Rose** comes as a basis for justification of the church itself. It is said that the church is a perfect society. She is not dependent on the permission of the state for her existence, but holds her charter from God. As a perfect society she has a right to all those means which are necessary for the attaining of her end. **(3)** It is assumed by some that the **Order of the Green Rose** was established as an Order of Chivalry directly under Papal protection.

Two such Orders are known today as the *Sovereign Military Hospitaller Order of Malta*, and the *Equestrian Order of the Holy Sepulcher*. These Orders are under the protection of His Holiness as Supreme Pontiff and are not considered to be wards of the Vatican State. The Order of Malta is a sovereign independent entity in International Law which enjoys mutual diplomatic relations with sixty-seven sovereign states, in addition to being an Observer Member of the United Nations. The Grand Master of this order is elected by the professed, religious members of the Order and serves for life. His election must be approved by the Supreme Pontiff. The Grand Master of the Holy Sepulcher, however, is appointed directly by the pope and serves at the pleasure of the Pontiff. **(11)**

Among the other powers of the pope, as regards the **Order of the Green Rose**, are that he dispenses the treasury of the Church and the grant of plenary indulgences is reserved to him, he can legislate for the whole Church with or without the assistance of a general council, he has full authority to interpret, alter, and abrogate both his own laws and those established by his predecessors, and he can dispense individuals from the obligation of all purely ecclesiastical laws granting privileges and exemptions in their regard. **(3)**

Also, as the supreme governor of the church, the pope has authority over all appointments to its offices including the approval of new religious orders, and can, if he sees fit, exempt them from the authority of local ordinaries. And, although certain titles and insignia have over the spans of time become assigned to the pope alone, the phrase *Servus servorum Dei*—Servant of the Servants of God—is an entirely papal title yet once was applied to others. **(3)**

Servus servorum Dei is the motto of the **Order of the Green Rose** although it does not appear on the Order's shield or banner.

Pope Gregory VII and his reformation efforts led to the "Conflict of Investitutes," a struggle between the popes and the German kings Henry IV and Henry V during the period 1075-1122 and, while the prohibition of investiture occasioned the conflict, the real issue was whether the imperial or the papal power was to be supreme in Christendom. **(4)**

The powerful pope sought to realize the Kingdom of God on earth under the guidance of the papacy. As successor to the Apostles of Christ, he claimed supreme authority in both spiritual and secular affairs. In seemed, as the successor of Peter, he could only act according to the dictates of justice, goodness, and truth. It was in this spirit he claimed for the papacy the supremacy over emperor, kings, and princes. **(4)**

Of course that did not sit well with the emperors, kings and princes for

"Investiture" at this period of time meant that on the death of a bishop or abbot, the king was accustomed to select a successor and to bestow on him the ring and staff.

Since the time of Otto the Great (936-972) the bishops had been princes of the empire, had secured many privileges, and had become to a great extent feudal lords over great districts of the imperial territory. The control of these great lands, of both economic and military power, was for the king a matter of importance impacting the core existence of his imperial authority. **(4)**

The pope's object was to save the Church from the dangers that arose from the undue influence of the laity, and especially of the king, in strictly ecclesiastical affairs. The king, on the other hand, considered he was contending for the rights of civil government which controlled his supreme authority. **(4)** Needless, to say a great political battle ensued with both sides trying to eliminate the other.

It was into this fray that Pope Gregory VII created and enlisted the aid of the **Order of the Green Rose**. Based on his background in politics before he was elected pope, Gregory knew the value of sending representatives openly, and in secret, to assess and influence the ultimate political and military outcomes—hopefully in favor of the papacy.

There are some suggestions that the **Order of the Green Rose** was so successful in its quests on behalf of the papacy that it still exists, in some form, today.

The selection of a green rose to identify this Order is also important to this story. *Rosa chinensis viridiflora* is a chance mutation of the rose identified officially before 1856, and introduced into culture in 1856, but its exact origins are still unknown. The strange blooms are made entirely of sepals rather than petals. It seems as though it forgot to make petals and simply used the sepals instead. In the real world it seems to have evolved from *Slater's Crimson China* rose as they share common growth habit. It is a twiggy shrub that branches freely, forming a small, tidy bush of about 3 feet in height. It is not hardy in cold climates and is known to die back to the ground in some climates. Foliage is a bright clear green with a hint of red in its young leaves. It is also disease resistant. **(5)**

What better symbol, and symbolization reigned supreme in the Middle

Ages, could there be for a secret society. A rose of unknown origin, not recognized at the time, with blooms unlike any other rose, and never fully developed into full blossom so that it could be identified. It hugs the ground to remain inconspicuous and even seems to die out at times, but resurges with renewed vigor when needed. Further, it cannot be destroyed by internal disease. Could there be a better weapon for waging a political war?

Followers of history will know that *The Eleusinian Mysteries*, the greatest of all the ancient secret societies, established one of the highest known standards of morality and ethics unlike the obscene rites later practiced by Bacchanalia and Dionysia. These mysteries made great use of symbolism with father, mother, and child constituting the natural trinity. The Pythagorean and other schools of philosophy conceived the one divine nature of God to manifest itself in the threefold aspect of Father, Mother, and Child. These constituted the Divine Family, whose dwelling place is creation. **(6)**

The cross, itself, is considered the oldest of phallic symbols and the lozenge-shaped windows of cathedrals seem to be proof that yonic symbols have survived the destruction of the pagan Mysteries. Only those conversant with the secret language of antiquity are capable of understanding the divine significance of these and other yonic symbols. **(6)**

Flowers were chosen as symbols for many reasons. The great variety of flora made it possible to find some plant or flower which would be a suitable figure for nearly any abstract quality or condition. A flower may be chosen because of some myth of its origin, the particular environment in which it thrived, its significant shape, or because of its unusual characteristics.

Of all symbolic flowers, the lotus blossom of India and Egypt and the rose of the Rosicrucian's are probably the most important and, in symbolism, these two flowers are considered identical. The rose and the lotus are yonic emblems, signifying primarily the maternal creative mystery. The Rosicrucian's used a garland of roses to signify the spiritual vortices, referred to in the Bible as the seven lamps of the candlestick and the seven churches of Asia. **(6)**

In the Hindu philosophy, each petal of the lotus bears a certain symbol which gives an added clue to the meaning of the flower. As the lotus exists in three elements (earth, water, and air) so man lives in three worlds—material, intellectual, and spiritual. Thus, the rose and the lotus represent spiritual enfoldment and attainment. When the flower had nine petals, it was symbolic of man, twelve petals was symbolic of the universe and the gods, 7 petals was symbolic of the planets and the law, and five petals was symbolic of the senses and the Mysteries. The heraldic rose of the Middle Ages generally has either five or ten petals showing its relationship to the spiritual mystery of man through the Pythagorean pentad and decad. **(6)**

The rose symbol in Christian history—in this case a blue rose—is also symbolic of Mary Magdalene. The rose also is a mark of the 7th son and the blessings of hope and joy.

Thus, again, it would seem the rose would be an ideal symbol for the **Order of the Green Rose**.

The War of the Roses, the political era when this story takes place, is not connected with the origins of the **Order of the Green Rose** and only incidental to the involvement of the Order. However, there was one adaptation of the rose symbol of the Order during this time and that was the coloration of one leaf of the rose white and the other leaf red to symbolize the two sides in the war. It is believed that this change was made deliberately by the Order to demonstrate to both sides a greater power or simply to lend more mystery and intrigue to the battlefield where such colors were so significant.

Chapter 1—A Troubled World

When Tommaso Parentucelli, an Italian intellectual, was elevated to the papacy in March of 1447, and assumed the name of Pope Nicholas V, he inherited a troubled world.

In 1450 Pope Nicholas V proclaimed a Jubilee to honor the last submission of the antipopes, Felix V, and the recognition of the papal rights concerning the appointment of bishops and other officers of the church. Vast multitudes flocked to Rome in the first part of the year, but the hot weather brought on an onslaught of the plague which panicked the pope and he left Rome and visited various castles in an effort to avoid the infection. When the pestilence abated he returned to Rome. **(7)**

As with previous Jubilees, vast sums of money poured into the treasury of the Church, and the Pope used the Jubilee as proof that Rome was the center towards which all Christendom was drawn. At its conclusion, Nicholas dispatched legates into the different countries to assert his authority and to bring about the reform of abuses. Cardinal Nicholas of Cusa, one of the most devout and learned men of his day, was sent to North Germany and England. **(7)**

And, while these men held provincial and other synods and assemblies of the regular clergy, in which wholesome decrees were made, word finally reached the Pope that Cardinal Nicholas never made it all the way to England.

In the meantime, the Ottoman Turks captured Constantinople and ended the Byzantine Empire on May 29, 1453. Students in Paris, mostly foreigners, were rioting due to harassment by authorities. The final battle of the 100 Years War took place on June 17, 1453, when Talbot was defeated and slain at Castillon in Gascony. **(7)**

In England the two most powerful personages were Cardinal Beaufort and the Duke of Gloucester. The Cardinal was promoting the marriage of King Henry VI to the Princess Margaret of Anjou, a proposal strongly objected to by the Duke. After the marriage took place, a bitterness sprung up between Queen Margaret, who felt slighted, and the Duke, an equally proud nobleman. As a result, two factions were formed with Cardinal Beaufort leading one side and the Duke of Gloucester on the other side. **(8)**

The Cardinal was supported by the Duke of Suffolk and Queen Margaret and, representing the king, gained mastery over his opponent. In a plot to rid the opposition, the wife of Gloucester was accused of witchery and banished from the kingdom. Then the duke was charged with high treason, thrown into prison, and murdered in his bed. This bloody deed aroused the long slumbering hatred against the House of Lancaster. Although the House of Lancaster was represented by a weak and peaceable king, it was held responsible for the work of the Queen and her confederates. **(8)**

The issue came to a head when a state secret was revealed about an agreement whereby the father of Queen Margaret was to receive the French provinces of Maine and Anjou as a bonus in exchange for allowing his daughter to marry Henry VI. This enraged the Duke of York, now regent of France, and it was known he would never approve such a plan. Thus it became necessary for Margaret and the Duke of Suffolk to get the Duke of York "out of the way." They did this by depriving him of the regency and appointing the Duke of Somerset in his stead. **(8)**

The Duke of York, who had remained loyal to the House of Lancaster, was justly offended. He rekindled a desire of his own claim to the crown, supported by general sentiment in the kingdom. When Parliament assembled in 1450, Suffolk was charged with treason and imprisoned in the Tower. However, the queen's influence was sufficient to reduce the penalty to banishment for five years. However, he was pursued, overtaken at Dover, and slain. **(8)**

The kingdom now became a scene of confusion and the stage was set for the Wars of the Roses.

When the Pope's legate failed to reach England, and upon learning of the problems between the Church and state, Pope Nicholas V knew he had to take some action in order to reserve the authority of the Church.

Sometime in the latter part of 1450, a boat bearing a white flag with a triple gold crown, set sail from Naples via the Balearic Islands, through the straights of Cadiz, along the east coast of Portugal and Spain, through the Bay of Biscay, along the coast of France, crossed the English channel, and sailed up the west coast of England, following familiar and well-traveled trade routes of the Middle Ages.

Aboard the ship was a special, trusted legate representing the pope, himself. He had made the arduous journey with the fastest speed possible encountering some delays for re-provisioning the ship, and for entering selected ports in Portugal, Spain, and France where several individuals were clandestinely summoned on board. One stop was made in England where three trusted associates of the legate were placed on shore with horses and equipment all armed with special messages from the Pope. And, somewhere along the voyage, the pennant bearing the triple crown was replaced by the flag of Italy.

The ship finally entered a small harbor, somewhere on the west coast of Scotland, arriving on a cold, wintry day in 1451. Upon reaching the calmer waters of the inner harbor, the captain ordered the flag of Italy struck and a bright yellow banner with a single green rose was run up the mast.

A lookout, posted at the top of a cliff overlooking the harbor, soon reported the arrival of the ship flying the green rose. Not long after that, three mule-drawn carts crossed a long drawbridge, spanning a deep chasm, and headed down a narrow hand-built road to the harbor where the ship was docked.

Chapter 2—Abbey Magdalena Rosa

The three mule carts struggled back up the cliff from the ship heavily laden with both men and supplies. In truth, they would make several more trips to the ship and back before their work was done.

None of the occupants of the carts, except the drivers, had ever seen the Abbey Magdalena Rosa and not many outsiders had ever had the privilege of entering its fortified walls. The abbey was under the immediate jurisdiction of The Holy See in Rome which provided its financing. The bastion had been attacked in its early days on two occasions, but those were quelled quickly each time by the mounted religious knights inside.

That it was situated in an excellent position, with only two easily defended approaches, was a tribute to the tall, dark-haired man, dressed in traditional monk regalia, who greeted the wagons at the entrance to the abbey. Those occupants, who were alert, noticed the green rose emblem embedded in the huge wooden doors that were opened at the approach of the wagons after they crossed the drawbridge.

Through the entranceway was a grand courtyard in which various activities were underway including training in marital arts, weaponry, and—of all things—diplomacy. Surrounding the courtyard were the walls of the various structures of the abbey arranged so that they were incorporated between the outer and inner walls in a five-sided pentad.

The wagons were pulled to a halt inside the courtyard and the guests were invited to step down by the tall monk. The legate from the pope was the first to step forward.

"Sire, I bring you greetings from *Pontifex Maximus.*"

"Welcome to our humble abbey, your highness. It has been sometime since we've had such a distinguished visitor. And," stretching out his arms, "let me welcome your distinguished friends to our humble home."

"We have come a long way to see you, but I pray you have time to show us to our quarters so we can refresh ourselves before we broach the manner for our appearance," the legate said.

"Of course," the monk replied. "We will have dinner in the Great Hall after Chapel. After we have given our thanks to God and eaten our repast, we can begin our discussions. I will show you to your rooms and our servants will see to your needs. They will summon you in time for Chapel."

"We are very grateful," the legate said.

Without further hesitation, the monk turned and led the way over to one side of the courtyard and entered an arched doorway leading them down a set of stairs to a long corridor with a series of doors along each side.

"This is your room," he said to the legate. "You others can take any of the rooms along this corridor that suits your purpose. We are several feet under the earth and the temperature here is a constant sixty-five degrees so you will be comfortable. There is a communal bath at the far end of the corridor or you may take individual baths in your room. Clean robes and sandals are available in each room. Just ask the servants inside for whatever else you are in need of." With that he turned and strode back up the stairs.

The Chapel service was unusually crowded that night after all the guests had arrived. The tall monk invited the legate to lead the service and stood by to assist. After the service, which included several chants, the group moved across a corridor and entered the Great Hall.

There was a difference in this Great Hall from those found in most of the castles in Europe. There were huge fireplaces, with chimneys built into the walls, on all four sides of the chamber and no elevated platforms at either end. Tables, with white linen cloths, were set up in the center of the room and huge chandeliers were hung from the high ceiling and fueled by natural gas. The floor was solid stone.

When asked about the flames, the monk replied: "When we were digging out our subterranean chambers we accidentally discovered a natural pipe leading downward. One of the digging tools struck a spark and we nearly lost several of our workers before we discovered how to cap, and subsequently put to use this wonderful discovery. Now we are using pipes made of copper, from our own mines, to distribute the gas to various parts of the abbey for lighting, cooking, and heating. You will note the fires in the fireplaces seem to be burning rocks instead of logs. That's because they, too, are fired by the gas."

"How fortunate you are," the legate said.

"We have made some other discoveries, too, that you will need to pass along to His Eminence. I will show you them in the days to come, depending upon how much time you have to spend in our house. I am particularly enamored with one discovery we came on by accident. We have both copper and iron ore mines and we process those metals in the same shop. One of our workers accidentally dropped a cauldron of molten copper on a form where iron was being molded. We thought we had ruined the iron mold, but when it cooled we found we couldn't dent it even with a chisel. We experimented with it and now use a combination of the two metals to make all of our arrow points, our swords, lances and other weapons. It is too heavy for armor, but we can make rims for our wagons that seem to last forever," the monk said.

"I'm impressed and it seems I have a lot to learn before I return to Rome. I'm looking forward to it," the legate responded.

At that time a row of servants, dressed in white, entered the Great Hall with platters of meats, vegetables, soups, and breads and the meal began. Wine and ale were provided along with water to help wash down the food.

"The water comes from the mountain streams and is as pure as can be," the monk explained. "Most of our people prefer it to the wine and ale although both are of excellent quality and made with the same water."

As the meal proceeded, and it was excellent, the legate brought up the people who had arrived with him.

"You have noticed that I brought several people along with me. Pope Nicholas decided the task he is giving you will need more than one set of hands to accomplish. He has sent some personally selected, skilled members of your Order to accompany you should that be your wish. He conveyed to me that he has complete faith in your abilities and loyalty and it will be up to you whether these people stay and assist you or go home with me," the legate said. "In keeping with the laws of your Order, there will be no introductions of these people, but I am to assure you they have been tested in the past and have proved worthy of their rank."

"I have noticed they seem to be fully aware of their surroundings and alert to any unusual things. I will test them on their negotiating skills and their battle prowess before I decide. And, I will listen to our leader's instructions before determining how many I might need," the monk said. "If you have had enough to eat, I suggest we retire to my chambers and we can begin our work. The others are free to roam the abbey as they will until we have need of them. My assistant will provide them directions and information as they wish."

The legate briefly relayed the information to the guests and he and the monk retired to private quarters to examine their task.

When they were ushered into the library of the abbey, the legate was enthralled by the shelves of rare books and documents. "You know that Pope Nicholas is an avid collector of books and artwork. He might be envious of your collection if he knew of its existence," the legate said.

"His eminence is welcomed to visit at any time," the monk said. "However, it would be hard to educate our monks if they had to visit these books in Rome."

The legate laughed. "I understand and will say nothing of them. If you will send a messenger to my room to bring forth the locked, wooden case with the triple crown insignia, I will be grateful. In the meantime I would like to peruse some of these pages."

"Certainly. I will be just a minute. Would you also care for a glass of wild mountain berry wine? I can guarantee you have tasted nothing like it before," the monk said.

"Excellent. I will look forward to the pleasure," replied the legate.

The wine arrived before the wooden case and both men were enjoying the luxury when a porter entered the room, after knocking, with the object in hand.

"Thank you," said the legate taking the case in hand. He proceeded to retrieve a key from the pocket of his robe and unlock the case. It was full of papers and maps.

"May I first show you my official identification as verified by the papal seal," he said, taking out one parchment roll. He slipped off the gold ribbon around the roll and stretched it out on one of the library desks.

The monk stepped up to the desk and examined the document carefully. It was a simple introduction of the legate written in the pope's own handwriting, signed, witnessed and sealed.

"Congratulations on your office," the monk said. "I know the pope has great faith in you to send you on such an arduous mission and I can see you are welcomed into his confidence."

"Yes, and now this is for you," he said, handing over a sealed packet with the unbroken mark of the pope on top.

"I assume you know the contents of this packet?" the monk asked.

"I know only in general what those instructions are. The pope feels the fewer people that know the complete assignment the better. My mission here was carried out in utmost secrecy as will your mission in England. It will be important that none in England suspect that the pope is behind your efforts. For this reason you will be operating under the colors of your Order and not the papacy," the legate said.

"Then I shall read this packet in private, after we have finished our conversation," the monk said.

"Do you have other instructions for me?"

The legate pulled out a small gold key from the case. "This key is your identification badge to all of those who are trusted to provide assistance to you in your quest. And here," he added, "is a map of England showing those places that have agreed to house you and your knights throughout your stay in England. All are considered safe, but unless they produce a matching key, they are not to be trusted."

"Further," he instructed, "there is a key to this key. If you twist this little part here, the handle of the key will separate. Any keys that do not have this feature are obviously fraudulent. You will also note that the handle is attached to a four-inch blade for use in any emergency."

"Wonderful," exclaimed the monk. "What exquisite workmanship." He examined the key closely and tried out the mechanism a couple of times. "I could have used something like this in the past," he added.

"There is one more item of interest in this key," instructed the legate. "If you press on this part of the handle you can release a liquid poison that is contained in the handle. You are instructed to use this opportunity only as a last resort."

"I understand," replied the monk.

"I also have the latest maps we have been able to obtain for the territories in England that are most likely to be involved in your task. You can examine them at your leisure and perhaps with those you decide to accompany you. And, the last thing I have for you is this summary of events, as we know them, which have led up to the current problems in England facing the Church. It would be dangerous for this document to fall into the hands of the nobles, so I suggest you leave it here when you depart. You are free to provide this knowledge to your men, but the information in the pope's packet is to remain with you only," the legate said.

"I have also brought you a chest of 'coin of the realm' which we have gathered and should be sufficient for your needs. If not, we will rely on you to use your key and resourcefulness to obtain more. If there are to be any need of large bribes to achieve your goals, we have provided a special cache, the location of which is within the pope's documents to you. Again, the pope is relying on your discretion in the use of these funds," the legate added.

"With that, I'll shall take my leave and return to my rooms. We will meet again tomorrow and I will endeavor to answer any questions you may have after you digest all of this information. And, on behalf of his eminence, I wish you God speed in your quest and tell you that I have been instructed to stand by in the event you have need of my ship to reach England."

The monk and the legate shook hands before the legate took his leave.

"My man is outside waiting to show you back to your rooms or to conduct a tour of the abbey if that is your wish," the monk said.

"Thank you," the legate said, "I appreciate your kindness."

After the legate had departed, the monk was wrapped in thought. He then read the lengthy document outlining the problems with the English crown versus the Church. After that, he was ready to open the packet from the pope.

Chapter 3—Preparing for Action

The next morning, after a breakfast of cold cereals and fruit juices, the monk invited all of his guests to a formal meeting of the **Order of the Green Rose**. The one exception to this invitation was the Pope's legate, who was not a member of the Order.

"You will have to excuse us for a time," the monk told the legate. "I must reassure myself that all of the people you brought are true members of our Order. As soon as we have finished the formal business of our meeting, we will adjourn to a separate room and you will be invited to rejoin us."

"I understand completely," the legate said. "Besides it will give me more time to peruse the volumes in your library if you would be so kind."

"Absolutely, and you are welcome to the facilities. I will send a man to get you when we are ready. That's when we will discuss our upcoming venture," the monk said.

With that the monk announced his intentions to the assembly and asked that the legate be escorted to the library and requested that any of his needs be attended to. He then led the remaining group through a doorway in the Great Hall and down several flights of narrow stairs until they were well underground. Eventually he arrived at a door where two guards were posted. On the door, in thick stained glass, was the emblem of the green rose.

The guards stood aside while the monk opened the door. But, instead of entering he stood at one side and shook hands with each of the guests as they entered. He was using a secret handshake known only to members of the Order and each person who entered the room was thus screened as to their membership. Further screenings would occur inside during the rituals practiced at these meetings. It would not be fair to the Order to try and describe the interior furnishings and decorations in this room, but suffice it to say they were elaborate and sacred to the Order. As soon as all had entered the chamber, the door was closed and locked from the inside.

What transpired next we do not know.

As soon as the meeting was over, all of the men filed out of the chamber following the monk, who led them up several flights of stairs to a meeting room. In actuality, this was one of the classrooms built into the abbey and used to instruct candidates for the Order. The monk then sent for the legate. Wine and ale were brought in large pitchers and each of the members were allowed to help themselves to the refreshments.

As soon as the Pope's legate arrived, the monk called the meeting to order.

"All of you know, or have guessed, that you have come to our abbey for a special purpose. The fact that many of you sailed here on the Pope's ship has undoubtedly given you notice of how serious this business is. As for my own folks here at the abbey, they will be learning of it at this time, the same as you," he told the forty or so assembled people.

"I have learned that all of you have been knighted and that many of you have served the pope well in the past. I can assure you that the task before us will call on you for all of your skills, your patience, your knowledge, and perhaps your cunning in order for us to be successful. I have great confidence that each of you will carry out your assigned mission, in the spirit of the **Order of the Green Rose**. I have not yet decided which of you will be individual group leaders, but since our quest is in English, and we will have to pass primarily as Englishmen, it is apparent that command of the English language is essential to our success. We will be learning more about each of you, and your individual skills, in the few days to come before we depart. It will be a dangerous mission and secrecy will be paramount to its success. If there are any among you who do not wish to participate in this challenge for whatever reasons, now is the time to speak up and you will be excused without any blemish to your name.

"Seeing no raised hands, I will assume you are all equal to the challenge. Now, I would like to have our honorable legate, who sits at the right hand of our Pope, come forward and brief us as best he can on the necessity of our services," the monk said, gesturing for the legate to come forward.

"Fellow churchmen," the legate began. "It is trying circumstances in Rome that have brought us to this spot on the coast of Scotland. Our Pope is besieged on all sides with forces that would destroy our Church. We have invading Turks on the east and we have feuding nobility on the remaining flanks of our great citadel. You are not the only parts of this Order that have been called upon to serve in these moments of extreme danger.

"But, you certainly are being handed one of the more important and difficult tasks which, as your good monk has said, will surely tax all your skills to the utmost. And, speaking for Pope Nicholas V, I can assure you his Holiness feels you are up to the task or I wouldn't be here before you now.

"I don't know all the details of what you will be expected to do. I only know in general what difficulties you will be facing with the jealousies, corruptions, and misuse of our Church rules that now exist in England. Clear lineage to the throne of England has always been in doubt and it is even more so today.

"I know only that the desires of our Pope are for peace and for the confirmation that the Church is an entity unto itself and not dependent upon the nobility or Kings to decide who should fill our posts. Yea, there is plenty of political intrigue in the Christian world without involving the church in local politics.

"Our Pope, and the predecessors who have gone before him, have had great visions of the world and the role of the church in peace and prosperity. We are prepared to pay the price in men and money to achieve these lofty goals entrusted to us by God. Therefore, it is by the grace of

God and Pope Nicholas V, that your Order once again is called into service.

"The Pope has seen fit to summon some of you from other countries to participate in this quest. But I must tell you that the monk who stands here beside me is the final authority on which of you, or any of you, will go on this journey. He is a wise monk who has served the church, God, and his family well these past few years and I beseech each of you to put your faith and your lives in his hands.

"May God bless each and every one of you and bring you success for His glory."

With that the legate stepped aside.

The monk again stood before the group. "I can tell you now that our job will be to help bring political stability to England and we are to employ whatever means to that end. I have some specific instructions from the pope that I cannot share with you at this time and lack of that knowledge will not have an adverse impact on your assignments.

"Before I commit to those of you who will be accompanying me, I have need to test your fighting skills, your mental prowess, and your ability to turn what comes your way into an advantage for accomplishing your mission instead of an impossible hill to climb. I have arranged several contests, something as knights you are all used to, to see what skills you bring us. It is not proper in these tests to injure, maim or kill your friendly opponent. If you do, you will immediately suffer severe consequences. For the rest of today, you may practice any or all of your fighting skills. I know many of you have spent long days aboard ship so you may need to hone your instincts.

"Tomorrow you will be put to the test by my men, who have been especially trained by me, and I warn you they are in top form. Should you successfully pass that test, you will be divided into groups of three or four and given certain problems to solve. These will be problems where the answer is never clear and much initiative on your part will be needed to solve them. I will give you this much information and that is it takes teamwork to be successful. After that, you will be tested on social and political skills. I can promise you a grueling few days, but you will be glad for them in the end. In our library, under guard, will be this copy of information sent to us by the pope that underlines the political problems we will be facing when we arrive in England. I will expect each of you to read this document thoroughly and be conversant with it before we work on the political strategies in three days time. Any of you who fail to succeed in these rigorous tests will remain behind when we leave, if you are of this abbey, or will board ship and be returned home without any dishonor. Do you have any questions?"

There followed an extensive period of questions and answers by both the legate and the monk mostly about the routines the knights would be facing in the coming days. There were no questions about the assigned quest itself.

The next few days were busy days for everyone at the abbey. At the conclusion of each day's activities, and after the evening Chapel and meal, everyone again assembled in the meeting room and objectively discussed their progress. The monk was pleased to note that, despite the severity of the testing, every one of the knights successfully succeeded in their tasks. There was little socializing after the nightly meetings as everyone was tired and wanted only to seek their beds for the night.

On the fourth day, the group was divided into teams of two. One member of each team was given a task to negotiate while the other member was instructed to obstruct the completion of that task unless outmaneuvered or out thought by his opponent. After the first go around, the teams were mixed and the tasks reversed. It was a grueling day, but a rewarding one for the monk since it showed that these chosen men were exceptional in meeting challenges thrown at them. He concluded to take all thirty-nine of them, and himself.

On the fifth day, they once again assembled in the meeting room after breakfast.

"I want to congratulate each of you. I have watched you work for the past four days trying to find a reason to eliminate each of you on the basis of your failure to rise to the occasions we set before you. I must say that you have astounded me with your skills and I will be proud to be serving with you.

"Based solely on language skills, I appointed myself and nine others to be team leaders. And while this selection in no way indicates the superiority of the team leader, I remind you that each has taken the vow of this Order to serve in whatever capacity he is called upon to serve. Therefore, I want no jealousy or hard feelings among any of you as a result of this selection.

"The legate and I have conferred. Based upon his recommendations and those of my own people, I have arbitrarily assigned each of you to a team. We will have ten teams of four knights each so that, if needed, we will be forty strong in battle along with any locals we may be able to recruit and train and that will be one of the tasks assigned to each team. A copy of this team assignment list will be going back to Rome with the legate so that the Holy Father can appreciate and pray for the service each of you will be giving.

"Further, I have a map, provided by the Holy Father, which shows the safe places in England for each of our groups. I have assigned each group to headquarter in one of these safe places. And there are others in the event one or more of these places is deemed unsuitable. The map also depicts the territorial assignments for each team by the number corresponding to the county or province in England. We have excluded Wales from our activities. I understand that has been assigned to be handled in a different way. I will ask each of you to commit these names and places to memory as this map will not be going to England with us.*

*** Note: See Appendix I for a copy of this map and the team assignments. This map is not an original, but a replica.**

"I have asked His Excellency to post this list and map upon the wall so that each of you can find your team members and locate your initial destination in England. From this point on, except for some joint exercises, you will be working as teams. His Excellency has kindly agreed to delay his departure back to Rome until next week so that we may accompany him as far as the coast of England. I have made arrangements to have good horses waiting for us where we offload the ship. Each of you will be allowed to take one squire, from this abbey, as your personal assistant. As with all of our staff, he will be a skilled archer and warrior regardless of whom you select. I will be taking my personal assistant. I would urge you to treat them as partners in this venture and I can personally assure you of their loyalty to you and to our Order.

"Please take time to review the posted lists, get acquainted with your team members, and maybe do a little research in our library about your headquarters destination. There is a packet of information already assembled for each point on this map. Pay special attention to your team location, but make sure you know about the others, too."

"We will meet here each morning after breakfast and outline a day's activities. I can assure you we will also get in some special military maneuvers and equip each of you with our latest in developed weapons. I will see my team in this room and I suggest each team meet separately in one of the rooms along this corridor making sure to retrieve your destination packet from the library. I would caution you to return those packets to the library at the end of the day."

The meeting was then adjourned and the knights spent the rest of the day getting acquainted with their teammates and studying information on their destinations.

The remainder of the time passed quickly with the days of training and the nights of study. Team members expressed delight with the battlefield maneuvers they learned in conjunction with archers and there was a general air of confidence when it came time to board the ship to leave.

Chapter 4—The Journey to England

When all was said and done, it was a crowded ship that took its leave from the harbor below Abbey Magdalena Rosa. Crammed aboard the ship were forty knights and all their armor and equipment, forty hand-selected squires along with their equipment, the legate and his assistants, the crew of the ship, the three mule carts loaded with equipment and supplies, plus all of the other materials necessary for the campaign.

On top of that it was another blustery day in January of 1451 with the seas high making conditions on the ship deplorable at best. Most of the men, including some of the ship's crew, were seasick. For the first two days of the voyage not much was accomplished. By the third day sea conditions were much improved and life aboard the ship began to return to normal considering the crowded conditions.

The monk and the legate began to brief the seventy-nine other members of the Order, primarily in regard to the doctrines of the Orders they would be encountering upon their arrival and their stay in England. We know that one such session had to do with the Benedictines and another with the Cistercians, an offshoot of the Benedictines. There were also briefings on the landing port, transport to the various assigned abbeys, and customs involved in abbey life in these Orders. Several of the sessions dealt with team assignments and how they were to blend into the countryside and still accomplish their goals.

We can only speculate as to most of what was said at these sessions;

however, some exhaustive research has uncovered much of the information that must have been imparted in order to prepare these individuals for their tasks. Certainly some of these sessions were devoted to the very instructions sent to the monk by the Pope although we cannot be sure of just what this information was. However, we will do our best with the information we have at hand as it is important to the story.

During this time in the high Middle Ages, the church was the main focus of community life. And, although the Abbeys were not "in the middle" of community life, the actions of the monks and friars heavily influenced that life. Abbeys were nearly always self supporting and the inhabitants had to work to maintain themselves and their Order.

"We will be dealing with two Orders," the monk told his associates. "The first is the Order of Benedictine; however, we will have direct dealings with only two of its abbeys. When the Vikings invaded England some 600 years or so ago, religion was nearly wiped out. It took the great Benedictine monk St. Dunstan, Archbishop and advisor to the royal house of Wessex, to revive monasticism. And, while each abbey is an autonomous body, it is tied to other Benedictine communities by a mutual adherence to the 'rule'." **(9)**

At this point the legate stepped forward and indicated that Pope Nicholas V had great faith in the Benedictines knowing that from their ranks have come emperors, kings, dukes, earls, empresses, and queens. He also pointed out that in England, Benedictine monasteries were usually quite wealthy and exerted a great influence on society. "Special envoys," he told the group, "have been sent directly from Rome to these to Benedictine Abbeys and we have been assured of their cooperation." He turned the deck back over to the monk.

"Benedictine life," the monk said, "centers upon liturgical celebration and scholarship. This group copies ancient manuscripts and through its educational efforts, learning has been kept alive in our time. Even today," he said, "there are literally hundreds of Benedictine abbeys located throughout Europe and in foreign lands. I want to assure you that I am personally acquainted with the heads of the two Benedictine houses that will be involved in this venture. I have done them services in the past and they will be eager to return those favors."

He proceeded to brief them on the two Benedictine fortresses that were involved.

"This ship will make landing at Whitby Abbey in Yorkshire. Yorkshire is the headquarters destination of Team #2 although that is not where you will be headquartered. As you know you will be further inland at Byland Abbey which is under the Cistercian Order. We will come to that Order in another session, but you should know that all of our headquarter abbeys are run by the Cistercians. I think the reasons for that will become clearer as we proceed. There is one exception and that is the Abbey at St. Albans, to which my team #6 has been assigned. It is under Benedictine control, but it is central to our efforts. I will talk about that next after we finish with Whitby."

Once again the legate stepped forward. "Let me assure you again that St. Albans has been contacted and agrees to assist us in every way along with Whitby," he said.

"Whitby Abbey," the monk continued, "is located along the east coast of England in Yorkshire. There is a safe, all weather, landing area there just inside the mouth of the River Esk. The Abbey also controls a small village at the landing area where we will receive whatever assistance we need. This is an old Scottish heritage area and I am personally acquainted with many of the members of this Order who have pledged their allegiance in this matter. Those of you who want to quickly retain your land legs will find the 199 steps leading up to the abbey a chore, but you will quickly become acclimated to the land again by the time you reach the top.

"We will also pick up our horses there. They have been sent from the nearby Cistercian Abbey of Jervaulx, also an area where I am acquainted due to past experiences. Let me assure you these will be some of the finest horses in England and you and your squires will be proud to have them. The monks of Jervaulx are famous for their breeding of horses and we have been promised the finest of their lot. They have been schooling them for the past few weeks awaiting our arrival. I sent word to them prior to our departure of our likely arrival date, so I'm confident our mounts will be waiting. And, I would remind your Highness here of the obligation to pay for these horses," the monk said.

The legate again stepped forward. "I have been assured via the master of the ship that arrived in Scotland a few days before we departed that payment already has been made. In fact, he said, considerable payments were made to all of the abbeys and safe houses at the time we secured their pledges to help us," he said.

"Thank you," the monk said. "It is better to have a well-fed ally on our side than one who is hungry for his supper."

"Without going into unneeded detail, suffice it to say Whitby Abbey has seen its share of turmoil since it founding in 657. As I said earlier it has a lot of Scottish tradition and has been heavily involved in the English politics since its beginnings. It is for that reason it will not be one of our main headquarters, but you can consider it a safe house in any emergency in addition to those we have already fixed. I will tell you that my own father is buried on the present grounds of the abbey. He escaped the black death only to be struck down in a building accident," the monk said.

"I can assure you that our arrival will be quietly celebrated by the monks in residence and will be a welcome break in their daily lives although I would plead to you to be as unobtrusive as possible in order to maintain their good will. We will be there only long enough to get each of your teams outfitted, provide the necessary travel papers, and help you on your way," the monk said. "I'm also hoping we can purchase seven more carts, along with animals to pull them, so we can equip each team with an easier job of transporting its equipment and goods. That may take more time, but we will send each team out as soon as it is equipped so that we all won't be on the roads at the same time."

"Do any of you have any questions?" the monk asked.

"Where will we be sleeping and eating?" asked one of the squires.

"Good question," the monk replied. "Most of these abbeys have guest quarters for nobility and their servants. The knights, as befitting their status, will occupy the spaces for the nobility. You squires will be housed in the laity quarters, but I have been assured they are spacious and clean. We will all eat together in the refractory. And," he added, "that reminds me that each team will be supplied with spare food and blankets in the event it has to camp out while on the road to its destination. Your leader will be supplied with money and we encourage you to stay at the various inns and pick up the 'talk' along the way. A party of eight is sometimes difficult for some inns to accommodate, so you likely will have to split up for sleeping. You can make your own arrangements as you go."

There being no further questions, the monk continued with his explanations.

"The second major Benedictine site we will be using is St. Albans just outside of London a few miles. Since this is a focal point along the normal trade and travel routes, it is central to our efforts. Sooner or later most of the 'talk' in England reaches this site. I am also a personal friend of the bishop of St. Albans and, in fact, we are distantly related. The abbey has a large membership of monks with several hundred volunteers, some of whom will be placed at our disposal. The bishop maintains close ties with both the King and the Papacy and will be a great source of information for us as well as provide introductions as needed. This Abbey will be used as a 'clearinghouse' for our efforts and I will send word to each of you who can be entrusted to receive your information. In all likelihood the Abbey will be a central meeting place for all of us periodically. It has large landholdings and good accommodations in unobtrusive buildings away from the places where nobility often comes to seek solace. Pilgrims come to the Abbey from all over England to seek cures and to give thanks. It will be a great source of information and it is used to seeing strangers within its famous marketplace and walls of the Abbey.

"Besides, there is something sporting about establishing a base in the heart of the political intrigue in the country and so close to the royal houses," the monk laughed. "There is also a chapel there devoted to our Saint of the Blue Rose," he added.

"I have asked his Excellency to visit with you a bit about the second Order with which we will be more intimately involved—The Cistercian Order," the monk said, stepping aside. They were meeting on the "gun deck" of the ship so there was very little room to maneuver with the seventy-nine attendees sitting on the floor or gun platforms.

"The Cistercian Order is the most important of the new religious orders which have developed in western Europe since the late 11th century," the legate said. "It began in response to the movements for reform in our church. It has spread rapidly from its origin in Burgundy as some of you here know, I am sure. The monks in the Order own no personal property and work with their hands to support themselves. All successful monasteries have depended upon benefactors to donate enough lands to support the community. It is regulated by statues produced in Burgundy. This is the only Order emerging since the 12th century that has made a long-lasting impact on Britain and it was, in fact, in Yorkshire where it first took hold in England. **(10)**

"They are conspicuous in their dress with white habits and you will have to wear those at all times when you are on the grounds of the abbeys. They are fairly Spartan in their furnishings and their food, but there will be plenty for all provided by their personal labors. They have a written Constitution—*The Carta Caritatis* (Charter of Charity)—and are centrally controlled by means of an annual meeting of the abbots. This governmental system has been approved by papal seal," he said. **(10)**

"Members of this Order are extremely 'forward thinking'. It was from their stronghold in Yorkshire that the Order expanded throughout Britain. The eight original Abbeys in Yorkshire drew recruits and benefactors from neighboring towns and villages. In the early days they were particularly noted for sheep farming and extensive contribution to the wool trade. The Cistercians are a reformed Benedictine sect and were founded at Citeaux, Burgundy in 1098 by St. Stephen Harding, an Englishman. Most of their monasteries are located in wild, remote regions, which serves well your cause of secrecy. And, that is precisely why we are using this Order," the legate said. "With that, I will turn your attention back to our grand monk who, I understand, will review the information about the Abbeys to which you are assigned."

The monk struggled again to his feet on the deck of the swaying ship. "I have been informed by the first mate that we expect to make landfall off the mouth of the Esk River sometime late tomorrow evening. We will enter the river after dark and offload at the landing. The captain will signal the Abbey of our arrival before we enter the river. God willing, tomorrow night we shall sleep on dry land."

A warm cheer was roused from the seventy-nine men who had been in cramped quarters for what seemed like an eternity to some of them.

"You will only need to carry your personal gear off the ship with you.

The monks from the Abbey have been instructed to unload the ship and transport all of our equipment and other freight up to the Abbey—no small task, I might add. The ship carrying his Excellency, who has been so kind as to expedite our transport to this venture, will slip its cables and be at sea before daylight.

"Now, let's get back to talking about the Abbeys. You will find the Cistercian Abbeys are somewhat different in their organization from our Abbey in Scotland. Most of them are constructed on the same scale, but may have minor differences. I have taken the liberty of drawing a sketch of the Byland Abbey which will be occupied by Team 2, because it is one that I'm most familiar with. If I can get our learned legate here to help, I will unroll and hold it up so that all can see," the monk said.

With that he picked up a large roll of parchment and handed one end to the legate and it was held between the two of them while he continued.

"As you can see from this drawing, the precinct around Byland is about 110 acres and it is enclosed by this perimeter wall," he said, pointing to the map. "Most of the buildings are in the center of the enclosure and were placed there to help shut out outside noises and disturbances for the monks. There is an outer court and an inner court accessed through this inner gatehouse. It was once surrounded by swamp and woodlands, but the swamp has mostly been drained and a lot of the woods have been cut to supply building materials and for heat. As you can see there are several outbuildings beyond the Cloister. This one is the infirmary and here is the guest house. To the north of the church are three large ponds which are used to collect water. Other buildings in the compound, besides the church, include the Cloister, Sacristy, Library, Chapter House, Parlour, Dormitory, Warming House, Day Room, Refectory, Kitchen, and Lay Brothers' Range. All of these buildings can be accessed from the cloister, but entry is restricted. The south, east and west cloister walkways are primarily used as walkways, but the north walkway is used by the monks for reading, meditation and work. The cloister is also used for washing and shaving.

"The sacristy holds the liturgical vessels and vestments. Across here is the library. The chapter house here is the focal point of abbey life and all the monks gather here for an hour each day to attend a meeting. It is also used for business and to formally greet visitors. There are tiered stone benches around the walls. And, some of the past abbots are formally interred here," the monk said. "It is one of the most sacred places in the Abbey and you will not want to raise any alarms.

"You will not find much loose chatter throughout the abbey although the monks do communicate as necessary. Idle chatter," he said, "is believed to lead to sin, drinking, and debauchery. Along the east here is the monks' dormitory and it is accessed by this staircase from the cloister. It will house about eighty to ninety monks and you will find it is lighted at night at this end which is the redorters (toilets). Over here is the calefactory (warming house) on the south side with a large fireplace. One thing I should caution you about Cistercian abbeys. At least four times a year, and sometimes more frequently, they practice bloodletting as a preventative and restorative treatment. They believe it sharpens the senses, provides longevity, and quenches any sexual urges. This usually occurs in February, April, June and September, but can happen more often than that. I warn you not to become involved in that practice as you can lose your life and, at the very least, it takes a long time to recover your strengths.

"This large space here is the day room which is used to copy manuscripts and other work of the abbey. There is usually a water trough here used in the weekly foot washing ritual in memory of Christ. The refectory is here," the monk pointed, "and the kitchen is here. You will eat in the refectory for lay brothers and your daily food will be vegetables and fish. There is meat cooked in a special room for the sick and those of you who want meat can obtain it there. We have received special permission for that from each abbot. Here is the western range at Byland and that's where the lay brothers normally live. There are accommodations in this area for each of us, separated by a temporary wall that has been constructed. We will have our own redorters, sleeping area, and running water in each abbey, but will share meals with the lay brothers in order not to raise more suspicions in the Abbey," the monk concluded. "The meeting is now open for questions," he added.

"Will we be required to participate in the daily activities of the abbey when we are in residence?" asked one of the knights.

"No. In fact you will be excluded from most activities as for any other guest of the abbey. You will have direct access to the abbot at all times, you may come and go as you please bearing in mind you will have to produce a pass, which the abbot has prepared for each of you, in order to gain entrance to the abbey after dark. Should you not want to be seen leaving or arriving there is a secret access to each abbey which you will be shown, but you should exercise great care when using it. You may freely mingle with the monks during their outside day activities and, on occasion, you may even want to lend a hand. Each abbot has given special permission for the knights to train lay workers in the use of arms and military tactics and that will be one of your assigned tasks. Some of the monks may also voluntarily participate in these exercises as defenders of the abbey. Each abbot will instruct you as to the extent of this training and when and where it can be carried out," the monk said.

With that the meeting was dismissed and the group was free to examine the map of the abbey and carry on with life aboard the ship. All, it seems, had been heartened by the news that the voyage was drawing to an end.

Chapter 5—Whitby Abbey

On the evening of the next day, as promised by the captain of the ship, those on deck spotted land. Not long after that, with the use of a spyglass, the Abbey on top of the cliffs was in plain view. The ship's captain ordered the colors of Italy lowered and again the yellow banner with the green rose was slipped up the mast. Watchers kept their eye on the abbey until it, too, hoisted a similar banner at the top of an old Roman signal tower now a part of the fortress wall.

The captain acknowledged the sighting by dipping the banner three times before lowering it and replacing it again with the banner of Italy. Observers noted the yellow banner at the abbey, too, was quickly lowered and replaced with its normal colors of the Benedictine Order.

The ship continued to ghost slowly toward the mouth of the river Esk and the harbor. It was fully dark by the time the ship reached the torch-lighted quay at the foot of the village below the domineering walls of the great abbey. The quay was already lined with horse-drawn carts driven by monks in black robes waiting to unload the ship.

When the crew finished cabling the ship to the quay and placing the gangplank, the legate and monk stepped off to greet a small group waiting to receive them. The abbot of Whitby, escorted by two armed knights, was among those in the group. As soon as he saw the monk, he stepped forward and opened his arms. The two warmly embraced.

"When I heard we would have visitors from Scotland, I was hoping it would be you," he told the Monk. "I have been praying that God has been good to you," he added.

"Thank you, your highness," replied the monk. "It is good to see you and your brothers again after all these years."

"We have taken special care of the memory of your loved ones while you have not been among us, and you are indeed welcome on your return. Our monks have been greatly excited over seeing you and I've had to reprimand them on occasion, but not too harshly," the Abbot smiled.

"Your love and prayers are greatly appreciated and returned in full as you know," the monk said. "But I am forgetting my manners. Let me have the honor of presenting our special legate representing Pope Nicholas V. In our tradition we have not exchanged names so I will leave that to your wills in private."

The legate stepped forward and stretched out his hand which the Abbot proceeded to bow and kiss the ruby ring on his hand. "We are greatly honored to have you in our presence," the Abbot said. "We are sorry that you have so hasty a departure, but we understand both the necessity for your speed and the secrecy of your mission. You will have time to share some bread and wine with us while my brothers unload and transport the supplies and equipment from your ship?" asked the Abbot.

"I would with pleasure," accepted the legate. "It is a great relief to have my feet on solid ground if but for a few hours."

With that the Abbot turned to the monk. "Your men can ride on the carts up to the abbey and then we will begin unloading the ship," he said.

"If your highness pleases," the monk said, "my men can walk up the steps and the process of unloading the ship can begin immediately. The captain has been instructed what is to be unloaded, so we may proceed to the abbey." With that he turned and waved to the ship and the men on board began to file off. The monk pointed them up the street to the stairs to the abbey. It was an impressive sight as the knights and their squires filed off the ship, past the group, and on towards the abbey.

"I have transport for us to the abbey, but I think it most likely you will prefer to meet us there and will climb the stairs with your men," the Abbot smiled. "I will take charge of his highness and will meet you at the top."

"Thank you. Your memory suits you well," the monk said. He then stepped into line with his group and climbed the steps to the abbey as he had them do.

When the group reassembled in the inner courtyard of the abbey, the knights and squires had already been assigned to quarters and were getting refreshed for a meal to be served in the huge refectory at the abbey. The legate and the monk were escorted to their quarters and invited to assemble in the chapel before the meal.

In the meantime, the unloading of the ship was fully underway. Each cart driven by a monk would pull up to the quay alongside the ship and the ship's crew would use a wooden crane, attached to the main mast, to swing a net load of equipment out of the hold of the ship and directly into the cart. Crew members would remove the net, reattach it to the pulley apparatus of the crane and hoist it aboard for the next load. The loaded cart would pull away and begin its arduous journey up to the abbey and another would be pulled into place to be loaded. It was a fairly efficient process although somewhat encumbered by its extensive manual labor. It wasn't long before the drivers of the waiting carts, used to such labors, got down and helped the ships crew load each cart. After that, the process went much faster.

Most of the materials loaded from the ship to the carts were heavily wrapped in oiled canvas to protect them from the damp of the ship's hold so the monks were somewhat disappointed in not being able to discover what they were handling. That disappointment was alleviated later when they were allowed to unpack the heavy crates and bundles.

A couple of the carts had to make two trips up to the abbey and back before the job of unloading the ship was complete and it was in the wee hours of the morning when the job was completed. The monk and the Abbot had returned, via one of the carts, with the legate when it was time for the ship to cast off for its return to Italy. Fond farewells were said at the dock along with assurances from both sides that the efforts to come would be successful. The legate reminded the monk that the Pope would be anxious to hear news of his progress and that **The Order of the Green Rose** would be in papal prayers from then on.

The monk assured the legate that he would keep the pope informed.

"The trade routes will be busy with our messages although some of them may come in strange form. Be aware that all messages from us will be embossed with the rose," he told the legate.

With final goodbyes to the Abbot and the monk, the legate boarded the ship and the crew pulled in the gangplank and untied the bow and stern lines. The ship slowly drifted away from the dock as the crew began hoisting the sails. A fair wind was blowing so the ship quickly scuttled back out to sea and was soon lost in the darkness except for a bobbing lantern in the stern.

When the ship had gone, the monk and abbot re-boarded their cart and returned to the abbey for the rest of the night. Activities would resume after the Noon chapel at the abbey, they agreed before departing to their respective quarters for the remainder of the night.

It was closer to 2 p.m. when things got moving at the abbey the next day. Everyone, it seems, had been tired out from the night long activities and even the monks had been granted a dispensation to sleep-in throughout the morning. Nevertheless, there was quite a bit of earlier activity at the abbey. Some of the monks were out working at their daily chores and some of the knights and squires were out working the kinks out of their legs and systems.

The Green Rose monk had arisen about ten a.m. and strolled up the hillside to a small grove, overlooking the abbey and the sea, where there were two well-maintained gravesites. A monk had been working at the site when he arrived and greeted him before leaving him in solitude. He looked at the graves for a long time and then sat in repose for a time on a stone bench beside the graves. It was a time of remembrance back to his childhood when he lived at the abbey with his parents. His father had been a skilled craftsman responsible for supervising much of the reconstruction of the abbey which had been destroyed by the Danes in 867 and stayed deserted until the Norman Conquest. In about 1078 the restoration had begun with the leveling of the old buildings. It wasn't until the 13th and 14th centuries that the massive rebuilding effort took place. It was interrupted in 1349 when the plague hit the abbey as well as most of England and Europe.

Only about twenty monks were housed in the abbey at this time, but a number of lay volunteers worked tirelessly to maintain the grounds and the farms that supported it. When the monk arose to return to the abbey he found several monks quietly waiting along the path to greet him as he wound his way down the path. He had known them, and they had cared for him, when he was in residence. He gave each of them a familiar greeting and hugged them soundly. He knew they were responsible for the fine care of the graves he had been visiting and was spiritually lifted by their prayers and affection.

He was all business by the time he returned to the abbey. While he was descending the hill, he spotted a cloud of dust in the near distance and saw that it was a large herd of horses being driven towards the abbey. He watched while the horses were directed through a secondary gate in the fortress walls and entered a grassy courtyard in which a large pole corral had been hastily constructed to accommodate them.

He hurried on down and over to the courtyard to greet the Cistercian monks, robed in white, who were herding the horses. The lead monk spotted him approaching and rode over and slid off his mount.

"I bring you greetings from Jervaulx and our Master," he said. "It is our privilege to serve you and your men. Along with the horses I have brought guides who will lead your parties to our abbeys so that it will appear we are religious travelers. Our Master thought it would be the best way to preserve the secrecy of your missions in 'gossipy England,' as he put it."

"I am honored by your presence and the wisdom of your Master," the monk said as they shook hands. "That will indeed be a great assistance. I had been pondering how to get our men to their stations without arousing undue concern along their routes. And, I see your Master has sent some fine looking horseflesh in the bargain."

"He told me to tell you that next to serving the Lord and our Order, he is privileged to serve you and your cause and reminded me of the great service you have provided to our Order in the past. He says this is but a fraction of the repayment owed. I was instructed to select the finest of our stock and that's what we have brought. And, he said, there is a descendent of an old friend of yours in the bunch. The Master said he would not be surprised if your eye could single him out," the Cistercian said.

The monk cast his eye over the herd stirring in the corral. "You have actually brought two descendants of my old friend," he said. "The first is that large bay with the white blaze and the second is that sorrel with the white foreleg."

"The Master will be pleased. He had thought to trick you, but decided your squire should also be well horsed so he had me bring both. I see you have not lost your keen eye," the Cistercian smiled.

By this time the Abbot had also come to see the horses and was greeted with a deep bow by the Cistercian.

"You and your brothers are welcome and we thank you for bringing our friends such fine horses. You must come as it is time for our main meal of the day and we have specially prepared fish and vegetables in honor of your presence," the Abbot said.

"Our Master sends his greetings to you. He will be pleased that we are being so well received," the Cistercian said. "I will signal my brothers to follow us." He turned and waved at the dozen or so riders who had dismounted and turned their horses into the corral.

"Let us go and break bread together," the Abbot said, catching the monk and the Cistercian by the arms on either side of him.

After the prayers and the meal, it was time to get down to business. Besides the three carts brought on the ship, the abbey had provided five of its own carts and had obtained two others in good condition from the villagers along with horses to pull them. The monk immediately provided money to pay for the carts and animals so they could quickly be replaced. He added a couple of extra shillings to give to the villagers who had made such a sacrifice by giving up their carts, too. The Abbot immediately dispatched a lay volunteer to the village to pay for the two carts and animals making certain the man understood he had to pay over the bonus too.

The monk assigned a cart to each of the teams and gave each team leader a list of the supplies they were to load including the personal armor, banners, and weapons of the knights. Included on each list was a special gift meant for the Master of each abbey. Each team was introduced to its Cistercian guide and they all immediately set to work.

The knights were primarily interested in the horses so they soon induced their Cistercian guides to help catch their mounts and mounts for their squires. There was a spirited contest over the horses and the Cistercian had to intercede to protect the sorrel and the bay for the monk. At last the teams were all satisfied and the work went quickly after that.

Team 2, which only had a few miles to travel, was enlisted to help the others, and it was only a matter of a couple of hours before the teams left, one-by-one, along the routes that would eventually lead them to their assigned abbeys. Each group was formidable with four armed mounted knights in black robes, four armed mounted squires in black robes with their bows tied to their saddles, and a Cistercian guide in a white robe driving the heavily loaded cart with his horse tied on behind.

First to go was Team 8 which had to travel several days almost to the southern seacoast of England to Forde Abbey in Dorset (#10 on map). Next to leave was Team 1 which had to travel northwest to the western coast of England to Calder Abbey in Cumberland (#7 on map). Third to leave was Team 3 which headed south and east to Kirkstead Abbey in Lincolnshire (#21 on map). Next was Team 9 which also had to travel the length of the country south to Netley Abbey in Hampshire (#14 on map). Team 5 was ready next and headed southwest to Croxden Abbey in Staffordshire (#31 on map). Sixth to leave was Team 4 heading south to Little Coggeshall Abbey in Essex (#12 on map). The next departure was Team ten which had a long journey south to Hailes Abbey in Gloucestershire (#13 on map). Team 7 headed towards London and would settle just south of there at Waverly Abbey in Surrey (#33 on map). Team 2 finally got its chance to depart heading across Yorkshire to Byland Abbey (#39 on map). Last to leave was Team 6, headed by the monk and guided by the Cistercian monk, which left on the road to St. Albans Abbey just to the north of London in Hertfordshire (#16 on map). Although St. Albans was a Benedictine Abbey, the Cistercian monk was ordered by his Master to personally guide the monk's party along the road because he knew several places where the group could camp or receive housing. He also was bearing a special gift to the Bishop at St. Albans from the Master.

Thus, all of the teams were finally on the road. Some arrived relatively quickly and were operating within just a week. Others had further to go and it was as much as three weeks before the last of them arrived safely at their destinations. It was not until three months later, when all the teams gathered for their initial session at St. Albans, that the stories of their travels became known.

Travel in medieval England was fraught with dangers and some of the teams encountered more than their share of difficulties. Were it not for the Cistercian guides, so thoughtfully assigned to the task by the Master at Jervaulx Abbey, it is certain that some of the teams would likely not have arrived intact. But, as the saying goes, all's well that ends well.

Chapter 6—The Journeys

It wasn't until sometime in May, 1451, that all the teams gathered for the first time at Abbey St. Albans in one of the guest houses on the east side of the great court and in an isolated part of the grounds. The teams had been arriving for the past two days and the monk had been inquiring as to their activities in the three months since he had seen them.

All of the teams, it seems, had experienced some difficulties with the exception of Team 4, which had traveled the length of England without the slightest hint of trouble, a journey to which they credited their Cistercian guide who led them cross country and away from many of the more traveled roads. They were comfortably situated at Little Coggeshell Abbey in Essex close to the sea.

The leader of Team 4 reported to the monk they already had been introduced to a number of notables in their assigned territory by the Abbot and at least one of the knights, with Norman Ancestry, was making the social rounds. Two of the other knights were regular visitors to the local villages, and the team leader was busy training several of the lay workers of the Abbey in the use of arms and battle tactics. They were, he said, also keeping an eye on the seaport shipping since many "interesting" travelers were visiting the English king these days. He gave the monk a complete report of the political and social scene as it had been reported to him by his team.

The squires attached to his team, he added, were making some interesting contacts in the villages and had their fingers on the pulse of the "gossip" taking place among the villagers. They had been invited to converse with several of the town boards and had even "taken tea" with a group of the more influential ladies in one of the villages. One squire had increased his popularity by entering and winning a local horserace in one of the Sunday afternoon sporting events. Lay volunteerism at the Abbey had increased significantly since their arrival and the Abbot, he said, was quite pleased with that turn of events.

Team 1 from Holmcultram Abbey in Cumberland was the second group to arrive at the meeting. It had perhaps the furthest distance to travel to reach the St. Albans meeting site and had been on the road for several days. The team leader told the monk his group, which had to cross several mountains to reach the abbey, had been delayed for a few days by a rockslide which had dammed up a mountain stream and created a huge lake making it impossible to cross.

The team's Cistercian guide had been leading them across the mountains using some little traveled trails and paths which had made for some tough travel anyway. The crossing he took them to was all flooded and impossible to cross and they had to make an extensive and difficult detour in order to cross the river and eventually reach the abbey. This time, the leader said, the team had traveled the more used roads, as instructed by the Abbot, and had made good time arriving without any difficulties. It had helped out several travelers along the way after their coaches had become mired down in the spring mud.

He reported the abbey was fairly isolated, but several larger villages were reachable within a day's ride. The knights and squires had been pressed into "police" duty when several monks of the abbey had been subjected to attacks while they were traveling to and from the villages performing their duties. He reported great success in stemming the tide of those attacks, capturing and killing a number of the bandits, and receiving the gratitude of both the Abbot and the villagers.

"My people are certainly welcomed already in the villages and are being confided in by the people and nobles alike. One of our knights is providing military training for one of the castles and the Lord of that manor is very grateful. He invited us all, including the squires, to his

Easter feast and our ears were ringing with the intrigue in the region," the knight said. "I have brought you a complete report and any of our team members will certainly substantiate it."

"Thank you," the monk said. "Congratulations on your progress. We'll talk more of this after I read your report and we hear from the rest of the teams.

Next to arrive at St. Albans was Team 7 having come a relatively short distance from Waverly Abbey in Surrey. The team leader reported his group had "made quite a scene" in London on their journey to the abbey as one of the squire's horses stampeded when frightened by a group of street evangelists pounding on metal drums—wash tubs and the like, he laughed.

"I'm telling you we all had a time controlling out mounts when those people let loose with all that banging just as we were passing through. It is a good thing we had time to get acquainted with the beasts before it happened or we all would have been unceremoniously embarrassed," he said.

As the story unfolded, it got funnier and funnier and both of them were soon sore from laughing. It seems the squire was hanging on as best he could to the crazed horse when they crashed full into a fruit and vegetable stall on the side of the street scattering produce everywhere and making a grand mess. The produce made the footing even more slippery for the horse, who was beyond caring, and for the squire who eventually landed in a spot of fresh tomatoes that were not actually all that fresh, the knight added.

The street vendor was very upset and physically attacked the squire, who defended himself quite ably, despite the slippery footing. Both, the knight laughed, were rolling around in the muck before it was over. Before we could intercede a local constable showed up and soon restored order.

"I had to pay for the damage and set things right with the vendor. When we finally sprang free, the vendor was cleaning up the mess and the evangelists were still banging away on their drums all excited at the growing crowd they thought they had attracted," he said.

"We finally made it to the abbey without further trouble, but our squire has maintained contact with the street vendor—they are friends now—and is picking up some wonderful street gossip for us. We are experiencing the annual spring flooding at the abbey now, which is making life more difficult for the monks, but we are coping with the situation. We have been able to recruit quite a few lay brothers to help out and the Abbot is pleased with that. One of our squires can read and write and he has attracted a number of child and adult students to a class he conducts in the evenings at one of the larger villages. Our knights have seen service in protecting some of the villagers from attack by thieves and our arrowheads have attracted the interest of one of the more powerful lords in the area. We have an appointment to demonstrate them at one of his feasts coming up after planting time," the knight reported.

"This area is highly involved in the politics of London and the Royal Court and we are having to tread quietly lest we stir up any interest we don't want. I have here the latest in political intrigue, but I fear there is a lot more to come in the near future including the measure of a royal wedding," the knight said. "We also are training some of the lay brothers and monks at the abbey in the handling of arms and fighting tactics and they are taking to it quite well. This is a large abbey and we can field more than 100 men just from here if we need them," he concluded.

The monk expressed his gratitude for their progress and provided some additional insight to the knight to put into practice upon the teams return to Waverly Abbey.

Team 5 from Croxden Abbey in Staffordshire arrived next. This team had encountered some difficulties getting to Croxden while crossing some mountains and spending the night in one of the mountain villages.

"One of our squires," the leader said, "approached a woman to buy bread for our camp. The woman was startled and dropped a pan of hot water she was carrying. When that happened they both jumped, slipped in the mud, and got tangled up on the ground. This enraged the husband who, with some of his friends, confronted us later at our camp. It is thanks to our Cistercian guide, who stepped into the breach, and convinced the villagers we were "men of God" that a real serious problem was averted.

"We stayed there two more days to make certain all hard feelings had been soothed and by the time we left the villagers were bringing us fresh bread, ale, fish and other commodities. I think they would have liked us to stay," the knight added. "We had no more difficulties on the journey."

He went on to explain that Croxden is a small abbey and has not always gotten along with some of the local lords or their descendants. "Since we've been there two additional monks have been initiated into the Order and several more have become candidates thanks to one of our knights who speaks fluent French—for the abbey is located in a French-speaking area. The Abbot has expressed his pleasure and our knight is now giving him and the monks' lessons in the language. He has also recruited one of the monks, who knows French, to help and eventually take over the teaching task.

"Our other knights have been visiting and smoothing relations with the lords and nobility in the area and we have made some inroads in that effort. Some have taken a special interest in our weapons and we have promised to show them more upon our return. Our squires have pitched in to help repair some of the structures at the abbey and have generally improved our living quarters. One squire set himself to sell items in the villages made by the monks and he has contributed greatly to the income and industriousness of the abbey also much to the pleasure of the Abbot, who had some doubts when we arrived.

"As you requested, I have written a full report of our activities and stand ready for your advice," the knight concluded.

"Your efforts are much appreciated. After I have read your report, and listened to the others, perhaps we can develop strategies together," the monk said.

Team 2 from Yorkshire and Byland Abbey was next to show up. This was the area where all the teams landed in England and the monk was anxious to hear how they were doing as Yorkshire was one of the key spots in England indicated by the Pope in his message to the monk.

The team leader indicated no problems in reaching Byland Abbey except that nobody told the Abbot when they were coming. His group, after helping launch the other teams, arrived at the abbey well after dark and were refused admittance. It had to camp out all night until the morning before they were permitted to gain entrance to the abbey.

"When the Abbot found out who we were, he apologized profusely," the knight reported. "This abbey has seen hard times and the monks that are left there are having a hard time making a go of it. Some of the lands are even now in litigation so we are having to help restore the confidence of both the monks and the Abbot. I believe they are not only glad to have us, but are quite relieved we are there," the knight added.

"It is a beautiful and very large abbey, but woefully undermanned. We have made it our first priority to recruit lay brothers to help and hopefully some of them can be convinced to join the Order. Myself and my knights have made pilgrimages to all of the nearby manor houses and we have been promised some financial help for the abbey as well as the opportunity to visit with the peasants and recruit.

"So far we have more than twenty who are working daily at the abbey and things are beginning to look a lot better. The Abbot told me before we left that three of the laity had approached him about entering training to become monks and he was ecstatic with the progress," the knight said.

"It sounds as if you've had your hands full," the monk said. "Do you feel you would be better off being situated at another abbey?" he asked.

"I don't really believe so," the knight replied. "Our pilgrimages have really paid off and we are building a lot of support now. There are still quite a few important personages and nobility that overnight at the abbey and we've been able to be introduced to all of them by the Abbot. In fact, I have a report here of the political influence of the Duke of York who seems to hint that he might revive his efforts to gain the throne. At least this seems to be what he told the Abbot in confidence."

"That is very important news and I congratulate you for gaining the confidence of the Abbot so quickly. I will read your report and we will compare notes with our other teams. But, I believe you are well situated at least for the present," the monk said.

Just then Team ten from Hailes Abbey in Gloucestershire arrived at St. Albans and the monk excused himself to go and greet them.

The monk noticed that only six men were in the group with one knight and one squire missing from the assembly.

"Has something happened to members of your team?" he enquired of the team leader after the two were alone.

"No, except circumstances seemed to merit leaving them behind. The abbey has been raided on a number of occasions by bandits who come out of the surrounding hills. So far we have been able to stem the tide of those raids and I was fearful of leaving the abbey unprotected until we are able to locate the reasons behind these raids," the knight said. "I asked for volunteers and the whole team stepped forward so I selected the knight and his squire to remain behind," he said.

"We seem to have been besieged with this kind of luck since we landed. Our Cistercian guide actually saved us during out trip to the abbey and we felt we had some need to repay his alertness," he added.

He then relayed the story of their trip to Hailes Abbey from Yorkshire which was uneventful until one evening they were camped in a grove of trees when a band of thieves, dressed as Benedictines, rode up and asked to share the campsite.

"Our guide became suspicious that they were not acting in the manner of monks and alerted me to possible danger. I told our members to have their swords and daggers ready in the event of trouble and arranged with the squires, and their bows, to separate and maintain a watch throughout the night. Sure enough in the early morning hours they left their beds and were prepared to murder our knights in their blankets. Our alert squire put an arrow through the leader and awakened the rest of us. We sprang up and managed to kill three more and wound two others. One of our knights sustained a leg wound, but was still able to travel although it was painful for awhile. He is fully recovered and with us now.

"We made the wounded dig a grave for their comrades and then cut off one of their hands as a reminder not to pursue their criminal ways. They were grateful for their lives," the knight added.

"The abbey remains a popular pilgrimage site as a repository for the *Blood of Christ* from Jerusalem presented by Edmund of Cornwall as a result of the Crusades. That may be what is attracting all of the bandits who are preying on the pilgrims," he said. "We have organized and trained a number of lay members of the abbey to patrol the access routes, but they still are in need of encouragement and supervision. We have one pilgrim, a former knight, who has shown an interest in the abbey and we may be able to press upon him the job of leading these volunteers.

"In the meantime, the Abbot is greatly pleased with our help and has promised to provide letters of introductions to the nobility in the area and to help us become integrated into the social structure. We think he will be a great help. He already has provided us with some important information, which I have written in my report. It concerns the infirmities of the King and the controversies in his Royal Court so it should be of some interest," the knight concluded, handing over the report.

"I thank the brave knight," the monk said. "I shall read your report with interest and commend you for your foresight in not leaving the abbey unprotected. I trust you will fill in your comrades on what transpires here when you return."

"I assure you that is my intention," the knight replied.

Team 3 from Kirkstead Abbey in Lincolnshire also reported problems along the road with bandits. It seems the guide was leading them through a forested area when bandits came at them from the trees near a small village. The knights quickly responded to the attack giving the squires time to aim their arrows and the bandits were dispatched via sword and arrows. They were buried in the trees and the Cistercian guide provided a burial rite. None of the team was even scratched although the battle was fierce for awhile.

"They were surprised that we were armed and by the fierceness of our attack. Our squires put five of them out of action with their accurate shooting and that took the heart out of the rest. They will not bother any more travelers," the knight said. "Had they known we were knights, instead of wearers of the robes, it is doubtful they would have had the spunk to attack."

The knight then related the experiences of his team since arriving at Kirkstead Abbey. He said the abbey was well populated and the "attitude" was one of defiance to the local authority. "We expect if the nobility tried to storm the walls of the abbey they would meet with quite a bit of resistance from the monks. We are capitalizing on that attitude and have been schooling the entire community—monks and laymen—in the use of weapons and warfare. The Abbot is very grateful for our efforts and has been encouraging. I'm just hoping he doesn't want to start a local war," he said.

"Because of this thought, we have begun visiting all of the noble houses in the area and assuring them of the peaceful intentions of the abbey. These nobles are quick to recognize the possibility of another fighting force at their eventual disposal and are promising both military and financial aid for our efforts. We are accepting only that aid that comes without conditions so as not to put our Abbot in an untenable position," he added. "Much of the equipment we have received is pretty much outdated, but our squires are reworking it into useable condition and adding a few touches of their own.

"The abbot has promised to parade his new might whenever we say it is ready for such a showing. In the meantime the word of our activities has gotten around and we have several knights from nearby manors that are actually helping with the training and, more than 100 volunteers have already been recruited for the training and to work on the abbey grounds and granges (farms)," the knight concluded.

"I would caution you to make sure your Abbot doesn't have royal visions himself," the monk said. "And, if he does, to put in place some measures that will quickly turn his attentions elsewhere. I have a plan for that which we will discuss at our general session after all our teams are here," the monk said. "In the meantime it sounds as if you are doing good work. How many men could you field if we needed them?" the monk asked.

"I feel certain we would be more than 200 strong and, in all likelihood, some twenty or more knights would be happy to join with us," the knight said. "Those numbers are increasing almost on a weekly basis,' he added.

"Excellent," replied the monk.

Team 8 from Forde Abbey in Dorset was next to last to arrive at St. Albans. It too had some problems on its original trek to the abbey, the team leader told the monk.

"We were approaching the coastline near the abbey when a gang of pirates attacked us," he said. "We think they were scavenging on shore from their ship. Our quick reactions probably saved us from harm," he added, "and there are now two less pirates to be concerned about. The rest of them scurried back towards the sea through a marshy area where we didn't care to follow for fear our horses would get bogged down. I think it will be awhile before they restore their courage enough to attack what looks like an unarmed group," he said. "We did bury the dead and our Cistercian said the proper prayers.

"That said, we have been busy. The Abbey is in dissolute condition and we have had to spend much time in repairing our quarters and purchasing food, not only for us, but for the fourteen monks who are left. Some of them were too weak to work from the bloodletting operations, but they slowly are returning to health.

"The Abbot gave us permission and introductions to several of the wealthy estate owners and some of them already are coming to the aid of the abbey. We have recruited lay help and the rebuilding of some of the structures is well underway. I expect in another couple of months we will be free to extend our efforts full time to the task for which we have been sent. I apologize to you," the knight added, "for not being able to make good headway right away."

"You have done well and have had similar experiences with some of our other teams. Had we known the sad shape of some of these Cistercian abbeys, we might have gone elsewhere. However, it appears each of you has made sufficient progress that we will be better off keeping with our original plan, but we will discuss this at our general conclave. I presume you have maintained contact with those wealthy estates and that will certainly help our cause," the monk said. "Rest easy," he added, "you are not alone."

"Thank you, sire," the knight responded.

The leader for Team 9, the last group to arrive, from Netley Abbey in Hampshire, told of narrowly escaping a waterfront riot en route to his assigned station.

"We were staying overnight in a hostel recommended by our Cistercian guide when sailors in the port rioted against the gambling halls claiming they were being cheated. And, as things go, they probably were being taken advantage of. Anyway one of the taverns was set on fire next door to the hostel and we had to run for our lives. Fortunately, we had left most of our gear in the cart under guard of one of the squires and the Cistercian. They had our mounts saddled and the cart hitched by the time we arrived there or we probably all would have been burned to death. As it was the cart hit the side of a building as we were making our hasty retreat from the blaze and damaged a wheel. It took us two days to find a replacement wheel of the right size and we had to bargain it off the cart of a peasant for a substantial fee.

We had no further trouble reaching the abbey.

"We have made some progress in our quest; however, Netley Abbey is suffering from a lack of financing and has had to sell off some of its land. It's position near the coast makes it a way stop for nearly every mariner in the vicinity and such hospitality has cost them much of their livestock used to feed the freeloaders and/or stolen from them.

"Since our arrival we have convinced to Abbot to charge rent for overnight stays and that has added considerably to the income of the abbey. There presently are twelve monks and the Abbot in permanent residence, but on an average night there are from seven to twelve visitors looking for overnight accommodations. We have induced several of them to stay on as laity and they have taken on the job of feeding the visitors each night and morning and that has made the monks quite grateful for our presence as it has relieved them from a burdensome daily task.

"We are treating these visitors in a welcoming fashion and already the word is getting out of the changes in the attitude of the abbey which is being welcomed by the other landowners who also have been subject to the high rate of freeloading. Some have begun to send food, clothing, and blankets. One has even lent his chief cook to help train our laity brothers in preparing meals. We think, by this means, most of the news in the area, as well as the gratitude of the nobility, will mostly be coming to us rather than us having to seek it out. I have the information in this report," he said, handing the report to the monk.

"That is an unexpected twist that should prove to be valuable. We will share your success at our conclave and perhaps some of the others can pick up on it," the monk said. "Congratulations on turning a bad situation into a positive," he added.

"Please tell the other team leaders to join me after supper and we will lay plans for our general conclave tomorrow," the monk said. With that he returned to his rooms to read more fully the reports he had been handed. He would tell them tomorrow about the experiences of his team in reaching St. Albans and what his group had been doing. In some ways he felt fortunate to having selected St. Albans as the abbey was thriving and had more than 100 monks in permanent residence.

Chapter 7—The Conclave

The meeting with team leaders stretched far into the night as they discussed the various reports and hatched out their future strategy. When, at last, all were in agreement, the monk dismissed them and told them to assemble their teams at ten o'clock later in the morning. It was 2 a.m. when the meeting broke up and everyone sought their beds.

Promptly at ten a.m. the teams assembled in the Chapter House of St. Albans Abbey. It was a spacious room with vaulted ceilings and tiered stone steps around three of the walls where the team members could sit. The Abbot himself was in the chamber when the team members began to arrive and he greeted each of them personally.

The monk called the session to order and asked the Abbot to say a few words.

"On behalf of our Benedictine Order I want to welcome each of you to St. Albans. We have a long history of service to God, El Papa, and our Order. I am somewhat aware of your service, thanks to my family relationship with your leader, and I want to assure you we stand ready in all ways to help your cause. You have my full support and that of my brothers in this abbey who have been praying many years that God will bring peace and contentment to our brethren and country.

"I know you are in capable hands with my nephew here who has done outstanding services in the past to this precinct and to some other of our

Benedictine precincts in England. He is quite revered by our brothers in his own right and his prowess is unmatched in the protection of our Order. We are all grateful for his services and we know your trust in him is well placed.

"May God grant you the wisdom and prowess for a successful and lasting conclusion to your quest and please know that all of us here at St. Albans will be sending our prayers for your success. May God bless you all," the Abbot concluded before departing the Chapter House.

"I didn't count on such a testimonial from my esteemed uncle, but you can see now see how important our mission is in the eyes of our colleagues," the monk said as he addressed the group. "Your team leaders and myself met for long hours last evening analyzing and comparing experiences and we have come up with an overall program which we think will further our cause. But first I want to congratulate each and every one of you for rising above the difficulties you have encountered thus far and working to advance our progress in ways of which we did not conceive when we began this venture. Your success, in so many ways, will be used to guide our future activities. As we proceed some of you will be called upon to give the rest of us a first-hand account of your experiences so that we may be guided by your experience in our own areas. But I will let it be known at the outset that all of you have distinguished yourselves in your own manner and we are both thankful and grateful for your actions," the monk added.

"I have read the accounts of each team and heard directly from your leaders as to your activities, your successes, and the job still ahead. From this we have developed a strategy; however, I want you to know this strategy is to be considered as general direction and in no way should it hinder your own initiatives in seizing upon opportunities that present themselves in the future. It will be those initiatives, I believe, that ultimately will determine the successful outcome of our assignment. I already have encoded a report to Pope Nicholas and it will be on its way by courier this afternoon.

"Since I have heard from all of you, and you have not heard of the activities of me and my distinguished team members, I want to begin this session by bringing you up-to-date with our activities. I, too, have written a report as have all of our team leaders. These reports will be made available for you to read at the conclusion of our meeting. I think you all should read them or have them read to you. There are some amusing moments in some of them, but I digress.

"All-in-all we had an uneventful journey here from Yorkshire except for one incident near Nottingham. I thought at the time that perhaps Robin Hood had brought his band of merry men back together; however, I know that is not the case. Our Cistercian guide had found us a spot to camp by a stream in Sherwood Forest—probably one of the spots favored by Robin—and we had bedded down for the night. We always set a watch at night, changing it every two hours so that it was not too hard on any of us, and that precaution paid off. It was just before dawn, when we were all sleeping soundly, that our guard heard some suspicious sounds and aroused us. We pretended to be asleep in our blankets when the attackers stormed our camp. We had set two of our archers behind trees, just outside of the firelight, after stuffing their blankets with saddles. They scored the first two kills and pretty much forestalled the robbers. We were able to throw off our blankets and bring our swords into play to finish up the surprise. We killed one more of the murderers and captured five of them. Under questioning they revealed they were really after our horses, but would have enjoyed our money, too. We cut off one of their ears as a reminder not to attack religious men in the future and turned them loose. We can only imagine the stories they related about the monks who faced them down. We made them take the bodies of the others with them after they promised they would receive a Christian burial. It was quite a sight to see five one-eared men lugging off three bodies," the monk said.

"We had no more trouble after that and have received a warm welcome here at St. Albans as you can see from the words of the Abbot. We have been amazed at what we already have learned here. I will have a surprise for you when we gather tomorrow morning in the orchard area of the abbey, but you will have to wait until then to discover what it is. The abbey is also hosting an experimental printing press that appears to be a marvelous invention and could be very useful to our cause. Instead of hand-lettering, multiple copies of a notice can be printed on the press in just a short time. It is wonderful and you will have a chance to see the prototype right here at the abbey. This event precipitated an audience with the King here at the abbey, at the invitation of the Abbot, and I have been able to learn much about him that should be useful to us in the coming months.

"Our knights and squires have also been busy teaching military tactics and armed combat to the monks and laity of the abbey and to a number of lay brothers in the village. Pilgrimages to the abbey have increased by at least half since word has gotten around that we are here. The King was quite interested in our swords and arrowheads and has commissioned a group of experts to work with us in developing the techniques for making them here. We also have a school that has begun with the aid of our knights and laity volunteers and we have more than fifty boys attending on a daily basis. They will become our eyes and ears of the future," the monk concluded.

"I know you are anxious to hear our suggestions for our future course of action, but the Abbot has been kind enough to send us some refreshments so I suggest we take a short break and then reconvene in a few minutes," the monk told the group.

When the conclave reconvened in about thirty minutes, the monk called on various team leaders to lead the discussions and sometimes it was a team member—knight or squire—who gave first-hand accounts of their activities and fielded questions from the assembled team members. It was a slow process, but it led to a complete understanding of what had been accomplished and what could be accomplished as well as a number of techniques to use for those purposes.

Without going into the various discussions, suffice it to say there were two main initiatives discussed with a number of alternatives under each one. The main discussion centered on the local initiatives each team could take in their assigned areas and there was less discussion regarding some important political initiatives and follow-up that needed to be taken. One other discussion was held regarding establishing a system of communications so that messages could be relayed back and forth between the teams and St. Albans as needed and there was an agreed on signal that would summon everyone to a designated assembly point post haste with an addendum if they were to bring as many armed men as they could muster.

The first and longest discussion concerned local initiatives the teams either were conducting, or could be conducting, to further their relationships with the communities surrounding their abbeys. An outline of the points and sub-points subsequently agreed upon include:

1. Local initiatives seem to be helping the cause and permitting the teams to become firmly established in their abbeys and the surrounding communities. For this reason they should be continued and even expanded where possible. They are to include:

a. Visitation opportunities with manor lords and knights in the area of the abbey. These visits are to provide:

(1) Assurance that any military training conducted in the castles, villages, or abbey is to establish a system of security for residents as well as traveling pilgrims;

(2) The offer of training assistance to any of the lords and their knights who may wish to take advantage of the opportunity presented;

(3) Demonstrations of new developments in weaponry and the hardened arrow points, swords, knives and axes used by team members;

(4) Generating opportunities for invitation to feasts of the manor lord as respected and welcome guests; and

(5) Gaining permission from the lords to visit with the villagers.

b. Visitations to the local villages to gain the confidence of pub owners, vendors, magistrates, and others in a leadership role and to develop them into "eyes" and "ears" for the team;

(1) Recruiting lay brothers to help out at the abbey and receive military training. Encouragement for laity workers to enter the abbeys as trainees to become monks in cooperation with the Abbot;

(2) Arranging local contests that identify military prospects—horse races, jousting, swordsmanship, archery, wrestling, knife and axe throwing, etc.;

(3) Establishing schools to teach the young men of the village in their responsibilities and in the opportunities to:

(a) Read or write;

(b) Develop skills as known by the monks and team members;

(c) Learn wrestling and self defense;

(d) Learn how to observe and pass along information of an unusual nature.

c. Establishing a system of security patrols and watch stations throughout the various territories with a means of communicating, by signal, any information of note.

(1) Set up a paid system of watch keepers and volunteer mounted and foot patrols to respond to emergencies;

d. Due to the increased traffic by soldiers and sailors returning from France and other pilgrims using the abbeys for food and shelter, establish a system whereby some reimbursement for these services is possible. Also find ways to bring more income to the abbeys to assure their continued cooperation.

(1) Set up a standard charge for room and board either in cash or services from those seeking shelter at the abbeys.

(a) Some abbots might prefer a voluntary "contribution box" for those who occupy the beds and partake of the meals.

(2) Most monks are skilled craftsmen and all abbeys have the right to "market privileges" in the local markets. Therefore, establish local markets for their goods and get the monks engaged in selling items in the local village marketplaces.

(a) Teach the locals how to make and sell their own crafts.

2. Political initiatives are particularly important and special attention should be paid to information regarding changes in:

a. The Royal household affairs

(1) Rumors of an upcoming wedding

(2) Any illness of the king

(3) Decisions of the king's Council

(4) Changes in residence of the royal family

b. The Duke of York's affairs

(1) Rumors of designs for the crown

c. Local government officials, particularly sheriffs or constables

(1) Unrest in any of the shires.

d. Summons to the court for any of the abbots where our people are being sheltered.

3. Communications with the various teams and the St. Albans headquarters for the Order. Messages need to be weekly and a system of couriers using recruits in the various villages along the way should be established.

a. Contract with local farmers or peasants to become couriers as a paid service.

b. Train them on how to deliver in secret.

There were other ideas approached at the conclave, but these were the major agreements of the day with each team responsible for carrying them out in their own way. Other initiatives were encouraged, but the chief theme was to develop a system for gathering and coordinating information from the various parts of the country.

On the next morning, the teams gathered in an isolated area of the orchards where the monks had erected ten large targets. Most thought there was to be an archery contest, but were quite surprised when the monk arrived carrying a piece of equipment they had not seen before. He had with him another man who was pushing a covered hand cart.

"This is a new kind of firearm," the monk said as he stepped before the assembled group. "It hasn't yet received a name although it works on the same principle as the cannon except it is small enough to be carried by a foot soldier. The inventor is here with us this morning. He has been working on the piece here at St. Albans for a couple of years in the utmost secrecy. He brought the idea to the Abbot and was granted an opportunity to develop it under the auspices of the Church. After he demonstrates the weapon, each of you will be given an opportunity to use it."

The man brought by the monk stepped up at the monk's nod, raised the weapon, aimed it at the center-most target and fired it. The noise made several of the party jump, but they were awed with what they had just seen. It was even more inspiring when a large hole appeared in the center of the target about fifty feet away. Most of the group walked down to the target and examined the hole. When they were through, the monk addressed them again.

"Now you are going to see how to load and prime the weapon which uses lead balls like this one as the force instead of an arrow. It is driven by a charge of black powder which pushes the ball through the barrel and towards the target with great force," the monk said.

Once again the man stepped forward and demonstrated how to load the weapon. He first cleaned out the long barrel and then poured a measure of black powder down the barrel. A lead ball, wrapped in a piece of leather was next and this was pushed down gently using the same staff he used to clean the barrel. Powder was then poured in a "touch" hole at the top of the barrel. He then handed it to the monk who stepped forward, aimed the weapon using both hands, and fired the weapon at another target using the lighted end of a stick—mounted in a small metal container on the side of the barrel—to ignite the powder at the hole. The lead ball hit the upper half of the target also making a large hole.*

"I'm not as skilled as our learned blacksmith here," the monk said, as he handed the weapon back to the man.

"I made arrangements to purchase ten of these weapons when the Abbot introduced me to this craftsman and he has worked night and day to provide them." With that he stepped over to the hand cart and provided one of the weapons to each team leader.

"Our friend here will conduct training on how to load, aim, fire and care for these weapons. Each of you will take turns firing it and the best man on each team will be placed in charge of it for his team. I warn you it is not to be used except in an emergency and must be kept out of sight at all times. It has been provided for your defense only. This weapon ultimately will change warfare as we now know it and we don't want it to get into the wrong hands. I have commissioned our friend here to make 100 more of these contraptions, but first we need to learn how to use them. Each of you must become an expert before we allow this weapon to be used in battle. There's no question it will make even the weakest man strong in terms of military importance," the monk said.

With that the training and firing began and lasted for the better part of the next two days. Even the monks at the abbey began to complain about the noise.

When the conclave reassembled for the final meeting, all of the team members were excited about the new invention and there had been a spirited competition between the knights and squires as to who could handle it best. In the final outcome eight of the squires and only two of the knights were chosen as keepers of the weapon—a fact which made the squires quite proud.

The teams said their goodbyes and left St. Albans for the return travel to their home abbeys, but only after a special chapel service presided over by the Abbot himself.

A special messenger was soon dispatched from the Abbey headed for London and the seacoast with a message for the Pope.

It was almost four years to the day before the entire group was once again assembled at St. Albans and much had changed in England with war in the immediate future.

***Note: Handguns were first used in the Second Battle of St. Albans when the Earl of Warwick had 500 Burgundians, some armed with the devices, among his troops. It was snowing during the battle and some of the handguns misfired with wet powder and others apparently simply blew up. (12)**

Chapter 8—The Far North

When Team One left St. Albans, it returned to the far north of England and to the stronghold of support for the Lancastrians and King Henry VI, one side of the battles involved in the later Wars of the Roses. The team had been warned to "tread cautiously" in its pursuit of information. The northern areas of Britain were heavily wooded and the people were of the "rough and tumble" variety not much for niceties of civilized society or for obeying the laws of the land.

Cumberland, where the team was located in Holmcultram Abbey was both a maritime and border county with Scotland. The Solway coast is low and sandy, but lofty and rugged on the Irish Sea. There is open and flat country in the northwest, watered by the Eden River, which flows through meadows and arable land. To the east and south the countryside changes into a region with deep defiles or dales, which form the mountainous district known as "The Lakes." The wet climate restricts most agriculture to the rearing of sheep and cattle. Carlisle was the principle town with 17 other market towns scattered over the landscape.

Also bordering Scotland to the east of Cumberland is Northumberland, another county with a history of warfare between England and Scotland. It had some twelve market towns with the northernmost town in England being Berwick on the Tweed. It is a hilly countryside although there was much corn and wheat grown in the eastern part with rich meadows on the banks of the rivers. The western part, next to Cumberland, was mostly barren, heaths and mountainous and a haven for border raiders.

South of Cumberland is Westmorland which consists of a continuous succession of mountain, moor and fell, intersected by deep winding vales with numerous streams including the Eden, Lowther, Lune, and Kent which forms a broad estuary terminating in Morecambe Bay. The western part of the area is also within "The Lake District." Arable land in the moist atmosphere is mostly confined to the valleys and is suitable for turnips. The greater part of the land is natural pasture and woods.

South of Northumberland is Durham which borders on the east coast of Britain. It, too, is hilly and some points reach about 2,000 feet high. There are wide moors among the hills with lots of timber. Principle streams include the Wear, the Tees, the Tyne and the Derwent.

All-in-all, this was rough country in the 15th century and Team One was subject to attack whenever it was moving around the countryside. For this reason they almost always went as a complete team with the four knights, four squires, and whatever other mounted guard they could muster which often included the Cistercian monks and/or conversi (lay brothers) from Holmcultram Abbey.

Holmcultram Abbey was founded in 1150 by Prince Henry, son of David I, King of Scotland. The abbey was intended as an affiliation of King David's own foundation of Melrose and the first monks came from this abbey. However, the abbey did not remain a purely Scottish institution as it had friends and benefactors on both sides of the border. It was the richest and most influential of the religious houses in Cumberland and Westmoreland, yet it also suffered greatly during the years of hostility between Scotland and England. Despite the problems, the abbey was favored by many of its aristocratic contemporaries. It served as a base for English invasions of Scotland and the Abbot had great political influence in Britain.

And, as a house of the Cistercian Order, an offshoot of the Benedictine Order, it had close original ties with the Knights Templar founded during the Crusades. Therefore, it was not adverse to warfare providing it was performed with the will of God. The Holmcultram

Abbey was therefore a "wise choice" to harbor Team One.

In the years after the conclave at St. Albans, Team One proceeded to establish a network of trained security forces in the areas it serviced, built up great trust by the local lords despite the ill feelings between those loyal to the side of Lancaster or to the side of York. It seems in this turbulent North Country there were plenty more sides to go around and the centuries of warfare had built up great emotions between families of note in the area.

Team One maintained a strict neutrality at all times and managed to build up a solid network of spies which tapped the heart of most of the households of notables in the area. It could be a maid, a wardrobe mistress, a sergeant of the guard, a gardener, a knight, or even a peasant who became an informant for Team One. All who served in this capacity were well rewarded for their information and it soon occupied at least four monks full time at the abbey to compile the reports from the various sources in the area.

During the period from the conclave at St. Albans until the first battle of the Wars of the Roses at that same St. Albans, Team One operated with impunity and little suspicion thanks to the training provided. There was one notable exception that took place in 1453-1454 when a jealously erupted between well-known "border reive" families in Northumberland. Both families were well known for their stealing of livestock on both sides of the border. Since tensions were high between Scotland and England during this period, Team One was dispatched from its abbey to try and mediate the dispute which involved some pasture rights in a wild mountain area known as Kidland. Since part of the area belonged to the monks of Newminster, who handled rentals of the properties to the various clans, the feud was a great concern to the peace of the area and to the church.

Team One gathered its weapons and armor and headed for the trouble spot as soon as an emissary, dispatched from Newminister, arrived. Besides the knights and squires there was a baggage cart and twelve other armed monks and lay brothers from Holmcultran Abbey. Their travel took them through Carlisle, Brampton, Greenhead, along the length of Hadrian's Wall, and over to Chollerford. From there the group turned north to Rothbury where they were to engage in pre-arranged peace negotiations to take place at Brinkburn Priory, now largely deserted except for occasional worship services in the priory church.

Brinkburn was an Augustine priory located in an isolated valley in a loop of the Coquet River. It, too, suffered greatly over the years from Scottish raiding parties, but it had been re-built from an earlier disaster and the buildings were still standing, could house a goodly number of people, and there was good pasture for the livestock.

This turned out to be one of the rare times prior to the first battle of St. Albans, which officially began the period of the Wars of the Roses, that the Green Rose battle banner was displayed in armed conflict. When Team One approached the priory the two opposing sides were already there and engaged in a pitched battle on the grounds. Team One donned its battle harness and rode into the midst of the battle in full dress and with banners flying and effectively split the two warring factions causing them to lay down their arms after about ten minutes of fighting. Whether it was the force of twenty knights, squires, and others that turned the pace of the battle, or the shock and awe of the resplendent knights in the full battle armor of the Order of the Green Rose, is still undetermined. Regardless, the sudden appearance served to stop the fighting in progress and effectively brought the two parties to the negotiating table.

Team One's forces remained in full dress and on the alert throughout the three days of intense negotiations and an agreement was only reached when the monks of Newminster threatened to withdraw the rights of either party to use the Kidland pastures. A pact was agreed to, but neither party was greatly satisfied with the results and there were skirmishes among them even as they left Brinkburn priory to return to their border homes.

Nor, was that the end of the story. The monks riding with Team One spent a lot of time examining the buildings and basements in the old priory. Some of them were examining a group of small basement rooms by candlelight one night as they were preparing for the trip home when an apparition of a woman appeared before them, dressed in 13th century battle dress, and carrying a silver sword. When the monks recovered from their shock, they observed she was pointing the sword towards one corner of a basement room.

The monks called in the other members of Team One, who didn't see the apparition, but decided at the monk's insistence to explore the room further. They finally used some old boards to scoop away the soft dirt in the corner and discovered a large chest covered with about a foot of dirt. When they opened the chest they found it was filled with silver and gold coin and exquisite jewelry. This money was used to finance the activities of Team One, and several of the other teams, during the remainder of their time in England.

However, getting the treasure back across England to Holmcultram Abbey, and eventually to St. Albans, was another story. Finding the treasure was one thing, keeping it secret was another matter entirely. Although the monks were sworn to silence, getting the lay brothers to keep the silence was another problem. It was later learned that one of them, sent into Rothbury to purchase supplies for the journey home, had an encounter with a linen maid in an Inn where he stayed overnight. By the time he returned to the priory with his load of supplies, the word was fast traveling around Rothbury.

Residents of Rothbury, in former times, were among the wildest and most ferocious in the country. For fighting, drinking, and gaming they had a reputation worse than Tynedale and Redesdale with little regard for the laws. Poaching venison was one of their delightful pursuits and religion did not have a strong influence on them.

Team One was packing up their cart, preparing to leave, the morning following the return of the man sent to purchase supplies in Rothbury, when the first attack came. Eight armed men came charging from the woods towards the Team One party intent on surprising them. However, they had misjudged the time it took to cross the open area to where the priory buildings were located and the Team had plenty of opportunity to arm itself. Arrows quickly dispatched by the squires quickly killed two of the attackers and the Knights and monks, already mounted, but not in harness, took care of the rest. One was left alive, although gravely wounded, and he relayed an account of how they had found out about the treasure. The lay brother quickly fell on his knees and offered his head for betraying them, but he was forgiven since they needed all their manpower for the journey home.

The dead, including the wounded bandit who died shortly after relaying his story, were left where they lay after the monks said some words over their bodies. The team quickly finished loading and soon left the priory taking the same route since there was only one travelable entrance/exit to the isolated buildings.

Although they kept a sharp eye and their weapons at the ready, it was not until they reached the beginning of Hadrian's Wall that a second attack came. This time it was launched from the ruins of one of the old Mile Castles along the wall and consisted of close to twenty men on foot armed crudely with clubs and spears. Again the archers created havoc among the attackers and they never got closer than about fifty yards to the group before they were repulsed. The knights restrained from routing them further, but three of the monks dispatched about five of the attackers and hastened their retreat.

It was the first of three more attacks Team One repulsed during its eighty mile traverse of Hadrian's Wall. All but one of the attacks was launched from the ruins of the wall itself. The other came from a wooded area and forced Team One to set up a defensive line behind part of the old earthworks barrier of the wall with the squires taking up archery positions high in an old turret which gave them a clear shot at the approaching attackers. The knights were able to don their harness (armor) and, mounted on superior horses, were able to drive off the attackers. The archers, from their vantage point, decommissioned at least twelve of the bunch and the knights and monks dispatched many of the rest. It was a bloody battle for a time, but the attackers were mainly unskilled in professional warfare and had been assembled in haste. They attempted to regroup in the nearby woodlands, but the archers discouraged any further attack.

The Team had no further problems returning to Holmcultram Abbey with the treasure, but was dismayed to learn that the negotiated pact between the warring families was largely in vain after one family gathered all its members and successfully stormed the stronghold of the other killing most of the members. It was said they did it in revenge for missing out on the treasure recovered at the priory. It did, however, resolve the question of disputed pasturage for the monks.

When news of the treasure reached St. Albans by messenger, the monk himself lead a group of fifty archers and swordsmen from the abbey to escort it to St. Albans. The jewelry and coins were identified as Scottish in origin and were divided among the ten teams to finance their operating activities with a due reward to each host abbey which greatly cemented the good relations they enjoyed.

In addition to the treasure, Team One managed to curb much of the violence in its assigned territory, it discovered a plot of the Scots to link up with King Henry VI before the Wars of the Roses, and its mapping and charting of the defenses of the various castles along the Scottish border ultimately helped the Yorkists reclaim them towards the end of the Wars of the Roses.

The spy system established in the area by Team One was ultimately responsible for the capture of King Henry VI and his attendant who spent a year hiding in safe houses in Lancashire, Yorkshire, and the Lake District in 1465. Most of these spy systems ultimately became linked with those in other territories and when Henry and his companion posed as monks in a monastery in Yorkshire, he was discovered and tracked from then on utilizing these systems until he subsequently was captured.

Carlisle, close to the Holmcultram Abbey, was a main center for Team One activities during its earlier years. It encouraged the monks to market goods at the main marketplace and also set up schools to educate the children in the area. This technique eventually spread to other main marketplaces throughout the territory as other Cistercian and Benedictine establishments followed suit after they learned of the successes at Holmcultram Abbey. These efforts greatly enhanced the recruiting of lay brothers at the various abbeys and soon most of the monks were engaged in producing goods to sell along with the fresh farm produce they grew on the grounds.

The only downside for the monks was finding they were not as cut off from society as they originally intended since they had extensive estates to run and numerous workers to supervise. The additional revenues were welcomed at the abbeys and the lives of the monks were enhanced, especially in the winter time since they could afford to maintain more heat in their buildings. However, their successes also led to jealousies and criticisms. And, there were rumors about the found treasure which eventually spread all over England causing more and more pilgrims to visit the abbeys and permitting most abbeys to have a "contribution box" instead of a flat charge for overnight accommodations and meals for those who had no monies.

In addition, some of the monks felt they no longer wanted to endure the discipline of monastic life since they were thrust back into civilization through sales activities of their goods and teaching the children. Some even left their orders and some tended to ignore their vow of giving up all material possessions or even their vow of chastity. However, there were plenty of recruits to replace them and for a time, the populations of involved abbeys rose until eventually they again began a decline.

Chapter 9—Yorkshire

There is little question but that Team 2 played a vital role in the events leading up to the Wars of the Roses when it returned from the conclave at St. Albans to Byland Abbey. Yorkshire was a haven for political intrigue dating back to the times of William the Conqueror who, in subduing northern rebellions, scorched the earth and caused great destruction in the area. The Doomsday Book, King William's census of 1086, indicates that half of York was owned by the King and the other half by influential Normans.

It was this division that carried on into the 15th century and had such a profound impact on the Wars of the Roses. With half the countryside backing the Lancastrians and the other half devoted to the Yorkist's, it was a trying time for the operations of Team 2 which had to quickly become aware of where loyalties fell.

Yorkshire is a maritime county bounded on the north by Durham and the Tees River, on the east by the North Sea, on the south by the Humber River and Lincolnshire, and on the west by Lancashire. In the interior is a great central valley stretching southeast to the Humber and bounded on either side by heights—the Cleveland Hills and the Wolds on the east and the Pennine mountain chain on the west. From its very beginnings Yorkshire has been divided into three areas—east, north and west—besides the independence of the City of York.

York was the second largest and likely the most important city in England even though London was larger in population. The stone walls enclosing the city and the Bars (medieval gateways) protected its residents and Kings and Queens were frequent visitors. The Dukedom of York was already, by custom, conferred on the sovereign's second son.

In this instance, that was Richard Plantagenet, born September 21, 1411, as the son of Richard of Conisburgh, earl of Cambridge, and Anne Mortimer. He married Cecily Neville in 1424. Two of his sons later became kings of England.

York was growing in population and was a busy port city exporting mostly wool and other manufactured goods. There were more than forty parish churches, an abbey, priories, friaries and religious hospitals located within the city walls and trade was flourishing with more than 100 crafts being practiced, each controlled by its own guild. The wealthiest and most powerful of these was the Company of Merchant Adventurers, the guild of overseas trading. It was this guild that was to play another important role in events leading up to the Wars of the Roses.

Despite a poor beginning having to camp out all night before receiving permission to enter the Byland Abbey upon its first arrival, Team 2 had already made great strides in securing the cooperation of the Abbot before it left for St. Albans by recruiting several "lay brothers" to help the monks at the abbey as well as working to secure financial help.

Even more recruits had arrived at the abbey by the time Team 2 returned and there was much for the team to do. One of the squires, who they found was knowledgeable in construction and carpentry, was assigned to repair some of the aging buildings at the abbey. One of the knights volunteered to help in the litigation of lands held by the abbey, which were under fire, and to eject trespassers who were trying to illegally farm and pasture some of those lands.

The precinct at Byland included about 110 acres and was enclosed by a perimeter wall. The church and cloister area stands at the middle of the precinct sheltered from the noise and activities in the inner and outer courts where industrial and domestic work was carried out, where guests were accommodated and alms distributed to the poor. The cloister was one of the largest in England. The church was laid out to represent the various distinctions in the community. A feature of the Cistercian Order was its incorporation of lay communities and the abbey church accommodated both groups separately. The monk's cloister was in the eastern part of the church, the lay brothers' was in the west, and were divided by a large partition. The church itself was built in a cruciform shape and the aisled nave was divided into eleven bays and stretched roughly 100 meters in length. The lay brothers' choir occupied the six westernmost bays with the next two forming the retro choir and the last three were occupied by the monks' choir. The north and south transepts (side arms) each had two chapels where ordained monks could pray and celebrate masses. A square-ended presbytery was situated at the east end of the church and steps separated this, the holiest spot in the precinct, from the monks. It was here the high altar was built of stone and mass celebrated and Communion received. The abbey church was innovative and impressive in its size, scale and the quality of the masonry work and sported a beautiful "rose" window.

Byland Abbey was once a vast and busy hive of industry, but had fallen on ill times. The members of Team 2 set out to restore the abbey's prominence and importance so that once again it would be one of the "three shining lights of the north" along with Fountains and Rievaulx abbeys.

One monk, Team 2 discovered with the help of the Abbot, was a descended from a Templar knight assigned to the abbey in 1311 when the Order was dissolved and the knights dispersed among the various religious houses. The team immediately recruited him to help train recruits and monks in the use of arms at the abbey and found that he was quite skilled in the art.

By August of 1451, the Templar monk was conducting regular training sessions with about thirty monks and lay members participating. The blacksmith at the abbey had been quite busy making swords and other armored gear using metallurgy formulas brought from Scotland by the team. The lighter weight and superior strength of the arms had delighted the Templar monk and he was making good use of the new weapons in his training program. Several of the trained lay brothers were later dispatched to other abbeys in Yorkshire to begin training programs there after Team 2 knights and squires had reached agreements with the abbots.

The recruiting campaign in York, a few miles south of the abbey, and in some of the surrounding villages was showing positive results by

September. Half of the original military class of thirty had already been dispersed to other abbeys and the other half was busy training more than 100 new recruits sent to the abbey by the recruiters. About twenty of them came from the castles of lords in the areas after they came to Byland to observe the training class.

Progress also was being made in promoting the production of various crafts by skilled monks and lay brothers, the agriculture harvest was proceeding smoothly thanks to the extra help, and repairs to the abbey buildings, including the infirmary, were progressing. The western range, where the lay brothers were housed, had been expanded in order to accommodate new recruits.

One of the knights had visited with the Abbot at Jervaulx Abbey and secured the loan of enough horses to establish a scheduled messenger service between Fountains, Jervaulx, Kirkstall, Rievaulx, Roche, Sawley, St. Mary's, and Whitby abbeys which increased communication, cooperation, and exchanges of ideas greatly between these institutions. These abbeys were located within a 75-mile triangle of each other at the outer extremes of the triangle; however, no abbey was further than thirty miles from another in the group. The key to gaining the confidence of the Abbots was the need for additional protection due to the increased tensions between the political groups in the country and the lasting fear of another invasion from Scotland. Each abbey would write a report of its weekly activities, including political and economic information, and riders would make a complete circuit of all abbeys each week carrying the reports which were available for all abbots to read—much like a round robin letter. This meant each abbey was updated on the activities of the other abbeys within a two week period at the most.

Special messengers were dispatched from any abbey needing immediate help and the response to such pleas could be rounded up and provided in a limited measure within twenty-four to forty-eight hours depending upon the urgency of the need. The military training and the recruiting efforts also assured enough armed forces within each abbey to hold out for the time necessary for aid to arrive.

In November of 1451, Team 2 had to muster its forces to repel a group of armed men intent on trying to occupy lands belonging to the abbey by force after the knight assigned to resolve disputes had ordered them to pack up and leave. The four knights and four squires of the team were in full armor and backed by the mounted Templar monk in armor along with forty foot soldiers armed with swords, pikes, and axes and protected by chain mail. Arrayed against them were about fifty armed brigands, some apparently recruited from the pubs at York. When the trespassers saw the armed force of Team Two approaching they immediately dispatched a horseman to negotiate. In the meantime the Team Two force formed a battle line, but such efforts were not needed.

The trespassers quickly agreed to continue working the land on a rental basis with the abbey. The lead knight ran a hard bargain and collected a year's rental in advance in an amount nearly twice as much as normal rent charged by the abbey. Needless to say, the Abbot was quite pleased, and an armed conflict was avoided although the Templar monk had been itching to see how well his trained recruits performed in a real fight. The trespassing group continued to work the land and paid its rents on time for some years to come.

From that point on the Abbot of Bylands was extremely appreciative of Team Two and worked actively to support it. This helped cement the importance of the information network as the Abbot personally visited each abbey to work out the final arrangements and set up the plan. It turned out to be a great strategic victory by Team Two and before long weekly reports from the entire Yorkshire were being gathered and summarized for a weekly report to St. Albans. One of these reports was instrumental at a later date in alerting St. Albans to the coming opening battle of the Wars of the Roses.

By February 1452 Team Two had assembled a chart identifying York vs. Lancaster supporters in Yorkshire which greatly eased the tensions of their work. In addition, maps were drawn and copies dispatched to St. Albans of several of the Lancastrian castles in the area showing defenses and possible weaknesses that could be exploited in the event of war. These were to prove valuable towards the end of the Wars of the Roses when the Yorkist's were "mopping up" after their victory.

Another challenge developed for Team Two in May 1452 when some of the guilds in York began to demonstrate against the sale of goods made by the monks of the various abbeys and sold at marketplaces in York, Whitby, Leeds and other smaller villages in the area. Of special concern were the woolen blankets being produced at the abbeys and exported via special ships primarily from Whitby. A month later, through the auspices of St. Mary's Abbey in York, a soup kitchen was opened in York in cooperation with the Mariners Guild and another one began operating shortly after that in Whitby by monks and lay brothers from Whitby Abbey. The kitchens catered to mariners sent there by the Mariners Guild; however, they were open to other needy people, too.

It was about this time that a monk overheard one of the sailors, off a ship recently arrived at Whitby from the coast of France; tell others how badly England was faring in France in the battles to hold onto its conquered lands. Word was immediately dispatched to Byland and an urgent message was forwarded to St. Albans. The monk at St. Albans dispatched a secret note to the Duke of York in London advising him of the news. In this note, embossed with a green rose, was a veiled suggestion that England would be better served if the Duke resumed using the surname Plantagenet. Shortly after that the Duke complied and the royal circle became concerned about its claim to the throne which further aroused the political tensions.

Shortly after that Team 2, with the assistance of pressures applied on the Mariners Guild by the Abbots at St. Mary's and Whitby, secured a long-term agreement allowing the monks to sell their goods in all marketplaces in Yorkshire as well as export their blankets. No further trouble was reported and the soup kitchens continued to serve as valuable sources of information.

The agreement was further extended in January of 1453 when Team 2 finalized arrangements with mariners to carry dispatches directly to Rome. This arrangement was used on occasion when St. Albans could not find an available ship south of London for this purpose.

It was in March of 1453 that a strange occurrence called Team Two to action. A dispatch rider arrived from Roche Abbey, about sixty miles from Bylands as the crow flies, reporting the abbey was under siege from a troop of mounted knights armed with shields, standards, helmets and coats of mail. The Abbot was requesting immediate help to defend its walls and drive off the attackers.

Team 2 immediately dispatched riders to Rievaulx, Fountains, Kirkstead, and St. Mary's abbeys requesting an armed force be sent to Roche. Then it assembled its own force consisting of ten knights, ten squires, and 100 foot soldiers supported by four horse-drawn supply carts and headed towards Roche Abbey planning to send the mounted knights and squires at a fast pace with the foot soldiers to follow under the command of the Templar monk, who had trained them.

The mounted force overtook a force from St. Mary's Abbey just south of York which added twenty knights and sixteen squires to the ten knights and ten squires from Byland, so it was a considerable number of horsemen hurrying down the road to Bylands. As was the way in medieval times, forces tended to grow as others learned of the impending threat and there were fifty knights, 43 skilled squires/archers and a large number of volunteer foot soldiers on the march by the time the mounted group reached Roche.

This abbey is situated in the valley of the Maltby Beck, about nine miles from Doncaster and thirteen miles from Sheffield. The site is enclosed by steep limestone cliffs and bordered on Burneswald which became known as Sherwood Forest. The abbey was close to several well-traveled thoroughfares although it was located in a remote area.

The mounted group approached the gates of the abbey and identified itself. Immediately the gates were thrown open and they rode into the outer courtyard where the Abbot of the community was waiting to receive them.

It seems the attacking force had been made up of ghosts!

The Abbot explained that one of the monks had seen a ghostly apparition of a fully armored troop of knights descending out of the hills toward the abbey walls in the early evening hours of the day before. He immediately raised the alarm by ringing the church bells and the monks and lay brothers assembled to man the battlements. A number of them also confirmed seeing the approaching mounted troop and a dispatch rider was immediately sent to St. Mary's Abbey at York and then on to Bylands Abbey to sound the alarm and call for help.

All of the abbey defenders watched as the mounted troop simply rode on past the abbey and off into the night without even a glance toward the defenders. It was then they realized it was a revisit by a similar ghost group recorded at the abbey more than 200 years earlier, but there was no way to recall the courier.

Over the next twelve hours more riders and foot soldiers arrived to help defend the abbey until the final assembled force numbered a few more than 1,000 who had arrived within the 48-hour target period for such support. All-in-all Team 2 found it to be a very successful test of its system and a new confidence was installed in all of the affected abbeys.

There was, however, a few of the foot soldiers who were tired out from the forced march and not in the best frame of mind at the false alarm. The monks at Roche had not wasted time after they realized the mistake and had been busy assembling ample food and drink for the troops. It ended up as one of the largest picnics in the history of the Middle Ages and some "spirited" competitions were arranged for entertainment among forces from the various abbeys. The celebration lasted for three days and everyone seemed in a good mood as they departed to return to their home abbeys.

Word soon got out about the false alarm and some ribald humor made the rounds for a time, but most citizens were grateful for such quick response to defend their homelands and it is said, despite the political unrest, that much of Yorkshire slept better at night for several months afterwards.

The well known rock quarries of Roche Abbey were busy for years supplying stone for building projects at the other abbeys in an effort to pay tribute for the efforts of its neighbors.

Needless to say, recruiting for the abbeys stepped up and even more lay brothers were schooled in the military arts. In fact, some of the lords who were Yorkist supporters also stepped up the training of their own forces and the members of Team Two and the trained men of the Templar monk were kept busy advising and instructing at several of the county castles.

It was not long after, in August of 1453 that King Henry VI suffered a mental collapse at his royal manor in Clarendon which threw all of England in a state of alertness and concern. When news of the collapse reached Yorkshire there was immediate unrest between the houses of York and Lancashire.

Word came almost immediately from St. Albans for Team 2 to begin a propaganda campaign on behalf of the Duke of York to encourage the King's Council to appoint him as 'Protector of England' until such time as the King recovered. This, of course, was firmly opposed by the Queen and leaders of the Court party. There were a number of clashes around Yorkshire between the Lancastrians and Yorkists, but these were mostly due to excess zeal fueled by alcohol at the local pubs. None of them involved Team 2; however, some of the forces trained by the abbey did push to try out their new skills and were able to put down most of the problems, but the area was full of unrest.

In February of 1454 Team Two received its share of the monies earlier discovered by Team 1 and this permitted a quicker expansion of the spy network and financing for the propaganda campaign in favor of the Duke of York.

A month later, on March 27, 1454, the Duke succeeded in his quest to become 'Protector.' Within two days of assuming the post he had imprisoned Somerset in the Tower of London and appointed the Earl of Salisbury as 'Chancellor." These events were to lead directly to the Wars of the Roses although no one was suspecting that at the time. The Duke was busy instituting a number of welcomed reforms in the government when the King recovered his wits on Christmas Day.

Prodded by the urging of the Queen, the King released Somerset from the Tower and in April of 1455 paid a visit to Parliament where he summarily dismissed the Duke of York. It was no surprise to the Duke as in January he had received a second message embossed with a green rose warning him that the King was going to act and that he would be in "danger" from that point on.

Team 2 received a dispatch from St. Albans, as did the other teams, two days before the King's actions requesting their immediate march to St. Albans bringing their armaments.

Shortly after that the Duke of York returned to his estates and began raising an army to march on London. It was later learned that many of the troops trained by the monks joined with the Duke and fought in the first battle of the Wars of the Roses at St. Albans.

Chapter 10—Eastern Midlands

As unlikely as it may seem, the production, processing, and sale of wool played an integral part in the Wars of the Roses because it provided revenues for the Cistercian Order to finance the training and arming of lay brothers and to spread that training to other areas of the Midlands.

In June of 1451 Team 3 returned to Kirkstead Abbey in Lincolnshire to find that the abbot had not only continued with the training schools it had started prior to the St. Albans conclave, but had increased the recruiting efforts and had even more lay brothers eager to undergo the training. It appeared the abbot wanted command of his own personal army so Team 3 had to take immediate steps to forestall any such efforts, yet not jeopardize the training programs already underway.

The lead knight immediately resorted to the plan mapped out between himself and the monk at St. Albans and increased pressure on the abbot to double the production of wool, wool products, and other agriculture efforts of the Order thus diverting the abbot's attention from his military pursuits. Each time the abbot would focus his attention on raising and training more armed men, the knight would redirect his attention to some phase of agriculture production.

In the meantime, many of the already trained lay brothers were assigned to work in the various "granges" of the abbey, with the distinction of carrying arms and adding to the protection of their fellow workers. The plan worked well and eventually trained lay brothers were sent to other abbeys for the same purpose.

In the meantime the knights and squires of Team 3 began a calculated campaign of visiting other abbeys and strongholds in the Midlands. Gaining support and trust from the nobles was a slow process and the team would get together and map out a campaign for each stronghold after assessing the mood of the noble and the knights of the household. Each campaign was tailored to the household and more times than not, the plan was accepted with little alteration once it was presented.

It was a slow process and could take up to several months just to convince one noble he needed help. Egos were such during the Middle Ages that Team 3 had to develop a technique of highly praising the efforts of the noble while showing him areas where his defenses, his leadership, and his opportunities to enhance his power and prestige would be advanced through their help. Once the noble was "sold" on the plan, a group of trained lay brothers from the abbey, led by a member of Team 3, would literally "move in" to the noble's household for the time necessary to execute the plan. Usually, the noble was so pleased with the progress of his "troops" that he would recommend it to his friends.

This had the distinct advantage of identifying who supported whom in the territory and proved to be a valuable insight when it came time for fighting in later years.

In July of 1451 another unique opportunity opened up for Team 3 when the abbot of Kirkstead insisted they accompany him to the annual fair at the market and seaport access village of Boston located a few miles to the south of the abbey. The abbot used the annual market to promote the higher grade wool produced by the abbey and was keen to show Team 3 he was working to increase the revenues as it had suggested.

While Team 3 was reluctant to take the time away from its other activities, the event turned out to be one of the biggest advances for its efforts.

The Cistercian reputation for producing fine wool and other agricultural products was well founded. After the initial gift of land to a Cistercian abbey, the monks worked hard to develop it into a profitable piece of real estate despite the fact it likely was not the best land available.

Their work brought additional endowments of all types of lands, but usually scattered and some distance away from the abbey. Considerable effort was expended to consolidate these lands in order to not be associated with peasant agriculture in the area. These land holdings were known as "grangia" or granges. The Cistercian granges were among the best and most economically successful in the country.

One particularly competitive advantage for the Cistercians was that its granges were staffed by lay brothers who were not paid wages and this was a key element in expanding the system. Usually, each grange was worked from a set of buildings including barns, animal sheds, sometimes a mill, housing for the lay brothers, and occasionally a chapel. The granges served a secondary purpose as handy places for the abbot or lay brothers on business to stop for the night during their travels. This regular travel between the granges and other Cistercian houses allowed the Order to "hear" news of what was going on in other parts of England and abroad and members not only were knowledgeable of the politics of the age, but learned about newly developed crops and methods of farming.

The system proved especially valuable for the teams of the Order of the Green Rose as it was the nucleus of every spy system they established and each team, with the exception of Team 6, merely had to expand on an existing system.

The agricultural success also had some drawbacks for the Cistercian Order as it led them away from their original pursuit of isolation; however, this also proved valuable to the efforts of the various teams to improve the financial lot of many of the abbeys, which by this time, had begun to decline from earlier triumphs.

All of the Cistercian abbeys held market privileges which enabled the monks and lay brothers to sell surplus produce and to purchase any goods they lacked. This proved to be the third tool needed by most of the Green Rose teams to revitalize these abbeys and achieve political objectives. It is doubtful the Pope could have chosen more wisely when he committed the teams to the Cistercian houses.

Since much of the English landscape was suitable only for grazing, sheep farming and the production of wool became the most lucrative product for the Cistercians after they realized the opportunities afforded to them. Each sack of wool probably contained about 200 fleeces so it was relatively easy to pinpoint the numbers of sheep on each grange by what was marketed. The Order developed a method of washing and preparing the fleeces and graded them into three classes—best wool, medium wool, and lock wool. This usually brought them higher prices than the competition as knowledgeable merchants would seek and bid on the Order's wool first.

Most of the abbeys also dabbled in brokering wool produced by others such as peasant farmers with limited animals. This wool was called "collecta" and was kept separate from the wool produced by the abbey. This added to the incentive of the merchants to deal with the white-robed monks at the marketplace.

Wool was stored in "houses" before being transported to the ports to be shipped abroad. Boston and Lincoln were two of the major collecting points for export wool and the reason for the importance attached to the annual fair at Boston by the abbot.

The fair was set up around St. Botolph's Church and featured hundreds of booths rented for the event by both local and foreign merchants. It was one of the top three most important commercial gatherings in England during the Middle Ages. Besides produce from the surrounding countryside, the fair featured imported goods of cloth, canvas, linen, iron, copper, timber, dyes, wines, dried fruits, spices from the East, and fish being brokered and sold at the various booths.

Merchants visiting the fair were also eager to purchase the wool, wool products, grain, lead, and salt exported from Boston. It was a time of serious business, but also a time for merriment with various entertainments offered throughout the days of the fair. Local inns and pubs did a large share of their annual business as a result of the influx of participants to the town. Most of the religious houses from Lincolnshire, Yorkshire and beyond held special tenements in Boston which were primarily used to expedite the sale of wool and other products produced by the abbeys and priories. Piers on the east side of the Witham River were being used for unloading and loading of goods for transshipment on the river to and from the coastal areas where the ships were waiting. This activity was ongoing constantly. Thus, the fair at Boston drew a mixed crowd of English and foreign visitors each year.

Members of Team 3 spent their days, and sometimes far into the night, striking "deals" with visiting ship captains and merchants for delivery and sale of goods produced by the abbey. Before the event was concluded they had written agreements for the sale of wool and barley for all that could be produced for export in the next five years. The abbot was greatly pleased with this marketing expertise, but not so pleased when he had to mortgage some of the abbey granges to assure he could deliver what was purchased and to cover the advanced deposits made to secure the agreements. He vowed he would not be so anxious to take the team to next year's market. He made sure the monks and lay brothers took special care with the lambing process the next spring and even visited some of the granges to encourage them.

One of the team's contacts at the marketplace was the owner of a tannery at Grantham, in south Lincolnshire, who also agreed to work with the abbey in the preparation of leather. This increased the productivity of several of the lay brothers who were put to work making leather trade goods—belts, shoes, purses, quivers, harness, and some protective military gear. It also opened the door to establish a spy cell in the village, a traditional overnight stop for kings and nobles traveling the countryside to and from London.

When harvest time rolled around in September and October in 1451, even the members of Team 3 had to pitch in to guarantee enough barley was separated to assure meeting the export quota agreed to at the fair. The abbot was greatly relieved when he didn't have to forfeit any of his lands since the harvest was plentiful with enough surplus to provide for the abbey needs for food and seed and a surplus to help allay any shortages the next year.

One wintry day in February 1452, six of the Team 3 members were making contacts at the noble houses near Stamford in the southwest part of Lincolnshire, a main coach stopping point on the road from Nottingham to Boston. They were just about to cross the River Welland, which runs through the town, when they spotted a stopped coach on the road ahead under attack from highwaymen. With drawn weapons they immediately launched an offensive attack against the robbers catching them focused on subduing two armed knights escorting the coach.

One of the squires scored a remarkable hit with an arrow loosed from the back of his galloping horse and that alerted the robbers to their approaching danger. The team swooped in and managed to capture six of them, including the one hit by the arrow, but the others sped quickly away from the scene. One of the defending knights was badly wounded and they immediately rendered aid.

A noblewoman riding in the coach demanded to know who they were and the team leader identified his group as lay brothers from Kirkstead Abbey. They loaded the wounded knight onto the floor of the coach while the lady tried to reward their efforts by offering her purse, which they refused. They escorted the coach into Stamford and to a hospital operated by one of the religious groups in the town. Then they delivered their prisoners to the local constable, filling him in on the details of the attack, and telling him where he could locate the lady and her injured knight. The team then went on its way thinking little more about the incident.

Later, a message was received at Kirkstead Abbey, that the highwaymen had been convicted and hung at a set of often-used gallows on High Street in Stamford. The message was sealed with the well-known "falcon in a fetter lock," the personal insignia of the Duke of York.

April of that year was sheep-shearing time and Team 3 was busy protecting the wool shipments to Boston for export and making sure they got to the correct warehouses at the port village. They also spent some time escorting foreign buyers to the abbey to bargain for wool until the abbot finally called upon them to bring no more buyers as his supply for the next eight years had already been sold and he was afraid he would have to mortgage the church building itself in order to assure delivery of the goods as contracted.

The one advantage enjoyed by Team 3 was the opportunity to visit with the buyers as they traveled to and from the abbey and to learn about things happening in the world, especially France, where the English troops were losing ground in the battle to save possessions. Many details of just how bad the war in France was going were relayed by messenger to St. Albans. The monk at St. Albans, in turn, relayed some enquiries to

Team 3 to be asked of the travelers and that added to the bank of information.

It was in early June of 1452 that the next incident of interest happened to Team 3 during a visit to Newstead Abbey, an Augustinian Priory in Nottingham, where the team had been invited to begin recruiting and training some of the monks and laity at the abbey. This was in response to the abbot at Kirkstead who set up the opportunity during the fair at Boston the previous year. The team knew the abbot was motivated to keep them from participating in this year's fair, since the resources of the abbey were already sold out, and he had arranged this effort as a distraction. The team later learned the abbot had been well aware of the team's efforts in distracting him into agricultural instead of military pursuits, and this was his way of evening up the opportunities.

Anyway, it provided a good opportunity to work with the Order of St. Augustine and the team was looking forward to the challenge. The monks at Newstead had been subjected to a growing series of assaults from a gang of thieves and had been seeking protection as they worked the abbey's lands. It also established a new chapter in the Order of the Green Rose for being the only time its knights and representatives hastily withdrew from an ongoing battle.

The team was leading a new group of recruits through Sherwood Forest en route to the Newstead Abbey when it was attacked by a huge band of armed brigands—numbering close to fifty or more. While there were the four knights and four squires of Team 3, plus two monks from the abbey, and six recruits, they were seriously outnumbered especially when it came to close-in combat. Hence, the team leader made the decision to withdraw as quickly as possible to the old castle in Nottingham where they stood a better chance of defending themselves. The knights kept the brigands pretty much at bay during the flight, except for one of the recruits who was killed when he disobeyed orders and chose to do battle instead of retreat.

The team became trapped in the upper bailey of the old castle and was still holding its defensive position as darkness fell. One of the Augustinian monks approached the Team 3 leader and outlined a plan for escape using a secret escape route known as "Mortimer's Hole" which led to the village below via a series of tunnels entered through a secret door known to the monk.

During a lull in the fighting, the monk led the Team 3 party through a series of dark tunnels and caves which eventually led to an old and respected Crusader era Inn in the village below. The team came up through a trap door in one of the cellars of the Inn and slipped unseen out a back window into the street. The only casualties, besides the slain recruit, were the loss of their horses and much of their gear which had to be left behind at the old castle.

The team was not very pleased when it had to return to Kirkstead Abbey in a donkey cart driven by one of the Newstead monks. The team spent several weeks purchasing new horses in the area and replacing their gear before it returned to Newstead Abbey to finish the job. Ultimately, it was the results of the training that finally caught up with the thieves when a mounted troop of monks and lay brothers from the Newstead Abbey surprised their camp one morning in Sherwood Forest and captured a number of them including most of the Team 3 horses. They also found a hut containing the lost armor belonging to the team. One of the monks led the captured horses loaded with the armor back to Kirkstead Abbey and returned it to Team 3 relating how they had recaptured it. Those bandits, not killed in the clash, were hanged.

In September foreign merchants again began visiting Kirkstead Abbey to deal for wool, only this time it was for the "collecta" wool being held by the abbey for smaller wool producers in the area. This trade had increased nearly 100 fold as peasants and small farmers learned they could get higher prices for their wool by brokering it through the abbey, even after paying the monks to clean and grade it as they did for the abbey produced wool.

The news from the fighting in France, brought by the merchants, was that England was losing the war and this news was immediately dispatched to St. Albans.

Early in 1453 Team 3 was urged by the monk at St. Albans to redouble its efforts at recruiting and training more military prospects. The Team was busy rotating its services between the castles and abbey programs it had established and soon more than 1,000 lay brothers, monks, and even knights from the various strongholds were actively pursuing training. Team 3 set up a series of "contests" and these were carried on throughout the spring months as entertainment in the market towns in Leicestershire, Nottinghamshire, and Lincolnshire. The only time anyone got hurt was when a local farmer or peasant entered the competition without the proper training and ended up on the casualty list although there was only one serious such incident when one of the peasants subsequently lost an arm.

Surprisingly enough, it was these contests that added to the opportunities to recruit and the progress of the military training escalated. Many of the trained lay brothers from Kirkstead Abbey were called into service to help train these recruits and soon, upon short notice, more than 5,000 trained fighters could be summoned to combat. This proved to be the greatest military success by any of the teams.

In June Team 3 received word from workers at one of the abbey's granges near Gainsborough, on the River Trent, that they were constantly being pillaged by a group of river men who were breaking into the storage buildings on the farm and stealing stored wool and barley, loading it on a barge, and moving it down the river leaving the monks no method of catching them. The Abbot at Kirkstead arranged for Team 3 to use one of the narrow barges contracted by the abbey to transport wool to Boston from some of its granges.

Team 3, along with a couple of armed monks from the abbey and a group of twelve lay brothers, boarded the barge at Lincoln, leaving their horses at one of the abbey's stables. The barge crew, made up of six burley hands plus the master and his wife, made their way upriver to a junction with the Trent and then moved downriver to the granges near Gainsborough docking their barge below an old manor house standing high on the east bank of the river. From there they could see the buildings on the abbey's grange on the opposite bank of the river.

The group set up a camp along the river for its vigil. It was four days later when they saw a barge being pulled up on the opposite bank and the barge crew loading up sacks of wool from the abbey's storage house.

Team 3 immediately boarded its barge and the river men steered it across to the opposite bank arriving just as the other barge was pulling away from the bank. Needless to say Team 3 gave chase and it was a couple of miles before their lighter barge began gaining on the crooks. When the crooks became aware of being chased they started dumping cargo over the side in an attempt to lighten their barge so it would move faster in the river's current.

Finally, the leader of team 3 called over one of his squires who was in charge of the new hand gun the group had received at the conclave in St. Albans and asked him to see if he could do some damage to the other barge. The squire braced his weapon on the prow of the barge and loosed a lead ball. It missed the other barge completely and the squire reloaded for another try.

"This time allow for the movement of the barge up and down," the team leader told him. The squire apparently was a fast learner for his next shot struck the arm of the river crook manning the huge tiller bar in the stern of the craft sending him to the bottom of the barge. The barge quickly swung sideways in the current and before another crook could right the tiller the barge grounded on a sandbar. The barge men for Team 3 quickly brought their barge alongside the grounded barge and Team 3 boarded and soon took the other barge by force. Some of the crooks jumped into the water to avoid the flashing swords. Most of them couldn't swim and drowned when the current pulled them under. The three that could swim were quickly dispatched with arrows fired by the squires.

It took quite an effort by the lay brothers, working in conjunction with the barge men, but the captured barge was towed back to the grange and left there for the monks and lay brothers to use in the event another raid was made on the storehouses. No attempt was made to recover the cargo floating down the river, but there was plenty in the captured barge to replace what had been stolen.

The abbey group was pretty joyful on its way back to Lincoln via the borrowed barge and returned to the abbey without further incident. A report of the encounter was sent to St. Albans and, as a result, each team involved in water traffic soon set up a barge of its own, filled with armed lay brothers, and designed to police the river problems. Some of the teams, including Team 3, operated multiple barges if there was more than one navigable river in its assigned territories. The barge teams also picked up quite a lot of "river gossip" along their various routes.

Other than attending a renown sheep fair at Corby Glen in Lincolnshire during October, things ran pretty normal for Team 3 until early in December when a special messenger arrived at the abbey bearing an invitation for the members of Team 3 to attend Christmas festivities at Fotheringhay Castle in Northamptonshire as the honored guests of the Duke of York and his wife Cecily.

Since Christmas festivities in the Middle Ages lasted for several days, Team 3 spent the next week getting all in readiness for the trip to Northamptonshire. A dispatch rider had been sent to St. Albans to report the invitation and word was received back that both the abbot and leader of Team 6 also would be attending the festivities along with some of the other members of Team 6. All were looking forward to a reunion of sorts as it had been nearly two years since they had seen each other. They arranged to arrive separately at the castle so as not to divulge their connection unless the Team 6 monk leader decided to do so during the festivities.

The village of Fotheringhay was about seventy miles south and west of Kirkstead Abbey and Team 3 set out on December 18th for Fotheringhay Castle, located on a man-made hill just outside of the village overlooking the River Nene and a lake in a beautiful setting. There were no problems along the roads as most people preferred to travel in warmer weather. News of their approach reached the castle before they did and a large welcoming party was in the outer bailey as they crossed the moat and entered the castle grounds through the large gatehouse. Included in the welcoming party were the Duke and Duchess of York, several of the castle knights, and the monk and abbot from St. Albans. After the introductions, grooms took the horses to the stables and the guests were escorted to the Great Hall for the first of several banquets held during the Christmas season.

As honored guests, members of Team 3, along with other visiting dignitaries, were seated at special tables located just in front of the elevated table of the Duke of York and his family and were served the same fare as the Lord's Table. All-in-all, there were more than 200 guests dining in the great hall throughout the festivities. The highlight of the Christmas day feast was the parade with the traditional boar's head, but there were many other exciting dishes served throughout the season at the various feasts including cockentrice, live birds in a pie, a peacock in full feathered dress in honor of the duchess, and several courses of venison, ox, pheasant, coneys, and even mutton.

Team 3 members were honored on Christmas Day with special presents offered by the Duchess including suits of clothes and specially cast silver daggers emblazoned with the fettered falcon insignia of the Duke. Other guests received gifts, but not as lavish as those handed out to members of Team 3. The monk from Team 6; however, received a specially cast gold coin with the rose emblem of the Duke of York.

To most of the members of Team 3, the festivities tended to run together. There were chapel services, hunting parties, masked balls, contests, feasts, and several conferences with the Duke and Duchess of York during the nine days Team 3 spent at the castle before being allowed to return home. Both the knights and squires acquitted themselves well in the hunts and contests and more often than not it came down to members of the two teams combating each other for the championships in archery and various mock battle contests. Team 3 bested Team 6 in archery and ring spearing, while Team 6 upheld its honor in horsemanship and sword dueling so it was pretty much an even split. None of the knights were allowed to enter the jousting for fear of injury. In truth, none of the local knights were eager to compete with them anyway due to the prowess demonstrated in the other contests.

In addition, there were three night-long sessions with the monk and members of Team 6 comparing notes and assessing the current political situation in the country. Based on information picked up by Team 3 from its contacts with ship captains and merchants, it was decided to issue another "Green Rose" declaration to the Duke of York advising him of the inherent dangers caused by the ill-run war in France and the apparent intent of the Court Party which controlled the King's Council.

As a result, the monk from Team 6 had a secret meeting with the Duke and Duchess, handing him a special sealed report embossed with the green rose. He then proceeded to outline why the Order was in England, briefed the Duke upon its activities and potential for raising military troops, and offered his assistance. To say that the Duke was astounded is to put it mildly, but he quickly foresaw the advantages of working with such an organization and a deal was struck.

Soon special messengers could be seen leaving Fotheringhay Castle bearing requests for a council among the Duke's supporters and such a council did take place about a month later. However, no member of the Order of the Green Rose was in attendance as part of the secrecy arrangement between the Duke and the monk. A message was dispatched to St. Albans at the conclusion of the council and further instructions were sent to all of the teams at the various abbeys throughout England.

It was soon after Christmas when the whispers began about the Duke of York's aspirations to the throne of England. Not long after that the King, or in this case the Queen, was seen to send a special envoy to Scotland and the word came back she was seeking a special alliance to help the mentally ill Henry VI retain his claim and possession of the throne.

Team 3, upon its return to Kirkstead after the Christmas season, started an intensive propaganda effort, along with all of the other Green Rose teams, to get the Duke of York appointed as "Protector of England" while the king was ill. Team 3 used the theme: "Don't let the Council pull the wool over your eyes," as the theme of its campaign and that struck a real strong response from the many York supporters it its territory since wool was perhaps the most important commodity of the area.

The campaign was intensified in February of 1454 when Team 3 received its share of the monies discovered earlier by Team 1. Some of the money was paid to the Abbot at Kirkstead to repay his efforts in sharing wool profits to finance the team's activities. The remainder was used to purchase arms and armor for trained lay brothers and other military volunteers in the area. In addition, recruitment and training in military tactics was stepped up still another notch. It is estimated there were currently more than 2,000 men undergoing training during this period in addition to about 4,000 that already had received training and were being armed as fast as possible.

An emissary from the Duke of York arrived at Grantham for a meeting with the Abbot of Kirkstead and leader of Team 3 to quietly discuss military affairs in the area and to deliver a large cash grant to the abbey to expand its mining of coal, lead, and iron in the Ashby Wolds area in Leicestershire to be forged into weapons and military harness.

The abbey proceeded to double its production of these minerals and smelted the iron into pigs at its foundry near Coalville. The cast iron pigs were then shipped by cart and barge to Lincoln where lay brothers from Kirkstead supervised an iron works on one of the abbey's granges. By the end of the year more than 200 lay brothers and hired workers were producing an array of arms including, in its later stages, cannon. Team 3 played an important part in the design of these arms and Lincoln-produced swords and arms became well known by the end of the Wars of the Roses. Each piece was embossed with a special copper rose, which turned green over a given period of time.

By April of 1455 the Duke of York was personally raising an army. By the time Team 3 was summoned to St. Albans, the Duke had already called more than 5,000 men to arms including most of those trained through the work of the team.

Chapter 11—East Anglia

When Team 4 returned to Coggeshall Abbey after its return from the Green Rose Conclave at St. Albans Abbey, it immediately resumed its efforts at contacting the various manor houses in its assigned territory, known primarily as East Anglia, but consisting of the counties of Essex, Suffolk, and Norfolk along the East coast of England.

While the abbey had continued to work with monks and lay brothers on military training, the team's dreams of spreading such training over its territory were soon shattered as visits continued to the various nobles in the area. What it found out was that most manors were well built and had protective walls, but they were thinly manned for defensive purposes. The territory, with the exception of the various abbeys, were primarily limited to 800-acre estates—especially in Norfolk—when the territory was split among the followers of William the Conqueror. These smaller estates made it economically hard to maintain even a small military force although, in some cases, wise landowners had arranged for parts of the estates to be sub-divided among small "freeholders" who, in time of conflict, could be called on for defensive purposes. However, these were largely poorly armed and minimally trained.

At first the team was excited about the need for military organization, but found considerable resistance from most of the land holders due to the memory of a 1381 peasant revolt caused by taxes levied at the time.

This revolt, although short lived, had widespread destructive impact on the area including the sacking of several of the abbeys, churches, and manor houses including Coggeshall Abbey itself. Landowners wanted no part of arming the peasants in the area and raising the possibility of another such revolt.

The team considered this a setback and its leader rode directly to St. Albans to consult with the lead monk and to come up with a possible alternative plan. In the meantime, horseracing was catching on in the area and the other members of the team, including the squires, were often winning small purses at the local marketplaces for their superior horses. All this had been started by one of the squires on the team shortly after the team had arrived in the area.

The popularity of the races increased speedily as many of the nobles in the area had fine horses and loved such competitions. And, this proved to be the solution to Team 4's work with the local towns and villages—not only horse races, but other sorts of contests including "sack races," relays, archery, spear and hatchet throwing and other skill competitions and demonstrations encouraged by the local guilds. One village even sponsored a "bread baking" contest which attracted bakers from all over the countryside to compete for prizes. Many of the parish churches jumped into the fray and there were even "singing" contests before long. All-in-all it was a "masterful stroke" and still provided some of the rudimentary military and defensive training needed, but in a more "spirited" form.

Team 4, in order to maintain its own status in the area, sent for some specially bred horses from Jervaulx Abbey in Yorkshire and entered them in local races. One of the monks at Coggelshall, was only 4-feet, 6-inches tall and weighed less than 100 pounds. He was enlisted to ride in several of the races and became quite well known as one of the first jockeys in the racing sport. He also designed a lightweight saddle which allowed him to control the horse yet maintain his balance. Many of the competitors admired the saddle and ordered them specially made and this became one of the industries for the abbey.

Most of the summer of 1451 was occupied by Team 4 with encouraging and promoting the seemingly innocent contests. By the end of the year more than 100 local marketplaces featured some type of contest each week, but horseracing remained the overall favorite.

One of the problems observed by the members of Team 4 during visits to the manor houses was that many of them were in need of repair. When the team leader visited with the abbot about the condition of these houses, the abbot immediately asked if they were made of bricks. It seems a lot of the construction in the 12th and 13th century used bricks from an old brickworks at Coggelshall Abbey and the monks had once been well noted for their masonry work.

"Is the brickworks still standing?," enquired the knight.

"I think the shell of it is still there and, of course, the clay pits are still open. Our monks have been using a hand made form to make bricks for our own use, but nothing like we produced before," the abbot said.

After receiving directions to the old brickworks on a nearby abbey grange, the members of Team 4 did a walking tour of the area with the assistance of one of the older monks who pointed out the features of the former operation.

"Why was the operation discontinued?" the team leader asked.

"Most of the richer nobles began importing stone and bricks from France and other parts of England and our demand fell off. Also, the decline of our membership in the Order has played a part," the monk said.

"If labor was not a problem, could the brickworks be restored?" asked the team leader.

"We would have to reinforce the present structure, rebuild the linings in some of the ovens and find some source of fuel to fire them. We used to use peat, but that was such an uneven heat they had trouble with quality. If we could find a reasonable source of coal and labor, we could be back in production within a couple of months," the monk added.

"With the abbot's permission, would you be willing to direct the operations?" the knight asked.

"With the grace of God that is one of my specialties," the monk said.

Team 4 held another meeting with the abbot, who had begun to warm to the idea of further restoring the abbey to its former prominence, and permission for the monk to proceed was immediately forthcoming. Four of the lay brothers at the abbey, under direction of the monk, began working to rehabilitate the brickworks which lay alongside the bank of the Blackwell River not far from a huge pole barn on a grange adjacent to the abbey grounds. Team 4 divided into two groups with the team leader's group assigned to discover and secure a supply of coal and the other part of the team was to begin recruiting new lay brothers to operate the brickworks.

At the recommendation of the abbot, the coal seeking members of Team 4 left for Kirkstead Abbey in Lincolnshire, to negotiate an exchange for coal produced by one of the abbey's granges near Coalville. It was a successful trip and an agreement was concluded to swap fired bricks for coal. The processed coal was to be shipped by wagon and barge to Boston, transferred to seagoing vessels at the mouth of the river, and shipped along the east coast of England to the southern town of Malden and up the Blackwater River to the brickworks. Finished bricks in payment were to be returned in the opposite direction, but via the same vessels. It was a system that worked out well for both abbeys although Coggelshall's lay brothers had to train those at Kirkstead in the art of masonry.

In the meantime, the other half of Team 4 had been busy recruiting lay brothers to run the brickworks, but had run into some difficulties since traditionally the lay brothers at the abbey were non-paid workers. Finally, in cooperation with the abbot, an agreement was reached whereby the lay brothers would receive no direct compensation for their work, but indirectly would be allowed to share in the profits of the brickworks either in goods received or ultimately, a small land grant, depending upon their years of service. It took a few months, but the abbey soon had more than 200 lay brothers actively engaged in digging clay, making bricks, or working on specialized masonry teams repairing buildings in the area.

The first word of a smuggling operation stealing market wool from abbey and private storehouses reached Team 4 in February of 1452. Early reports told of smugglers stealing the wool and woolen cloth and transporting it to Norwich in Norfolk County for shipment to France and other European countries. This turned out to be a false report and by March the members of Team 4 had pretty well pinpointed Lynn, a port located on the shoreline of an area of the North Sea called "The Wash," as the primary destination for the smugglers. Since many of the local manors were impacted by the thefts from centralized storehouses, it was pretty easy for Team 4 to secure needed cooperation from the nobles in the area to try and catch the thieves.

Norfolk is an extremely flat countryside broken by low swells and depressions and it was very hard to spot and track smuggler caravans en route to King's Lynn until Team 4 hit upon the idea of using the many round towers constructed years earlier in various spots in the county—as many as 75 of them throughout the county. Believed to have been constructed for defense, lookout, signaling, or simply to shelter the water wells inside each of them, Team 4 concluded they were ideal for the purpose of tracking the illegal caravans.

Since there were more than 600 local parishes in the county, Team 4 worked with the various religious leaders to utilize parish members to man the towers in six-man teams assigned to keep watch over the landscape on a twenty-four-hour a day basis until the smugglers were stopped. Each tower was supplied with food and the team provided the material to light a signal fire, if at night, and was furnished a bright yellow and red striped flag if an illegal caravan was spotted during the daylight hours. The flag was to be flown with the yellow stripe up if a caravan was simply spotted or the red stripe up if emergency assistance was needed immediately and the tower was under attack. Since each tower had its own enclosed water well, it was easily defended and the six-man team could hold out until help arrived.

Such help was probably the forerunner of the mounted posse as Team 4 recruited and trained groups of ten members each with good mounts and weaponry. Most of these teams were housed at the manor estates throughout the county and many were led by the noble himself. It was felt that at least one team, and possibly two or more, could converge upon an impacted tower within and hour's time after the alarm was sounded.

Team 4 was in demand for some time providing military training and attack tactics to these teams which turned out to be a great substitute for the military training the nobles were reluctant to allow in the first place. All of the towers were manned and the response teams were in place as early as the last of April.

The system worked well, and the armed men in the watchtowers were changed every two weeks on a rotating basis. Although there were a couple of "false alarms" when tower occupants believed they had spotted a caravan, the alarms proved only to be a good test of the system.

It was in June of 1452 when the first real alarm was sounded and a train of smuggler carts was spotted moving through Norwich after a raid on an Augustine abbey holding house where processed wool was being stored awaiting shipment. The band of smugglers broke into the house during the night and stole some fifty sacks of processed fleeces, loaded them on carts, and headed overland towards Lynn (now known as King's Lynn).

With the advance knowledge of where the train was heading, and warning signals along the way to note its progress, Team 4 quickly gathered up some twenty of its mounted teams and headed towards Lynn by a more direct route than the slow overland train. The pursuing group was more than 200 strong by the time it reached the outskirts of Lynn and stopped by pre-arrangement at a grange near West Winch, about a mile south of the port town. The grange was operated by a Carmelite Friary which had established a precinct in South Lynn before 1260. The grange had a large pasture, barn, dormitory building and chapel and was able to accommodate the Team 4 force. It was also along one of the main roads to Lynn and the South Gate entrance to the town. The Team 4 leader and one of the nobles attached to the group rode on into the Friary to pay their respects and to seek help.

The Friars in their white robes were known all over the area and had freedom of movement throughout the town including the waterfront areas without raising suspicion. They were all briefed on what to look for and how to report the information to the armed force. The Friary also supplied food to the grange to feed the men. It was two days before the Team learned that the smugglers had apparently loaded the wool on two small barges along the Great Ouse River, above West Winch, and were floating them down river to Lynn for eventual loading aboard a ship.

Fortunately, the loading of the barges had been spotted through the efforts of one of the parish churches and they were being shadowed as they moved down river. The barges were easily identified and friars were alerted as to what to look for.

It was after dark on the fourth day, when word of the final destination of the stolen wool was received at the grange. In the meantime, the armed force had been put to work rebuilding walls and repairing structures on the grange, much to the delight of the friars.

The barges had drawn up to a dock near an area on the waterfront known as the Saturday Market and an old stone warehouse on the public quay operated by the Hanseatic League. The Hanse merchants were a powerful German trading organization made up of merchants from North Germany and had been operating from Lynn since 1424 (or earlier) and was well established and respected.

Since their involvement in a smuggling operation was highly unlikely, the Team 4 leader contacted one of the wealthier German merchants in the town regarding the barges. The merchant assured the knight the League did not engage in thievery and pledged his full cooperation, and that of other League members, to find out about the barges and their loads of wool. The merchant knew, if they were docked at the League's warehouse, the contents of the barges would be scheduled to be transshipped on a merchant ship.

The next morning, the 200 members of the armed force surrounded the League's warehouse, led by the merchant, and stormed aboard the two barges capturing the bargemen without a struggle. The team leader identified a mark on the wool sacks to assert claim to the wool and an extensive investigation followed.

The merchant demanded to "see the books" kept by the warehouse and discovered the wool had indeed been consigned to be shipped to Germany by one of the smaller merchants associated with the League. He was immediately arrested and subsequently hanged, but not before giving up other members of the smugglers including the captains of two private merchant vessels regularly sailing out of Lynn. The two vessels were seized by the armed force and confiscated. They subsequently were used to carry coal and bricks for the Coggelshall Abbey. In all, some forty plus people were detained, tried, and hung as a result of the investigation carried out by the Hanseatic League. And, while it did not stop all of the robberies, it certainly decreased the raids on the abbey wool.

Most of the armed forces were released to return home shortly after the initial raids, but members of Team 4 were occupied with the investigation and carrying out of justice for the thieves until late in August. When they left Lynn it was only after a large banquet had been held in their honor courtesy of merchant members of the German organization who were grateful to be cleared of any association with the smuggling.

The tower spy system continued on for a few months, but eventually ceased to be effective as most of the parishes abandoned their assigned watch after things calmed down. It was said that the "threat" of renewal of the system held crime to a minimum in Norwich for several years after that.

In September word came by special courier from the same German organization of merchants that the English war effort in France was failing badly. While this information was passed along to St. Albans, the monk there already had been updated with the situation by another team. It was proof; however, that the spy system established by the Order of the Green Rose had far reaching tentacles into other countries. The team did receive a special assignment from St. Albans to increase its efforts to "spread the word" of the corruption by the King's Council and Court Party for refusing to properly fight the war. It was not long before many of the parish pastors were offering opinions and prayers on the war. This did not do much to lessen growing tensions and there were many "faction" fights in the local pubs throughout the country.

Team 4 had many other enterprises claiming its attention and in December of 1452 much of its time was devoted to the growing "weaving industry" being spearheaded by many of the local parish churches in Suffolk. The production grew so fast that weekly "cart runs" had to be made to pick up finished goods produced by the women of the parish churches and a collection point and warehouse was established at Ipswich to be used in the exporting of the goods. The abbot himself concluded a lease for a large brick warehouse constructed years earlier with bricks from the abbey and contacted Ipswich merchants who were eager to participate in the purchase and export of the fine finished cloth produced by the churches.

Materials produced by each parish church were carefully indexed and cataloged upon receipt at the warehouse at Ipswich and one-half of the proceeds were dutifully returned to each church. This had a secondary impact of providing money for the many churches to improve and repair their buildings and demand for abbey bricks and trained workmen escalated, too. About a quarter of the proceeds were dispatched to St. Albans to help prepare for any contingencies involved in the current political unrest in the country and the other quarter was invested in the abbey lands and industries.

By February of 1453 the restored brickworks at the abbey was in full operation, although it had been producing quality bricks for some months. Some 200 or more lay brothers and share workers were busily engaged in the production of bricks and barge loads were shipped almost weekly to the port in Malden for shipment to foreign and domestic ports as well as to Kirkstead Abbey to fulfill the exchange agreement for the coal, which had greatly improved the quality of the fired bricks to the extent it was rare when a problem occurred. This increased production by more than twenty percent and permitted the abbey to consign bricks for its local building and repair contracts.

Even the masonry guilds were "on board" with the program as demands for their workmen also increased and many of the parishes were willing to pay a premium to secure craftsmen for their projects. Times were good and the abbot was very pleased with Team 4.

One of the biggest projects was secured in May when the lord of an older manor in the area of the abbey pleaded with workmen to repair his buildings and build a new chapel within the enclosed walls. This project alone necessitated the abbey to pull out old molds, long in storage, and to produce a limited number of bricks with "knocked-off" corners for chamfers, "rounded" corners for door posts, and even more elaborate moldings used to create some of the Gothic style arches of Coggeshall Abbey itself. These bricks were sold at a higher price. The bricks produced at Coggeshall were slightly larger than the old Roman-produced bricks and the only competition for the locally produced bricks were those imported into the area from Flanders, known as "tall bricks."

Bricks were used to supplement the locally produced "flint" stone used for construction. It was easier to use bricks to form the angles of buildings, both inside and out, including quoins, window jambs, door jambs and arches. Guild workers were used for the stonework while abbey artisans did the more complex brick work.

In May of 1453 the members of Team 4 were asked to expand the work of the parish churches in weaving cloth from wool. The wool project had been "the talk" of many of the villages participating and others, hearing about it while visiting the various marketplaces, were eager to get involved. By July the industry had grown to the extent that at least six shiploads were being sent abroad from Ipswich every month and the abbey had spearheaded the biggest economic boost the local areas had ever seen. There was no unemployment and workers were sometimes brought in from the London area to help out.

In July the brickworks received a large order from Scotland which necessitated the abbey opening a second brickworks near Sudbury on the River Stour where the barges of bricks were floated down river to Harwich and subsequently shipped to Scotland and other markets.

Abbey revenues were at an all-time high and the abbot was looking for other investments so the second brickworks was a natural expansion. The abbey also made an investment in more ships and ended up with a fleet of ten seagoing merchant ships by adding eight to the two it had received as a result of putting down the wool smuggling operations at Lynn earlier. Coggelshall one of the few abbeys in England known to have had its own merchant fleet. Although the upkeep for the ships was high, it still was far less expensive than shipping through private merchants and the ships were soon paid for and making another nice profit for the abbey.

Of all the Order of the Green Rose teams, Team 4 produced the most economic return for the host abbey and the Order. In fact it later returned its share of the monies secured by Team 1 as "not needed" to fulfill its mission.

By January of 1454 Team 4 was highly engaged in using its opportunities to spread propaganda in its three counties to secure, with other teams, the appointment of the Duke of York as "Protector of England" while the King was ill. It was later learned that petitions from parish churches, several bishops, and about twenty percent of the local nobles and freeholders put direct pressure on the King's Council to secure the appointment.

In March an order came down from St. Albans which asked Team 4 to "secure secret sites" to begin weaving military coverlets with the insignia of the Duke of York. Within a few weeks secret shipments were being made to a castle in Wales. The Team also received a representative from several of the noble manors asking for help in training military forces based upon the contacts made earlier and the success of the ten-man teams organized to protect Norfolk during the time when smugglers were active.

One knight and squire from Team 4 was all that could be spared to meet this request and they were quickly dispatched to the manor of one noble who had the facilities to train and arm and number of fighting men. Several of the trained lay brothers from the abbey also were sent along with a training plan hatched out at night by members of the team.

This plan charted a six-week training program based upon establishing ten-man squads and setting up competitions as part of the training. The plan also allowed for the awarding of special "badges" for those who excelled in the training. Each badge was adorned by a tiny "green rose." They were made of fired porcelain and supported by a decorative ribbon of green and white, green and yellow, green and red, or green and purple depending upon the level of the award. They were much sought after by the combatants and worn proudly. Many such badges subsequently appeared on the chest plates and coverlets of soldiers supporting the Duke of York in the first battle of St. Albans and later battles during the Wars of the Roses.

After the initial training session conducted by members of Team 4, and the successes of the training methods, three additional camps were established and training in each camp was limited to 100 soldiers each so that some 400 militarily trained men were graduating every six weeks. Those already trained were allowed to return to their homes, but some were held over and paid to help with the training at the camps.

In July of 1454, the industries of Coggelshall Abbey had grown so large that it was natural that some labor disputes developed. One such dispute involved the owners and operators of the wagons and carts handling both the cloth pick up rounds and the shipments of bricks overland. The dispute was not over payment of services, but rather the "overloading" of the carts and wagons. Many of the vehicles were not built for heavy loads and were usually drawn by one ox or horse and couldn't handle the heavy loads.

Team 4 immediately instructed each teamster to have loaded only such amounts as he could safely haul which corrected the problem immediately, but severely reduced the amount of goods going to market.

Ipswich had a wagon works operated by a private merchant with whom Team 4 visited. A deal was struck whereby the wagon works would accept trade-in's of old wagons and carts towards the purchase of a new, heavy duty vehicle. Since the wagon masters were paid for hauling their loads, they had ample funds to purchase the new wagons and pay for them in installments, deducted from their reimbursements by the monks, and paid directly to the wagon works. Under this arrangement it would take an average of two years for a teamster to pay off his new wagon. With the life of the vehicle from ten to twenty years, based upon good maintenance, it was a boon to the teamster and a real rise in his social prestige.

The old carts were turned over to the monks by the Wagon Works for about half the cost of what the teamster was allowed on his trade-in. These carts were either rehabilitated or pirated for parts to make repairs to the more serviceable vehicles which, in turn, were donated to the various parishes to help in their collection efforts of locally produced cloth since the parish church was usually the "pick-up" area for the weekly shipments to the warehouse in Ipswich.

While it took some time to accomplish, the wagon works "sold" more than 400 wagons in the next few months and the monks were able to salvage and repair about 300 of the "trade-in" vehicles donating them to grateful parish congregations. Some of the parishes even took to "renting" the refurbished carts to their parishioners for special occasions thus increasing revenues for the church.

It became a very "popular" thing for a parish church to receive a cart from the abbey and the Abbot himself attended ceremonies held when each cart was delivered to the various churches. They were called "white carts" after the robes worn by the Cistercian monks who rebuilt them. Some of the parishes even whitewashed or painted their cart white.

Sometimes the name of the parish church was painted on the side of the wagon to identify it as belonging to the church and to make it harder for the carts to be stolen.

Another problem, even more serious, arose in October of the year when a delegation from the Court Party in London visited the abbey and asked for a tour of the various activities. Team 4 had been forewarned of the visit by a courier from St. Albans so the Team, conferring with the abbot, had hatched an inspection tour that would show the various activities underway, but would steer the committee away from the war goods with the Duke of York design emblazoned on them.

Sure enough, a five-member entourage arrived from London on October 5th, to visit with the abbot. He insisted on conducting a prayer service at a small chapel on the precinct grounds to open the tour, not knowing that Team 4 had finished military gear stored in a basement of the chapel. The Team sat through the service on pins and needles hoping none of the delegates would want to tour the facilities of the chapel.

As soon as the service was over the Team leader steered the tour group to the nearby grange barn, an old surviving timber-framed structure dating from around 1140, the earliest days of the abbey itself. The barn was a huge structure measuring 120 feet long by forty-five feet wide and thirty-five feet high at the apex of the roof. The lower part of the barn was still being used for animals, but a loft had been constructed and this was where the abbey did its own cloth weaving. Blankets, instead of military goods, had hastily been threaded onto the looms and monks and lay brothers were busy producing colorful blankets from died yarn. A pile of blankets was stacked along one side of the loft after being hurriedly "carted in" from nearby parishes where they had been woven. Each member of the delegation was invited to accept a new blanket as a "gift" of the abbey and this helped to assuage any ill feelings toward the abbey and made the tour a lot more pleasant and less stressful on all.

Special ceramic vases had been fashioned and fired at the brickworks, leather jackets were made at the leatherworks, specially made fireplace pokers had been fashioned out of wrought iron at the foundry, and an array of other gifts, including craft items made for local marketplaces, were gifted to the visitors. One even commissioned a "racing saddle" with a promise to pay for it. The saddle was specially made and delivered, but no payment was ever forthcoming. Nevertheless, the King's delegation completed its tour and was sent back to London with a whole cartload of gifts from the abbey. Abbey records show that several other delegations were dispatched from London in the ensuing months as soon as word got around as to the benefits endowed on the first delegation. Subsequent gifting was more limited and the delegations soon fell off. In the meantime, the making of the materials for the Duke of York was moved to one of the more remote granges, which also had a barn suitable for the work, and all shipments of finished goods were made after the cover of darkness from then on.

Team 4 was kept busy supervising and encouraging the various abbey enterprises until in April 1455 when word came the Duke of York was personally raising an army and the team was summoned to St. Albans.

Chapter 12—The West Midlands

Who would have thought that high taxes, floods, and bad harvests would have caused economic hardships in the Middle Ages? But that's exactly the situation Team 5 encountered on its return to Croxden Abbey in Staffordshire after the May 1451 Green Rose conclave held at St. Albans. In fact, life was so strapped at the abbey that the team leader decided to split his forces and send one-half of his team to Whalley Abbey in Lancashire, the team's back-up safe house.

Croxden Abbey, styled as "The Abbey of the Vale of St. Mary at Croxden, was dedicated in 1181 after moving to its present site from its initial site established in 1176. While life had never been easy at the abbey, it seems no more than twelve or so monks lived at the monastery throughout its history until the arrival of the Green Rose team. The two previous centuries were times of highest prosperity for the abbey with much of its profits coming from sheep farming. Now the abbey was trying to recover from a series of set backs and the population was reduced to an abbot and five monks who could barely sustain themselves let alone provide for eight full-time visitors.

Yet the facilities of the abbey, copied from the Aulnay mother house in France, were perfect for the operations of the Green Rose team. The site was surrounded by a thorn fence, erected by the monks to prevent theft and entry to the precinct in earlier times. It had a large mill pond and dam and the buildings were more elaborate in design than most Cistercian churches in England. It had a large church and claustral ranges with a detached abbot house. A large barn was also a part of the precinct. The abbey buildings were on the north bank of the Teen River while one of its large granges was on the south side of the river. An old Roman Road ran along the south side of the grange, so the abbey was quite accessible to travelers.

After dispatching the four-members of his team—two knights and two squires—with a pack train to Whalley Abbey, the main team set about an economic revival for Croxden Abbey as its first task.

Since sheep and wool were the main sources of income for the abbey, the team leader decided to concentrate on those areas as the first order of business. Team members scoured the countryside purchasing new breeding stock for the abbey as well as recruiting lay brothers to help with the care and maintenance of the abbey and flock. By October both efforts were beginning to pay off. Besides bargaining for an additional 200 prime ewes and six quality rams, the team managed to convince a dozen locals to sign on as lay brothers at the abbey.

This, of course, put an additional burden on the five permanent monks and they were not that happy with the changes; however, the abbot could see the upcoming financial benefits and lent his full support to the efforts. The monks soon got into "the spirit" of the job and things proceeded fairly smoothly although a large share of the monies left with the main team had to be expended for general upkeep and food. However, more support had been promised from St. Albans if needed.

While scouring the countryside for desirable sheep, the main part of Team 5 became pretty well acquainted with the area which was to serve them well as time went on. Croxden Abbey was located in an area with very few close neighbors. Uttoxeter to the south was perhaps the closest village and Ashbourne-on-the-Water was about eight miles to the northeast. Crakemarsh Hall to the south was about halfway between the abbey and Uttoxeter. Other tiny hamlets included Rocester, Denston, Alton, Alton Towers, and Oakamoor.

The team was able to explain what it was doing to these neighboring villages and soon a number of volunteers began appearing at the abbey gates to assist in the work as lay brothers. And, there was a lot of work to be done since the work ability of the monks had been diminished in proportion to their dwindling numbers.

With an increased sheep herd to take care of many of the new flocks were dispersed to granges owned by the abbey, but previously leased due to the low manpower. One of these was north of Ashford-on-the-Water and a large group of the animals was sent there along with two of the new rams. While this was going on the team also encouraged the repair of the storage sheds and the barn on the home grange at the abbey. Repairs were also done on the mill at the abbey and once again farmers were able to bring their grain for milling although they mostly had to work the mill themselves. Nevertheless, it brought in a welcome supply of grain to the abbey in exchange which was used to help feed the new workers.

In late October the team was busily engaged in the repair of abbey properties, increasing the sheep herds, and getting things ready for shearing and processing the wool the following spring when the abbot at Croxden received word of the kidnapping and ransom demands for the abbot at Buildwas Abbey, a fellow Cistercian House located in Shropshire County along the banks of the Severn River. A messenger from St. Albans brought word of the kidnapping along with a request that Team 2 investigate the matter and see if it could be brought to a favorable conclusion.

The team leader immediately summoned his fellow knight and the two squires from their work on the abbey granges and the four of them set out, with one additional lay brother from the abbey and four pack horses, on the trail to Buildwas Abbey. Their route led them southwest from Croxden through Uttoexeter and Stafford to just south of Telford and the abbey. The monks at the abbey made their expenses by charging tolls on a bridge crossing the Severn River at the abbey. It's location near the border of Wales had seen a rather turbulent past from Welsh raiders.

In fact, kidnapping the abbot at Buildwas was not new. In 1406 raiders from Wales had kidnapped the abbot and in 1342 one of the monks actually murdered the presiding abbot. He managed to evade arrest and later petitioned for reinstatement into the Cistercian Order. It is an imposing abbey with rows of Norman columns; however, only a few monks were actually living there when the team arrived.

As the story unfolded, as told by the noticeably upset monks, the abbot had been visiting one of the granges on the north side of the river near Saplins Wood when a group of thieves attacked his party of three other monks. Finding they had no money, they kidnapped the abbot and rode off to the west toward Wales. The three monks were tied to trees in the woods and only managed to free themselves when another monk came to check on the party which was late returning to the abbey. The alarm was immediately sent out and an organized search had failed to turn up any evidence. Two days later a note had been attached to the abbey main gate demanding a ransom for the abbot's safe return.

One of the monks had overheard one of the bandits telling another one to "give the abbot the Llanfair horse" for his mount before the party rode off. He recognized the name as being located in the area of Clun, a village in the southwest part of the county in a remote area. Since Clun was also near the border with Wales, it made good sense to follow up on this information.

This gave the team a direction in its search for the abbot and it set off early the next morning leaving the abbey at dawn with the blessings of the monks. The group headed west towards Shrewsbury and turned south after bypassing the town hoping not to be noticed. It took a little used route south past Bishop's Castle and to a wooded area, Sowdley Wood, outside of Clun. From the top of a big rock they could clearly see Clun and the adjacent castle. The group set up a camp in the woods.

Since the festival of Martinmas (November 11) was only a day away, the team leader designated one of the squires to ride into Clun and pose as a traveler. His objective was to scout the area and to see if he could stumble across any information which would help their quest.

The squire took his job seriously and although he scouted both sides of the river, even paying a toll to cross the pack horse bridge that separates Saxon Clun from Norman Clun, he did not come back "sharper than he went," which is an ancient saying about whomever crosses the Clun bridge. What he did learn was there were lots of pilgrims gathering for the upcoming festival and it would be a good time for the entire team to attend the fair and visit with the people who would be asked numerous questions on each of the three days of the fair so the team's efforts in this area would not be unduly noticed.

When the team met back at camp on the following night, one of the knights had a visitor with him, a local farmer he had met while examining some of the locally grown produce. It seems the farmer had lived all his life in the area, as had his parents, grandparents, and ancestors before that. The knight asked the farmer to tell the group what he had learned as they had supper around the campfire.

"I don't know how true it is, but the word around the area is the Baron has a new religious guest at Clun Castle and he is a recent arrival. One of the peasants apparently saw a white-robed monk being escorted by the Baron's horsemen into the castle early one morning. The monk's hands were free, but he was surrounded by the horsemen which is unusual. The white robe also was different because local friars are garbed in brown," he said.

"It would appear that might be our missing Cistercian abbot," the team leader told the farmer. He then related the entire story to the farmer.

The farmer was appalled that a religious leader would be so treated "in these times." Upon hearing the story and the purpose for the arrival of the team, he offered his help.

It seems Clun Castle, a typical motte and bailey type structure, was built on one of the rocky mounds overlaid with morainic deposits from the last ice age existing east of the curve of the river Clun. What the farmer knew about the castle was handed down secretly in his family for many generations.

"It so happens," he told the group sitting around the fire, "there is a tunnel under the castle with a hidden entrance in one of the cliffs below the castle keep. My 12-year-old son says he has entered the dungeon area of the castle through the tunnel although I have never even thought about entering it."

"Do you think he could get in there again?" asked the team leader. "We will reward both of you quite well if that is possible."

"I would help you without any money," the farmer said. "And, yes, he has been in and out several times since he was six years old."

"Is it possible to get an armed man through the cave?" asked a knight.

"My son says there's plenty of room for him and he's already nearly six feet tall. However, I would doubt that anyone wearing armor could make the trip, especially the climb up the face of the cliff to the entrance of the cave," the farmer added.

"There are torchlight ceremonies at the fair tomorrow night," added one of the squires. "One of them is an archery contest and I understand one of the castle knight's is the champion from last year. It is likely he'll be on hand from the castle and I imagine he'll bring his own supporters since the Baron is not very well liked in the town."

"Well, then, tomorrow night it is," spoke the team leader. "Can you bring your son to our camp tomorrow evening?" asked the leader.

"We will be here, answered the farmer. Do you need any other assistance?" he asked.

"No," replied the team leader. "We are well equipped to handle the situation. We will break camp after your arrival and make our way, with your leadership, to the riverbank below this cave of yours and see if we can't rescue our abbot. Then we will be on our way, hopefully, before any word gets out. We have two extra packhorses, since we have been so long on the road. We'll use one of the them for the abbot to ride, but the other is a gift to you and your son along with its pack saddle," the team leader said.

"You are very gracious and your gift will be much appreciated as my son is of the age he needs his own horse," the farmer said, before he left for his home.

After he had left, the team gathered again around the fire and laid out its plan for the rescue. The escape route also was planned after the leader decided to stay away from the traveled routes, such as the Clun-Clee Ridgway, the historic route where cattle were driven from Wales to markets in the Midlands and London. It was decided to head across country on lesser known trails, asking directions along the way, until they reached Church Stretton and could link up with the main road leading to Shrewsbury.

They spent the next day breaking camp, packing the horses, and making preparations for that night's foray into Clun Castle. It was decided to give the best packhorse to the farmer's son in grateful thanks for his help, and he could use it to get to the river as the farmer had said he and his son would be riding double on the farmer's horse when they arrived back at camp. The team leader knew the abbot would be thankful for his rescue and wouldn't much care about the horse he was riding as long as it could do the job. The team also planned to give a gift of about half the money they had with them to the farmer for his efforts. One of the squires was sent into Chun to purchase a supply of good wax candles to be used to light their way in the dark caverns under the castle.

That evening, when the farmer and his son arrived, the team immediately presented the horse to the son who was so overwhelmed he began to cry which embarrassed the entire team. The purse of money was also given to the farmer and, he too, was grateful.

"I have been thinking about your escape," he told the team leader. "I don't recommend you travel any of the main routes until you get well clear of Clun as the Baron has spies nearly everywhere. Thanks to your generosity with the horse and the gift of money, I feel as though I should do something to help your cause. I am no friend of the Baron as he has confiscated some of my lands and refuses to even compensate me for them. All of this," he said, "is leading up to let you know I have traveled the back hills from Clun all the way over to Church Stretton where you can pick up the main road again safely. I would be more than happy to guide you there, if you will put your trust in me."

The team leader immediately embraced the farmer and said they had planned on traveling that way, but would have to ask directions along the way.

"We accept your offer with our thanks, and it is we who will be grateful to you," he said.

So it was decided. Just as it was growing dark the group left the campsite near the Rock of Woolbury as the farmer told them in was known. The farmer and his son led them down to a road that by-passed the hamlet of Woodside and followed a small creek to where it converged with the River Clun. The son led the way to a little known ford in the river and they crossed to an area known as The Green on the east side of Clun. It was well after dark by the time they crossed Shropshire Way, a main road to Clun, and made their way past the north side of Clun to the river below the Castle Clun standing high on the opposite bank.

The farmer took a long rope from behind his saddle and handed one end to his son who plunged into the river and began to wade across until he reached the channel in the middle and then he had to swim. The farmer had also waded out to the edge of the channel so the rope would not be too heavy for his son to swim with. The channel was only a few yards wide so the son was soon pulling the rope onto the far bank where he secured it to an outcropping of rock.

The two knights and one of the squires used the rope to get themselves and their swords, or bow, across to the other side. The farmer had hitched the other end of the rope to his horse and they held it taut as the trio edged their way across the stream to where the boy was waiting. After that the rope was allowed to trail in the water, but secured on both banks, so that it wouldn't be spotted by anyone floating the river even though there wasn't much chance of that. Sometimes, the farmer explained, fishermen used the river at night for illegal poaching.

After the river crossing, the men followed the boy up a fairly well defined, but narrow, trail leading up the side of the cliffs. The trail had some switchbacks and was quite hazardous in spots, but the group had no trouble in negotiating it in the dark. The entrance to the caves was behind a narrow niche in the rocks and could not be seen from the river so the group paused to light the candles it had brought. The boy showed them the stub of a candle he had used to explore the caves which he had hidden at the entrance under a rock.

It was pretty eerie inside the cave. The boy told them there usually were bats sleeping in the cave during the day, but they were outside now. It took about fifteen minutes of walking to reach a crack in the wall, which had been enlarged big enough to accommodate a man sliding through. It was concealed by a slab of rock, which the boy shifted to one side, but only after the men had extinguished the candles.

The boy carefully looked up and down a long corridor underneath the castle which was lighted by a torch at either end with a series of cells along one side. He carefully eased his way through followed by the three men. The squire immediately strung his bow and got an arrow ready in the event a guard appeared, but the two knights kept their swords sheathed so as not to make any undue noise.

There was a small window in each of the cells and the cell doors were secured by a bolt mechanism on the outside. The team leader examined each of the cells which were empty except for one at the far end of the corridor which was close to the guard station. Peering around the end of the corridor, the leader saw there was one guard who already was asleep at his post. He drew his blade quietly and snuck up on the guard clipping him on the back of his head and knocking him unconscious using the flat of his blade.

The squire stood at the ready with his loaded bow while the two knights dragged the guard to the far end of the corridor and locked him in a cell where even if he yelled his head off it was unlikely to be heard. After that the knight opened up the cell where the abbot had come alert to the noises made outside.

The knight identified himself and the abbot immediately fell to his knees in tears. The knight allowed him a moment and then helped the abbot to his feet and the escape was on.

The abbot had been living in some sparse conditions, but had been well fed in his captivity and even explained that once or twice he ate at the same table as the Baron although he preferred the isolation of his cell. Even at that, it took about thirty minutes to make their way back to the cave entrance, carefully replacing the rock that had allowed them access to the corridor. The abbot was having a difficult time making his way down the side of the cliff until the boy took him by the hand. After that progress was quicker. The group had signaled those on the opposite bank and once again the rope was taut as they made their way safely across the river. The boy came last after untying the rope from the rock on the bank and his father simply dragged him across as he held onto its end.

Once they were assembled on the river bank, the abbot was helped to mount his horse and the group left leaving the boy to carefully make his way home with the story that his dad was out buying cattle in the event enquiries were made.

The group made good time and it was on the morning of the second day when the farmer stopped the group as they topped a hillside.

He pointed to an old hill fort in the distance.

"That's Caer Caradoc," he told the team leader. It is located about two miles northeast of Church Stretton. If you follow this path it will take you past the fort and will connect you with the main road to Shrewsbury. Just remember to keep the old fort on your left side and you won't have any trouble reaching the main road. I will head south from here and buy a cow on the way home just to be sure."

The farmer shook hands with all and the abbot left him with a blessing and a pledge if the farmer ever needed help just to send word or come with his family to the abbey. "I can assure you we will have an armed force in the future to protect us," he added.

It took two more days for the team and the abbot, now dressed in the spare clothing of one of the squires, to make it to Shrewsbury and another day to return to the abbey at Buildwas where he and the team were welcomed with open arms and the lay brother became an instant hero and was offered acceptance into the Cistercian Order, which he accepted. He was later put in charge of an armed group of lay brothers, which the team trained at Croxden Abbey, at the request of the abbot.

When word got around of the daring rescue and of the new trained fighting monks at Buildwas Abbey, there was no further trouble.

Busy with its activities of training monks and lay brothers in the skills of fighting and supporting the ongoing work to improve the wool production at Croxden, the main bunch of Team 5 were quite busy. They did manage to meet up with the other members of the team when they held some joint training maneuvers at Alderly Edge in January of 1452, but that is another story.

Things were going well at Croxden by February when the abbot suggested he might like to revive an old pottery operation. More than thirty lay brothers were now engaged in abbey activities and he asked the team leader to look into the possibilities after leading the team on a tour of the old "pottery works" the abbey owned on a grange at nearby Denstone. The abbot also indicated the library at the abbey contained a book on pottery making and the various clays and glazes used at the time the pottery works was in production. The old kiln, used in firing, was still standing in the corner of an old barn—in fact it was the corner of the barn—on the grange and shelves held some of the old forms used to shape pots and decorative items the pottery produced. In addition, there were two old double-wheeled potters' tables (wheels) which were driven by foot power. They appeared to be in good condition, although quite in need of cleaning.

The abbot thought most of the earthenware pottery used at the abbey had been made in the barn which would give the team and idea of a lot of the items that could be produced. The clay, he said, was dug on the grange itself and they had used at least three different kinds.

The team leader, working in the abbey library later that night, discovered in a "potter's journal" kept by one of the earlier monks, that the monk had been working on a formula using powdered sand to make a glaze that covered the pots in a "highly polished" finish. While no pots had been produced using this glaze, the book indicated at least three experimental pots were produced each using a slightly different formula and had been taken to the abbey for examination.

Not having even suspected such a product, the team leader took his candle and examined the library more closely. Sure enough, on one of the high shelves in the library, were three pots which fit the descriptions in the journal. He got them down and examined them closely in the candlelight and determined they were not of the kind that was seen in the area or that he had previously seen. He was pretty excited and disturbed the sleep of the rest of his team and the abbot with his find. It was at that moment a new pottery industry was born for the abbey that would turn out to even surpass wool in annual revenues for the establishment.

The next morning, they invited all the monks—now numbering fifteen—and the lay brothers housed at the abbey to a meeting to explain the idea for the new pottery works showing off the three pots found in the library. It was enough to excite the group anew and when the call came for volunteers some twenty stepped forward including two of the monks.

The team leader decided to talk to each of them to learn if they had special artistic skills and what he found out simply amazed and excited him even further. One of the monks was a skilled artisan and had learned pot making before he joined the Order, but had never been called upon to utilize his talents since the pottery had long been closed before he arrived. One of the lay brothers was a skilled artist and had been painting pictures in his cell, using paints he devised from raw materials found around the abbey grounds. He was asked to get some of his works for the group to see and it turned out he was quite professional. Another of the lay brothers knew about clay and had worked at brick making before coming to the abbey. This was the nucleus of the industry which eventually employed some 200 peasant workers in addition to the monks and lay brothers who were not paid.

The group was escorted to the old pottery works where they began to rehabilitate the facilities including sleeping quarters in the loft of the old barn which they later learned was quite adequately heated in the winter as long as the kiln was being used.

The "potter's journal," it turns out not only identified the clay types, but the sources where they could be obtained on the abbey lands. Besides the three identified clays, two other types were eventually found and incorporated into the pottery works. The special experimental sand was found along the banks of a small creek running past the barn and soon clay and glazes were being worked. Some of the old molds were fixed up and the first pots began to appear. After the clay was plastered into the molds, it was set out in the sun to dry. Then one of the lay brothers was recruited to clean up the resulting pots and get them smoothed out for the painter. He had prepared each of the three glazes listed in the journal and, after several tries, produced a set of pots almost exactly like the ones found in the abbey library.

The team leader had found a reference in the journal mentioning crushed lead ore and some of this was brought to the abbey. When added to the glaze mixtures, the pots came out much darker, but were much heavier and sturdier. When the artist added brick dust to the glaze, the pots turned a beautiful dark red. Eventually he used other substances to produce green and yellow pots and had also produced a sickly looking blue which he was still trying to enhance. The glazes actually made the outside of the pots have a "glassy" look and they were quite easy to clean.

The team scoured the countryside to secure materials for the pottery. At the same time they questioned some of the residents as to what kind of pots they were most in need of to make their work easier. Most indicated they wanted a lighter weight water jug and a pot with legs and a vented cover they could put at the edge of the fire for baking. This required new wooden molds and a local carpenter was found who dabbled in wood carving and he was induced to become a lay brother at the abbey. It took him three months of work to produce the first prototype mold. The pottery used it to make twelve pots of varying colors—four pots of each of the three major colors—and these were given to some of the peasant wives in nearby villages to try out.

The pots were an immediate hit, especially the three-legged baking pot, but the housewives began squabbling over which color was the prettiest and for awhile there was a lively "trading game" going on until each finally ended up with a favorite color. It turned out the dark red pots were slightly favored over the others not because of their color, but because they were less likely to darken in the embers. The pottery leaders finally decided to make the baking pot only in red and use the other two colors for the water pots and that system worked well.

After the experimental pots were placed in homes around the area, word soon got around as the housewives were prone to brag about their new acquisition and soon a number of enquiries began to arrive at the pottery to buy the pots. By this time the carpenter had completed two more baking pot molds and three more water jug molds so the pottery could turn out as many as three baking pots and four water jugs every day. Potters would fill the molds each morning and lay them out in the sun to dry. By the next morning the clay would be hard enough so the mold could be removed although the raw pots were left for another forty-eight hours to dry before they were sent for cleaning, painting, and firing. As the demand rose more molds were crafted, more workers were hired, and more pots were produced.

By the end of the first year, the pottery had repaid all of its start-up costs, was paying good wages to the hired workers, and was turning a profit for the abbey. As time progressed the painter had several assistants and they were using the four colored glazes to paint landscape scenes on the pots so that buyers came from all over England to purchase the pottery's work. It also was a pay-as-you-go process whereby the pottery took orders if it didn't have the desired pots on hand and then notified the buyer when they were ready. The buyer paid for the pots when he picked them up as the pottery did not ship any pots nor did they sell them in the local marketplaces although several customers began re-selling the pots at an increased price at some of the larger fairs in the county. But any customer could travel to the pottery and buy any of the available pots at the pottery price.

After a time some more artistic creations were added to the pottery line and some of these made it into the royal households as well as the kitchens and great rooms of many of the lords and nobles around England. No potter's mark was ever used by the pottery and all sales were by "word of mouth."

One dispute arose when a potter in the next county claimed the pottery had stolen his specialized glaze; however, when he was invited to bring samples of his pots to the pottery, it was soon discovered there were many variations in the glaze and the pottery's product was far superior. When he was shown the entries in the "potter's journal" from a century earlier, he conceded he did not have a claim.

While the main team was busy with the new pottery, it was learned the Duke of York, also in February, had begun to raise an army in Shrewsbury and other towns. They later learned that many of the men they had trained to handle arms has been drafted by the Duke for his march on London. No fighting actually occurred and the Duke ended up signing an oath not to rebel against the King in an agreement negotiated when the two armies finally met face-to-face outside of London. This gave a renewed incentive for nobles in the area to train more men and many requests from the various manors surrounding the abbey were honored by the main team. As soon as one group was trained it would, in turn, be used to train other groups which greatly speeded up the process.

By May of 1452 this effort was well underway and some ten or more teams were actively training men-at-arms for the local nobles who, in turn, were responsible for arming them. It was later estimated that more than 3,000 men were trained as a result of the combined divisions of Team #5's efforts in this area. It was about this time that the abbot at Croxden decided to expand the lead mining activities at Wirksworth, owned by the abbey, and enlisted the team to assist. This industry was actually owned by the crown and the abbey paid a fee for the privilege of producing lead. In turn, the abbot had rented out the lead works since the abbey didn't have sufficient manpower to operate it themselves. However, the success of the wool expansion and the pottery potential made the abbot take a second look at the lead business in hopes of revitalizing it. In truth, it was not profitable and the team members were dispatched to Wirksworth to see if the works could be salvaged.

When the four members of the team arrived at Wirksworth, along with one of the monks from the abbey, they were amazed at the extent of lead mining activities underway especially in the area north of the village stretching about three miles up to Matlock. The monk guided them about two miles northeast of the village to a grange owned by Croxden and called Grangemill, because of the mill erected on the property.

Large areas of timber on the grange had been harvested in order to plant forage for cattle and to feed the fires for smelting the lead ore.

Pure lead is a soft, heavy metal, easily worked with a low melting point. It was extensively used for plumbing, roofing, and creating paint pigments in the Middle Ages. It is not found in a pure state and near Wirksworth was usually bonded to Sulphur in a lead sulphide ore termed "galena." Ore veins, the team discovered, usually contain about ten percent galena and eighty to ninety percent of the galena could be smelted into pure lead. However, for every ton of lead ore mined, nine tons of waste materials were heaped up in mounds outside the shafts. Most of the digging was in horizontal shafts lined with waste materials along the sides. The shafts were dug down as far as the local water table as there were no means with which to drain the water.

At Grangemill were two horizontal shafts actively being mined and a smelting operation of sorts had been set up outside a large barn. Chunks of rock were brought to a large stone buried in the ground and were crushed manually by workers pounding them to pieces. The ground ore was then scooped up and layered with wood in a sloping stone hearth built into the side of a small hill, facing west to catch the prevailing winds. When the wood was fired the temperatures melted the crushed ore and produced the molten lead and Sulphur. The molten lead was poured into iron "pigs" and allowed to cool. When cool it was removed from the "pigs" and stacked for shipment or to be re-melted and poured into molds used to make products of the day.

The team made camp in an area near the grange and spent a few days observing the operation without making their intent known to the operator of the lead works. It observed two things:

1. About ten peasants worked in the two horizontal shafts each day removing the ore and loading it on hand carts used to move the ore downhill to the lead works. About two cartloads of ore were produced daily from each shaft.

2. The smelting process was fired up each morning to work the previous day's ore production after another five peasants took turns—two at a time—working the hammers to crush the ore. The fifth member scooped up the crushed rock and piled it on another cart. When the cart was loaded—not two heavily—he was assisted in pushing it across and up to the hillside oven. There the ore was layered with split wood until it was filled and the fire was then kindled allowing the molten ore to flow out the bottom where it was captured and poured, using giant iron ladles, into the "pigs." Each firing of the furnace would produce from thirty to fifty pigs, depending upon the quality of the ore so the daily output from the lead works was in this range.

After the team had satisfied itself about how the operation worked, and how much was produced on a daily basis, it rode into the grange and sought out the lead master. The team leader identified himself and members of the team and introduced the Croxden monk. Then he asked to see the records of production which were quickly produced. Together with the monk they studied the journal and discovered the records showed daily production at the mine and works only recorded from eight to ten pigs of lead produced each day.

When confronted, the lead master immediately produced his sword and yelled to the other men who came to his aid wielding hammers and shovels. The team had not been caught by surprise and soon dispatched all but the lead master himself, who was wounded on both arms and legs as the team had wanted him left alive to talk.

As the story unfolded, they found the lead master was only one part of a larger scheme to loot many of the lead mines in the area. At least two-thirds of the daily production was being stolen with no payments made to the crown for that lead. Of the eight to ten pigs of lead claimed, one-tenth went to the crown, six-tenths went to the mine operator, and three-tenths was credited to the abbey which did not cover operating expenses of the mine. The lead master identified his connection to one of the town officials at Matlock so the team began a more extensive investigation leaving the monk behind to clean up the mess and perhaps to get the mining operation moving again on a more profitable basis.

The first job for the team was to load the wounded lead master on a horse-drawn cart and haul him into Wirksworth to the officials at the Barmote Court which had operated in the village since 1266. While it met only twice a year with a jury of twenty-four persons, it was always open for the filing of claims. The lead master told his story for the second time and the court immediately issued a warrant for the arrest of the Matlock official. This, in turn, led the team along a line of widespread greed resulting in twenty-four more arrests and the implication of one of the nobles, although a direct connection could not be proven. A special session of the Barmote Court was held and all twenty-four were convicted. Twelve of them were hanged outright, ten were sentenced to a lifetime of "hard labor" in one of the king's mines, and two subsequently escaped and were hunted down and killed resisting arrest.

In the meantime, one of the squires had been assigned to recruit new workers for the lead mines. And, although they were a motley looking lot, production at the works was soon up to an average of thirty pigs of lead per day with no work on Sunday. This provided 180 pigs of lead per week and immediately began bringing substantial revenues back into the abbey even after the king's share and expenses of operations were taken out. In addition, two other veins of galena ore had been discovered on the grange property which made the long term prospects for the operation excellent. One cartload of the ore from the mine was brought to the pottery works each month where it was hand smashed by the artists who used a number of combinations of the crushed ore in the glazes used in the pot making.

It was a couple of years later when a secret operation was established in the nearby barn at Grangemill making small round balls for the hand-operated guns and larger round balls for cannon. In addition, a side industry was started making gunpowder.

It was November of 1452 before the main team was ready to return to

Croxden Abbey after successfully getting the lead works back in Croxden hands. The monk stayed behind to permanently supervise operations there and the team, thinking it deserved a break, decided to ride north to Castleton and visit some of the caves they had heard about.

It was a crisp morning when they rode toward Matlock from their camp at Grangewell just outside of Wirksworth. As the crow flies, Castleton was little more than ten miles, but by the time they traveled the roads through Matlock, Bakewell, Baslow, Calver, Grindleford, Hathersage, and through the Hope valley to Castleton it was more like twenty miles and they camped for the night along the Noe River near the ruins of an old Roman fort before reaching the objective. Castleton was less than a mile away, but they wanted to enter the village in daylight.

It was a good thing all of the Green Rose teams arranged to stand watch during the night and this team was no exception. One of the squires was standing his watch about 6 a.m. in the morning, just as the dawn was breaking, when he spotted a bunch of horsemen crossing the valley from the direction of the small hamlet of Hope and heading toward their camp. He immediately roused all the team members and they carried their valuables and led their horses into the ruins of the old fort where they proceeded to saddle and get into fighting harness. By the time the mounted party arrived they were ready and spoiling for a fight.

Bedrolls and camping gear had been left at the campsite and it soon became apparent the visitors were bent on robbery and murder. A couple of them loosed arrows into blanket rolls and others speared them from horseback. There were about twelve in the gang versus the four team members; however, it was an uneven fight from the start. Two of the bandits were immediately felled by arrows and the others quickly took flight when confronted by the armed knights and squires. A running horse chase thundered up the banks of Peakshole Water, a branch of the Noe River, toward Castleton, but the gangsters soon veered off to the left, over a ridge, and thundered into the entrance of a cave underneath the dominating edifice of Peveril Castle.

Since the cave was located under the huge fortress on the hill above, the team leader dispatched the other knight and a squire to climb the hill to the castle and ask for help in the event there was an entrance to the castle dungeons via the cave.

After about an hour, the squire came back down the path leading a squad of six armored soldiers. There was indeed an entrance to the caverns from the castle, the squire reported, and the Duchess of Lancaster, currently in residence, was organizing another such team, led by the knight, to enter from the other side so as to entrap the bandits in their own web.

One of the castle guards was familiar with the caverns. Torches brought with the group were lighted and the group launched its foray into the cavern expecting trouble at any time. The entrance to the cavern was huge and there actually were cave dwellers living inside. The guard accosted one of them and asked where the mounted bandits had gone. He soon had the information from the poor creature that was in fear for his life.

Actually, the sights within the giant cavern were awesome including a waterfall in one of the inner caverns. It was behind the waterfall where the bandits had disappeared which also led to the castle entrance above. Soon the cavern team heard the sound of fighting ahead and hurried around the corner of the cave where there was a battle ongoing between the group from the castle and the bandits who, up to this time, had been holding their own. Once the new fighters lit into them with a vengeance, the fight was soon over. One of the castle guards had been injured and the team knight, who was in the forefront of the fighting, was wounded on one arm. There were no other casualties on the team side, but the robbers did not fare nearly as well. Of the ten who had fled into the cave, 8 were killed outright and two others, including the leader, were wounded and captured.

Some of the cave people were summoned to clear out and bury the bodies and the rest of the group, except for two of the castle guards, were left to return to the castle via the underground cave. The two guards were assigned to escort the cave people in carrying out the grisly work of clean-up and then to bring up the horses and gear of the team to the castle which had been left outside the cave entrance.

When the team encountered the Duchess in the Great Hall of the castle, it expressed thanks to her for the assistance in running down the thieves.

"We should thank you for ridding this bunch of bandits. I presume they are the ones that have been hanging out in the hills around Hope?" the Duchess asked.

The team leader acknowledged that was the direction they had come from to raid the camp.

"Good," the Duchess added. "We have been trying to catch up with this bunch for several months and you were nice enough to bring them to us," she smiled.

She indicated the two wounded bandits to one of her guards. "Take these scum away and find out if there's any more of their bunch and where they are hiding out," she commanded.

"Perhaps you will be kind enough to be our guests during your stay?" she asked.

"We would be very pleased and honored your grace," the team leader said. "However, we are merely tourists having come here to view the caves and, from what we've just seen, they are indeed as marvelous as has been said."

"Nonsense," the Duchess said, "you have done us a great service and you will be my guests. I haven't toured the caves in several years and I would be proud to show them to you."

And so it was decided. The squires were sent with spare horses back to the old campsite to collect the team's gear while the two knights were shown to spacious quarters in the keep of the castle. The poor squires were put up in the servant's quarters upon their return from the camp site.

The next three days were spent in the presence of royalty touring the innermost secrets of four main caves near Castleton—Blue John Cavern, Cliff Cavern, Speedwell Cavern, and Peak Cavern beneath the castle itself. The Duchess kept the second knight from the team within reach and seemed to be quite attached to him and the team leader began to fear he would lose him from the team. After the third day he announced their departure back to Croxden Abbey in the morning, much to the disdain of the Duchess who seemed to want to keep them around for awhile longer.

Nothing was said to the knight and, sure enough, he was ready to ride off with the team the next morning. He later explained it was a great relief to be back on the road and asked the team leader why it had taken so long before they left. He said the Duchess was extremely sweet to him and seemed to want a closer relationship, but he just couldn't get past her strong body odor masked in heavy perfume.

The team had a pleasurable journey back to the abbey and were soon immersed in other adventures.

Several months later a personal note from the Duchess was delivered to the second knight in which she indicated the two captured thieves had been hung in front of the parish church at Hope along with a dozen or so others who had been found hiding out in the hills around the village. The note concluded that she "hoped to see the knight again."

In January of 1453 Team 2 got a request from St. Albans to participate in a public market and fair at the marketplace in Ludlow in Shropshire County near the border between England and Wales. It seems the Lady of Ludlow Castle, wife of Richard Plantagenet, Duke of York, had heard about the Croxden pottery during Christmas celebrations of the family in Fotheringhay Castle in Northamptonshire attended by members of teams 3 and 6. As a result the Duchess of York had made a special request of the lead monk of Team 6 to see if the Cistercian monks at Croxden would be willing to display samples of their pots at the marketplace located in the square in front of the main gate to Ludlow Castle the following month—during the Festival of St. Valentine celebration.

Since it was considered a near Royal command, the abbot declared he had no choice but to comply with the request and enlisted the knights and squires of Team 5 to represent the abbey along with a couple of the monks who would actually display the pots on behalf of the Order. It was quite a pack train that left Croxden Abbey on the morning of February 8 and made its way via Ketterling, Coventry, Birmingham, and Kidderminster over to Ludlow arriving on February 12th. It was slow traveling with the two knights, two squires, two monks, and four mounted and armed lay brothers to handle the pack animals. They made a train of twenty-five horses, including ten mounted and fifteen for pack purposes. Travel was slowed one day due to a snowstorm encountered en route.

Ludlow Castle was located in an area known as "The Welsh Marches," the term "March" derived from the Anglo-Saxon "mearc" which means boundary. The Welsh in particular did not gracefully submit to Norman control until King William created the Marcher Lordships, granting virtual independence for petty kingdoms handed to 150 of his most valued supporters. The lands were collectively referred to as the "Welsh Marches." Marcher lords ruled lands as they saw fit, unlike counterparts in England who were directly accountable to the king. Ludlow was one of the border castles created during this period. The Marcher Lords were not only allowed to build castles without royal grant, they were also allowed to raise militia and to exact taxes for their own cause. They became a powerful factor in English politics.

Since they were to be guests at Ludlow Castle, the train moved right up to the main gate and announced its arrival. They were quickly admitted into the outer bailey of the castle and shown a wooden stable for the animals. Leaving the lay brothers in charge of stabling the animals, the members of Team #5 and the monks were shown to quarters on the lower floor in the North Range of the castle's inner bailey which looked out over the River Teme below. In fact, the narrow windows provided a rather spectacular view of the surrounding countryside.

The lay brothers were accommodated in the servant quarters built into the lower levels of the Great Tower or Keep next to the Gatehouse entrance to the inner bailey. However, they also were allowed to eat with the other castle occupants in the Great Hall located in the North Range which also housed the family living quarters. The Duchess of York greeted each member of the team and monks personally at the first meal. She also issued a challenge to the two knights to enter the jousting and skill tournaments to be held in the outer bailey during the festival. There was also an archery contest for the squires. Since the note from St. Albans had forewarned the team that such a challenge might be forthcoming from the Duchess, the team had brought along its full dress armor and banners.

The monks and lay brothers were quite busy setting up a pottery display in the local marketplace, just outside the castle. Their efforts proved to be the "hit" of the market and they received more than 200 orders for various pots despite the fact that buyers would be required to journey to Croxden Abbey to pick up their pots. They only had a few pots on actual sale at the festival, since the Duchess of York—upon viewing their wares prior to the market—had purchased most of them on the spot. She did allow them to be displayed throughout the festival so the monks merely had "order opportunities" to sell requiring a ten percent deposit on each order. They had so much coin to transport back to the abbey it required one of the pack horses to carry it, especially since the Duchess insisted on paying for her order in full.

The festival had begun on Valentine's Day and ran for four consecutive days. Each day there were tournaments held on a field in the spacious outer bailey of the castle. The public was invited to watch.

Archery contests were held on the first day and the squires of Team 5, wearing their distinctive Green Rose breastplates, made quite a stir with the crowd as they worked their longbow magic until it was just the two of them competing for first prize. One finally beat the other by landing his final arrow just a quarter of an inch closer to the center of the bull's eye in the target than had the other squire. Both were hailed as heroes as they easily beat the other competitors in the elimination contest.

But the crowd was really stirred when the jousting contest began on the final day of the festival and knights from all over England and Wales had come for the competition. The appearance of the two silver and white garbed knights from Team 5, with their unique Green Rose banners and breastplates, made a spectacular entrance into the jousting arena, accompanied by the squires. They didn't disappoint the crowd either as each beat several other opponents to advance to the finals. When they were paired against each other for the championship, they both refused to challenge each other and were declared joint champions. Each was awarded a decorative medal and a scroll in honor of his victory. The two squires were each awarded a purse of gold and a scroll for their archery skills.

The crowd was so impressed it bowed in respect whenever a team member passed by during the closing hours of the festival.

On the day of February 19, 1453, the team left the castle about 2 p.m. and was given a rousing cheer by the residents of Ludlow as they rode out of the main gate of the castle once again dressed as Cistercian monks. This followed a final feast in the Great Hall of the castle where the Duchess took delivery of her new colorful pottery. The Duke of York had arrived at the castle, with a contingent of armed guards, on the day before the jousts and he sent his regards to the monk at St. Albans. He also conferred with the leader of Team 5 and an agreement was reached to secretly produce lead rifle and cannon balls at the abbey's lead works in Wirksworth to be delivered by the Duke's own pack trains directly to Ludlow Castle. The Duke pointed out that clothing for war purposes, produced by other Cistercian abbeys, also was being stockpiled in secret at the castle.

In May of 1453 the main team was busy at the abbey owned grange just north of Ashford-on-the Water where the main sheep herd was deployed in an area called "Eweclose" just to the right of the hamlet. The abbey monk in charge of the now sizeable herd summoned the team members and several lay brothers, who herded the sheep, together one evening and indicated everything was ready to herd the flock to nearby Ashford in the Water and across the Wye River to the shearing pens located just at the edge of an area overlooking the river.

The team leader, not that familiar with sheep, asked:

"Why do we need to move the sheep? Can't we shear them right here?"

"It is just a part of the process," the monk replied.

The next morning the mounted team members with the lay brothers and two dogs moved the herd about half a mile to some holding pens at the edge of the river next to an old packhorse bridge crossing. When the sheep were penned, the lay brothers carefully sorted out the new lambs and carried them two-at-a-time each across the bridge to some holding pens on the other side. It took several trips for each of the lay brothers to get the numerous lambs across and team members dismounted and pitched in to help.

The lambs put up a tremendous noise at being separated from the ewes and the ewes kept calling for their lambs so it was a pretty noisy spectacle to which no one in the nearby hamlet seemed to pay any attention. When all the lambs were across and penned on the other side, the monk lined the lay brothers up along the bridge with their sheep sticks and signaled to the team members to turn the ewes loose. The ewes bounded out of the gate, down the river bank, and started swimming across near the bridge in a frantic effort to reach their lambs on the other side. The lay brothers dutifully used their sticks to dunk each of the ewes several times during the swim.

It wasn't until the herd was once again assembled at the shearing pens that the team members understood the purpose of the "sheep wash" was to clean the wool prior to the shearing. It took a full two days to shear all the flock and there was quite a supply of fleeces to clean and grade before they were transported to an abbey collection point in Sheffield and subsequently transferred to Boston for export along with fleece and wool from other Cistercian abbeys.

It seems that Ashford had a long history as one of the major crossing points along the Wye River and the crossing and old pack bridge had been used for many centuries to dip the sheep before shearing. Ashford was also a source for black marble from a nearby quarry known as "Kirk Dale." Although not a pure marble, the limestone turns up a shiny black color when polished.

It was in August when a dusty messenger from Peveril Castle arrived at Croxden with a message that the Duchess of Lancaster had been kidnapped by the remnants of a bandit group which, everyone thought, had been hunted down and eliminated by the main part of Team 5 and the guards at the castle. It seems the Duchess had been riding in the area of Mam Tor, protected by two of the castle knights, when a dozen or so bandits challenged them and in a running battle, killed the two knights and captured the Duchess. Another traveler witnessed the event and carried word back to the castle. An extensive search had not discovered the raiders so the head steward at the castle sent the request for help to Croxden remembering the earlier adventure.

The main group of Team 5 left immediately with the messenger and traveled to Peveril Castle to organize a search and rescue operation. It's first effort was to round up a number of the villagers at the nearby hamlet of Hope for questioning. Not much progress was being made until one lad of 13 years of age was brought into the chamber where the interrogations were taking place. It was pretty obvious he was quite frightened. When he was treated kindly by the team leader he quickly started cooperating and revealed his uncle was one of the new gang, but it was now operating our of the hamlet of Edale on the other side of Mam Tor. He didn't know the exact location of the gang's camp, but thought it was somewhere along the Pennine Way above Edale.

The boy was sent to Edale, along with one of the castle guards who was a distant relative, to seek information on the whereabouts of his uncle. The effort was successful and the boy and guard came back to report the likely location of the camp where the Duchess was being held was located along Crowden Brook in the area of Upper Booth along the Pennine Way. They were not able to pinpoint the exact location for fear of arousing suspicion, but knew a search group could follow the creek from Barber Booth up to where a camp likely was located.

This was welcome news at the castle and the boy was well rewarded for his cooperation, but asked to remain at the castle until a rescue operation could be completed. The guard relative of the boy suggested they could "look down" on the Upper Booth area from Horsehill Tor to the south without being observed and that's what they did.

The leader for Team 5 organized his team plus ten of the castle knights and guards, including the guard related to the boy, and they set out early the next morning via the trail leading to Edale, but before reaching the hamlet they cut straight east through the heavy woods to the top of Horsehill Tor. It was ten a.m. by the time they reached the summit and all were glad to rest. Upon looking down the valley towards Upper Booth, about half-a-mile away, they immediately spotted a large campfire and group of men along the creek and just to the side of the path known as the Pennine Way.

"We can cut down the hillside until we get to that path and then approach their camp from three sides attacking at my signal," the team leader told the others. He then divided them into three groups for the attack putting his archers in a group to open the attack. It took about an hour and a half to get everyone into place. As they grew close to the camp, the bandits all seemed to be busy preparing their Noon lunch around the fire. There was a stick and stone covered hut just inside the edge of the trees and it was presumed that was where the Duchess was being confined. The team leader designated his fellow knight, who knew the Duchess well, to sneak up on the hut and be prepared to defend the

Duchess in the event the gang tried to dispose of her during the attack. When all was ready, the team leader gave a sharp whistle and almost immediately two of the gang at the fire collapsed as they were struck by arrows. In just seconds, two more were killed causing a panic among the ten remaining men at the campfire. They started to scatter and run for the trees when the two other attacking teams all converged on them from those same trees. Those who resisted were quickly cut down and two trying to escape across the creek were felled by arrows. The entire incident lasted less than three or four minutes before the camp was taken.

About that time the other knight on Team 5 came from the trees escorting a dirty, but greatly relieved Duchess who was warmly greeted by her knights and by Team 5. It was a happy group that gathered back at the castle that night. The next day the Duchess showed her appreciation to all who participated in the rescue operation at a large feast in the Great Hall of the castle. Seated at the head table was the youth who had provided information on the whereabouts of the gang and he subsequently went into the service of the Duchess. All of the castle guards were given rewards of clothing and money and the Duchess offered quantities of gold to the members of Team 5, which they respectfully rejected saying their efforts had been solely due to their appreciation for the help of the Duchess earlier and they would accept no reward.

Some week's later four fine stallion horses were delivered to Croxden Abbey with leather saddles imprinted with the names of each of the team members. The team leader received a fine white stallion with Arabian bloodlines, but the second knight was given a spectacular palomino stallion with a silver studded saddle. They all knew where the gifts had come from and that it would be impossible to return them for fear of breaking the rules of Chivalry.

About a month after that, a heavy wagonload of fine polished marble slabs from the quarries at Ashford was delivered to Peveril Castle by a Cistercian monk. What it was used for by the Duchess was never found out by Team 5 although rumors in later years indicated the Duchess had a fine, polished, black marble table in her bedroom.

In November, at the request of St. Albans, the main part of Team 5 was engaged in setting up courier routes along some of the old Roman

Roads near Hayfield, working an old route from Buxton to Glossop where an old Roman fortress of Melandra Castle had been located. They were establishing a relay station at Hedfield (Hayfield today) when they happened upon thieves attacking a pack train loaded with leather goods en route from Glossop to Yorkshire via Hayfield and Chapel-en-la-Frith.

At first glance it appeared the thieves had already captured the train, but upon closer scrutiny the team spotted two monks engaged in a sword battle with two of the gangsters while the other were cheering on the two fighting members of the gang and ready to intervene if the monks happened to get the upper hand. That was all it took and the squires began loosing arrows into the fray while the two knights drew their swords and swept down on the train and bandits. Even though the team was badly outnumbered a steady aim by the squires was bringing down crook after crook while the knights were steadily closing in.

The knights quickly dispatched from horseback the two thieves battling the monks and then turned their rage on the rest of the bandits still milling around on their horses. The squires kept calmly picking off bandits until they finally realized they were outmanned and made off at a fast gallop on the trail leading toward Chapel-en-la-Frith. The knights managed to hack off a couple of the rear riders of the gang before returning to the pack train. And, one of the squires made a remarkable longbow shot and put an arrow into the back of the leader of the gangsters riding at the head of the pack. He immediately fell off and was run over by the others in their haste to escape.

The final casualty toll was two monks killed and two monks with minor wounds from swordplay. The bandit total was eight dead, four wounded and captured, and about eight more who escaped. The two monks left with the train had some cuts and scrapes, but had acquitted themselves well in the ensuing fight to save their train and the knights were respectful.

They loaded the wounded men on captured horses, after burying the dead, except for the two dead monks who also were loaded on pack horses, then Team 5 escorted the train along the trail to Chapel-en-le-Firth where they hired some armed horsemen to escort it along the trail to Yorkshire, its original destination.

The two dead monks were buried with ceremony in the church burial yard located on a ridge of land overlooking the upper Blackbrook valley and close to the junction of the Buxton-Glossop road with the old salt trail which came from Cheshire and crossed Rushup Edge into Edale on its way to Sheffield and Yorkshire.

The remaining monks were satisfied with the burial site and promised to erect a stone to commemorate them. Team 5 sent their request on to the quarries at Ashford and it wasn't long before two black granite polished crosses were erected over the graves. The two live monks visited the grave sites upon their return from Yorkshire and then detoured down to Croxden Abbey to give their personal thanks and to tender an invitation for Team 5 to visit Basinwerk Abbey in North Wales which was the home abbey for the monks. The monks were made welcome at Croxden and stayed for two days observing the work of the monks in the pottery before starting their long journey home.

Things remained quiet although the rumors of impending war were building all over England. A respite was offered in January when the team was employed in building support to appoint the Duke of York as Protector of England in view of the king's continued illness. It was in January when the gift of money arrived from St. Albans which had been found by Team 1 and Team 5 sent half of it north to Whalley Abbey to the other half of its team. The amounts were used in both locations to promote an increase in the military training and manufacturing currently underway.

It was in July, after sheep shearing time, when the main team members received a special command invitation from the Duchess of Lancaster to join her and other nobles in a game hunt at Cannock Chase in Staffordshire. The event, a three-day affair, was to be headquartered at Fairoak Lodge well within the protected area of Cannock Chase and a place the Duchess had secured for the event.

When the four members of Team 5 arrived on the night before the hunt was to begin, they were assigned to one of more than 100 tents and pavilions erected around the grounds of an old three-story hunting lodge which was used to house the Duchess and other members of the King's immediate court. The king, being ill, was not in attendance, but most of the higher members in the Court Party were in attendance. Lesser nobles and invited guests were all housed in the tents, which suited the members of Team 5 well.

They were all dressed for the occasion in black wool pants with dark green tops and had all brought their longbows and swords for the hunt.

There was much merriment that evening around the score of pavilions as the guests ate and drank and caught up on gossip. Team 5 worked a pavilion near their tent and ran into many of the nobles from Lancashire, London, and other areas of the realm. Team members managed to glean as much information as they could as to the protocol involved in the hunt so as to not become a social liability to the Duchess who had been kind enough to invite them. In the process, much information was gained on the current health of the King, the Queen's efforts to enlist Scots to help preserve the crown, and a number of other "rumors" making the rounds. Much of this information was later dispatched to St. Albans.

The hunting party did not get underway the next morning until about ten a.m. The invited guests were assigned to one of six areas within the Chase—Haywood Warren, Strawberry Hill/Wolseley Plain, Wolseley Park, Brockton Coppice, Brindley Heath, and Broadhurst Green. Team 5 members drew Haywood Warren for the day's hunt along with sixteen others so the party numbered twenty in all led by one of the permanent Foresters. Several Underkeepers and Rangers were to serve as "beaters" to drive the game into range of the shooters. The Forester lined all of the "shooters" with their bows in a long line in an open area above a place known as Dick Slee's Cave. Each was about 100 feet from the next so it was a pretty long line of shooters. When all was ready, he raised a horn to his lips and sounded three short blasts.

Almost immediately came the sound of shouts, noisemakers, and beaters moving through the brush and trees driving the game towards the shooters. It should be noted here that each shooter had differently marked arrows with the markings recorded in the Forester's book so that the dead game could be attributed to each individual hunter.

After about ten minutes you could feel the tension up and down the line of bowmen as they waited for wild game to break cover of the adjacent trees. Two wild boars were the first to break out of the trees and they made a wild dash parallel to the line of shooters and it looked as though they would make their escape untouched until one of the squires from Team 5 loosed an arrow that downed one of the boars almost immediately. A noble on up the line scored a second hit on the other boar and both fell victim to the hunt.

From that point on it became a melee as stags, more boars, rabbits, foxes, elk, and anything else that moved on four legs was targeted in the shooting spree. The second knight on Team #5 scored a kill on a magnificent ten-point stag and the lead knight scored on a bull elk with a massive rack. In all, there were thirty-five deer, six boars, fifteen rabbits, twelve foxes, one cow, and four sheep massacred by the hunting party. When all the kills for the day were gathered more than 200 deer, eighteen boars, 125 rabbits, thirty-eight foxes, fourteen cows, twenty-two sheep, and three squirrels were tallied. Special ceremonies were held including presentations of manure, sticks, and other "hunting lore" honors to some of the shooters. Since the first stag of the day had been scored by the second knight from Team 5, a special honor of presenting the *fewmets* (feces) of his stag to the presiding magnate (in this case the Duchess of Lancaster) fell to him. It was not something he really wanted to do, but custom demanded it so he did. The Duchess accepted the gift with "grace," but the poor knight had to spend the entire evening in her custody.

On the second day of the hunt, dogs were used to help locate and drive the game to the various hunter lines. Each group had been rotated to a new location for this day's hunt and Team 5 members were located in the Wolseley Park area along the edge of a broad meadow so that it took an exceptional bow shot to bring down running game. Only six stags and four roe deer were killed along with another cow and two seemingly unconcerned sheep that wandered out of the edge of the trees and made good targets for the lesser skilled bowmen. All four of the Team 5 bowmen scored kills—three stags and one roe. Points were being accumulated for all of the hunters and three of the top five spots were held by the two knights and one squire of Team #5 by the end of the second day. The other squire was in 7th spot in the point competition.

Day three of the hunt was held on horseback. Team 5 was assigned to

Brockton Coppice, a heavily wooded area of the Chase that held good promise for the hunters. Again a line of horsemen was sent into the trees, but any organized line soon erupted into chaos as individual hunters took off in chase of game they had scared up. Some tried to run down the wild, scared game while others took stances and fired arrows after the fleeing animals. Before the day was out, the casualty list of hunters was nearly as big as the killed game. In team 5's party, two horses had been run to death, three hunters had been seriously hurt when knocked off their horses by overhanging tree limbs, one horse stepped in a wolverine burrow and had to be dispatched, and several other hunters were sporting a series of arm and facial cuts where they had been whipped by branches. Relying on their archery skills, the Team 5 members had escaped unscathed. The team leader scored two stags—both hit by arrows and then dispatched by sword from the back of his horse, the second knight scored an elk and a boar in a similar fashion, and the squires each had a stag with one adding a boar and the other two foxes.

When the scores were tallied up that evening, Team 5 became the talk of the party. The second knight had edged out the team leader by three points to become the champion of the hunt and the two squires came in fourth and fifth in the rankings. The third place knight was one of the knights from Peveril Castle whom the members of Team 5 had worked with in the past. The Duchess seemed well pleased with her new "champion" awarded him with a gold necklace and a lusty "kiss." The team leader got a silver necklace and a handshake. The two squires received silver "medals."

The Duchess did her best to try and persuade her favorite knight to ride back to Castleton with her party, but the team leader convinced her he was needed elsewhere. The team packed up and left for the return trip to Croxden Abbey as soon as the ceremony was over. However, the prowess they showed in the hunt was to build as the stories were told throughout England after the hunt was completed. News of the team's success was quick to reach St. Albans and a dispatch rider carried a note of congratulations from the leader there.

Excitement pretty much died down after that as the main force of Team 5 became immersed in its activities of producing military supplies and training men for military service. There was one incident in October of 1454 while the team was working some of its trainees on field maneuvers in the Stiperstone Mountains. The team leader and one of the squires from the team had been drilling a group of twenty recruits in field battle maneuvers and the party had camped for the night near an Inn located in a mountainous area. Some of the trainees had been visiting with locals in the pub part of the Inn when a fight broke out between York and Lancaster loyalists. Interestingly enough part of the recruits had teamed with part of the locals on the York side and the other recruits and locals were on the Lancaster side so it turned into a full-fledged brawl before the knight and squire could rally the rest of the troop to break up the fight. Each of the fighters was forced to donate all the money they had on them to help pay the innkeeper for damages. The team leader added some of his funds to make sure the innkeeper was well compensated and would keep quiet about the reason—the rightful parentage of the new Royal infant—for the fight.

The troop was told to mount up and they started back toward Croxden Abbey in the dark. The team leader and squire drove them without rest all the way home until there was little fight left in them. For the next few days the chief lessons learned were discipline.

The main part of Team 5 also held a number of training sessions at the old castle in Stafford as a result of a request received after their participation in the big hunt at Cannock Chase. They were engaged in this activity in April 1455 when all the team members were called to St. Albans.

Chapter 13—The West Midlands: Part 2

Meanwhile, the second part of Team 5 had been equally busy since its timely arrival in June of 1451 at Whalley Abbey in Lancashire. Since its primary territorial assignments included Lancashire and Cheshire, it was in perhaps a more tenuous political position than the first part of Team 5 located further south at Croxden Abbey in Staffordhire.

This part of Team 5 found itself immediately embroiled in a feud between Whalley Abbey and Sawley Abbey located a few miles to the northeast. Whalley was founded in 1172 by Bohn, constable of Chester, and was colonized by monks from Combermere. The original site was at Stanlaw, on the Mersey estuary in the Wirral, an area of desolate marshland and susceptible to flooding. After enduring for 100 years, the monks petitioned for a new site and eventually moved to Whalley. The two communities were soon engaged in a bitter dispute over scarce building materials and construction at the new abbey progressed at a slow pace. When the Team 5 members arrived they found an abbot and some thirty monks residing at the monastery.

Lancashire was the heart of the political power for the current King and tensions in the area rose and fell like the tide whenever disputes arose. It was what one today would call a "political hotbed." Monks at Whalley Abbey were largely supported by sheep raising and the wool trade. Since the abbey was located on the banks of the Calder River, it was fairly easy to ship the wool off to markets.

The knight, who was the designated leader for this half of Team 5, immediately decided to encourage the monks in military training. It was fairly easy to receive the consent of the abbot who was already tired of the local dispute between the monasteries and who felt his abbey might have an edge if his monks were trained fighters. *[Note: This was a decision later regretted at the abbey, after the Reformation, when the military trained monks rebelled against the new king and the king's troops seized the property and expelled (or killed) the monks.]*

In the short run, the military training raised the confidence level of the monks and permitted Team 5 to branch out into several new ventures which greatly increased the income to the abbey as well as resulted in more than doubling the population of monks and greatly encouraging new lay volunteers willing to work the abbey lands.

The first real test for what we will call the "B Team"—the second half of Team 5—came in September of 1451 when poachers began to encroach on an abbey grange located some distance away from the current abbey on Morecambe Bay near Lancaster. This was a grange the abbey had operated since its original location and workers not only raised sheep, but harvested cockles from the waters of the bay to supplement the abbey's income.

Morecambe Bay is a large bay on the western coast of England and has the largest area of intertidal mudflats and sand in the country. Five rivers drain into the bay which is notorious for its quicksand and fast moving tides. The bay has rich cockle beds, which have been fished by locals for generations and "fishing territories" are well known and respected for the most part.

One of the monks from the grange at Morecambe Bay had arrived on foot at the abbey in late September to bring word that a gang of poachers had moved in on the abbey's cockle fishing grounds in the bay preventing the monks from working the beds. The abbot immediately sought out the knight team leader and asked for help.

By the next morning, the B team was on the march toward the grange led by the monk from Morecambe and followed by a supply wagon and ten of the monks from the abbey who had been receiving military training since June. It took a full three days for the group to reach the grange on

Morecambe Bay due to poor road conditions and frequent rains of the approaching fall season.

Team B leader visited with the Morecambe Bay monk during the overnight camps and, along with other team members, they evolved a strategy to drive off the poachers upon their arrival. The monk warned them of the dangers in the bay including the quicksands and moving tides which the team planned to use in retaking the cockle beds.

After arriving at the grange, the group stayed concealed while observing the territory and watching the poachers at work in the cockle beds operated by the grange. It was soon apparent the poachers worked until just before the tides came in and then moved off to the southeast over a narrow path bordered on both sides by quicksand. This is the same path the monks used to escape the tides on a daily basis and they knew it well.

Militarily, the plan was simple. The B Team would simply wait until the poachers were hard at work and then move in and block the path of escape from the tides. The poachers could either attack the armed monks, squires and the two knights, or they could attempt to flee in other directions although the incoming tides and quick sand would quickly prevent their escape. Timing of the approach to the blockade point would be crucial and since the tides varied in impact from day-to-day the monks at the grange were to use their experience to let the team know when to begin the blockade.

At the appointed time, Team B led the assault on the poachers successfully blocking off the 20-foot wide escape path backed by the armed monks. It was a formidable force and the poachers, as soon as they saw the opposing force, knew they were in trouble. To their credit they made two formal assaults on Team B, but were soon repelled with casualties including two dead poachers. They then tried to escape over the quick sands, but lost two more of their band in that feeble attempt. By that time the tides were running fast and the remaining members of the band tried to swim ashore—another fatal mistake on their part.

In the meantime, Team B and the monks kept retreating before the incoming tides, but kept up their blockade of the only escape path. The final result was no injuries on the side of Team B, but two poachers killed with swords, two poachers killed by quick sand, and 36 poachers drowned in the incoming tides. Bodies of the drowned poachers were spotted all over the bay and to Team B's credit they spent the next few days recovering the bodies and burying them in the sands.

The show of force by the abbey reinforced its claim to the cockle beds and no further encroachment was encountered. After a few days Team B and the monks marched successfully back to Whalley Abbey. Soon the word of what happened reached the countryside and the abbey was much more highly regarded.

In fact the king began a custom of appointing royal guides to help travelers cross the bay, a practice which has lasted for centuries.

The B Team began receiving many more volunteers at the abbey wanting to participate in the military training and by January of 1452 it was working with an entire mounted troop. Regular contact had been kept with members of the A Team at Croxden Abbey and it was jointly decided they would conduct a joint military training exercise between troops from the two abbeys at a place called Alderly Edge, a village on the edge of an escarpment that overlooks the Cheshire plains. The escarpment has been a site for copper mining since the Bronze age and is underscored with hundreds of mine shafts and tunnels.

This joint exercise was to have far reaching political impact on the area although none of the members of Team 5 had any such idea when they conceived of the joint maneuvers.

Alderly Edge is a small village in Cheshire which takes its name from the wooded escarpment towering above the Cheshire plain. None of the team members was aware of a local legend which tells of a wizard and sleeping warriors who will save the country in a crisis. It seems a farmer on his way to market was confronted by an old man dressed in white who wanted to buy his white mare. The man explained that one day when England was in great danger, the army would wake and ride out onto the Cheshire plain to save the country. But one soldier didn't have a horse, which is why the man wanted the farmer's horse.

The farmer thinking he would get a better price for his horse at the market refused to sell. Then the man in white predicted although the horse would be much admired it would not be sold and he would be waiting for the farmer's return. When the farmer was returning home with his unsold horse he again met the old man along the escarpment who renewed his offer to buy the horse. To help seal the bargain, the old man in white used his rod and struck the rock face of the escarpment which opened to reveal an entrance with iron gates.

The old man led the farmer inside where he saw knights of old, dressed for battle, asleep on the ground. By each knight was a white mare, except for one knight who had no mare. The old man (believed to be a wizard) told the farmer this was the last mare needed for the sleeping army of knights. The farmer was given gold coins and led out of the underground gates which then closed and were covered with rock face.

This legend was apparently well known in the countryside around Alderly Edge, but no one thought to mention it to Team 5.

It was just a "troop of recruits" that rode out of Whalley Abbey early one January morning heading for Alderly Edge, but it was a "ghost troop" that returned later on. Team B departed the Abbey with forty mounted troops on grey and white horses, and two supply wagons, making its way south through Manchester to an area outside of Wilmslow. In the meantime a similar mounted troop left Croxden Abbey and made its way through the countryside camping in an area just south of Alderly Edge.

Early the next morning the two troops met on a staged battlefield on a plains area and practiced mounted charges and maneuvers for more than four hours. The clanging of swords and the pounding of hoofs could be heard from some distance away from their battlefield and especially by one farmer who heard the ruckus while he was milking his cows and watched the event from the top of a small hill behind his farm. He soon mounted his horse and headed for Alderly Edge where he swore the country had to be in great danger because the great army of knights, mounted on white horses, had arisen and was engaged in a pitched horse battle on the Cheshire Plain—just as the old legend had predicted.

A volunteer dispatch rider was sent immediately to Beeston Castle perched on a rocky crag a few miles away. The castle was built in 1225 by Ranulf de Blundeville, the 6th Earl of Cheshire on his return from the crusades. Beeston crag is one of a chain of rocky hills stretching across the Cheshire plain and the castle was located and designed both as an impregnable stronghold and a symbol of power. It was to this "symbol of power" that the villagers of Alderly Edge were looking for help in this new crisis. Upon arrival of the messenger from Alderly Edge, the squire of the castle immediately assembled a troop which picked up more fighters en route to Alderly Edge. But, wasn't until twenty-four hours later when the castle army arrived at the scene of the Team 5 maneuvers and both of the troops were well on their way back towards their respective abbeys unaware of the excitement they had raised.

The castle army numbered more than 200 mounted knights and about 400 foot soldiers by the time it arrived on the scene. An inspection of the "battlefield" found numerous marks of horses and a few pieces of broken and discarded equipment, but no sign of any mounted army in the vicinity. This, of course, gave even more creditability to the old legend and villagers and recruits in the castle's army were pretty well "spooked" since superstition was a strong force in these times.

By the time the Team B forces returned to Whalley Abbey word had already preceded the news of a "ghost army" on the prowl. Troops from Beeston Castle patrolled the plains around Alderly Edge for the next few months, but no further signs of the "ghost army" became apparent. However, interest in military training increased greatly and the B Team from Whalley Abbey soon was working with three mounted troops as nobles from nearby strongholds were keen to increase their military prowess in the face of this "new threat."

The squire of Beeston Castle reinforced his defenses already consisting of two parts—a small inner bailey on the summit of the hill with a sheer drop on three sides and a defensive ditch on the other and secondly, an outer bailey on the lower slopes with a massive gatehouse and another ditch. The castle already had been described as *Castellum de Rupe*—the Castle on the Rock. The ditches were deepened, the walls were strengthened, and the gatehouses were reinforced.

The churches in the area of Alderly Edge and as far away as Manchester showed an increase in worshippers each day which lasted for several months until the excitement slowly faded away.

The excitement was further heightened in February of 1452 when York began soliciting an army in Shrewsbury and other towns to the south of Alderly Edge and eventually led it towards London where it met the Royal army and a peace was negotiated.

Military activities continued to build at Whalley Abbey as well as Croxden Abbey as the political tensions kept building. The leader of Team B was pursuing additional weaponry for his troops in training when he discovered one of the monks at the abbey was in fact a master bow maker before he joined the ranks of the monastery. He was given permission to construct a bow and soon produced a longbow with a superior range than those bows now in use. When questioned about his feat, he explained the materials found in the Forest of Bowland were superior to other woods used and permitted the stronger "pull" and range of the arrows.

In March Team B, along with about fifteen of the lay volunteers at the abbey and three horse drawn carts, left Whalley Abbey for the Forest of Bowland to secure materials for a bow making operation. In the meantime the monk was left with instructions to organize a crew and begin training volunteers in the art of bow making.

This particular forest was about thirty miles north and east of Whalley Abbey as the crow flies, but a little further by the few roads that existed in the area. It took two full days of travel to reach the edges of this particular forest and then another day to locate the particular trees they had been told to look for by the monk left at the abbey. The group worked for three days cutting saplings and loading up the three carts with several hundred small trees from which to fashion the bows.

The laymen didn't know it at the time, but they would be making numerous trips to the forest in the coming months as it took some months to cure the shaped wood and dry it for the bows. Once the bow making operation began it was a process that took several steps so there were bows in all stages of construction.

In the meantime members of the B Team were demonstrating the new bows in several of the local marketplaces and taking custom orders as they went. The bows were much in demand after the demonstrations and many of the nobles tried to corner the market, but were limited to no more than forty bows with each order. That was enough to fully arm a mounted troop although many carried spare bows whenever they headed towards a battlefield.

The bow making operation got so popular that it wasn't long before people were riding to Whalley Abbey to try the bows and place their orders personally. At the peak of this operation there were fifteen skilled bow makers working full time and as many apprentices in training. "Whalley bows" achieved a bit of notoriety in the process and continued to be in demand for long after the B Team departed from the abbey. Since a bow is not much good without arrows an offshoot of the bow making operation was the making of arrows and this, too, became recognized among the rank of superior archers of the era.

After the second year, revenues from the bow making industry at Whalley matched the income the abbey was receiving from its sale of wool from all of its various granges.

After the first bows were finally produced in July of 1452 and bows were coming off of the production lines on a daily basis, members of Team B took a few to a fair at Manchester to demonstrate. The two Squires were entered in a local archery competition along with a field of more than 100 competitors, including some of the more noted archers in the area. When they tied for first place and competed in a tie-breaker that took 100 shots to finally determine the winner, they instantly became famous and archers and would-be archers flocked to their demonstration area throughout the remaining days of the fair.

When Team B returned to Whalley Abbey it had only its personal bows left as all the others had been snapped up by buyers. In addition, the lead knight handed over to the abbot orders for several hundred more bows, mostly purchased by a representative of the Duke of York who wanted to capture the entire market. At the current output of about fifteen finished bows per day, it would have taken more than two years of work at the abbey to fill these orders alone.

The abbot immediately began to double the size of the workshop and storage sheds at the abbey for the bow making process which eventually employed nearly 100 skilled bow makers, 150 apprentices, and six carts which made round trips to the Forest of Bowland twice each month to maintain a steady supply of working materials. It was big business for the abbey and finally calmed the long standing feud with nearby Sawley Abbey after the two abbots combined efforts to find and train enough skilled bow makers to meet the demand. Eventually a separate operation was started at Sawley Abbey, but it never did achieve the reputation as for the bows made at Whalley Abbey.

The Duke of York himself paid a secret visit to Whalley Abbey during the winter of 1453 to observe the operations and to increase his standing order for more bows for his developing troops. This part of the operation, like that at other abbeys, was carried out in secret as were deliveries of the finished bows.

While at the Manchester fair, the Team B leader instructed the rest of his team to be "on the alert" for other projects that might lead to additional income for the abbey and that might help spread its influence in the area.

One of the squires, who was quite popular due to the archery contest, visited the poorer areas of the market place and found many struggling families with small gardens trying to sell their produce at the market to supplement their meager incomes. When he discussed this idea with the other team members they all thought it would be a good way to help both the abbey and the many peasants struggling to feed and clothe their families. They knew Team 4 was having some success with a similar operation involving the making of cloth and, upon inquiry, received permission from St. Albans to proceed with the idea.

Team B spent the winter months demonstrating the new bows at many of the local markets and at the same time working to organize and develop the idea of "market gardens" to be planted in the spring. They made arrangements with many of the local peasants to plant gardens and grow numerous of vegetables and fruits to be sold through an Abbey marketing system which would provide them the seed to plant as well as a permanent cooperative stall at the marketplace through which to sell their goods along with others. These two factors were the key to the eventual success of the "market gardens" idea since peasants had neither the resources to provide many seeds nor could they legally sell produce at the market places which were controlled and licensed by nobles in the area. Since the abbeys were granted free licenses as part of their agreements with the original landlords, it was an ideal opportunity for the peasants to join forces with the monks.

Markets had existed in England well before 1066, but most markets seem to have come into being in the 12th and 13th centuries. Towns had to be granted "market rights" and these town markets were in fierce competition with other nearby market towns. Many, in fact failed due to failure to attract buyers or due to illegal or unofficial markets in many towns. At one time, for instance, there were twenty-three official markets known to exist in medieval Cheshire, but there were probably twice that number if the unofficial markets are included.

In the first year Team B was able to organize "market gardens" to supply produce in ten of the larger markets around the abbey. This turned out to be quite successful with the abbey retaining 15% of the sales price of the vegetables and returning 85% to the gardener who was delighted since the produce sold for a much higher price at the co-op market than the individual and/or illegal sales of the past. It also gave the peasants a higher degree of respect and incentive to produce even more in the coming years now that they were assured of a fair market for their efforts.

When the word spread of the success of these markets, Team B had to recruit more lay volunteers to keep up with the demand and in many cases used the peasants themselves to not only supply the market booths, but to man them too. They had to make sure there was one lay volunteer from the abbey at each booth to handle the money, accounting, and distribution of the proceeds, but all-in-all the process went smoothly and began to multiply at a rapid pace.

There was so much demand that Team B had to devise a method to "screen out" the less serious of the peasants in order to assure the supply of vegetables to its markets was "top of the line" and thus could command the best price.

One of the squires came up with the idea of a competition to decide who was the best vegetable/fruit grower in the area with all peasants that wanted to enter given a chance to compete. What evolved was an annual "Harvest Fest" competition held on the grounds of the abbey with peasants from each of the various markets being invited to submit samples of their best produce. The first such event was held in October of 1452 and participants from each of the ten then existing markets entered the competition.

When it was over, the monks offered a cash prize for the largest vegetable in three different classes, the oddest looking vegetable in those classes, and the best tasting vegetable in each of the three classes—root vegetables, leaf vegetables, and pod vegetables. Fruit was not included although it would be in later years. The highlight of the event was the crowning of an overall champion who was presented with a cash prize and a carved sign with painted vegetables on it proclaiming him/her as the champion. The sign was to be posted at the outskirts of the village bringing notoriety to the champion as well as the village where he/she lived.

The Team B squire who came up with the original idea, the abbot, and two of the participating monks served as judges and the competition was fierce. At the end all of the vegetables were cut up and cooked in a huge vat of soup laced with mutton chunks and everyone had a celebration dinner.

Needless to say it was a huge success and even some of the surrounding nobles and their families came to view the judging. In later years they would be recruited to help with the judging and thus become a part of this effort. As the word of the "market gardens" and the annual competition spread, the abbey had no trouble in expanding its produce marketing and the annual competition became a recruiting ground to select the best local producers to supply the co-op markets so there was always an underlying competition in addition to the top prizes. Eventually, the event became so big that it had to be moved to one of the granges near Whalley and off from the abbey grounds itself. Many of the parishes and villages today still carry on competitions for the best flowers and/or vegetables and you can still see signs posted at the entrance to a village proudly proclaiming the prowess of its residents.

It was one sunny July morning in 1452 when the Abbot of Whalley sought out the leader of the B Team with another problem with one of the abbey's businesses that the team had no prior knowledge of its existence. It seems the abbey had a salt works at Nantwich located quite a distance south of the abbey, near the village of Crewe, and closer to Croxden Abbey than Whalley Abbey. According to the abbot, the Nantwich salt works, although owned and operated by the abbey, was actually contracted out to a private operator. In the last two years, the works had failed to yield a profit for the abbey and the abbot was finally getting around to wondering why that was so.

One of the squires from Team B was dispatched to "check out" the salt works and to report back before taking any action and he immediately left with one of the trained lay volunteers at the abbey and a packhorse. They would be gone for three weeks before returning to the abbey. Just as the Team B leader was about to send out a search party, the pair rode back to the abbey to report its findings.

The squire reported that he and the lay volunteer had "gone to work" at the salt works to learn and observe its operations. It was producing a sizeable amount of salt, he said, but it appeared the contractor is simply stealing the proceeds, underreporting the production, and multiplying the production costs to show there was no profit from which to pay the abbey. The two had followed one nighttime salt shipment to a warehouse in Nantwich and saw gold coins change hands, but when they checked the books on another night there was no record of such a shipment. After that discovery they had packed up and returned to the abbey with their news. Neither the squire nor the lay volunteer believed that any of the fifteen or so other workers at the salt pit were involved or had any knowledge of the thefts. They thought the thievery was pretty much handled by the contractor and his foreman at the salt works.

They also reported the village of Nantwich had a long history of violence and had been conquered and reconquered many times in the past so that villagers were somewhat "hardened" to such thievery and tended to turn a blind eye even though they did not approve of it.

Armed with this information, the leader of Team B gathered the other members of his team, including one monk and two other armed lay volunteers and set out for the salt works the next morning. They arrived two days later and simply rode into the works and captured the contractor and his foreman. Both men recognized the superior strength of Team B and simply surrendered without a fight. Workers at the salt pit actually cheered when they saw the two taken into custody and offered no resistance to the abbey takeover group.

Upon questioning, the contractor denied any guilt and offered the books at the salt works to prove he was operating honestly. However, the foreman apparently fearing for his life, told a different story implicating both himself and the contractor in the thievery which had been going on for several years although both had gotten even more greedy in the past two years and were stealing nearly all of the proceeds.

Team B turned the two thieves over to the local sheriff and both ultimately were hanged as "an example" to other would be salt thieves. The monk and one of the lay volunteers were left at the salt works to straighten out the operations and to secure the interests of the abbey.

Essentially, operating the salt works was fairly simple although the environment in which it was produced was fairly hot and dangerous. After watching the operation for a couple of days, the Team B leader encouraged the monk to raise the wages of his workers to compensate for the danger involved in their work. This was done and proved to be a good economic move as more salt was produced and profits from the salt works actually increased.

Salt brine, removed from the pits, was boiled in open "pans" until the salt crystals began to grow. Fires were kept burning under the floor at one end of a wooden structure and the heat was piped under the brine pans to keep them boiling. This created a hot, steamy environment and the men raked the salt crystals to the sides of the pans and then scooped them out into wooden boxes. Once the salt had "gone hard" in these boxes it was removed and further processed for sale.

Team B, minus one monk and one lay volunteer, subsequently returned to Whalley Abbey and reported its actions to the abbot who was greatly pleased with the efforts. He assured the team that he would relieve the two left at the salt works on a monthly basis from that time on and was true to his word.

In August word reached the abbey from St. Albans that the King had a mental breakdown and Team B was instructed to increase its military training efforts. Work began to expand the military group from one troop to two troops and the team members were quite busy at the marketplaces throughout the summer recruiting volunteers.

When the abbot decided to round up and drive the abbey's prime cattle to the Annual Cattle Fair at the marketplace at Tadpole, in Cheshire, the first part of September, team members were eager to assist so they could expand their military recruiting efforts.

The abbey had small herds on four separate granges and several days were spent in rounding them up, culling out the market steers, and gathering the herd at one of the granges. The drive itself also took several days, but the cattle were pushed hard and managed to arrive in good shape at Tadpole just as the fair was getting underway.

Now, Tadpole is located on the west edge of the Cheshire Plain overlooked by Beeson Castle—the castle master who sent the mounted troops in January of 1452 to Alderly Edge where teams A & B had been practicing military maneuvers. Although it was now nearly two years later, Team B found the rumors still "rife" about the ghost army and had little trouble convincing young men to join its military training efforts. Tadpole also was on the main coach route between London and the salt works at Nantwich.

The fair lasted for a full week and the abbot was so pleased with the sale price of his cattle that he purchased a new bull for the herd. He bought it at a bargain price and liked to talk about his prowess at the trading block. Members of Team B, accompanied by the five herders from the abbey granges, and about twenty-four of the young peasant men recruited for military training, began the trip back to the abbey about mid-September herding the new bull along with them.

When they established camp on their first night along the trail, they woke up the next morning and the bull was missing. It took three days of searching for the critter and he finally was found back at the farm of his original owner. Team B found out just why the bull was "bargain priced" when the owner finally confessed he had sold the bull twice before only to have it return to his farm unclaimed.

Team B repossessed the bull from the reluctant farmer, hobbled it, and led it back to the camp. The team members never told the abbot why the bull was so low-priced. It took three more days to make the return trip to the Abbey and the team members enjoyed many a private laugh whenever the abbot bragged about his "bargain bull."

About a month later, the abbot received word that the Queen had produced a male heir—Edward. However, the word on the streets and marketplaces was there were doubts about whether or not the King was the actual father of the infant. Team B kept up its training of the new military troop until just before Christmas when it rejoined Team A at Croxdon Abbey for the Christmas celebrations.

In February of 1454 a share of the monies, discovered by Team 1, finally reached Team 5 and was split between the two groups. The money was used to more fully equip the mounted troops being trained at each of the abbeys and training efforts were intensified as the political atmosphere was even more sensitive throughout the land. The Duke of York had been appointed Protector of the Realm about a month earlier and many changes in the government were underway in London

It was March of that year when Team B received word from St. Albans it was to travel to an old priory at Runcorn/Norton to establish a military troop there at the request from the abbot of the Augustinian Order.

The name Runcorn comes from the Saxon Rumcofan meaning a "wide bay or creek." The Constable of Chester, a man named Nigel, erected a motte and bailey castle on Halton Hill about 1071 to watch over the Lancashire and Cheshire plains and the river estuary. Conversion to a stone structure castle probably began in the later half of the 12th century. In 1115 Nigel's son, William Fitznigel, founded an Augustinian Priory at Runcorn. In 1134 the monks moved the priory to Norton, about three-and-a-half miles away. The barons of Halton provided Norton Priory with substantial amounts of money until 1200. In 1391 the priory was raised to the higher status of abbey.

Team B wasted no time journeying to Norton and getting established at the abbey. The abbot received them with a warm welcome, showed them to their quarters, and said he had a surprise for them after they were settled in.

The surprise came the next morning when a troop of forty men came through the front gate at the priory shortly before 9 a.m. They were volunteers from the surrounding area who had been recruited by the monks as soon as the abbot received word that Team B was coming to provide the training.

It was a good group of men, Team B decided, after about two weeks into the training. One young man had shown excellent leadership abilities and Team B soon designated him as commander of the troop, a job which he took very seriously.

The new Runcorn Troop, as they called themselves, proved to be innovative. During a time when Team B was back at Whalley Abbey getting more supplies for the new troop at Norton Priory, the new commander of the troop decided it was time to test his soldiers so he set up a field training exercise designed to capture the nearby Halton Castle overlooking the River Mersey about three miles away from the abbey. Neither Team B nor the abbot knew what was being planned.

Early one morning the newly formed troop moved out of the abbey and marched to the outer wall of the castle. It used scaling ladders to get over the top of the wall and was ensconced at the base of the inner wall when the Captain of the Guards at the castle became aware he was being invaded. He rallied the castle guard and a brief skirmish ensued before the leader of the Runcorn Troop called a halt to the battle by waving a white flag. Fortunately, no one was hurt, but the abbot was immediately called to the castle to explain the mock invasion.

The abbot, in turn, called on Team B for an explanation. To the credit of the new troop, it nearly captured the castle before the guards rallied to hold them off until the truce was declared. Team B, together with the abbot, made a sincere apology to the Captain of the Guards and invited his troops to participate in further training exercises to "sharpen up" all military skills. Although it is not known for certain, rumors in the pubs around the castle indicate that a large "bribe" in terms of new military equipment was donated to the castle by the priory which further appeased the hurt feelings.

The new commander of the Runcorn Troop was summarily dismissed from his leadership position although he was kept on as an advisor and strategist which was more to his liking anyway. From that point on, each watch commander at the castle posted a guard whose sole job was to keep an eye on the abbey at Norton to prevent any further "surprises."

The castle guard distinguished itself well in later battles during the English Civil War although it twice suffered defeats. It was probably a good thing the Runcorn Troop was not mounted on white horses when it attacked Halton Castle as that was near to the site of the Team A and

Team B joint military exercises at Alderly Edge in January of 1452 and rumors were still circulating about that episode. Had the Runcorn Troop been mounted on white horses it likely would have been a battle to the death.

It was May of 1454 before Team B was sent on another official Green Rose mission. This time it involved a small cheese making operation on a grange near the village of Chester in Cheshire. It was owned and operated by the monks from Whalley Abbey and had been one of the most profitable milk and cheese ventures of the abbey for a number of years. However, the operation had fallen on hard times and two of the monks at the Chester grange had been attacked and murdered by a gang of thieves while they were en route to a nearby market town with a cart load of cheese to sell.

Cheshire cheese, the prime cheese of England, dates back to pre-Roman times. It is said that soldiers at Chester, in the first century, stuck chunks of Cheshire cheese on their swords and roasted them over an open fire. As the soldiers knew, Cheshire cheese responds well to heating and is a traditional cheese topping for toast.

NOTE: It wasn't until the 16th century that cheeses became known by the name of the region or county where they were made. And, cheese making was a widespread farmhouse activity in England until the second half of the 19th century. Cheshire Cheese is Britain's oldest named cheese. It is mentioned in the Domesday Book of 1086 and was reputed to be the best cheese of Europe. It was a favorite at the Court of Elizabeth I in the 16th century. Originally the cheese was made near the village of Chester on the River Dee, but it soon spread to farms throughout the county of Cheshire. It is usually white or red in color, but there is also a blue Cheshire. The distinctive flavor of the cheese is thought to be due to the salt springs which run under much of the pasture land. These give the milk, hence the cheese, a slightly salty tang, which is still a characteristic of Cheshire cheese today. (13)

When Team B arrived at the abbey's grange at Chester, the monks had already been buried and the cart and team had been recovered when the horse had returned to the grange apparently of its own accord. The cheese itself was quite distinctive with a red-orange color and easily identified since most cheeses made in the area were white or blue in color.

The team made another pleasant discovery in talking to the monk in charge of the cheese making operations at the grange which was situated on a hill overlooking the River Dee just south of the main village of Chester, an important shipping and trading port. The monk told them the stolen cheese was easily identified in two ways—the unique orange-red color made by blending oils colored with annatto, an imported spice/ dyestuff, and the abbey's mark stamped on each round of the product—WA .

He told them the cart had arrived back at the grange's barn two days after the robbery and killing sometime during the night. There was no sign the horse had been abused and the cart was still in working order. Team B made a close inspection of the cart, but it yielded no clue as to where it had been. The dirt on the wheels was common to the Boughton Heath where the grange was situated. However, the cart was whitewashed and had the Whalley Abbey sign painted in small letters on each side so it was easily identified from other carts in the area.

Wasting no time, Team B rode over to Stamford Bridge located about four miles east of Chester to examine the site of the robbery. The head monk at the grange rode with them to show them the way and to locate the robbery site. Not much was left to indicate how many were in the party that stole the cart and killed the monks, except there were indications the thieves had been mounted on horseback. Recent rain had washed away all tracks, but there were a few piles of horse manure around the location which indicated a mounted attack.

The knight in charge of Team B decided it would be best if the team went in separate directions to begin questioning villagers and travelers along the roadways for any sighting of the cart or the cheese which may have taken place following the robbery, which occurred in broad daylight. The knight reasoned that someone must have seen something or the cheese itself might be a clue if some of it could be located. The thieves had already had plenty of time since the robbery to distribute and/or sell the cheese.

Since Stamford Bridge was located at a crossroads of the old Roman road, travel was fairly common in each direction from the small hamlet.

It was two days later when each of the team members returned to the grange. Each had made a number of inquiries and all had located some of the stolen cheese which had been rather widely dispersed after the theft. So much information was available that the lead knight decided to map out the locations where evidence was found and that took several hours with each of the team members making contributions to the sketch.

In the final outcome there were two reported sightings of the cart and horse and ten identifications that were credible for the cheese. Of the two cart sightings one was headed south on a small road near Tervin and the other was headed west on the road leading directly to Tervin. In addition, eight of the ten confirmed cheese possessions were in the close vicinity of Tervin so that's where the team decided to concentrate its further efforts at finding and dealing with the culprits that killed the monks.

Tervin (now Tarvin) is a small township about five-and-a-half miles northeast of Chester which also was noted for its cheese making and for the town's old parish church known as St. Andrew. It was originally called Tervyn by the Romans taken from the Latin "terminus," meaning "end." The head monk at the abbey's grange, when shown the marked map, indicated he wasn't surprised since the main competition for the abbey's red cheese came from an old barn in Tervin that had been converted into a cheese making operation about two years earlier by a returning knight who had served in France.

The knight, a royal knight by decree, had been awarded lands in the area. He quickly developed a dairy farming operation. He had visited the abbey's grange and asked for a tour of the cheese-making operations shortly after his arrival. The monk had conducted the tour personally, but had never revealed the formula for coloring the cheese which also gave it a special texture much favored by those who bought the cheese from the grange.

The monk surmised that the knight may have stolen the cheese in an attempt to discover just what made it so special or to re-package it and sell it under his own brand in an attempt to be more competitive. The monk also indicated the knight had surrounded himself with a band of about twenty armed men who apparently had served with him in France.

Upon hearing this, the Team B leader dispatched one of the squires to return to Whalley Abbey and secure the services of one of the troops currently in training. In the meantime, the remainder of the team set out for Tervin to scout the area where the knight was operating and to make a final determination about how best to capture he and his cohorts.

They scouted the barn where the cheese was being made and the manor house occupied by the knight and his men. The manor house was about one mile away from the barn/factory with a couple of intervening farms, probably owned by the knight. The general pattern they saw in two full days of observation was that the knight, accompanied by about five of his men, made the rounds of his farms each morning. He had a habit of demonstrating his power by lashing out at some of his workers whenever he felt they needed disciplining and seemed to rotate this discipline among his various farms each morning. His strict discipline was enforced by his men who rounded up the farm workers each morning for this particular display of authority.

After the tour of the farms, he would ride to the cheese barn and repeat his performance only he disciplined at least one of the workers at the cheese barn each morning so these workers received the full brunt of his wrath each day.

On this matter, the knight in charge of Team B reasoned that the knight's workers were probably no threat to them and the team would only have to deal with the armed guards in order to make a successful attack. However, he decided there would have to be a two-pronged attack on the cheese barn and the manor house. And, so it was planned.

It was another day before the squire returned from Whalley Abbey with a troop of forty mounted and armed men. It took another day to lay out the plan of attack and to coordinate the two-pronged effort against the manor and cheese/barn. The troop was divided into two forces with ten of the men assigned to accompany half of Team B (one knight and one squire) to attack the barn. The other thirty troopers were to go with the remaining knight and squire to attack the manor which was felt to be the more difficult of the two targets since at least fifteen armed men would likely be encountered.

Early the next morning the troop moved out long before daylight and rode as a single group along the old Roman road about a mile and a half past Stamford Bridge to a road leading south past Tervin Sands and into Tervin itself. The main body of troops dropped off at the manor house and surrounded it according to the plan with five skilled archers each posted at the front and rear entrances to the manor and concealed in groves of trees. The rest of the troop moved on towards the barn at Tervin and concealed itself inside a cattle shed about 500 yards away as planned.

It seemed like a long wait for both attacking forces as daylight came and the people began their morning chores. It was nearly 11 a.m. by the time the knight and his bodyguards arrived at the cheese barn. As they were rounding up the workers the armed men emerged from the cattle shed and quickly faced off against the knight and his men who were caught by surprise when the dismounted knight was using his whip on one of the workers.

The Team B knight and squire had their Order of the Green Rose banner flying and were dressed in Green Rose decorated white armor making a splendid sight in the mid-morning light. The other members of the troop also wore white pullovers decorated with the Green Rose so they looked like a regular military outfit. All were equipped with long bows as well as swords and other war materials. None of the knight's force was armored.

The knight demanded to know what was going on and, when he was told he was under arrest for murdering two of the abbey's monks, he immediately drew his sword and the fight was on. The first volley of arrows from the Green Rose troops dispatched all five of the knight's followers and he soon found out he was outmatched by the Green Rose knight in the hand-to-hand combat. However, he refused to surrender and was put to the sword by the knight. All of the peasants working at the cheese barn fell on their knees and paid homage to the attacking force letting it know they were not going to oppose it and, in fact, praising it for coming to their aid. The knight interviewed several of the workers and got a full accounting of how the knight and his men had stolen the cart full of cheese and killed the two monks. The cart had been brought to the cheese barn and unloaded before one of the workers wrapped the reins and sent the horse on its way. He was severely whipped by the knight for this brashness, but the cart and horse were long gone by the time it was discovered what he had done. The knight had ordered the workers to use the stolen cheese to discover "the formula" so that it could be duplicated. Some of the workers had, in turn, stolen part of the cheese and taken it to their homes and or relatives to eat.

In the meantime, the force surrounding the manor house moved in after a rider from the cheese barn informed them of the successful attack there. The trumpet sounded and all of the force emerged from hiding and surrounded the house. The Team B knight, also adorned in his white armor, rode up to the manor door and demanded the men inside come out. When the men wanted to parlay, he told them of the death of their knight and promised them they could ride away in safety as long as they left their weapons and agreed to leave the county. After a short time, this was agreed to, and further bloodshed was avoided.

The cheese barn was turned over to the monks at the abbey grange who, in turn, put it into the operating hands of the workers who profited greatly in the after years, but never did produce the quality of cheese made by the abbey monks.

The armor and weapons of the knight's troops were loaded onto pack horses and returned to Whalley Abbey with Team B and the troops and used to equip other troops in training.

There was no further trouble for the abbey grange in Chester as word soon got around the neighborhood the monks were under the special protection of a "white knight," which could appear and disappear as if by magic to protect them. The abbey's cheese became even more in demand as a result of this enhancement in reputation.

That was the last engagement for Team B before it departed for St. Albans in April of 1455 to meet up with the remainder of the Green Rose teams.

Chapter 14—The Heartlands

The reign of Henry VI was in political trouble by the time Team 6, led by the Green Rose lead monk, arrived at St. Albans, the Augustinian Abbey where they were to be headquartered. Just short of one year earlier on May twenty-four, 1450, three weeks after the murder of Suffolk while he was en route to exile in Calais, a political revolt erupted in Kent during the Whitsun celebrations all over England.

Hundreds of armed men assembled in Ashford in the Weald in Kent and marched towards London. One of the leaders, Jack Cade, inflamed the local populace by claiming the Queen meant to avenge her lover, Suffolk, by razing to the ground the homes of all Kent farmers and peasants.

It became known as Cade's Rebellion and succeeded in overwhelming the royal forces which demoralized Henry's nobles causing the king to leave London for Kenilworth. Cade's army occupied London terrorizing its citizens by their behavior. Londoner's turned against Cade and he later was killed resisting arrest.

The rebellion changed nothing and Henry's Court Party still ruled, but it was made clear that capturing London was not a difficult task. The Duke of York, who was blamed for the uprising, swiftly raised his own army of 50,000 and was welcomed into London as a "savior" to bring England back from the brink of political anarchy. York quickly gained control of Parliament and the king and queen were placed at a disadvantage promising reforms, but failing to deliver them.

So the political unrest in England was rife when the Green Rose team arrived at St. Albans. The team was well received by the Bishop, the actual uncle of the lead monk and soon settled in its new surroundings. Since it was a Benedictine Abbey most of the team was familiar with the architecture and had no difficulties in getting around.

On the second day, the Bishop himself, conducted a tour of the activities taking place at St. Albans. Two of the workshops were of special interest to the Green Rose team.

First was an area set aside where a group of monks was using a primitive printing press to reproduce a "NOTICE" that was to be passed around to the various parishes under the jurisdiction of St. Albans. What impressed the monk and the rest of the team was the speed by which the publication could be prepared and reproduced. This, decided the monk, could be an important key in keeping other Green Rose teams informed and so suggested the same to the Bishop who gave him "free reign" to use the press as needed.

Second was a workshop where only one man was employed—a layman and not a monk. He was working on what he mildly termed was an exploding stick. That didn't make much sense to the Green Rose team until the man took the four-foot long object outside for a demonstration. He pointed out an old apple tree at least a good bow's length away and suggested the team keep its eye on the lowest limb to the left of the trunk. He drew the stick to his shoulder and seemed to sight along its length. Then he took a lighted wad of cotton and touched it to a hole in the top. A loud explosion resulted which made the team jump, but the lead monk kept his eyes on the tree and saw a piece of the branch split off and fly into the air.

"That was a lucky shot," the layman said. "Most times I miss what I'm aiming at due to the wind or irregularities in the barrel here," he said, pointing to the stick. "If I can refine the firing mechanism so I can use both hands to hold the stick, I can be a lot more accurate."

The monk and his team immediately saw the advantages of such a weapon in armed combat and said so to the Bishop.

The Bishop smiled. "I thought you might see that right off. I am hoping that you and your team can help refine the process so we can be better prepared as defenders of the church. That's why this gentleman has come all the way from Burgundy in France to help us out," the Bishop said.

After the firing demonstration, the craftsman led the way back to his shop where he showed them the cleaning and loading system and explained all the working parts. The cast lead ball, used as the load for the stick, was round and loosely fit into the bore of the stick until it was wrapped inside a leather patch. It was inserted into the bore after a measured quantity of black powder was poured down first. A long wooden rod was used to push the ball down firmly.

All team members marveled at the invention and some even picked it up and handled it their mouths open in awe.

The rest of the tour was interesting and there was a lot to see at the Abbey; however, none of the Green Rose team could get his mind off the exploding stick and they talked about it for days making frequent visits to the shop. One of the squires even sketched out an idea of how to explode the weapon with a mechanical "triggering" mechanism that got the craftsman all excited and he promised to see if he could make it work.

The new press was soon put to use duplicating a notice to all Green Rose teams to meet at the abbey in St. Albans on May 1st and black-robed monks, in teams of two, were dispatched on horseback to deliver the notices with instructions to tell each team the best route to the abbey.

In the meantime the Bishop gave the team permission to organize a school for children in the town and neighboring countryside and about twenty children, mostly from the village, assembled in one of the abbey rooms in April to begin lessons in reading and writing conducted by one of the squires with two monks assigned to assist him and to learn how to teach the classes.

This is where things stood when the various Green Rose teams began arriving at St. Albans for their first and only joint session until the final assembly of the teams near the end of their assignments some four years later.

When the conclave was over, Team 6 settled down to its own efforts of doing what it could in order to further progress towards succeeding in meeting the commands of the Pope and the plan laid out at the meeting of the teams.

The monk made development of a communications system and military training as the top priorities for Team 6 and the group began immediately to work on that project. He split the team in half with two knights and two squires assigned to communications development and the other two knights, including himself, assigned to the military training. He called them his "C" and "M" teams and told them to come up with some initiatives to get the projects underway.

The "C" team had by far the hardest assignment as they had to develop a system that would reach all of the other Green Rose teams. They began by interviewing the monks who had been used to carry the original conclave notice to each of the teams and mapped out the most available, all-weather horseback routes to the abbeys where the teams were located. Since the goal was to be able to regularly reach each team within a span of three days the team, along with the monks, devised a system of relay riders who would each be capable of covering one-third of the distance to the furthest outpost within a day's ride.

The next job was to establish contact with various abbeys along each of the routes in order to recruit trusted riders and mounts to make the system operable. The task for the "C" Team was simplified greatly when one of the monks suggested using headquarter and/or safe retreat abbeys for the task itself due to their convenient locations throughout the countryside.

Ultimately, they designed four major communications routes, labeling them green, blue, red, and black with all originating at St. Albans and able to reach each of the headquarters abbeys within the allotted 72 hours including the sub-headquarters at Whalley Abbey established by Team #5. This is the way the "C" Team presented their suggestions to the monk for approval:

Route	**1st Day**	**2nd Day**	**3rd Day**
Green:	St. Albans	Kirkstead	Byland
Blue:	St. Albans	Croxden	(Whalley)Holmcultram
Red:	St. Albans	Hailes	Forde
Black:	St. Albans	Waverly	Coggeshell-Netley

The lead knight assigned to the "C" team gave full credit for the idea to the St. Albans monk who first suggested it and he immediately was put in charge of organizing the system. Since he already had nine other monks, who had made the trip prior to the conclave, he had a ready made team with sufficient back-up couriers in the event they were needed. There was only one route (Blue) where the full 72 hours would be needed to complete the route, but none could see a way to shorten the time since Holmcultram was far to the north against the Scottish border.

The only other innovation in the system was the route to Waverly (Black), where it was suggested that two couriers be kept at that abbey—one to head southwest to Netley Abbey and the other to head northwest to Coggeshall Abbey whenever a courier arrived at Waverly Abbey.

The monk was pleased with the innovativeness and congratulated the "C" Team giving them the go ahead to establish the system. Each member of the "C" Team was assigned one of the routes and was to be accompanied by two of the monks from St. Albans. They were to ride their entire assigned route, picking up additional riders at each abbey along the way until the entire route was established and a schedule confirmed. The original intent had been to run each route on a weekly basis, but the monk decided it would be less conspicuous if it were run every second week unless an emergency message needed to be sent up or down one or all of the routes.

Within two weeks all of the routes were operating and regular communications was established between all of the Green Rose teams. Riders who departed St. Albans for the first way stop on their route would deliver their message to the next rider and then remain at the way stop for a return communiqué two to four days later depending upon how far away was the end of the route.

All-in-all the system worked very well in the four years it was in operation. A code had been developed for the messages in the event one or more of the riders was intercepted, but that did not happen although two couriers had to outrun outlaws chasing them. One courier took temporary refuge at Cleeve Abbey on the red route and the second ducked into Tilty Abbey on the black route. Both were provided fresh horses and completed their missions.

The "M" team's task ultimately proved more difficult than that of the "C" team only because of the political unrest and suspicion surrounding any military training or activity in the land. Cade's Rebellion the previous year had made the King nervous about his tenure on the throne and his spies were everywhere in the land focusing mainly on any activities—namely military—tied to the Duke of York.

For this reason the "M" team decided it had to find a way to overcome this unrest so that military training could be carried out without suspicion from the Court party which supported the King. One of the knights, remembering the team reports during the recent conclave, suggested that a "watch and patrol" system be established in order to provide both security and an early warning system of any undue unrest in the land. This, he said, could be used as a reason to recruit and train military-type units without alarming the King.

The monk took this idea to his uncle, the Bishop, and the two of them traveled to London to meet with the King's advisors in suggesting the plan. They ended up meeting with the King himself and he instantly grasped at the straw he was handed and gave his royal consent to the project even issuing a proclamation to the Bishop commending him for the idea and granting him the express authority to establish the quasi-military system of patrols and watches throughout the realm. The Bishop and monk agreed to keep his Highness "informed" as to their progress and carried the proclamation back to St. Albans where the "M" team received the news and went to work. It was probably the first "deceit" that the Green Rose team imposed upon the royal authority, but it was not to be the last.

After receipt of the proclamation, the "M" team was free to develop a plan that would lead to the establishment of a trained military force. Monks at St. Albans carefully forged additional copies of the King's pronouncement and these were duplicated by hand and sent by courier to each of the other nine Green Rose teams giving them the authority to begin military activities. Each team reacted in varying ways to this authority, but the end result was hundreds of trained mounted and foot soldiers with rudimentary military skills within the next four years.

Military drills immediately were started at St. Albans among the eighty or so monks in residence as well as some 100 or more lay volunteers that worked at the abbey. Two troops of forty men each—one to be mounted and the other infantry—were recruited and began daily military exercises. Other Green Rose teams were not so fortunate as the population of their assigned abbeys would not support such a force. They had to resort to local recruiting, using the King's proclamation, to recruit volunteers.

An offshoot of the military training, was the second part of the promise to the King. That was the establishment of a "watch and patrol" system. In many instances these patrols were drawn from the troops being trained, but the monk and Bishop made visits to many of the nobles in the area and encouraged them to begin their own patrol efforts, dividing up the surrounding countryside into patrol responsibilities for each of them. The King's proclamation again proved its worth as the gentry either supported the King or were not prepared to rise against him.

The "M" team also devised an information and alarm system that would permit immediate response and pursuit as was needed whenever one of the patrols encountered a potential or current problem. This system mapped out the patrol areas and communication points to be used to pass along information. In most instances these points were located along adjacent patrol routes making it easy to access the nearest patrol areas to where the problem was occurring. One team even made use of fortified towers stretching across its assigned territory that were built long before current times. Thus, messages could be passed from patrol area to patrol area and eventually reached St. Albans where the entire effort was being coordinated.

The flow of information into St. Albans completely swamped the "C" team which was directing the courier route. The monk decided, with permission of the Abbot, to establish a formal communications center at the abbey staffed by the spare courier monks along with twenty volunteer laymen who were recruited and trained and sworn to secrecy. This team was housed right on the Abbey grounds and each member had to secure a "pass" in order to leave. The "C" team was used to oversee this operation.

The information was divided into categories as it came in and passed on to whomever could make the best use of it among the Green Rose teams. Among these categories were:

1. Civil unrest including banditry and law breaking.
2. Political Interest including appointments and honors.
3. Important changes in the countryside including transfers of land.
4. Royalty and Magnate daily activities.
5. Industrial opportunities and ideas.
6. Local, county, national celebrations, contests, fairs, etc.
7. Foreign interests including Scotland, Wales, France, and Spain among others.
8. Church vs. State problems and opportunities.

These categories, along with others not identified, served the Green Rose teams well in the field and a constant well of information was channeled to them through the Team "C" communications system.

The monk and the Bishop, due to their rounds of the noble houses and visits to London, soon became involved in most of the social and cultural events in the area and became privy to much "inside information" regarding the ruling Court Party. In addition, the monk made a special effort to pay equal attention to those York supporters who opposed the King.

The next problem faced by Team 6 was a shortage of military weaponry, armor, and other items needed for a properly functioning army and the monk detailed his personal squire, a skilled metal worker, to see what could be done.

St. Albans already had a working forge being used by the gun maker as well as for other transportation and building needs of the abbey. The squire made inquiries and found the materials needed to make the weapons serving the Green Rose teams in Northamptonshire about seventy miles to the north of St. Albans near the village of Corby. Since this was a long way to ship cartloads of iron ore, it was decided to set up a smelting operation near the mines and this was done a bit northeast of Corby on an old abbey grange along what is now known as Willow Brook, a fast flowing all-year round stream.

With a team of ten armed lay volunteers from the abbey, the squire loaded provisions, materials, and tools into three carts and the group set out for grange which was operated by another Cistercian abbey, but with permission from the abbot to establish such an operation. In addition, the abbot promised additional help from his own abbey.

[NOTE: A similar operation was established in Leicestershire by Team 3 with a foundry established at Coalville and the metal shipped to Lincoln for fashioning into weapons and supplies.]

Upon arriving at the Corby grange, the squire set his craftsmen to work building a water wheel with which to power a huge fan built to resemble a more modern windmill of today except with smaller blades and a lot more of them. Wooden chambers were built to funnel the air into the main foundry where the fire crucibles were busy melting the iron ore. Other members of the team were sent to the nearby hills to begin mining iron ore, chopping down and splitting up oak logs, and one team member was put in charge of bringing a load of chalk to the site.

The crude steel making process was set up similar to the process followed at the Green Rose Abbey in Scotland and followed a three step process. First the iron ore is extracted from the ore by smelting whereby oxygen is removed from the ore by combining it with carbon using a forced-heat process to increase temperatures of the oak charcoal to the desired temperatures. The molten hot metal is then quickly poured into molds submerged in a water bath to quickly cool it down. These "pigs" (molded metal) are then re-heated to a lower temperature and hammered to close cracks and produce a "tempered" metal which is much stronger than the original iron and known in the trade as "sponge iron." Small pieces of the sponge iron were then heated to even higher temperatures in crude vats known as "crucibles" using forced air to increase the temperatures that could be achieved and blowing air directly into the crucibles to help burn out the impurities.

In addition, because the English iron ore was not as good as that produced in Sweden, which is the ore that had been used at the Scottish Abbey by the Green Rose Order, the squire had chalk added to the molten iron in this final stage which burned off even more impurities, including phosphorous, which tended to make the metal even stronger.

In most of the early foundries, steel making was a "iffy" process and often batches turned out to be useless due to lack of temperature control. However, in the Corby foundry the steady flow of air and running water cooling vats added stability to the steel making process and it wasn't long before the squire had the process producing good batches of steel with great consistency.

This was a highly secret process and only a few of the monks were entrusted with the formula for producing this weapon-strength steel. The chalk also was used to form the molds in which the finished steel was poured in order to ready it for shipment to St. Albans where it was heated again and poured into whatever forms were needed at the moment or pounded into the various swords and other weapons used.

Some experiments were tried to produce steel armor, but the finished products proved to be too heavy to be used in battle; however, breastplates of steel were added to existing armor which gave superior protection to the knights as neither arrows, spears, or swords could penetrate them.

It wasn't long before wagon loads of steel "pigs" were arriving weekly at St. Albans from the smelter at Corby to be converted into wagon wheel rims, breastplates, arrow and spear heads, swords, war hatchets and other weapons including daggers. Soon after that some experimental molds were made and gun barrels began being produced by the "exploding stick" maker at the abbey. In fact, the steady supply of steel made him think in even bigger terms.

Two other immediate problems cropped up for the Green Rose team at St. Albans shortly before the beginning of the next year—1452. These were heavy carts for hauling mainly military supplies and paper. St. Albans had its own primitive paper-making operation, but it lacked a sufficient supply of water and raw materials to produce paper in the quantities now needed by the Green Rose team for regular communications. Most messages were being carried by "word of mouth" and that left a lot to be desired as important details often were forgotten or left out of narratives. Each team had members who were fluent in several languages and could read and write most of them, but the peasant population remained largely illiterate at this time in England. However, whenever the peasants would take news to their lords or masters, good reports would wind up at St.

Albans and they were in writing on paper.

Two of the team were dispatched to an Augustinian abbey grange at Huntingdon in Huntingdonshire, near a small ancient village along the north bank of the River Ouse. The monks at the abbey had set up a small paper making process on one of its granges located on the bank of the river and were using locally grown hemp to produce a superior quality of paper. The Bishop at St. Albans had obtained a small quantity of this paper and was using it for special causes instead of the coarser paper produced by his own monks.

When the team members—one knight and one squire—arrived at Huntingdon they found a shed on the river bank being used for the paper making operations. A small channel had been dug to divert river water through the shed to help with the manufacturing process, but only three of the abbey's monks were assigned to making paper. The knight negotiated a contract with the abbot to enlarge the operation and it is believed a sum of money changed hands to seal the bargain.

At any rate, the next morning ten additional monks and fifteen lay volunteer workers appeared at the shed ready to work. The knight assigned five of the lay volunteers to gather hemp plants for processing. They also were used each spring to oversee the planting of more hemp to supply the new facility. Others worked to enlarge the water channel and to construct large wooden table-like troughs through which the water was directed. From a nearby town came some huge copper vessels which were placed on steel racks over fire pits in which to boil water and pulp. Large fiber woven screens were made and encased in wooden frames that fit over the water trough.

As the process developed, the raw hemp would be cleaned and then introduced into the boiling vats and cooked until the fibers became separated into a loose mass. This mass would be poured and spread evenly over the fiber in the frames. The water running underneath the frames cooled the mass quite quickly. The cooled sheets were then draped over large wooden board frames to dry. The dried sheets of paper where then placed into a press and a heavy weight was placed on top. The paper was allowed to compress overnight and was a finished product the following day. The sheets were bundled into stacks of 500, tied, and loaded on carts for shipment to wherever the paper was destined, including St. Albans.

Soon the production of paper outstripped the quantities of raw hemp available and the abbey had to plant several more fields of hemp to keep up with the demand.

The next problem tackled by the Green Rose team at St. Albans was the production of heavy duty military wagons and for this they turned to a small village in Buckinghamshire called Wickham which was near a grange operated by St. Albans. The village had several skilled craftsman and they were called upon to begin building the military wagons although they were more appropriately called "freight wagons."

The lead Green Rose monk himself handled the design of the wagons which had several innovative features designed to adapt to "travel situations" across England at the time. Among these were three-inch wide wagon wheel rims to counter bad weather road conditions, a spare wheel and rim mounted underneath each wagon, a hinged storage box across the front of the wagon the top of which doubled as a seat for the driver and two other passengers, a tongue designed to accommodate four-to-six draft horses, hinged fold-down sides to allow easier loading, and a high rear panel that folded down to form a loading ramp or table. Each wagon was constructed of solid oak wood and iron/steel bracing and hinges.

Two of the Green Rose squires were dispatched to Wickham (later renamed High Wycombe) to oversee the establishment and early operations of the "wagon barn." It took a month to secure the use of a large barn and to gather enough seasoned oak wood to construct the prototype of the wagon. The head monk even rode over to Wickham to inspect the finished product and suggested a couple of modifications which would permit later models to be more easily adapted to military uses such as troop hauling and field hospital services.

After the prototype was finished, it took nearly another month to gather the necessary supplies of wood, hinges and braces required to begin the building of other wagons. It took nearly six months before the wagon barn was in full production turning out one completed wagon every six days with at least two more in other construction stages. A supply of seasoned oak wood for the wagons was another problem.

For this the team turned to the nearby forests and assembled two teams of local peasants to cut the best oak trees and drag them to a yard near the wagon barn where they were split into planks and allowed to dry before being worked into wagons. Many of the craftsmen became so skilled in shaping and smoothing wood that they used scraps to begin building furniture (mostly chairs) which they sold at the various marketplaces. These proved quite popular and became somewhat of a sideline as the proceeds were kept by each individual craftsman and added handsomely to his annual income. When word got around of how much money these men were making, there was always a waiting list of men wanting to work on the wagons.

The wagons themselves were quite popular and many a noble purchased one or more for his own castle or household, but the bulk of the finished wagons were used to move military supplies and goods to a castle in Wales. Some of the wagons never made a return trip although the wagon drivers always rode back on the team horses.

In the meantime, during the years of 1452 and 1453, the spy system initiated by the Green Rose team continued to expand. Each team had established its own controlled system independent of all others gathering information from the various abbey granges around the countryside, the markets, the village fairs, and through the every growing system of "patrols" being initiated by many of the nobles across the country.

So much information was being filtered to St. Albans that the communications system had to be expanded once again. The tentacles of this system had already reached into the court of the King and St. Albans received a weekly report of the scheduled events involving the King and Queen and many of the other nobles attached to the court. Information even reported pending changes of residence by the King so that spy systems were in place even before the King arrived.

In the fall of 1451 the spy system was already receiving reports about the instability of the King and a propaganda campaign was initiated entitled: *Fitter for a Cloister than a Crown.* Hundreds of leaflets were secretly printed at St. Albans and distributed to all parts of the country with a drawing depicting the King tilted forty-five degrees to his left side and walking a crooked path. These appeared in nearly every town and hamlet in the country and some were posted as fast as the King's supporters could tear them down.

A reward was finally offered for anyone found putting up a poster or even reading one, but it is not believed that anyone ever collected on the promise. Most thought the poster was quite funny and that added greatly to its effectiveness.

After Christmas in 1452 the lead Green Rose monk and the Bishop at St. Albans attended a session at court. Shortly afterwards a secret message was dispatched by ship to Rome reporting on the increasing instability of the King. The situation was deemed so bad by the York supporters that they encouraged the Duke to gather and army in Shrewsbury and other towns and lead it towards London. This effort did not lead to armed combat and the Duke was forced to take a pledge not to rebel against the King again.

By this time St. Albans was receiving an increasing number of visitors seeking overnight lodgings and work began on enlarging this section of the abbey. The monk, with permission of the abbot, put specially trained laymen to serve the guests in the quarters and was able to intercept many important pieces of information as a result.

One such incident involved Queen Margaret. Two of her royal emissaries stopped at the abbey overnight en route to Scotland to offer a Christmas invitation to Scotland's Earl of Douglas who was a long time enemy of England. When he heard this news, the Green Rose monk immediately surmised the invitation was a veiled opportunity for Margaret to try and enlist the support of the Scottish Earl to come to the aid of the embattled and fragile Henry VI. Special dispatch riders left the abbey the next afternoon to carry the word to all Green Rose teams to "be on the lookout" for any information they could pick up. Shortly after the Christmas celebrations word was received at the abbey that a deal was indeed struck between Margaret and the Earl of Douglas to come to Henry's aid in the event of an internal conflict in England. It was not immediately learned what had been promised the Earl for his intervention, but most thought it was disputed land along the border between the two countries which had been traded back and forth during the various border conflicts since earlier times. A special note was sent by courier to Fotheringhay Castle in Northamptonshire where the Duke of York was currently in residence and had spent the Christmas holidays. The note was signed only with the imprint of a hand-colored green rose.

As luck would have it the monk himself, along with two of the other Team 6 knights, were invited guests at Fotheringhay Castle as a result of earlier efforts by Team 3 which rescued the Duke's wife, Cecily, from road bandits. Members of Team 3 were honored guests at the Christmas Day banquet and all during the festivities and that also included the Team 6 visitors. Special presents were given out by the Duke on Christmas Day as a "thank you" to the Team 3 members and the lead monk himself received a beautiful gold coin embossed with a rose.

After three all-night sessions between the two team members discussing the current political unrest, it was decided the lead monk would hand the Duke another specially prepared "green rose" note outlining the order's true role in England to provide political stability to the country. By this time it was apparent that Henry VI's reign needed to come to an end for this to occur. A secret meeting was arranged between the monk and the Duke and his wife. The monk handed over another green rose embossed note to the Duke outlining some of the political implications that had been learned through the spy system and verbally reported on the Order's role in England.

When the Duke recovered from the surprise, he heartily endorsed the Green Rose effort and a deal was made which was to have a monumental and powerful impact upon the politics of the country although not much relief in the form of reforms to benefit its citizens.

One of the controlling influences in the English countryside was the actions taken by crown-appointed Sheriffs and/or Constables. These offices were designed to maintain peace among the populace although—as in the case of Cade's Rebellion—the office served to inflame the public instead. At the suggestion of the Duke of York the team at St. Albans determined to extend its spy system to this level of government. The effort met with limited success as holders of these appointments tended to be rather brutal in their treatment of the peasants and were out mostly for their own personal gains in both power and money. As a result, their actions largely were not predictable. Some important information came from these sources, but it was mainly at times when the opposing forces were recruiting armies across the countryside.

The Green Rose information team was all set to go to work when Queen Margaret finally produced a long-awaited heir to the throne in Edward. The birth took place in October shortly after King Henry suffered a longer and more complete mental breakdown than he had on previous occasions. Since the Queen had a long association with a lover, there was some question about the parentage of the infant and several bulletins were issued questioning the value of having a "bastard" as a future ruler of England. This raised quite a bit of discontent around the country and resulted in any number of "bar fights," but no armies were raised.

However, it did give emphasis for the push by the Duke of York to be appointed Protector of England while the King was ill. This effort finally succeeded in January of 1454.

In the meantime, St. Albans was quite busy with the various enterprises that had been started. The children's school had been quite successful and work was underway to expand this opportunity to other parts of the land. Politically, it was tough sledding for Team 6 since many of the nobles themselves could not read nor write and they sure didn't want their peasants to have that knowledge. Finally, educated monks were dispatched on a secret basis to many of the castles to conduct private reading and writing classes for the nobles and their families. This further delayed expanding the education system down to the commoners, but it did serve to enhance the power and prestige of St. Albans and the Green Rose teams. Soon, as many as thirty such schools were underway across the country which was about as many trained and educated monks as the abbey could spare for the six or so weeks it took to complete a training class. In some cases the class numbered up to forty students as nobles, especially those related to each other, combined families for the training.

It was in the fall of 1453 when a visitor arrived at St. Albans all the way from France where the war with the English had taken several bad turns. He was immediately shown into the workshop of the armorer at the abbey and they were secreted in the shop for several hours before the monk was called in. What the monk discovered was the visitor was actually the brother of the gun maker and he had come up with the idea and plans for an even larger exploding stick which he was calling a "mortar."

The trio soon called in the metal smith and the four spent at least two days discussing the drawings and the potential of the weapon before deciding to begin its experimental development. The monk made several suggestions on the development of a wooden, rolling carriage for the mortar and the process was soon sent off to the foundry and carpentry shops respectively where trusted monks and laymen were put to work on its development.

The most difficult part turned out to be casting the barrel of the mortar and making sure it was not flawed in any way. The first five castings turned out to have defects and it wasn't until the formula for the metal was adjusted that what looked to be a perfect barrel was finally cast some four weeks later. In the meantime the wooden carriage for the mortar was completed and the two were soon joined together to form the first cannon.

It was in January of 1454 when the first test firing was to take place. The new forbidden looking weapon was rolled outside the foundry at the abbey and pointed towards the apple orchards below. A barrier of bagged sand had been laid just behind the cannon for the armorer's protection when the contraption was fired. No one knew exactly how much black powder to load into the weapon so the monk figured out it should be in proportion to the size of the cannonball as compared to the exploding stick. That proved not to be the case as the first charge sent the ball outside the walls of the abbey proving that the cannon theory was workable. Unfortunately the charge also ruptured the barrel. The ball itself landed next to a startled deer in a forested area outside the abbey. A forester happened to see the deer bolt away and went to investigate. He found the iron ball and immediately assumed it had been "passed" by the deer in its frightened state. He wrapped a rag around the ball and took it to a village tavern where the metal "turd" became the talk of the village until the Bishop confiscated it as a "relic."

The armorer went back to work and it was another three months before the second test firing of the new "cannon," as it was now called. This test was more successful although the cannon ball shot straight out and bounced into the abbey wall loosening several of the stones although not crashing completely through. It took the monks two days to repair the damage. The monk and the armorer decided they had to devise a way to elevate the muzzle of the cannon so it was back to the drawing board to devise a new carriage. Several innovations for this process were tried before they achieved a workable, but crude, system which allowed the barrel to be swiveled upwards to four differing elevations.

The cannon was then loaded onto a heavy wagon and hauled to one of the remote granges belonging to the abbey before it was again test fired. The monk and armorer found that the highest elevation produced the longest trajectory for the cannon ball and lower elevations reduced its range considerably. They finally fired one ball from each of the elevations and measured the differences in where the balls landed to determine the range of the cannon. After that they adjusted the amounts of black powder used and discovered they could pretty accurately determine the range of each ball by the amount of powder used and the elevation of the barrel. They still had no way of accurately aiming the cannon except to adjust the direction of the carriage itself.

At any rate, the experiment was a success and the cannon was returned to the armory and locked away in a back room. The armorer was directed to make a few more "balls" for the device, but no further work was to be done.

Throughout the balance of 1453 the Green Rose Team 6 was kept quite busy with the expanding education system, increased military training, weapon and wagon making, spy and information gathering activities and other enterprises it had started.

In January of 1454, when the Duke of York was confirmed as Protector of England, he made a night visit to the abbey at the invitation of the Green Rose monk and the Bishop. During this visit it is believed he was shown the newly developed cannon told of its military potential although it was not demonstrated. But, after the Duke had departed back to London, the armorer was instructed to begin work on a second cannon barrel.

About a month later an envoy from the Pope arrived at the abbey and was received by the monk who offered his hand in greeting. The envoy had been expecting this and immediately delivered the secret handshake. When challenged for further identification by the monk, the envoy produced a replica of the gold key which had been given the monk in Scotland. The monk accepted the key, invited the envoy to be seated, and then entered an adjoining room to inspect the key. When he found it contained no secret compartment, he immediately became suspicious and decided to further test the envoy.

The monk returned to the room and struck up a conversation with the envoy asking him about his journey from Rome, what ship he had traveled on, and ports of call. The answers he received did not add up to his own experience, but still he kept silent. Finally, appearing to be satisfied, he asked the purpose of the envoy's visit expecting to receive some instructions from the Pope. Instead the envoy simply indicated he was here in order to observe and report back personally to the Pope. This immediately raised the monk's suspicions to a higher level since he knew the Pope would not send any envoy on such a foolhardy journey.

The monk then suggested the envoy was tired from his journey and would be shown to his quarters to rest before the evening chapel service and they would meet again later. The monk summoned an assistant who began to escort the envoy to the guest quarters in another part of the abbey where, upon the Green Rose monk's suggestion, he secured the guest room door when he left. In the meantime the monk inspected a small bag carried by the envoy and found its contents not suited to a long sea voyage so he consulted with the Bishop and laid out his suspicions.

Soon a squad of armed guards arrived at the envoy's room and escorted him to the lock-up in the lower level of one of the abbey's towers and shackled him, amidst violent protests, to the wall. The monk saw that he was treated well, under the conditions that existed at the time, and led several sessions whereby by envoy was interrogated. It turned out he was sent by the Queen—Margaret of Anjou—to learn the inside operations of St. Albans based upon a report from one of the "insiders" at the abbey who claimed the abbey was not supportive of the King. Further questioning revealed the source of the information was from one of the longtime monks at the abbey. He was quickly placed in isolation and remained there for the remainder of his life. The envoy was secretly transported to the coast and put aboard a ship bound for Rome to be dealt with there.

From that point on, the residents of St. Albans and the Green Rose team were "on the alert" for further infiltrations although none were discovered. Word was sent out to all other teams to "be sensitive" for similar attempts to infiltrate their ranks. A similar note was sent to the Duke of York by a special dispatch rider.

Not long afterwards, in February of 1454, the Duke of York appeared once again at St. Albans to meet with the Green Rose monk and the Bishop of the abbey. It was at this point that it appears a special agreement was reached that the Duke would support the Pope in return for formal, but secret support of the Green Rose efforts. No written evidence has ever been found that such an agreement was reached, but one of the monks noted in his personal journal that a summons had been sent from the secret meeting for pen, paper, and sealing wax. Not long after the meeting was concluded, a special courier was sent to Rome, believed to be carrying a signed and sealed copy of the agreement, and instructed it was to be presented for the personal attention of the Pope.

Also, it was from this point in the narrative that word also was dispatched to all Green Rose teams to increase their military training and equipping of trainees. At St. Albans the armorer was reinforced with additional volunteers and instructed to work on both the "exploding stick" and the new cannon. No other cannon barrel had been successfully cast although several attempts had been made, but each had some type of fault. The formula for the steel had been adjusted several times, but satisfactory and consistent results were still elusive.

One other industry of note was begun at St. Albans early in 1452 and that was known as straw-plaiting whereby hats, dolls, and various other designs were woven from straw primarily by peasant women. One of the St. Alban monks had learned the craft from a peasant woman, after he had admired her work, and spent some time weaving straw at the abbey. When the Green Rose monk saw examples of the monk's work, he immediately saw it as an opportunity for the peasant women to earn money at the various marketplaces throughout the land.

However, the Bishop felt there already were too many activities at St. Albans and suggested to the monk that some other Green Rose team might need income from such work or have the time to sponsor the activity. The straw-plaiting monk was asked if he would be willing to train others in his craft and he quickly accepted the challenge. After some enquiries, via the dispatch system, he was sent to Hailes Abbey where Team ten was headquartered.

It was about June of 1454, after the Duke of York was confirmed as *Protector of England*, that a courier was received at St. Albans carrying a message directly from the Duke. It seems one of the Crown's wildlife protectors had spotted a group of armed men robbing young Osprey's from their nests in a protected wildlife area known as "Rutland Water." The Ospreys, as well as Swans, were under the protection of the crown and the Duke was asking the Green Rose team for help as locals had tentatively identified some of the local "constables" as members of the gang responsible for the thievery.

Rutland Water was a natural swampy area near the Rutlandshire town of Oakham and served as an over-wintering site for many varieties of wild fowl as well as a breeding site for Ospreys. Many of the Ospreys were migrant birds from Scotland that winter over in the south of England and Wales, Spain and Portugal, and even North Africa. The return migration begins in March and the males return to breed in the same vicinity from which they themselves fledge, often returning to the same nesting site in Rutland Water.

The Osprey is a medium-large raptor known to feed on fish. It is also known by various other names including a "Fish Eagle." It locates its prey from the air and then plunges feet-first into the water to seize a fish. The fish is always turned head forward to reduce drag while the Osprey returns to its nest with the prey. The birds usually mate for life beginning in March or early April and spend about five months raising the young. Many Asian countries were known to train Ospreys to catch fish.

The main concern by the Duke was that the wholesale theft of the young birds would soon reduce the numbers in the Rutland Water area so that it would no longer be a breeding ground.

Two of the Green Rose team were soon dispatched—one knight and his squire—along with ten of the mounted and trained lay volunteers from the abbey. The Duke had provided the names and location of the reporting wildlife "protectors" in the area and this was to be the starting point for the Green Rose party.

The group made camp in a wooded area overlooking the Osprey preserve and the knight soon made contact with the two protectors who lived in the village of Oakham. Both rode to the camp with the knight in order to brief the Green Rose party.

From what the team learned, the thievery had been underway each spring for a number of years and the robbers would board log rafts and pole them out to the nesting sites, usually in dead trees, and steal the young birds out of the nest just before they were able to fly. Sheepherders grazing their flocks in the area had first reported the thefts.

One of the protectors led the knight and squire to an area being grazed and they visited with a shepherd who told them how the thieves were working the area. They would launch their rafts from various locations around the shoreline where the birds were nesting. There would be three men to a raft—one to pole it through the marshy waters, one to climb the trees and hand down the fledglings, and a third to receive the birds and stuff them in wooden cages on the rafts. When the cages were full they would pole back to the bank, unload the cages into a high-sided cart, and drive them away.

One of the protector's had tracked a cart load of birds to the south, but had lost sight of it on the streets of London near the dock areas, and he was "pretty sure" the birds were probably put aboard a ship for markets in Asia.

Since it appeared the thieves were well organized, the knight decided the best way to handle the problem was to set a trap. The shepherd reported the cart was left unattended on the shore while the thieves were stealing the birds so it was decided to use dye to put an identifying mark on the left rear corner of the cart where it would likely be overlooked by the thieves since they were working in the twilight anyway. The shepherd indicated there were usually two rafting parties which meant a total of six thieves; however, the cart left with only the driver on board. This meant there would be five locals to capture without alarming the cart driver, who would be followed to London to see where the birds were being warehoused or delivered.

The knight decided the team would hide in the woods until the cart departed and then move out and capture the local poachers. When they were in custody, the knight, squire, and three of the volunteers would follow after the cart while the others escorted the thieves to the local jail and would stand guard until a court was assembled. The plan for the followers was to have one tailing the cart as best he could, while the other four would ride on ahead and station themselves along the road to London. When the cart passed their hiding place, they would contact the trail rider and then ride on ahead and alert the next watcher by attaching a green scarf to their saddle to use as a warning signal. When the watcher spotted the scarf he would show himself and get ready to do the same for the next watcher. The first watcher would then ride on ahead and take up another watch station along the road. They would do this all the way to the dock area in London hoping to keep in contact with the wagon without alerting the driver.

A night watch was established on the camp and it was three days later that the group spotted two horse-drawn carts, one loaded with wooden cages and the other with what looked like logs, drive up and stop along the bank of the water in the preserve. Sure enough there were six men in the party. The logs turned out to be two rafts which were quickly carried down to the water and launched. Then half of the wooden cages from the other cart were loaded on each raft. Two long poles were tied along the side of the log cart and these were quickly carried down to the rafts. Three men piled onto each of the rafts and they were quickly poled out into the swampy waters to the trees where the Ospreys had their nests.

As soon as the rafts were far enough away, the squire used trees for cover and worked his way quietly over to the carts where he painted a small green rose on the right rear corner of each cart. In the meantime the Ospreys were kicking up quite a fuss out on the water as their fledglings were taken from nests and stuffed into the cages on the rafts. Several of the male birds made diving passes on the rafts and even pushed one man off the raft into the water. He grabbed hold of the long pole and was helped back on the raft.

All-in-all it took nearly two hours for the bandits to fill up the wooden cages with the baby birds and start their return to the bank. The team members had saddled their mounts and were waiting in the shelter of the trees for the moment to strike. All six of the bandits worked to load the cages back into one of the carts. When the cart was loaded they sent off the cart with its driver into the night and then the remaining five started loading the rafts and poles onto the second cart. When that was done, they all jumped into the cart and started towards the village of Stamford which was the direction taken by the first cart.

The knight gave a pre-agreed signal by simply moving his horse forward and the team quickly surrounded the departing cart. One of the volunteers was assigned to stop the horses pulling the cart and the rest stood by with drawn swords hoping for some resistance from the bandits. They were disappointed as they all recognized the futility of resistance and threw up their hands in surrender. They were all quickly bound with hands behind their backs and the entire procession started heading towards Oakham.

When all was secure, the knight, squire, and the three volunteers started after the cart loaded with the birds. When they got close to the cart in the dark, they had no trouble locating it since the baby chicks were still calling for their parents and some of the Ospreys were still making passes at the cart and driver which was making the horses a bit restless. As soon as the team came to a meadow area it split up. The squire was assigned to tail the cart. The knight and one of the volunteers broke off to the left to pass the cart and the other two went to the right. Since it was dark they had to be careful, but the cart driver was so busy ducking from the diving birds and with the din of the crying birds there was slim chance any of the team would be spotted.

The chicks proved to be a real benefit to the stalkers since they always knew when they were close to the cart. The hopscotch plan of trailing the cart was working so perfectly that the knight decided to ride on ahead to the outskirts of London to determine the most likely path to the waterfront and see where his trackers could hide without running into any of the night watch patrolling the streets.

It was very nearly dawn of the second day by the time the cart approached London along one of the old Roman highways. By this time all of the team had assembled just inside the city except for the squire who was still trailing the cart. Suitable hiding places had been scouted and selected and each of the four chose a site. The knight himself chose an alleyway right at the waterfront.

The cart plodded pretty much along the route that had been scouted until it reached the dimly lit entrance to a warehouse about two doors from where the knight had posted his lookout. The cart driver got off and entered by a side door. Moments later the two main doors to the building were opened up and the driver remounted his cart and moved it inside. By this time the birds were pretty well tired out and there was not much noise from them.

After the remainder of the team joined up with the knight, it was decided to enlist the aid of the London night watchmen to surround the warehouse. The knight hailed one of them, showed him a sealed authority signed by the Duke of York as Protector of London, and the watchman hurried off to round up other security officials. It took about two hours to assemble the local Constable in Charge along with some twenty of his men all armed with oak sticks.

In the meantime the Green Rose team had been scouting the pier behind the warehouse where a ship was tied up flying a Greek flag. The knight used his team to board the ship and overcome the crew. They were all asleep in the hold of the ship and were taken without a fight. Only the captain, who only spoke Greek, put up a fight when he was caught in his quarters. He was quickly subdued and bound and locked up in a brig in the bowels of the ship with his crew.

When that was accomplished, the Constable and his men entered the warehouse from the front while the Green Rose team entered from the rear. It turned out there were nearly twenty men being housed in the warehouse, most of them out-of-work seamen. A few put up a struggle, but were quickly battered to the ground by the Constable's men. The cart full of birds was standing in the center of the warehouse and the horses had been unhitched and were in a nearby manger area calmly munching hay. A second cart also was in a corner covered by a tarp. When the tarp was lifted the team spotted several cages of another type of baby bird which appeared to be Royal Swans.

The captain of the ship was questioned, using a Greek interpreter, he finally confessed this was his third trip carrying birds and they were being taken to Singapore where they were offloaded and sold on the open market. It turned out that two of the sailors housed in the warehouse were members of a Singapore gang behind the bird stealing.

When informed of the catch, the Duke of York immediately assigned a group of Royal Navy sailors to sail the ship back to Singapore, minus the load of birds, with the intention of advising authorities there of the thievery and to turn over the captain and the gang members to authorities.

Word came back to the Duke some two months later that a number of gang members had been seized by authorities in Singapore who had been upset by the illegal birds being smuggled into the country. Some twenty people, the dispatch said, were publicly hanged.

The owner of the London warehouse was arrested and publicly whipped along with three of his regular employees. Crew members of the ship were impounded into the Royal Navy and the unemployed in the warehouse were simply turned out to fend on their own.

The cart full of birds was returned to Rutland Water where the chicks were replaced in the nests, but the conservation officers did not know what fledglings to put into what nests so they ended up hand raising a number of them for a few weeks until they could fend on their own. They identified each of the hand-raised chicks by painting a green band around one leg and more than fifty percent of them returned the following year to Rutland Water. This time they apparently found the right nests. The other cart of swan chicks was taken to a special swan preserve, but only about half of the chicks survived the trip.

The Duke of York sent a highly complimentary letter to the monk at St. Albans thanking him for the action by his team and providing a number of gifts and invitations. A banquet was held at the abbey to honor the Green Rose knight, squire, and the volunteers for their superb handling of the Osprey Affair as it was termed.

The Osprey Affair was the last official action of the Green Rose Team 6 at St. Albans. The team members were busy overseeing all of the activities initiated for the remainder of the year. In late November 1454, the spy network reported the King was recovering his senses and dispatches were sent from St. Albans to all of the teams and the Duke of York. A few days later the King made a public appearance and the recovery was confirmed.

In February 1455 the King called a parliament session whereby he dismissed the Duke of York from his role as Protector. The Duke, fearing for his life, immediately began raising an army and by April the political tensions were so great that the supporters of the King feared the Duke of York would try to claim the crown again and also began assembling an army. The monk quickly issued a recall of all team members to assemble at St. Albans with weapons and armor, but to bring none of the troops they had trained.

Chapter 15—The Southeast

It was February 1451 before Team 7 arrived at its destination abbey—Waverly in Surrey—in the southern part of England. Waverly was the very first Cistercian monastery established in the British Isles in 1128 as a colony from the French Abbey of L'Aumone. The abbey is located in the valley of the River Wey and has sustained periodic flooding, crop failure and bad seasons throughout its life.

It was during one of these flood times when Team 7 first approached the main entrance gate at Waverly. The team had spotted the abbey from a low rise along the approach road and had seen the flooded conditions even in the main courtyard of the abbey. In fact, one of the monks at the abbey had to wade through knee-deep water just to admit them at the gate.

They were housed on the second floor of the visitor's quarters at the abbey, which was high and dry, but the horses had to be stabled at a nearby grange barn located on higher ground. It was an inconvenience for all and the team found most of the monks were suffering from exposure.

One of the first tasks for Team 7 was to see what it could do about the flooding. In surveying the abbey grounds the next day, it was discovered that a small stream flowing through the property was in fact backing up from the high river flow and flooding the abbey internally as well as polluting the drinking water supply.

The lead knight organized a working party and a temporary dam was constructed across the stream bed just outside the abbey wall with a gate that could be opened or closed depending upon the level of the river. A diversion ditch was dug which diverted the stream flow around the dam to another low-lying area which formed a pond. The pond was eventually deepened and stocked with fish to help feed residents and guests of the abbey, but that occurred several months later. The diversion ditch, when finished, immediately drained excess water from the abbey grounds and, as soon as the ground dried out, living conditions were much improved.

It was this action that quickly gained Team 7 the confidence of the abbot and the monks inhabiting the abbey.

A second problem that became quickly apparent to Team 7 was a predominance of crime in the nearby village and surrounding countryside generally performed by out-of-work mariners and organized gangs of pirates who made periodic raids in the area. One of the targets for the raiders was the children in the village who were kidnapped and apparently shipped off to foreign lands and sold into slavery.

With permission of the abbot, the Green Rose team visited the village and convinced the elders to establish an armed patrol system to protect the village. As a further protection, the children were transported by cart to the abbey each morning to learn how to read and write and returned each afternoon to their parents in the village. This gave the children added protection during the day and permitted parents to attend to farming or other pursuits in order to care for their families.

The Green Rose team immediately set about arming the best young men in the village and training them in fighting techniques. It was not an easy process and was only completed when the team returned from the May conference in St. Albans with a wagonload of donated weaponry ranging from broad swords to daggers and pikes to bows. Contests were held to determine which villager was best suited to which weapon and several spirited fights took place. It served to accelerate both the training and to elevate the confidence of the villagers to defend themselves. A watch system was soon established and quickly proved its worth a few weeks later when the village was attacked by a gang of pirates in broad daylight.

An alert watcher sounded the alarm and more than fifty armed villagers were ready when the gang rode into the village square. The gang immediately left the vicinity as soon as they saw the villagers standing against them, but not without some casualties. One of the neophyte archers of the village scored a direct hit on the gang leader when an arrow struck him in the shoulder. Two other villagers, armed with pikes, unseated one of the gang from his horse and other villagers quickly stabbed him to death. That was enough for the gangsters and they quickly departed.

There was jubilation in the village and Team 7, along with the abbot, were invited that evening to a local feast. The village men, who had imbibed heavily in the local beer, were soon bragging of their fighting prowess. It took the Green Rose team several days to "settle them down" so the military training could proceed in an orderly fashion, but the spirit was never again diminished.

In the meantime, the children were enjoying the school sessions each day and life improved for the entire area.

Waverly Abbey was not without its supporters in the country and its influence even reached to the Court Party and the King. The abbey and abbot had maintained an important political influence in English royal affairs for many, many years although its prominence had diminished in more recent years. The abbot, however, was well acquainted in the area and introduced the Green Rose team to a number of the notables living in the surrounding countryside. One of these nobles showed an exceptional interest in the swords and arrowheads used by the Green Rose team and the team promised to demonstrate them at the next festival hosted by the noble which was to take place in June.

In March word came to the abbey that a London street vendor, with whom the team had an encounter en route to the abbey, wanted to see one of the Green Rose squires. The squire was immediately dispatched to London and picked up news from the vendor about an impending royal wedding between Margaret of Anjou (French) and King Henry VI. The gossip also included a warning that the marriage was brokered via a secret deal of some type although that part had not yet been revealed. A courier was immediately sent to St. Albans.

By the time Team 7 left for the April conclave at St. Albans, it had more than thirty children regularly attending classes at the abbey and nearly 100 young men undergoing military training.

Farnham Castle was an impressive stone motte and bailey fortress formed around an old Norman tower and enclosed by a shell-keep, with buttress turrets and a shallow gatehouse. It has a triangular inner bailey and a range of domestic buildings with a newly constructed brick entrance tower. The formidable outer bailey curtain wall is flanked by square towers, an old gatehouse and a large, deep ditch. This is where Team 7 found itself in June 1451 after its return from the conclave.

The lord of the castle had arranged a special market day and feast in honor of completion of spring planting and had invited Team 7 for a demonstration of its arrowheads and swords. Most of the villagers from Farnham had been invited to watch and many were sitting or standing along the walls of the inner bailey where the contests were to be held. The four squires from Team 7 were to demonstrate the arrowheads while the knights were to demonstrate the swords. For the archery, the squires set up special targets about fifty yards distance from where they were to shoot. Each target was made of different materials. The first target was a two-inch thick slab of round wood about eighteen inches in diameter. The second target was a two-inch thick slab of local stone about eighteen-inches square. The third target was a leather breast plate commonly used by foot soldiers. The final target was a metal shield from one of the knights at Farnham Castle emblazoned with the coat of arms of the local baron.

All eyes were on the squires as they drew back their longbows and let the arrows fly. A gasp was heard from the watching throng as all four of the arrows struck their respective targets almost squarely in the middle. It was as fine a showing of archery prowess as any had seen and gained immediate respect from the watching knights and nobles who knew just how good a feat it really was. After the shot, the royal visitors, including the Baron of Farnham Castle, were invited to inspect the targets.

The arrow had gone completely through the slab of wood and nearly cracked it in half. The rock slab was completely shattered. The arrow had penetrated a full six inches through the leather breastplate. The metal shield was struck squarely on the emblem of the baron and the arrowhead was completely through the metal. The nobles were even more impressed with the results and insisted that arrows be fired at a number of other targets of their choice. In all, the squires fired ten arrows each and never missed a target although there was one shot landing on the outer edge of one target. Most were firmly planted in the center area of each target.

After the target shooting was the sword demonstration. In the first round, the four knights from Team 7 stood in full armor but without insignia. They were matched by four of the baron's knights from the castle. The contest lasted about two minutes before the Green Rose knights shattered the blades of the opposing knights with their swords. A second round found the knights up against four armored foot soldiers representing the baron all armed with long-handled pikes and battle axes. This fight lasted a bit longer, but ended up with shattered pikes, split shields, and bent axes for the foot soldiers while the knights were virtually untouched.

There was no need for further demonstrations as the nobles, including the baron, were suitably impressed by the Green Rose weaponry and by the battle tactics displayed by the knights. The Green Rose knights and squires were honored at a banquet following the contests and left the castle with the abbot and an invitation to train the baron's knights and soldiers. Three of the other nobles promised to contact them soon in regard to their own forces. It was a successful demonstration by the Green Rose team and the abbot was as impressed with its prowess as much as were the nobles. Word soon got around about the demonstrations and many lay volunteers began coming through the gates of the abbey hoping to be included in the training activities there. Since these volunteers also had to work the abbey fields and crafts as part of their mission, the abbey had plenty of labor with some to spare.

One of those crafts was the production of beer from special hops grown at three of the abbey's granges. One of these granges, known as The Sands, had been losing hops from the racks where the harvested crop was laid out to air dry. Thieves were apparently sneaking in at night, loading the drying hops in bags, and then disappearing in the darkness. When the abbot complained to the Green Rose team about the losses, the team sprang into action.

It seems the flavor of beer depends largely upon the quality of the hops used to brew it. Waverly hops, as the locals called them, had a distinct aroma and flavor when used to make beer and the abbey had enjoyed visits from royalty throughout its existence simply as a result of its quality beer which seemed to suit royal tastes. Even King Henry VI regularly bought Waverly beer for his royal household and several shipments were sent to London each year where they were distributed by the royal servants to the various establishments of the king.

Most of the beer was distributed to various pubs located in villages near the abbey, but some even made it to the more famous pubs in London, too.

At any rate, the loss of quality hops meant that revenues from beer production at the abbey would be less although the shortage worked to raise the price of the beer that was produced. Fortunately for the abbey, hops are harvested several times throughout the summer growing season as the plants continue to produce.

Since The Sands grange was the one most often hit, Team 7 began to "stake out" the drying racks at night after the second harvest period. The local sheriff was also invited to participate in the watch and two team members, four or five lay volunteers, and at least two of the sheriff's men were on watch each night while the hops were drying. It was on the third night of the hops watch that thieves again visited the grange. The watch group waited until the thieves had bagged up most of the hops before they launched a surprise attack from two separate directions. It was nine watchers versus four thieves and things were quickly brought under control after a brief struggle. The sheriff's men took charge of the bruised and bound thieves and marched them off to Farnham where they were convicted and publicly lashed before being released. Had anyone been seriously injured in the melee, they likely would have been hanged, although they quickly cooperated with the sheriff and confessed they were working for a local pub which made its own beer. The pub owners were arrested, tried and hanged.

After that episode the Green Rose team seemed to be surrounded by hops—something they had not previously noticed. Since many of the peasants grew their own hops, those not used in the production of beer were used for decorations at local churches, for weddings, for feasts, and often hung in local pubs and homes since they are reputed to help "cleanse" the air. The team also found out they had been eating tender hops "shoots" as a vegetable at the abbey that spring.

Beer was in constant demand at most abbeys since the monks wanted a pleasant tasting, nutritious drink to have with their frugal meals. Beer was also a fine substitute for water which was not considered fit to drink. Further, even when the monks were fasting, beer was permitted since liquid consumption was not considered a break in the fast. Some estimate that monks were allowed to consume as much as five liters of beer on a daily basis.

Early in the history of Waverly Abbey, the monks were granted the right to sell beer. With the superior hops they grew, it was much in demand and added a considerable profit to the abbey's finances. In fact, the Waverly grut—the mixture of all sorts of hops and herbs used the flavor beer—had received a special license from the crown and was a well kept secret at the abbey. As was the case with Waverly Abbey, like most of England, barley was the grain of choice for brewing beer. Some say a small quantity of a second grain was used at Waverly, but there is no record of the formula used there. The fact that hops were used was somewhat of a mistake.

One of the monks was experimenting and trying to develop a medicinal beer that would help fight off the numerous miseries at the abbey brought on by the cold, damp winter weather. He added hops for flavoring because it was considered a medicinal plant. The result quickly gained him the title of "master brew maker" at the abbey and the Waverly beer was born.

[NOTE: It wasn't until well into the later English wars with France and Germany that using hops in English beer became popular when returning soldiers from Europe, having sampled local beers made with hops on the mainland, demanded the use of hops in English beers.]

The reputation of the Green Rose team had grown after the "planting feast" demonstrations so much so that the baron of Farnham Castle once again invited it to participate in the Christmas festivities in December of 1451. The team accepted knowing that many other local nobles would be in attendance and it once again would have an opportunity to demonstrate prowess in archery, jousting, and other contests and hunts likely to be held during the twelve days of festivities and political intrigue that accompanied the Christmas season.

Since Farnham Castle was but a short ride from the abbey, Team 7 opted not to stay at the castle during the Christmas festivities. It did participate in the majority of Christmas events held during the Christmas period except for the masquerade balls held nearly every evening in the great hall. They were persuaded to attend the Christmas ball, after the main feasting event of the season, and were somewhat disillusioned at the level of intoxication, those sleeping in the corners after the exhaustive meal and celebrating, and the general stench that layers of Christmas greens could not quite disguise. Since the team members were guests of honor, based upon the prowess they had once again demonstrated in the many contests and hunts, they had to stay for the traditional awards and gift giving ceremonies held throughout the day.

The abbot had gifted the castle lord with two barrels of beer and the Green Rose team presented a specially made brigandine armored vest covered in fine leather and emblazoned with the coat of arms of the castle. It was indeed a magnificent gift and again raised the prestige level of the Green Rose team in the eyes of the local nobility. The metal plates on the inside of the vest were made of the special steel formulated by the Green Rose monks. The baron immediately donned the new vest and wore it for the rest of the evening in a token of showmanship and thanks.

In return, the members of the Green Rose team, and the abbot, were showered with gifts of clothing, medals and prizes won through the competitions, and the honor of sitting at the elevated table with the castle lord and his wife at one end of the great hall.

In all, it was a successful Christmas season as two more of the local nobles confided in the team they were ready to begin military training for their own staffs and appointments were made for later in the winter to meet at the various castles and assess the needs before committing to the actual training.

Several days later the lead knight and his squire from the Green Rose team were back at Farnham Castle to discuss training needs for the baron's armored guards. What they found was a dire state of outdated equipment, a castle guard that was not prepared to fight, and an extremely lax watch/guard system protecting the castle. They made several recommendations on the spot to the lord who, although taken somewhat aback by his lack of preparedness, nevertheless agreed with the recommendations and took steps to correct the problems.

This made the captain of the guard quite angry and it was several days before he began to get with the training program being heartened by the steady progress being made by the men under his command with the stepped-up training. New watch procedures were instigated and the castle staff, in general, became quite adept at security measures making several suggestions themselves as they continued to gain experience and knowledge.

It took approximately six months for the Green Rose team to "shape up" the castle, but the strategy paid off handsomely after a visit to Farnham Castle by King Henry VI at one of the spring festivals where the castle guards thwarted an effort by a "crazed Frenchman," as they called him, to attack the King. The Frenchman was immediately hanged after two days of severe questioning. It was said he was "acting alone" in his effort to assassinate the King. The prompt discovery and actions by the castle troops in protecting the King brought immediate royal favor to the baron and the castle and the King even made a grant of additional land to the baron. The baron offered to divide the new land among members of the Green Rose team, but the lead knight suggested he reward his own men instead including the captain of the guards. It was this action that cemented the relationship between the abbey, Green Rose team, and the castle and that closeness and support lasted for years.

In fact, the castle troop was a part of the King's army in February of 1452 after the Duke of York raised an army in Shrewsbury and other towns and led it towards London. A peace was negotiated prior to any armed conflict and the Duke agreed not to again rebel against the King.

However, the smartly outfitted troop from Farnham Castle was noted and many other requests for military training were funneled to the abbey by the lord of Farnham who was reveling in his new found recognition.

The Green Rose team was feeling pretty good about itself and it decided to lend a hand to the lay volunteers at Waverly during lambing season when nearly all the abbey's monks and laity were called on to work the 5,000 strong sheep herd on the various abbey granges. The team was sent to The Sands grange near the abbey where a sizeable flock of sheep was maintained in addition to the hops cultivation and drying.

The head monk at the grange, an experienced shepherd, looked over his Green Rose volunteers and assigned them to catching and marking lambs (using a red dye) with at "WA" standing for Waverly Abbey. At first the job was fun and a lot of laughs were expended at the antics of the Green Rose team for their ineptness in catching and handling the lambs. In the first place the mother ewes were resentful when the lambs were captured and often attacked from the rear. Many a team member ended up with a sore back or rear after an angry ewe had butted him.

After the first day, the lead knight consulted with the head monk and asked for advice on how to more easily accomplish the team's assigned task. The monk arranged a demonstration with his more experienced helpers and the Green Rose quickly caught on to the more conventional methods of catch, mark and release used by the shepherds. One of the shepherd's dogs was assigned to the team's use and this quickly nullified any ewe attacks on the unsuspecting team members. After that the job went quite quickly and the team gained valuable insight on sheep herding and care. The marking effort lasted for most of a week and the team returned to the abbey quite tired and sore from the physical activity, but proud of its accomplishments in an unfamiliar battle. The lead knight had actually refined the monk's techniques into a battle plan and the Green Rose team was soon "showing how" to get the job done at a much faster pace than normal. Even the monk was impressed by their industriousness and soon started training his own men using the team's techniques.

The experience with the sheep led one of the squires to dream up an idea to promote the abbey's plan for overnight hostelling of visitors which had steadily been increasing despite the imposition of a fee for such services. A new guest quarters was added to the abbey structures and anywhere from six to eight guests were accommodated on most nights. As a show of hospitality, the squire encouraged the abbey to send each guest on his way after a morning breakfast, gifting them with a lunch wrapped in a square of cloth, and wishing them a good journey. The lunch consisted of two breakfast biscuits, a slab of cheese made at the abbey, a square of fruit "leather" also made at the abbey, and a ginger cookie.

One of the monks, who worked in the kitchen, had begun the practice of painting a small cross on the cloth squares used to wrap the lunch. It wasn't long before word got back to the abbey regarding the "holy biscuits" they were gifting to the travelers. And, the cloth squares—neatly washed and dried—were becoming quite popular as gift wrapping, small flags, dish towels, head scarves, etc. Before long the cloths became so much in demand the abbey began producing them for sale in the local marketplaces. It is believed the revenues to the abbey from the sale of these cloths eventually exceeded that brought in by the hostel accommodations.

In September of 1452 the Green Rose team received a request from St. Albans to establish an oak wood milling process on one of its granges in Sussex which was blessed with an oak forest. The only other use the abbey had found for the grange was sheep grazing so it welcomed an opportunity to expand its revenue producing opportunities even more.

Six of the eight members of the Green Rose team left Waverly early one morning and headed south and east for a village in East Sussex known as Crowborough which bordered Ashdown Forest and was in the area where the abbey had a grange it simply called the Forest Grange. The team leader had in his belt a special grant from the King permitting them to cut selected trees not only from the land on the abbey's grange, but from Ashdown Forest itself which was owned by the crown. The permit had been obtained from the king by the baron of Farnsworth Castle at the request of the abbot as a return favor for protecting the king from an assault while visiting the castle. It was a distance of about thirty miles and took nearly a full day to reach. It would have taken longer except the abbot had provided a monk to guide the team. The monk had tended sheep at the grange in the past and was familiar with travel there. He led them through some pretty rough territory before they reached the grange. The head monk at the grange had been notified to expect them and had prepared special quarters for the team in the loft of one of the sheep barns and that's where it set up headquarters.

On the next morning the team, along with the monk guide, went looking for a suitable mill site which they found on the side of a wooded hill in an area known as Raven Wood where a year-round stream was tumbling down the side. The monk showed them a spot where he believed they could build a water-powered mill in order to establish a rough cut sawmill. While the monk returned to the grange, the team rode into the small rural market village of Crowborough situated on a high mound nearly 800 feet above sea level.

It so happened the market was in operation on that morning and the team had little difficulty in hiring a pair of master carpenters, along with about ten other workers, who were willing to set up a camp at the future sawmill site and begin its construction. They were all given directions and told to report in two days. It was a welcome opportunity for the recruits as wage-paying jobs were short in Crowborough. The team then proceeded to purchase the necessary foods, supplies, and shelter materials needed and hired a local cart driver to deliver them to the site later that afternoon.

In the meantime, the monk from the grange had returned to the site along with four of his brother monks and they had carried in a number of tools and supplies with which to begin setting up the camp. A crude "A" shaped wooden structure was built from logs and branches to serve as a kitchen and housing for the monk who would be assigned to the project. Four other straight-sided shacks were built to house the workers with dirt and pine branches used to form the roofs. When finished they were water tight on the slightly sloped roofs; however, there were a number of gaps between the side logs which would later be filled with mud from the creek. The camp was pretty much ready by the time the hired workers from the village began to arrive a couple of days later.

The carpenters were quickly set to work making a water wheel using building materials brought from the grange while all but two of the rest of the party were given buck saws and axes and sent into the nearby woods to begin felling trees. The remaining two were put to work digging a hole to house part of the milling apparatus. When the hole was completed, they were put to work using the dirt and water to chink the cracks in the crude huts used for temporary housing.

Considerable progress had been made by nightfall when the Green Rose team, the monks, and the crew gathered around a campfire for the evening supper. One of the squires had shot and killed a deer while one of the monks had gathered a number of greens and roots from the forest. Another of the monks had brought a fishing pole and the monks were well supplied with fish for their supper which they made into a fish stew. All-in-all it was a tired, but well-fed and happy group around the campfire. The lead knight took the opportunity to explain what was being built, showed them the permit from the King to cut trees, and suggested if they applied themselves the temporary jobs could be turned into permanent ones after the mill was up and running and producing a suitable income. It turned out to be one of the few Cistercian-owned industries that wasn't entirely staffed by lay volunteers. At first the abbot had refused to consider paid workers at the mill, but he was soon to change his mind when he learned it would take more time to recruit and train lay volunteers than it would to hire trained local labor. He knew there was some urgency behind the request from St. Albans.

It took several days to complete the water wheel, get it properly mounted on a stone foundation, and give it the proper balance to turn evenly. After that it was another three or four days to set up all the gearing and structure necessary to operate the large straight saw used to make lumber. When the mill finally became operational, it took several enterprising changes in order to make the blade go up and down at a pace fast enough to saw through the big timbers. The end result was a working, water-powered, sawmill that could saw into lumber about six big oak trees per day by operating the mill from daybreak until dusk.

About two weeks after the mill was operational, a wagon arrived from the St. Albans wagon making enterprise at Wickham in Buckinghamshire to pick up the first load of sawn boards. Since it was a milestone for the new mill, work was stopped and an impromptu celebration was held. After that a wagon would arrive each week to pick up the lumber and pay the monk in charge for the previous load. The monk, in turn, would pay the workers at the mill and send the balance to the grange for eventual transport back to the abbey.

When the milling operation was in full swing, the Green Rose team returned to the abbey leaving the guide monk in charge. Things went well until about November when a raiding party attacked the mill in broad daylight killing the monk and two of the mill workers before setting fire to the camp itself. The raiders probably would have destroyed the water wheel and mill itself except for other workers who attacked them with axes and drove them off.

When word of the raid reached the abbey a day later, the entire Green Rose team left immediately with four other trained lay volunteers and two supply carts heading for the mill site at Ashdown Forest. It took a day-and-a-half to get there due to the bad roads and the camp was in a deplorable condition when they arrived with no work being done.

The head knight quickly rallied the remaining workers, who had already buried the two dead workers and sent the body of the dead monk back to the grange for burial. They had saved most of one of the huts for shelter and still had plenty of food, but were quite dispirited and some were even ready to go home. The knight quickly put them to work using stockpiled lumber to construct a fairly large bunkhouse of logs with a lumber floor and roof and framed windows and doors. He also instructed them to build bed frames inside for bunks filled with pine bows. Since all were skilled woodsmen by now, the work went quickly and the bunkhouse was operational by the end of the third day, except for some finishing touches.

Another square building was constructed to serve as the kitchen and dining hall with a separate add-on room for the monk who was to be put in charge of the operation. After that, most of the crew returned to the job at hand—cutting trees and making boards and the mill was back in operation. Fortunately, enough boards had been stockpiled to complete the weekly deliveries as scheduled.

When things were back in operation, Team 7 began the work of identifying and tracking down the raiding party. They talked with each of the survivors and ended up with a pretty good description of three of the raiders along with good descriptions of the horses they rode. An examination of the forest floor found some distinctive hoof prints.

Leaving the four lay volunteers from the abbey to guard the sawmill, the Green Rose team began tracking the raiding party. There were quite a few signs left even though the actual raid had taken place a couple of weeks earlier. The trail led to the northeast through the trees towards an old ironworks site that was no longer being operated. The team made a complete circle around the area, but found no signs leading past the smelting site. One of the knights rode into the camp, pretending to be a traveler passing by, and soon spotted the horses of the raiders in a corral. He left quickly when three armed men demanded to know why he was there.

Reporting his findings back to the team, they spent the rest of the day observing activities at the smelter site and determined it was not being used at present other than as a headquarters for the raiders. They counted twelve raiders in all, but didn't know if there were more who could show up at any time. The lead knight left one of the squires to stand watch while the rest of the team returned to the sawmill site to get their arms and pick up the four armed lay volunteers. The now fully armed (and armored) group rode back to the smelter late that evening, made contact with the squire who indicated the entire band of raiders was housed in a crude shack behind the smelter site, but their numbers had increased by four during the day.

After sizing up the situation, the lead knight decided there was only one way to avoid a prolonged battle and decided it was more than fair to "fight fire with fire." He ordered the squires to prepare a number of "flaming arrows," by wrapping the front of the shafts with dry moss and binding it with vines from the forest. A small fire was built behind some sheltering rocks and when the remainder of the team, including the volunteers, had surrounded the shack, the squires began shooting fiery arrows at the roof and walls of the shack. The dried wood caught fire almost immediately and the shack's roof was soon ablaze.

By the time the men inside realized the shack was on fire, it was too late for them to put it out. When they tried to escape, they were cut down by arrows as all four squires were lined up on the only door to the shack, which had no windows. After the first two men to leave were downed by arrows, the remainder quickly announced they were ready to give up. They were allowed to leave the burning shack, were quickly searched, and then bound with tree vines by the team. There were twelve survivors in all who, after questioning, readily admitted they were the ones raiding the sawmill because "it was located too close to their home hideout."

The shack burned all night and the team members took turns watching the prisoners. Next morning they were marched into Crowborough and turned over to the town council who locked them up in an old barn while they sent for the constable. When the court convened the men were found guilty of murdering the monk and workers at the sawmill and were subsequently hanged. Most of the locals were glad to get rid of the gang who had been terrorizing the territory in recent months while hiding out in the woods although two of the gang were local to the area which caused some family concerns.

It was January before the Green Rose team once again was in the area of the sawmill. Only this time it was to see if the old smelter site could be revitalized. The team was accompanied by a monk sent from St. Albans who was an expert in the metal trade having set up a similar operation at Corby in Northamptonshire. This second request from St. Albans was a result of the Christmas gift presented to the baron at Farnham Castle by the Green Rose team—the armored brigandine vest. The baron had been bragging about the vest at the Royal Court in London and the King had shown an interest as well as the Duke of York. The Duke, especially, had asked for 500 of the vests for his personal archers. Since the Corby operation was mainly devoted to weapons and wagon tires, it was decided to investigate the old smelter site in Ashdown Forest which had been identified in reports by Team 7 to St. Albans after the sawmill incident.

It took the St. Albans monk two days before he was satisfied with the quality of ore available and the layout of the old smelting site. He had performed several tests with the ore and even crushed and melted some of it down before he made up his mind. In fact, he told the lead knight of Team 7 that the quality of ore was about two grades higher than that being used at Corby and he thought he could turn the ore into a higher quality and lighter weighing alloy which would be much more suitable for the brigandine vests and perhaps even long swords and pike heads.

With the aid of the four lay volunteers from the nearby sawmill, the monk set about obtaining what he needed in order to modernize the smelter site and get it operating. Since the old living shack had been burned to the ground, the sawmill was shut down for two days and the men were used to construct a permanent building at the smelter using harvested logs and green oak boards from the mill. A second building was constructed by planting ten-foot vertical logs in the ground and anchoring them with a pitched roof of boards and shingles. It was under this open-sided shed that the monk was to fire up the crucibles to be used in the smelting operation.

Meanwhile, the Green Rose team visited the marketplace at Crowborough again looking for additional items requested by the monk as well as some workers to operate the mine and smelter. The team was well received and remembered in the village and soon had the ear of the Town Council who identified several villagers who had been connected with the previous smelter. The team interviewed each of them, found most too old to be much good, but turned up about eight sons who were aged fifteen to eighteen years old and eager to work. Some of the sons knew quite a bit about metalworking as their fathers had brought their skills to the small farms they currently were operating. In addition, two of the older men were identified as expert in the smelting operations and agreed to help get the smelter operating.

In visiting with one of the councilmen, the team leader mentioned he was looking for a foundry site in which to begin building specialized military equipment as well as tools for the local trade. The councilman led him to a large cave on the edge of the village which had previously been used by owners of the old smelter to fashion the metal into armaments. The area had been pretty much "stripped" of its equipment, but enough was left that it could easily be converted into a workable foundry site.

When the team leader mentioned restoring the business and making it a village project, the idea met with instant acceptance by the councilman who promised he would make the necessary arrangements for a meeting in the town square the next day to discuss the proposition.

At the meeting the next day more than 100 people crowded into the village square. The councilman introduced the Team 7 knight and the monk from St. Albans. The knight told them of the orders for brigandine vests and the desire of the Cistercian Order to establish a cooperative industry with the people of the village whereby the metal produced at the abbey's smelter would be hauled to the foundry, operated by the village, and the profits would be equally shared when the finished products were sold.

The St. Albans monk, dressed in his white robes, confirmed the agreement. There was a lot of discussion among the townspeople, but it was all centered on how the foundry could be set up and operated instead of whether or not to enter into the project. The final decision rested on how the village could secure the necessary initial financing to acquire the needed equipment in order to operate the foundry. This was resolved when the monk offered to lend a substantial sum of money to the village with a small repayment deducted over a period of years from the town's share of profits from the enterprise—a proposition that would cost the village nothing. After that, the Council held an immediate impromptu meeting and voted unanimously to approve the charter for the new foundry. The monk, who had come prepared, handed over a bag of money to the Council demanding only that a complete accounting be established open to public inspection. This was quickly agreed and one of the Councilmen was immediately appointed the official treasurer of the Crowborough Foundry as it was to be called.

Since the establishment of the foundry was now in the hands of the villagers, the monk supplied the Council with a list of items that would be needed to properly work the metal from the smelter and volunteered to train a group of six villagers in the metalworking trade at the smelter site once it was operating.

The village had a noted leather craftsman who had a small shop. Team 7 next targeted him and convinced him to expand his operation to fashion the leather necessary to cover the metal plate brigandine vests. He wasn't sure he could do it until one of the knights unfastened his own vest and showed it to the craftsman. After a close examination he vowed he could do the job although it would cost him an investment in some new equipment. The lead knight made him the same type of deal the monk had made the village, only this time it was Green Rose money that was put to work. He asked to retain the vest for a couple of days and by the time the team returned to the village to pick it up, he had fashioned a sample which he showed the team. Actually, he had crafted a few improvements in the vest making pockets for the metal plates instead of riveting them on. This made the garment even more flexible and still afforded the same protection.

To the credit of the townspeople and the St. Albans monk, the first 500 vests for the Duke of York were completed and delivered within six months after the project was started. The sawmill also contributed by cutting rough oak planks to be shaped into pike poles by village craftsmen and soon the village foundry was producing the brigandine vests and the war pikes. Orders for more of these instruments were arriving almost weekly and all of the industries—sawmill, mine, smelter, foundry, and leather crafting—were soon expanding. The foundry had not yet gotten around to fashioning tools although it had designs for several that would soon become a part of its line. An offshoot of the leather business was an increased demand for sheep hides and the abbey was kept busy increasing its sheep herds to meet the demand for wool, hides, and meat.

The Green Rose team was recalled to the abbey about the middle of March, leaving the St. Albans monk in charge of the smelting operations. He was busy training another batch of metal workers after the first six had begun working at the village foundry. The one thing he kept secret was the formula for making the specialized steel and the workers were only taught how to fashion the metal, not how to make it. All was equally well with the village foundry and the leather maker had expanded his shop three fold and was training twenty additional apprentices.

But, the reason for the recall of the Green Knight team was a request from two local nobles for specialized military training for their castle guards. It seems the baron of Farnham Castle had so impressed them with the discipline and manners of his own guard they were jealous and wanted to be able to match the baron—a matter of medieval pride.

The two castles involved were located a few miles east of Farnham Castle and were about 4 miles from each other which made joint training exercises a good possibility. Reigate Castle was a stone motte and bailey castle. A large oval motte is surrounded by a deep ditch and it features an underground sally port. Head another four miles east and Bletchingley Castle rears its head up against an escarpment. It is built in typical Norman layout of two baileys with a large oval motte in between and defended by a deep ditch. It features a stone hall-keep and sits in a dense cover of trees.

Team 7 decided it would pit its own team members against each other in providing simultaneous training at the two castles in an experiment to see which half of the team could provide the quickest and best training for the castle forces and they would pit the opposing forces against each other in a number of exercises throughout the six weeks of planned training. Accordingly, the head knight of Team 7 divided the team into two knights and two squires each. The team choosing Reigate Castle headed for its assignment and the other team headed for Bletchingley Castle. They agreed to meet in an open field between the two strongholds in three weeks time.

The Reigate team assembled a force of eighty castle guards, knights, squires, and workers to begin its training program conducting schools in hand-to-hand sword and pike fighting, archery, and various horse fighting formations. The time went quickly and the Reigate troops assembled on the west side of an open field near a place called Redhill early in the morning on the appointed day.

The Bletchingley team had better luck and found an experienced cadre of knights serving the castle along with some twenty trained foot soldiers. It began instructing nearly 100 fighting men with about forty per cent claiming some military training. The team put its troops through similar drills, but it taught the knights some new encirclement tactics along with its horse maneuvers. The Bletchingley troops were eagerly waiting the start of a mock training exercise on the east side of the open field.

The Green Rose trainers were each flying their own castle colors when they met in the center of the field for a pre-battle parley and to review the rules made so that injuries would be kept to a minimum. The lords of each of the castles were also present at the exercise along with sizeable numbers of their retinues. It was a beautiful morning and the men were all eager to strut their stuff.

The Reigate team fielded eight knights at the front of its force, including the two team members, and an equal number of knights from the Bletchingley forces faced off. Behind the knights came troops of foot soldiers and backing them all up were the archers. The archers were using blunt arrowheads and all the swords and pikes were wrapped so that the usual "clang" of metal striking metal was nothing but a "clunk."

When the forces were about 100 yards apart, the archers from Reigate suddenly quick-stepped to the front and began laying arrows on the approaching Bletchingley forces. The blunt edges could strike with a heavy impact and the first volley actually knocked two of the Bletchingley foot soldiers unconscious. The sudden archery attack caused the Bletchingley forces to mount an immediate charge. The Reigate archers immediately wheeled to the rear while the knights and foot soldiers began hand-to-hand combat. Archers from both sides were mounting a liberal arrow attack.

For awhile it seemed to be a draw, but the Bletchingley forces began to lose ground to the fierce attack from the Reigate forces. Just as the Reigate team was beginning to think it was going to win the day, a troop of fifteen mounted knights emerged from the trees behind them and waded into the battle on the side of the Bletchingley team. It took but three or four minutes before the Reigate forces decided it best to surrender. The commander of the Bletchingley forces, the knight in charge of Team 7, had simply matched the knights in the battle line for Reigate with his own knights, but sent his other trained knights through the trees to the rear of the Reigate army and they attacked as soon as they were in position.

It was a celebration for Bletchingley and the lord of the manor proudly hailed his forces and their prowess over Reigate. Unbeknownst to the Team 7 members, the castle lords had made a wager on the outcome of the exercise and the loser had to supply the winner eight oxen for a picnic celebration to be held on the field with the winning lord in command of the event.

The castle staffs had been preparing for the feast and the Reigate lord immediately turned over eight of his oxen which were slaughtered on the spot and mounted on spits over a huge, previously dug, fire pit along the south side of the clearing—a part of the grounds belonging to Reigate castle. Staffs from both castles began arriving with tables, benches, food, drink, etc. and the beer and ale were soon flowing freely as the various nobles, soldiers, and even servants quickly got in a celebratory mood. It was a fine feast and all went back to their respective castles with full stomachs and a renewed enthusiasm for the final contest to be held in three weeks at the conclusion of the training. Needless to say the Team 7 members assigned to Reigate forces were determined to avenge their defeat.

For the graduation contest, Team 7 decided it would be a different type of field test with each of the "armies" leaving their home castles by a designated time and marching to a battle site to be determined by the rapidity of the marchers as to where it would take place.

The Reigate team decided it would attempt to ambush the Bletchingly forces somewhere along the march route and the two knights carefully spent at least two days scouting the terrain between the two castles looking for just the right spot. When that was decided they went back and drew the layout in the dirt in front of the troops and carefully explained how the ambush was to take place.

The night before the contest, all the troops from Reigate assembled in the castle yard and marched triumphantly through the gate using torches to light their way as it was after dark. As soon as they were away from the castle the torches were extinguished and they marched through the night in the dark following a blazed trail through the trees. It was just about daylight when they reached the designated ambush site and began to deploy to their assigned spots. The instructions were to remain concealed until the Bletchingly forces reached a certain position and then to attack from three sides with the archers to remain just inside the tree line to launch their arrows. The other troops were divided into three twenty-man divisions of knights and foot soldiers.

It was just daylight when the sleepy-eyed troops from Bletchingly came marching down the road and into the trap. It was a complete surprise and the battle lasted only a few minutes. The first hint of trouble for Bletchingly was when the troops were stung by a barrage of arrows coming from three sides. While the arrows caused a great deal of disarray among the Bletchingly forces they were suddenly attacked from the same three sides by knights and foot soldiers that dispatched them without mercy. The leader of Team 7 soon saw his troops, although a superior force, were in such disarray as to be no longer effective as a fighting force and surrendered. The only casualty of the affair was one of the Bletchingly mounted scouts who had been suddenly pulled from his horse inside the trees when he was about to discover the hiding Reigate forces. He was quickly muffled so as not to spread the alarm, but suffered a broken leg in his fall from the horse.

Later in the day, the lord of Reigate Castle received back his eight oxen and the two lords declared they both were winners since each now had an experienced, field-trained force with which to defend their respective castles. In fact they worked out an agreement to assist each other in a time of attack. The troops were honored the next day at a banquet in the great hall at Reigate and several awards were presented. The members of Team 7 had gained a new respect for each other and that worked to their advantage during the remainder of their time at Waverly Abbey.

It was later learned the mock battle exercise between Reigate and Bletchingly castles became an annual event always followed by a huge feast. It became so popular that it was staged on an announced day, time and site so that local supporters could gather and cheer on their respective champions.

In July of 1453 came still another request from St. Albans to Team 7 at Waverly Abbey. This time it had to do with chickens. Even more important it had to do with the charcoal being produced daily from the slab and sawdust pile at the Abbey's sawmilling site at Ashdown Forest. It seems there were a number of old caves in the forest where bat and animal dung had accumulated on the floors which could quickly be turned into saltpetre (potassium nitrate) the most potent of the three ingredients required to make gunpowder—charcoal and Sulphur being the other two. The Team 7 operations had abundant supplies of both Saltpetre and Charcoal and St. Albans was calling on them to produce supplies for the weapons secretly being pursued at that abbey. Although Team 7 did not make the connection to gunpowder early on, it became clear for the purpose of its efforts after a personal visit by the Green Rose leader to review the Saltpetre operations.

Knowing that the dung supply in the caves would not be a constant source of Saltpetre, the leader for Team 7, at the suggestion of one of the monks working at the sawmill, had a large pit dug into the ground. Over the pit he had constructed a crude chicken coop with a slotted floor which allowed the chicken dung to fall directly into the pit, filled with straw and crushed limestone. The straw was kept wet with pig urine mud from an enclosed pen filled with the porkers used to feed the workers at the mill and nearby smelter. This was allowed to accumulate and fill for a year and then was dug out and the saltpetre refined in big tubs through a leaching and drying process eventually turning into white crystals. The same process was used to refine the saltpetre from the caves hauled to the mill site by wagons and teams.

It took most of a year to get the saltpetre process working smoothly and by that time the chicken pit was fulfilling its purpose. The original cages were moved over a second straw and limestone pit while the first pit was being worked to extract the saltpetre. A special slag burning charcoal oven had also been built at the sawmill site and soon bags of both products were being shipped via the lumber wagons to St. Albans en route to Wickham in Buckinghamshire.*

*** NOTE: It was later learned that a specialist from France, brother of the gun maker at St. Albans, had been brought in to help refine the saltpetre, charcoal and Sulphur, obtained from another location, into gunpowder. It was said that the three ingredients were mixed into gunpowder using a secret formula. Then the powder was dampened and pressed into "cakes" which were broken up into "grains" and these grains were then used to load fire the rifles and cannons. Another rumor says it was urine that was used to dampen the mixed powders—urine from monks and even better, from bishops. Medieval thinking would have supported this rumor since the clergy generally enjoyed a higher standard of living than common folk; therefore, clergy urine would be thought to be of a higher quality. Eventually, pure water was used as the mois*tener*.**

One benefit of the saltpetre project for the Waverly abbey was an abundant supply of fresh eggs which the abbey used for its own purposes selling any surplus at the local marketplaces. Since the abbeys chickens were mostly fed with a mixture of ground grain and dried hemp, the eggs were quite popular. The hemp was thought to increase the amount of poop from each chicken.

By this time King Henry VI has suffered his complete mental breakdown and the political turmoil in England was increasing.

In September of 1453 it came to the attention of the Team 7 leader that the abbey owned a hot water spring on one of its granges in Kent. Many of the Waverly monks had been sent there periodically to help recover their health after winter exposure. Others from the Royal family had also visited the site to "take in the waters." The knight proposed to the Abbot to turn the site into a spa for "holy healing," but the project never got off the ground.

Team 7 was constantly on the move during this period lending support to the various abbey industries and bearing an increasing demand for military training as word spread among the nobles of the successes of the team in preparing castle guards.

In February 1454 three more lords arrived at Waverly Abbey for a demonstration. By this time Waverly Abbey had two full troops of trained men—one horsed and one on foot. All were well equipped with some of the latest in weapons and armor and made quite an impressive sight when they were all lined up for inspection.

Team 7 used the troops to demonstrate the latest in weaponry and fighting techniques and the lords were quite impressed. By this time there were enough skilled monks to supervise the military training for the lords and they were quickly dispatched to three castles to begin work.

In May the King granted an export license to the Abbot at Waverly and the Green Rose team was asked to see about exporting some of the excess products being produced by the various abbey industries. Accordingly, the team left for Kent and eventually reached an agreement with the Hanseatic League of German shippers to export products to Europe. Principal exports from the abbey included wool, oak planking, leather goods, calicoes and beer. It was a simple business arrangement with the

Hanseatic League agreeing to ship and market the goods after purchasing them directly from the abbey at wholesale prices. The agreement worked well for both parties and lasted for many profitable years.

In August of 1454 came the strangest incident in the Team 7's activities. One of the knights and his squire were returning from Kent via a road along the Sussex coast when they spotted another knight engaged in battle against four would-be robbers. The knight was giving a good account of himself, but it was apparent he was tiring and couldn't last much longer against his aggressors. The Green Rose team immediately entered into the fray and soon dispersed the bandits, two of them severely wounded, but not before one of them mortally wounded what the team could now see was a knight of advanced age.

They helped the old knight off his horse and laid him beside the road. When they began to take off his armor so they could examine his wound, the knight stopped them saying he wanted to die in full armor. He asked to speak directly and in private to the Green Rose knight who sent the squire off for some distance and asked him to keep a lookout in the event the bandits wanted to try again.

In the time he had left, the old knight relayed a strange story after swearing the Green Rose knight to a vow of secrecy. Although there is no written record of this conversation, some of the details became known years after the incident. This is the knight's story as well as it could be pieced together:

"This is my dying confession," he told the Green Rose Knight.

"A long time ago my father and grandfather were returning from the Crusades via a secretly chartered ship that set sail from the east coast of Arabia (now Ethiopia) heading for Llandaff Castle in South Wales where our lord made his home. During one of the battles in Arabia, my lord's troop became separated and lost. We made for the sea knowing we could pick up a ship of some type and at least return home. We suffered terrible hardships, lack of water, and severe sandstorms, losing many men and animals along the way. It was during one of these sandstorms that our troop stumbled into the mouth of a deep crevice through majestic rocks. We were sheltered from the wind and traveled along the bottom of the crevice until we found a huge temple carved in the face of the rock.

"Thinking there might be food and water in the temple, the lord ordered us to dismount and go inside. The mouth of the temple led to a large cave where there indeed was water and a large supply of dates, cheeses, and other foodstuffs and we gorged ourselves until we could eat and drink no more. Then a few of us got torches and set out to explore the cave. We must have walked along a well-trod path for more than several leagues before we came to a huge room. There was a fire burning in the center of it and three monks were sitting around drinking a hot soup of some kind. When they saw us they jumped up and immediately drew their swords and fought us to their death.

"When we investigated the cavern we found the bones of six giants resting on rock beds in what looked to be a shrine of some type. I immediately sent back for our lord and when he came he was astounded at the sight. Further investigation turned up several urns filled with scrolls and gold and jewels of all descriptions. It was indeed an awesome sight and we were struck with the wonder of it all.

"Our lord immediately sent most of the troop on to the coast to secure pack animals and other foodstuffs while twelve of us remained behind to stand guard over what we had discovered. We were there for thirty days before our lord returned with supplies and pack animals. We carefully fashioned stretchers—at least twelve spans long—to carry the giants and packed most of the filled urns on the back of our animals before we set off for the coast where the lord had chartered a ship. We moved only during the night and rested in the day.

"We reached the coast safely, although we saw any number of scouts from our enemies along the way. I think our numbers were too great for them to mount an attack although our scouts said they were assembling a force to attack us. We reached the coast and had our ship loaded and sailed before they were ready.

"Our crossing was very rough and all of us got sick. We were cheered when told we were approaching the coast of England after weeks at sea. It was then we encountered a severe storm and we were blown onto the rocks near Cardiff where our ship foundered and sank.

"We spent days salvaging what we could from the timbers of the ship and lost three of our brave men in the process, but we managed to salvage the bones of five of our giants and most of the sealed urns containing scrolls. We only managed to find two of the heavier urns with gold and jewels and we have been using that money since to survive.

"But, now I must once again have your pledge as a knight to honor our bond," the knight said weakly.

The Green Rose knight once again offered his pledge, and the story continued.

"In the vestment under my armor you will find a secret pocket. I have spent many idle hours drawing a map of the entrance to the cave where we were able to preserve the remains of our giants. Inside this cave are the sealed urns with the scrolls and what is left of our treasury. We did not unseal the urns containing the scrolls for fear the damp air would destroy them, but inscribed upon the sides of each urn is the word 'Henoch.'

"One of the dying monks at the original cavern died with this word on his lips although we did not understand at the time what he was saying. Our lord, a devoutly religious man, believed Henoch walked with God so it has been our command as a Knight of the Realm to protect these artifacts. We have done that for many, many years and I am the last of the lot.

"You now must assume that charge and do your best to preserve these artifacts so that the non-believers cannot get their hands on them. You must…you must," the old knight said in his dying breath.

The Green Rose knight was astounded at what he had heard and even more astounded that he had given his word to protect whatever was in hiding in a cave at Cardiff. He carefully summoned the squire back and the two removed the breastplate and vestment of the old knight. The Green Rose knight searched the vestment and found the hidden pocket. He carefully removed the map, unfolded it and looked at the drawing, but could make little sense of it all.

After briefly relating the story to his squire, the two decided the best course of action would be to ride directly to St. Albans and turn the information over to the leader of the Green Rose team. So that's what they did after burying the old knight in his armor and marking the grave with his sword and shield.

It was later learned that a secret mission set sail directly from Rome, armed with the map, and landed at Cardiff. Armed monks were seen loading up a ship which quickly sailed away from the coast.

Team 7 heard no more about the cave or what actually was inside, but a secret message was received at St. Albans with the seal of the Pope sometime later and reportedly detailed what was found including mention of the writings of Enoch.

About this time it was learned the King had recovered his health.

In February a courier from London arrived at Waverly Abbey with news from the London street vender that the King was about to imprison the Duke of York who had been dismissed earlier that month as Protector of England. A courier was immediately dispatched to St. Albans and a Green Rose embossed message was forthwith carried and handed personally to the Duke.

By April the Duke was personally engaged in raising an army and Team 7, along with the other Green Rose teams, was recalled to St. Albans.

Chapter 16—The Southwest

Forde Abbey in Dorsetshire was a welcome sight when members of Team 8 spotted the buildings from the rim of a heavily wooded valley through which runs the River Axe winding its way past the front gate of the abbey. The team was quite tired from its travel south across most of the length of England and after having been put upon by a gang of pirates which they speedily dispatched sending the bandits on their way minus two fallen comrades.

From a distance the abbey appeared to be quite spectacular, but as the team approached it soon dispelled the beauty of the place spotting several places in the surrounding wall where there were substantial breaks and some of the buildings in sad need of repair. The 200-year-old abbey church appeared to be in the best shape of any of the structures.

Team 8 really didn't know what to expect as they approached the gate to the abbey. They rang the gate bell for admittance although it would have been just as easy to ride through one of the breaches in the wall. Pretty soon one of the Cistercian monks appeared along the road to the abbey buildings and opened the gate after the team had identified itself.

"I give you greetings from our humble house," the monk told the lead knight of Team 8. "I'm afraid we are not in condition to celebrate your arrival, but you are indeed welcome. He gestured the team inside, closed the gate, and slowly followed them up the road to the abbey where the abbot himself was waiting to greet them.

"You are a welcome sight," he greeted them. "We are ill prepared to serve your needs, but we hope you will be content with what we have to offer. After you are settled in and have had a chance to survey our sad state of repairs, you may present me with a list of your needs and I will see about obtaining them."

With that he gestured to the monk who had opened the gate and he led them to the guest quarters at the abbey which, although livable, were in a sad state of repair as were most of the abbey's buildings.

"What has happened here?" the team leader asked the Cistercian monk.

The monk merely indicated the abbey had come on hard times and he and his thirteen brothers had been having a hard time making ends meet for a long time. He asked forgiveness for his appearance and physical weakness and indicated his brothers were in similar shape due to the periodic bloodletting process, but all would soon be fit again. With that, he turned and left.

The Green Rose knight and team leader held an impromptu session with his team. It was finally decided to divide up and perform a complete survey of the abbey, its state of disrepair, and its stock of supplies including food. The team spent the rest of the day conducting its survey and met again after a supper of soup and bread.

Each team member had made a list of the conditions he had surveyed and had listed them as "urgent needs" and "needs" so they could be addressed by the team. It soon became apparent that the abbey was seriously short on food, had no fresh running water, and had little strength with which to earn the monies needed to sustain a livable life.

The next morning half the team, including the lead knight, set out for the nearby market village of Chard, about three miles distance from the abbey. The remainder of the team was put to work organizing priorities for the repair of abbey buildings, including its own living quarters. The village was quite productive and the lead half of Team 8 was able to purchase fish, vegetables, fruits, and cheeses in plentiful quantities to restock the abbey's larder. When it conferred with village leaders it was able to recruit several skilled masons and carpenters willing to work at the abbey repairing and upgrading its buildings. The team provided a pretty good description of the work that needed to be done and one of the village elders, a skilled mason, took charge of things and promised a crew would arrive at the abbey the next day with the necessary supplies and tools to begin the repairs.

When the team returned to the abbey it had two large cartloads of foodstuffs with them and the monks at the abbey were very grateful. Since most of them had recovered much of their strength after their bloodletting experience, the remainder of Team 8 had put them to work, with the blessing of the abbot, in clearing out debris from the dilapidated structures in preparation for beginning the repair work. The abbot had been somewhat skeptical since there was no great supply of building materials at the abbey, but he thought to take advantages of the fresh bodies of the 8 team members and quickly gave his permission. He, too, was cheered when he saw the supplies from the village and ordered a special "prayer of thanks" at the nightly prayer session.

Things were much more cheerful when the villagers began arriving with their carts full of building materials and supplies the next morning and Team 8 was on hand to show them which of the structures were in need of priority attention, including their own sleeping quarters. The villagers, paid for their labors with Green Rose money, turned to the work with enthusiasm and much progress was being made at restoring current buildings by the time Team 8 left for the Green Rose conclave at St. Albans in April.

In the meantime, the abbot escorted the Green Rose team around the countryside to visit the various nobles. This was a turning point for the abbot who had been very reluctant to make this move although precedent in the Cistercian Order was to seek such help.

Many of the barons were absentee landholders in Dorsetshire during this period, but the team found other landholders at Chard, Winsham, Ilminster, Crewherne, Hinton St. George, and Beaminster who willingly gave money, supplies, skilled labor on loan, and other favors in return for the promised military training to help fend off an increasing number of pirate raids, for the creation of a traveler's guest house open to all visitors at the abbey, and to receive penance for past sins.

By April there was a steady stream of volunteer workers at the abbey along with trains of supplies arriving daily. This was the scene when the Green Rose team departed for St. Albans.

May and June were busy times at Forde Abbey after the Green Rose team returned with new enthusiasm and new funding. Work was proceeding smoothly at the abbey and the new guest quarters construction was nearly complete. Living quarters for the team had been upgraded and the walls surrounding the abbey had been completely repaired.

Before the end of that period the foundations had been laid for a new visitor's chapel and a new barn on a nearby grange as well as re-pointing most of the stonework on the older abbey buildings. The team had convinced the abbot to begin charging a "fee" for overnight stays at the new lodging quarters at the abbey and it was this income that provided permanent upgrades for the food and other supplies needed. A few of the lay volunteers had joined the ranks of the monks and the permanent abbey population was now increased to twenty monks and about forty lay volunteers mostly engaged in building repairs or working on the various granges owned by the abbey.

While most of the granges were "leased" out, many of the tenants were behind in their rents. The abbot, lacking manpower, had made no effort to collect these back rents for some time so the tenants simply didn't pay. Four of the Green Rose team—two knights and two squires—set out to make the rounds of the granges and collect the rents. While they did not run into any armed resistance, in many cases they simply could not locate the current tenants on the abbey lands. After a few such diversions, the team merely adopted a practice of collecting the rents by taking an appropriate number of sheep and lambs in order to meet the overdue charges. These were herded to a grange adjoining the abbey grounds and served to bolster the abbey's supply of meat, wool and hides. It also served another purpose by bringing the tenants to the abbey itself in order to try and reclaim their properties. If the back rent was paid in coin, then the animals were released and the tenant was afforded an opportunity to sign a new lease and renew his vow to pay future rents in a timely fashion. For those tenants who failed to show the next fall to pay their rents, the team simply cleared the grange and offered it to new tenants under the abbey's lease terms. Word soon got around that the abbey was enforcing its rents and things quickly turned around. The abbot was pleased.

The other part of the Green Rose team, not engaged in enforcing the rents, met with the various nobles who had come to the aid of the abbey to fulfill the obligation to provide military training. They selected the three barons who had contributed the most for the start of the program. The team rotated between the three castles offering training at each one on two days of the week. They would work at Castle 1 on Monday, Castle 2 on Tuesday and Castle 3 on Wednesday often spending the night at the castle where the training was to begin the next day. When the first circuit was completed, it would be repeated so that Sunday was always a day of rest when the team would return to the abbey. This went on for six weeks until the team thought most of the troops were prepared to demonstrate their skills in a friendly contest.

The team arranged to hold a summer fair at the marketplace in Chard and sent word all around the countryside that there would be contests with prizes awarded the winners. The three castle barons had lent their support to the idea and put up most of the prize money and gifts to go to the various champions. There was to be Jousting, Archery, Sword Play, and Military Squad maneuvers along with lesser contests in the use of long-poled pikes, knife throwing, and hatchet throwing. Teams from each of the three castles were given special training by the Green Rose team and entered in the contests. The prizes were good enough to draw interest from the ranks of other nobles throughout Dorsetshire and the entry lists were quite long for each contest.

It had originally thought the contests could be completed in two days during the regular marketplace hours, but there were so many entrants the two days actually stretched into four days. The contests would begin each morning at ten a.m. and would run throughout the day and sometimes into the evening hours around a bonfire. There were separate venues established for the horse contests, the archery, and the hand-to-hand combat and these were operated simultaneously each drawing good daily crowds of spectators.

Besides operating the contests, the knights and squires of Team 8 also entered into some of the competition since they had a reputation to uphold. It was a grand time! Injuries were held to a minimum and the crowd was highly entertained. But it was the final results of the various competitions that virtually made the reputations of the Green Rose team in that area of the country.

In the jousting events, using blunted poles, two of the Green Rose knights battled for first place with the team leader actually coming in second as the other knight scored a "lucky" hit in the final run. A third Green Rose knight scored 5th and the last Green Rose knight scored 8th in the list. Knights from the three castles under training scored 3rd, 4th, 6th, 7th, and 9th in the competition with an outside knight placing 10th. It was the custom in these contests that defeated knights forfeit their horse and armor; however, this custom was waived in favor of prizes awarded to all of the top ten finishers.

The archery contests were divided into four separate divisions because of the large numbers of entrants. There was the older division, the fighting division, the youth division, and the youngster division based on age and experience of the contestants. The four squires from Team 8 did not enter the actual matches, but gave an impressive demonstration of archery to open the events. When the crowd demanded they compete against the winners of the two older divisions, they easily outscored each of the champions.

Archers from the three castles, where the team was training them, scored the first five places in the older division and the first four places in the fighting division. In the youth division, the son of one of the castle barons took the top prize. Other contestants completed the prize list in each of the four divisions. In the youngster division, the six-year-old son of one of the castle knights scored an impressive victory.

The horse/cavalry teams were perhaps the most interesting to the crowd as they had never before seen anything like them. In this competition six teams of riders were pitted against each other and judged on the basis of appearance, maneuvers, style, and difficulty. Each team had four assigned maneuvers it had to complete, but the rest of the competition was free style. You could see the teams practicing all during the fair. Of the eight teams entered in the competition, the Green Rose trained troops took first, second and fourth. The four knights and two of the squires opened the competition with their own demonstration and drew thunderous applause and admiration from the crowd for their daring maneuvers and skilled horsemanship.

In the hand-to-hand competitions, the teams from the Green Rose trained castles acquitted themselves well and all the barons were pleased with the newfound respect for their manors.

All-in-all it was an excellent test for the castle troops and they acquitted themselves well. The Green Rose team had no further difficulty in finding clients for their training programs and was busy at this for the rest of its stay at Forde Abbey.

Shortly after the conclusion of the four-day fair/contest, the abbot from Cleeve Abbey at Washford paid a visit to Forde Abbey seeking help. It seems Cleeve Abbey had been lacking for some time in internal discipline and the various enterprises by the abbey had fallen into debt to London merchants who were threatening to foreclose those debts on the abbey. The abbot at Forde immediately summoned the lead Green Rose knight, appraised him of the request, and asked if help could be provided.

After a long talk with the visiting abbot, the Green Rose knight agreed to return to Cleeve with the abbot and see what his team members could do to alleviate the situation. The next morning they set out along with the abbot, the lead knight, and another knight and their two squires and arrived at the abbey with no difficulties.

The Green Rose visitors found much the same conditions at Cleeve as they had found at Forde Abbey upon their initial arrival so they knew what had to be done. The job here was a bit more difficult as Cleeve was never a rich house, but it did have a limited number of granges which were producing little income due to back rents and poor management by the monks. The Green Rose team once again made the rounds of the grange tenants and returned with quite a bit of coin and a large herd of sheep. In addition, all tenants were instructed to visit the abbey for new lease agreements or to forfeit use of the land. This effort provided emergency funding for the abbey allowing it to stave off immediate foreclosure. After that, the team mounted a similar effort to visit nearby nobility and ask for help and enjoyed some success in that venture especially since word of the contests at Chard has preceded them. Many more military training agreements were struck and aid began pouring into the abbey at Cleeve much to the delight and grateful thanks of the abbot and monks.

One of the unusual sights at Cleeve Abbey was a wall painting in one of the rooms of the newly built refectory hall sporting a magnificent arch-braced timber framed roof with carved angels protecting the ends of its main trusses. This structure had a special "painted chamber" with a wall painting that was quite old. The wall, some six feet thick, had been part of an old Roman structure on the site and had been incorporated into the new building as part of the architectural plans. When the Green Rose knight viewed the wall, there was something about the artwork that was "unsettling" in his mind, but he couldn't quite put his finger upon it.

He did suggest to the abbey that the wall be incorporated into a "holy shrine" that could be used by "paying visitors" to the abbey and this eventually became a favored site for those seeking penance. He asked the abbot about the meaning of the painting, but the abbot did not know saying it was already there when he came to Cleeve. The knight suggested that the colors might be restored if the abbot had a monk who could do the work and this was eventually accomplished although it took several years.

The year was quite busy for the Green Rose team and it was August of 1451 when more pirate trouble broke out in the Cornwall area, the most southwestern shire in England. Cornwall had for a long time claimed its independence from English rule. It is bounded by Devonshire on the east and surrounded by water for the rest of it. It's coastlines sport excellent harbors and some of the coast is bounded by granite cliffs of up to sixty or more feet in height. There are many caves along the coastline, especially along the southern coast, and age old tin and copper mines have been dug to a great depth and some have been carried even beneath the sea.

It was near an area now called Land's End where the Forde Abbey had been granted a sizeable acreage of land which it used primarily for grazing sheep. And, it was sheep from this grange that were disappearing at an unusually high rate. And, this was where the Green Rose team established its headquarters in a barn near the coast as the only other structure on the grange was a small hut used to house the monks who tended the flock. The loft in the barn served as suitable sleeping quarters and the horses could be stabled below although the barn primarily was equipped for shearing the sheep each spring. One of the squires was appointed cook and he became so good that even the two monk shepherds regularly ate in the barn with the team.

One of the shepherds was quite familiar with the area and adjoining cliffs and was used as a guide while the team explored the area. The other monk indicated the thefts had been occurring at night and the stolen sheep just seemed to "disappear into thin air." When the Green Rose team found a well-trodden path leading down the side of a cliff from the main pasture at the grange, it surmised that may have been what happened to the sheep—they were simply grabbed and carried over the side of the cliff and down the path.

One of the knights and a squire were delegated to climb down the path and explore the coastline below. This took them more than half a day, but all they could find were some marks in the sand where it looked as though small boats had been beached. Nevertheless, the lead knight decided the best course of action was to set up a watch over the cliff path and that's what they did.

It was a week later before the watch system paid off. One of the squires was serving as lookout late one evening, with one of the herd dogs as company, when he heard noises about 60 feet below the edge of the cliff near the path. While he couldn't see in the darkness, it sounded like two small boats had been beached below with several men involved. He could hear them begin to climb the path to the pasture and quickly sent the dog back to the camp which was the pre-arranged alert signal.

The other men from Team 8 arrived in just a few minutes while the pirates, upon reaching the pasture, spread out and began driving one bunch of sheep towards the cliff's edge. The team was not in time to stop the pirates from pushing the dumb sheep over the edge of the cliff—about six of the ewes—but it launched an attack from the rear of the pirates and about five of them went over the cliff as well. The others began to put up a struggle, but most were soon either killed or mortally wounded in the hand-to-hand combat. Two of the raiders managed to scramble down the cliff and into one of the boats making their escape.

When morning dawned, Team 8 surveyed the results of its night's work. That's when they found seven bodies on the beach below, and five bodies in the pasture at the edge of the path. Upon examining the bodies on the beach, they found one man with severe injuries, but still managing to survive the sixty-foot fall. They summoned one of the monks, who administered last rites, but the team still worked to try and save his life. The pirate was grateful for the efforts, asked to be remembered to his wife and son in London, and told of a cave about two miles to the east, along the cliffs, that was used by the pirates as an operating base. He died about noon in the arms of the monk. Team 8 buried the dead pirates where they had fallen after first searching them for information.

In the pouch of one of the dead men, presumably the leader, was a scrap of paper with the name of one of the coastal barons scrawled upon it. The monk from the grange indicated the baron was well known and had a large coastal manor house along the south coast just about two miles from the grange—the same distance as the pirate cave. The baron had a nasty reputation, the monk said, and his armed men were known to mistreat travelers at times. But he was a powerful lord and controlled a lot of territory in Cornwall and Devon shires.

Knowing it couldn't scout out the pirate cave from the land, if indeed it was located below the manor house of the baron, the Team 8 lead knight decided to use the captured pirate skiff, still beached below, to move up the coast just before dark. Now, none of the team were sailors, so there was quite a bit of trepidation among them about the boat trip. However, the monk said he knew of a boy in the nearby village who was an excellent boatman and would be willing to take them for a small fee. This was agreed upon and the monk set off to fetch the boy.

He returned with the youngster in the late afternoon and was shown the boat, which he deemed seaworthy. He was invited back to the barn and the team discussed the strategy. As luck would have it the youth had sailed along the coast all his life and was quite familiar with the baron's house although he told them he took great pains to avoid it as his father had been mistreated by the baron and his men. After a lamb stew dinner, using meat from one of the dead animals—a meal avoided by the two monks—the boy and four of the Green Rose team—all volunteers—set off in the boat.

While it was dark out it was a clear night and, after the eyes adjusted, the coastline was plainly visible. The youth quickly hoisted a sail in the captured skiff and began working the boat up the coast. Due to the tides and only a slight breeze, it took the craft about two hours to make its way to where the baron's castle was clearly visible looming above the cliffs. The knight motioned to the boy to take the craft further out to sea and then to move along the coast past the baron's castle. When they passed the first time nothing was visible and the knight asked the boy to reverse course and sail past again. This time they spotted a glimmer of light at the base of the cliff about 300 yards west of the baron's castle. The knight signaled the boy to head inshore and they landed quietly on a small beach about another 100 yards west of the light.

The team, leaving the boy to guard the boat, began working its way quietly toward the source of the light. They had nearly reached the site when they heard a noise and sought immediate cover behind some rocks. They watched as a boat, identical to the one they had captured, seemed to magically appear from the side of the cliff and was rowed out to sea. The boat was manned by four men at the oars, one man in the prow and one man at the tiller—six in all. There was a small lantern hung from the top of the mast and, as the team watched, the men in the boat shipped their oars and raised a triangular sail. Looking out to sea the team spotted a small brigantine sailing slowly about a mile offshore. It, too, had a light attached to the top of its main mast.

After the boat was about half way to the ship, the members of the team entered into the mouth of a cave carefully avoiding the lantern left standing on a rock at the entrance. The water flowed right into the mouth of the cave, but there was a well worn path along the side of a large cavern. The team had brought along its own candles and cautiously lit them after they were inside the entrance and out of sight of the pirate boat. What they found was a veritable living quarters for the pirates along a wide shelf in the cavern and a continuation of the cavern. Two of the team began examining the pirate quarters while the lead knight and his squire continued to explore the cavern. It was another 300 or so feet before they came upon a carved staircase leading upward and surmised it must lead to the baron's castle on the cliff above. With that they returned to the pirate camp, checked with other members of the team who had found a leather pouch full of papers, and they decided to leave before the boat returned and they were discovered. The lead knight took the pouch of papers with him.

They had snuffed out their candles before approaching the entrance to the cave and had made their exit just in time as the pirate boat was well on its return trip from the ship, which already had sailed on. The team watched as the pirates lowered their sail and again rowed the boat inside the cave. A few minutes later, one of the pirates appeared at the entrance and secured the lantern from the rock and disappeared inside. The team returned to where the boy had been anxiously waiting, climbed aboard the boat, and quickly set the sail returning down the coast and arriving at the foot of the grange path just as dawn was breaking over the horizon. The again beached the boat where it had been left by the pirates and climbed up the cliff.

The captured papers proved to be a real bonus to the team. Among them were several maps, a letter of commission signed by the baron giving permission for the raiding of ships along the coast, and lists of names under various headings which, upon a more careful examination, turned out to be the various branches of a pretty widespread pirating venture coordinated and sponsored by the cliff baron. Cargo manifests from several ships were also in the bundle of papers and the Green Rose team decided these were ships captured and looted by the gangs.

Knowing the team was not strong enough to mount a force to capture the baron's castle, the lead knight dispatched one of the knights and his squire to carry the information back to Forde Abbey and on to St. Albans with a request for help. The knight and squire were to obtain fresh horses at the abbey and then continue on to personally deliver the papers and explain the problem to the lead monk at St. Albans. In the meantime, the rest of the team would stay and guard the sheep in case the pirates returned.

About a week later, as one of the knights was standing guard in the pasture, he spotted a ship just off the coast which had lowered its sails and was launching a longboat over the side. He immediately dispatched the dog to warn the others and there were six fully armed men waiting at the top of the cliff when the longboat, carrying at least twelve men, made landfall below. Some of the men began climbing the steep path and Team

8 could hardly wait to spring into action. When the first of the climbers reached the top of the path, quite out of breath, he was smacked in the midsection by the blade of a sword yielded by the head knight. The blow forced him off the edge of the cliff and his fall picked off three of the others climbing up the path. By this time the three squires were firing arrows, a difficult shot nearly straight down, but were finding at least one mark with each volley. This totally disrupted the would-be raiders and they quickly descended the path and began piling back into the boat. Two of the men ran over and launched the captured skiff and both boats moved quickly out to sea although one of the squires scored a great long-distance arrow shot taking out the pirate at the helm of the longboat which temporarily caused a problem as the boat turned sideways against the waves and nearly swamped. Another of the occupants quickly seized the tiller and the boat made its escape.

While the pirates recaptured their lost skiff, it was a costly price to pay and the team tallied six more bodies the next morning not counting the one in the longboat felled by the arrow who was tossed overboard in the resulting confusion. The ship, upon recovering the two boats, hastily made sail and slipped away in the darkness. The team leader couldn't be sure, but he felt it was the same ship they had spotted lying offshore from the pirate cave.

Word came a week later via the knight and squire sent to St. Albans that a Royal army force was en route to lay siege to the baron's castle and the Green Rose team was to assist in any manner possible, but not to identify themselves as other than Cistercian monks even though they were permitted to bear arms.

The Royal troop was commanded by one of the barons whose troops had been trained by the Green Rose Team 8. His force consisted of a Royal Guard troop from London and all of the trained troops from the three castles where the Green Rose training had taken place. It was a formidable force and one that had been strengthening along the road as was fairly typical of the Middle Ages when the King commanded. Their were some eighty knights, 200 archers, and about 400-foot soldiers when the troop arrived. They were joined by another 120 or so men from local villages as soon as the villagers found out the purpose of the troops. Most of these locals simply wanted a chance to repay the baron for his cruelness in the past.

The Green Rose team had also been spending some time analyzing the baron's defenses and had found a couple of weak spots that could be exploited by any attacking force. The plan of attack was for the army to surround the baron's castle and attempt to negotiate a surrender. Failing in that, it was to launch an attack. In the meantime, the Green Rose team would utilize the 120 locals to mount a flotilla force of small boats from the villages which would approach the baron's stronghold from the sea, capture the pirates in the cave below, and mount an attack up the stairs leading from the cave. The time set for a coordinated attack was at dawn in three days.

Preparations were made, the boats were easily secured from the cooperating villagers, and both friendly forces were in position. Although negotiations were ongoing after the Royal force surrounded the castle, neither side had been willing to give in. The leader of the troops sent one of his men to alert the Green Rose team of the impending assault the next morning.

That night the Green Rose team loaded up the villagers in the boats, assisted by the youth who had helped them previously and his dad, and they worked their way up the coast with the Green Rose team in the lead boat. It was a long procession as the boats were all sizes holding from four-eight armed men each. One boat got too near the shore and swamped, but another quickly rescued the occupants and towed the boat after bailing out the water. The Green Rose team located the cavern entrance and quietly beached its boat. The other boats followed although not without some noise. It was the noise that decided the Green Rose leader to go ahead and enter the cave and they managed to surprise the pirates in their sleeping rolls. The team quickly took the camp, killing two of the pirates in the process and taking the other five prisoner. By this time the villagers were arriving from the boats and the ledge was becoming quite crowded.

One of the pirates was "encouraged" to explain the step passageway to the castle above and he quickly outlined the procedures for gaining access to the castle. It seems there was a barred door near the top that was guarded and a "password" was used to gain admittance. It seemed quite fitting that the current password was "attack!"

Two of the knights of the Green Rose team, backed up by their squires, led the way up the stone stairway at the back of the tunnel. When they had climbed several steps and turned two corners in the ascending stairwell, they spotted torchlight ahead. The two knights, followed by the squires a few paces back, climbed almost to the stairwell and hailed the guard. He peered at them, but couldn't see them in the darkness.

"What is the password?" he asked.

"Attack," replied the knight.

The guard used a large key to unlock the iron-barred gate and opened it to admit them. When they were nearly up to him he saw their armor in the torchlight and started to slam the gate closed. Just then he was cut down by an arrow from one of the squires who had drawn his bow anticipating such a problem. The guard dropped without uttering a word although the key bounced along the stone floor making quite a racket. The two knights quickly stepped over the guard and into a passageway along which there were several cells with barred doors.

They quickly motioned the rest of the troops to enter the passageway and follow them to another staircase that led up to the main floor of the castle keep and opened to the inner bailey of the fortress. From an escarpment the Green Rose team could see that the attacking forces had breached the outer walls and were forming to attack the main gate leading into the inner bailey. As soon as most of the villagers had joined them, the Green Rose knights led an assault across the open court quickly reaching the main entrance gateway and overpowering the guards. Before the other castle defenders were aware of what was happening, the villagers had unbarred the gate and dropped a drawbridge crossing the moat. Fifteen minutes later it was all over and the superior Royal forces had subdued the castle defenders and taken the baron into custody as he was trying to escape down the same passageway entered by the villagers and Green Rose team. The villagers immediately recognized him and would have beaten him to death if the Green Rose knights had not stepped in and rescued the badly bruised baron.

The commander of the Royal troops quickly took the baron in charge, chained his hands, and told the villagers he would be taken to London for justice. After that it was a matter of cleaning out several pockets of defenders who knew to surrender probably meant eventual death. The Royal army marched off early the next day with the baron leaving the Green Rose team and villagers in possession of the castle. By this time the dungeon cells had been opened and several villagers were reunited with their families and the mood of the people was joyous.

It was about four months later that a message from St. Albans confirmed the baron had been convicted and hanged, the King had reclaimed the baron's land for the crown, and several of the pirate branches had been raided and broken up. The ship that had visited the castle was captured at a port in France. All-in-all some 120 in the widespread pirate syndicate were hanged, another fifty or sixty were imprisoned, and nearly 200 others operating on the fringes of the pirate organization, some not even knowing the connection, were convicted and released on conditions of parole. It was the largest and most successful clean-up of coastal pirates in the history of England and the King, it was said, was "quite pleased."

One of the disappointments for the Green Rose team is that no cache of pirate wealth had been uncovered at the baron's castle although several other caches were discovered in the various raids on the branches of the organization. The Green Rose team returned to Forde Abbey satisfied with its success, but sorry it had no treasure to present to the abbot.

The next months were kept busy as the team supervised much of the now completed construction work at the abbey. A new type of treasure was discovered one afternoon in early November when one of the squires was passing some idle time in hiking around the abbey grounds. He was somewhat "in a dream world" while viewing the beauty of the valley floor until he suddenly realized his feet were all wet. When he looked for the cause of the marshy area, he discovered a spring of fresh water flowing from the ground. He cupped his hands and enjoyed the sweet taste of the water before returning to the abbey to report his find. When the lead knight heard of the find, he immediately went to the abbot and asked permission to develop the spring into a permanent water supply for the abbey.

A team of volunteers began enlarging the hole around the spring until it was at least twelve feet in diameter and about six feet deep. This was quickly lined with stone around the edges and the abbey had a permanent cistern. The volunteers were next put to work constructing an aqueduct leading down hill to the abbey structures while others were set to work forming crude "gutters" of copper to be used to pipe the water to the various abbey buildings. One of the first projects impacted the Green Rose team when water was piped under the garderobes in its sleeping quarters to carry waste off and into a sewage pit lined with stone and gravel. Smaller branch lines were dug and filled with gravel to serve the overflow. It wasn't long before the abbey's residence and the sleeping quarters for the monks and lay volunteers also were attached to this system by a series of pipes. Thus, Forde Abbey had one of the first complete sewer systems in England and living conditions were much improved. The fresh water also was piped into the kitchens and living quarters where it collected in specially constructed "drinking pools." A dipper was kept at each of these pools and used for drinking and for dipping clean water into a wash basin beside the pool.

The lay volunteers asked if somehow the fresh water could be piped to the village. The Green Rose team decided this was probably not feasible and nothing further happened with this idea until one of the volunteers came up with the idea of constructing a "water wagon" to haul the liquid to the village. Since this was workable, two of the heavy wagons were quickly converted into copper-lined water wagons which were hauled to the village square and the villagers were allowed to purchase fresh water for a small fee. It wasn't long before there was quite a demand for the "soft" spring water and three more wagons were purchased and equipped to haul and deliver the water. Some of the volunteers who had been engaged in the construction process were re-hired to operate the water wagons and allowed to share in the profits.

After the Christmas celebrations, the members of Team 8 decided to ride down to the Cornwall area once more to examine the captured castle more closely for pirate treasure. That effort proved to be unsuccessful; however, the team did re-discover fairly rich tin and copper veins in some of the old caves. One cave led under the sea and the team explored it until it emerged on a small, unoccupied island just off the coast. This information was immediately dispatched to St. Albans, but neither the records of Team 8 nor those at St. Albans reflect whether or not this information was ever put to any use. The team did set up a small mining and smelter operation in one of the ore rich caves, but it was only developed enough to serve the needs of the abbey although some "copper piping" was sold to nearby nobles.

The team also discovered one of the "sheepherder" monks at the grange, previously attacked by pirates, was a skilled fisherman. Since a constant supply of fish was necessary to feed the increasing numbers of monks and lay volunteers at the abbey, the team secured permission and re-assigned this monk to set up a fishing and drying operation. The two principal species of fish caught were mackerel and pilchard and in the period of several months the monk had expanded his operation to include six small fishing boats and a drying operation in one of the caves along the shore where the gutted fish were dried and smoked on huge wooden racks. This operation solved the food problems at the abbey since it also produced sufficient vegetables in its own gardens. It also allowed some of the dried fish to be sold in the various marketplaces especially during the winter months.

In September of 1452 the team learned the abbey also owned a grange in Devon with a large grove of apple trees. They had been drinking cider with their meals at the abbey, but none had thought to enquire as to the source of it. When they rode over to Devon to examine the grange, they found several acres of apple trees that had not been worked for several years. Some of them were in bad shape with lots of dead limbs, but the bulk of the trees appeared to be healthy. The grange ranged a herd of sheep and also a small herd of hogs and these activities had occupied the monks most of the time. Enough of the apples were picked each fall to press a supply of cider for the abbey and the rest were allowed to fall to the ground where they were gobbled up by the hogs.

While most villages had one or two apple trees, used mostly for cooking and eating, not many had access to enough of the fruit to make cider. The Green Rose team sensed a new industry for the abbey and presented a plan to the abbot who immediately agreed. There was a surplus of labor available at the abbey, due to the end of the major construction projects, and a number of lay volunteers agreed to move over to Devon and establish a cider works.

Since the apples were already ripening, there was some urgency to the project. A somewhat crude "cider barn" was quickly constructed near the orchard and two large cider presses were built by the volunteers. Some of the volunteers were delegated to pick apples in the orchard and it wasn't long before the first cider began flowing. However, there was a shortage of vessels in which to store the cider until one of the other abbeys shipped several wagon loads of earthen pots to the mill. These pots held about a gallon-and-a-half of cider and had loose-fitting tops. One of the monks devised a system whereby melted wax was used to seal the lids and the first load of "pot cider," as the locals came to call it, was sent to market.

It was an immediate success and the mill was formally in operation. It became even more successful when one of the monks heated a pot of cider on a cold winter morning and then got called away before he could drink it. He dumped it into one of the jugs thinking he would come back in a few minutes and enjoy his refreshments. The pot sat there for several days before the monk remembered it. When he tasted the cider inside he found it perfectly preserved. After that, the mill workers heated the cider before sealing it in jugs and it had a much greater market life allowing them to sell the cider on nearly a year around basis.

As an offshoot, the apple pulp was dried and fed to the pigs and these pigs commanded a higher price at the market since the meat was considered "sweet." The hides were cured and shipped to other Green Rose teams who had developed leather industries. In later years the abbey began dry-curing hams and smoking them with apple wood and this, too, became a successful enterprise.

The Green Rose team spent the last several weeks of 1452 working to establish a watch/guard system along the lengthy coastal areas of its assigned territories. The defeat of the pirate baron had seemingly put some coastal dwellers to "sleep," but the numbers of pirate raids did not diminish and, in fact, in some areas these raids were increasing.

Visiting with nobles, whose estates bordered the coastal areas, the Green Rose team was able to get an informal agreement to establish a system of "coastal watchers" along long stretches of Lyme Bay on the south shore and about half of the northern coastal areas starting at Bridgwater Bay and working west along the Bristol Channel.

The team got permission from most of the nobles to utilize their castles and/or manor houses as staging points for the Coastal Watchers, as they became known, and then established temporary shelters for intermediate points in between the main staging points as required. In all, there was some type of "watch point" about every five miles along the coast. Due to the ruggedness of part of the coastline, some of the watch points were within observer distance of each other and signal fires and flags were readied at each one for emergency use. Stone huts with no doors, but a narrow, defendable passage to the interior were hastily constructed for these watch points and the ruins of some of them lasted for generations. Some of the Coastal Watchers were in the pay of their nobles, while some were recruited from the ranks of the volunteers undergoing military training, and others were obtained by word-of-mouth through the market places. Other than those under control of the nobles, a minimum wage scale was set up for volunteers that increased based upon the length of their continuous service.

While replacements were continuously recruited and trained, the paid wages with incentives to stay, held it to a minimum. In all, more than 5,000 armed soldiers and civilians were at one time engaged in this Coastal Watch service.

The end result, in the first two years of the system, was the identification and capture of more than 2,500 pirates or coastal raiders, the early warning for more than 500 raids on manor houses, farmsteads, and small villages, and the public hangings of more than 500 of the captured pirates. Within six months of operations, the Coastal Watchers had all but eliminated coastal piracy much to the delight of the nobles involved. Without a doubt piracy increased in other parts of coastal England, but not in the area assigned to Team 8.

The lead knight of Team 8 had been haunted by the fact that no real pirate treasures had been uncovered in his area despite the fact that rumors abounded about buried treasure, ghosts, etc. It was in July of 1454 that he, and other members of the Green Rose team, had returned to Cleeve abbey to check on operations. Once again he visited the painting on the wall and sat for long hours studying each and every detail. He spent a lot of time asking others about the painting and then sitting again and staring at it. The Cleeve monks began to think he was obsessed and tried to avoid him.

The knight was sitting in front of the wall one evening, staring at the painting by candlelight, when he noticed a peculiar shadow at the far left side of the painting. He picked up a candle and moved closer to the spot and began to jostle some of the protruding stones. One smaller inset stone seemed to be loose and when he pushed harder on it, the wall just seemed to open. He was so surprised he dropped his candle and had to relight it. The wall opened inward on concealed hinges in the stonework and he found himself stepping inside and standing at the top of a stone stairway descending into the darkness. The stairway was only a couple of feet wide. What he found was amazing and he stared at it in total awe. An underground room at the bottom of the stairs was indeed a treasure trove with five small chests of various coins dating clear back to Roman times, one chest of gold and silver jeweled trinkets, several gold drinking cups, and other miscellaneous trinkets inlaid with jewels and gold. It was a fortune!

When he recovered his wits, the knight quietly withdrew from the treasure room, mounted the steps, and closed the stone door making sure it was firmly in place. The next morning he left the other team members at the abbey, without telling them what he had found, and rode directly to St. Albans to report to the lead monk.

About two months later a special ship again arrived from Rome and the bulk of the treasure was loaded onto a cart and transported to the seaport where it was loaded aboard the ship. The remainder of the treasure was then revealed to the abbot and used to finance the various businesses of both Cleeve and Forde abbeys for several years. The records seem to show that the treasure actually increased during this period as financial ventures of the abbeys were making a strong and profitable showing by this time.

Some of the money was used to open a new stone quarry at Bath in Somerset and much of the production from this works was used to build the more permanent watch stations along the coastal areas being loaded aboard ships and sent to the respective sites.

Another use for the money came in March 1454 when a message from St. Albans requested Team 8 to establish a glove making industry in Somerset, using pig hides from the cider mill. These were to be specially designed gloves in the form of padded leather with pockets for steel plates to protect the hands of sword and pike men while in battle. The note directed them to the village of Yeovil, located about fifteen miles northeast of Forde Abbey, and provided the name of an established glove maker with a shop in the village.

Since things were running pretty smoothly among the various industries at the abbey, the full membership of Team 8 was quickly on the road to Yeovil. It was March, travel was quite difficult, and it took the team nearly a full day to reach the village located on the banks of the River Yeo. The village name is believed to have been derived from an Anglo-Saxon word meaning "forked river." When the lead knight made contact with the glove maker, he was careful not to mention the abbey or the letter from St. Albans knowing that about 100 years previously the townspeople had rioted against clergy over the markets.

However, the glove maker already had been alerted he was to be visited by a team from Forde Abbey so there was no long-lasting animosity over previous village problems. When the lead knight explained the reason for the team's visit it wasn't long before a bargain was struck. The glove maker had been using only his family to ply his trade, but the requirements for the military gauntlets would necessitate an immediate expansion. The lead knight recalled the success of other teams in using villagers for home industry and suggested this might be a way to not only increase production, but bring added income to many of his neighbors as well. This was the turning point in the negotiations.

The glove maker invited the team to spend the night in his barn indicating they could use the tanned hides in there for beds and to keep warm against the chill and that's what they did. Each member of Team 8 had brought his own gear and supplies so all were quite comfortable. The next morning the team and the glove maker ironed out details and the lead knight advanced him a sum of money to purchase additional equipment, which would have to be hand crafted, and to pay villagers for their early labors in getting the industry started. The glove maker preferred to tan his own hides, so the agreement was that raw hides would be supplied by the abbey and the glove maker would set up a larger tannery as well as make the finished gloves.

The artisan had already conceived an idea of the design for the specialized gauntlets which turned out to be similar to the armored vests being made elsewhere. Only this time a small hammered steel plate would be inserted into a pocket on the back of each gauntlet to protect the back of the hand and wrist. The abbey would provide the steel plates and they agreed on the size that would be needed.

The glove maker called his four sons into the conference and the discussion continued for most of the day as final details were worked out. By that evening everything was agreed and the first money exchanged hands to seal the bargain. The glove maker sent his sons out in separate directions the following morning to find villagers and peasants with sewing skills in order to stitch up the gloves. It had been decided the glove maker and his family would tan the hides, cut out the glove patterns using specialized forms and tools, and the leather pieces would then be shipped out to seamstresses who would sew the pieces into the finished gloves. These workers would be paid on a "piece" basis with a sum of money allowed for each finished gauntlet, providing it was good quality work and returned to the artisan as completed pairs.

Several "prototypes" were cut from existing patterns, including a few innovations, and on the fifth day of the visit a number of villagers and farm wives began to gather at the leather works about ten in the morning. The team watched while the glove maker explained the proposed work, what it entailed, and how it was to be done. He then added information on the pay scale which was typical of the period. About three-fourths of the people at the meeting agreed to give it a try and the others were either too busy with their own work or didn't feel they could do justice to the work. Several of them indicated they knew of others who could handle the work and would pass along the information.

There were about twenty who started work immediately when the glove maker handed out the cut-out pieces of leather and began training his new apprentices. By the end of the day there were twenty new pairs of military gauntlets that had been finished and passed inspection. Eight of these were immediately snapped up by members of Team 8. Leaving the glove maker to continue training the glove stitchers, Team 8 took its leave. Four of the team headed over to Ashdown Forest and the St. Albans smelter site to arrange for the production of the steel plates for the gloves while the other four headed immediately for the abbey's grange in Devon producing cider and hogs. The latter purpose was to arrange for the shipment of pig hides to the glove maker at Yeovil. Team members had agreed to meet back in Yeovil in two weeks.

The first part of the team arrived back in Yeovil a day before the appointed time along with a pack train carrying a supply of the new armor plates specially designed to fit the gauntlets. It was not a large supply, but enough to take care of the glove production for several days until a larger shipment was scheduled to arrive. After that, the glove maker would receive weekly shipments of the plates depending upon how fast he could finish the gloves.

On the appointed day, the remainder of team 8 showed up with a wagon load of fresh hides. The team members were tired out since they were forced to help out the monks in skinning some fifty pigs in order to secure their quest. The wagon load of green hides didn't smell too good, either. When they arrived with the hides at the glove maker's barn, they were quite relieved to turn over their burden. However, the fresh hides made the barn pretty much untenable and the team decided it would rather camp in the nearby woods, which it did.

While they were gone, the glove maker had produced a number of additional pairs of gauntlets and the new metal plates were inserted to complete them. Members of Team 8 also acquired the metal plates in the backs of their new gauntlets, too. One problem had developed in the home industry part of the glove making and that was in "turning" each glove. The gloves were stitched while turned inside out and then "turned" on a special turning post designed for that purpose. The glove maker had agreed to turn the gloves at his shop after they were sewn and that speeded up production right away. The team arranged to have the finished gloves shipped by wagon to Forde Abbey on a two-week schedule and they were re-distributed according to demand directly from the abbey.

After word got around about the new armored gauntlets, it was not unusual for Forde Abbey to receive by courier traced outlines of hands for special orders for the sized-to-fit gauntlets from many of the knights and nobles in the area. These orders were transferred on to the glove maker who generally had them filled and delivered with the next shipment of finished gloves to the abbey. The "tailored" gauntlets brought much prestige to the abbey and Team 8 who spent a lot of time demonstrating them to the troops it was training.

In June Team 8 received a special courier from St. Albans regarding crates of cygnet swans recovered during a raid on a London warehouse by members of Team 6 following a wagonload of stolen Osprey chicks they had traced from the hatching grounds at Rutland Water. It seems the crates of swans were en route to a Swannery located on Chesil Beach near Abbotsbury just a few miles from Forde Abbey. The cartload of cygnets were being sent, by order of the King, to St. Peter's Abbey in Dorsetshire. St. Peter's was a Benedictine Abbey, founded in the 11th century, and an unofficial watcher over the King's swans who nested in a protected area near a marshy area sheltered by the tidal inlet of Chesil Beach.

Team 8 wasn't informed exactly what to do with the cygnets, but set out immediately for St. Peter's Abbey and Abbotsbury in order to be present when the cart load of birds arrived. It was understood they were to provide some sort of protection to the baby swans that were always under the protection of the King. However, none of them knew anything about such birds.

They headed southeast from Forde Abbey and rode through some pretty dense woods en route to Abbotsbury and had been directed to look for a landmark known as the "Grey Mare and her Colts" located about a mile from the village. The Grey Mare and her Colts, as it is termed locally, is a long barrow dating from around 3000 B.C. serving as a single burial chamber of sarsen stones. The Ridgeway hills stretching east-west just north of the village provided a natural causeway to Abbotsbury and a excellent vantage point from which to scan the surrounding countryside, and the sea, for approaching enemies. The abbey of St. Peters was located down on the coastal plains just south of the village and it was easy to spot the great Tithe Barn and St. Catherine's Chapel as the team drew near.

The team was impressed by the huge barn and one of the squires took time to pace off its measurements after the team was settled in the visitor's quarters at the abbey. He estimated the thatched roofed structure was more than 270 feet long and just over thirty feet wide. The chapel was equally impressive and its spire was long used as a lookout across the sea and by mariners as a course marker.

They had informed the abbot of the purpose of their visit and the cart full of swan cygnets that was en route from London by order of the King. The abbot immediately summoned two of his monks, who voluntarily kept watch over the Swannery, and the team had an opportunity to question them as to the missing chicks.

Neither monk apparently had seen any thievery from the Swannery although they had noticed a number of empty nests. If the chicks were from the Abbotsbury area, they had been removed in secrecy; however, both monks agreed to keep a closer watch over the area especially in the spring when the new chicks were hatching and maturing.

Team members had a chance to inspect the Swannery on the following morning and were impressed by the docile nature of the hundreds of cygnets still nesting in the area dutifully cared for by their parents. It was later that day when the cart arrived at the abbey from London.

The two Swannery monks were quite dismayed when they opened the cages and looked at the condition of the birds. They decided on the spot that the forty or so cygnets would have to be hand cared for as they would never survive if set loose in the Swannery in the poor condition they were in. They immediately directed the cart to move down to the barn were they hurriedly prepared a soft bed of dried grass in a corner of the huge structure where the sun warmed the stone base during the day and where they could build a warming fire if the nights turned too cold. They prepared a trough of fresh water for the birds and cooked up a corn-based mash with which to feed them. The members of Team 8 were called on to assist in the feeding of the chicks and that turned out to be a more difficult task than any of them would have thought. Some of the birds were pretty much too weak to eat and the mash had to be forced down their gullets and the necks of the birds stroked to make certain it went all the way down. It took the team and the monks more than two hours to feed all the birds and to get them safely bedded down. Those birds still in good condition were reluctant to stay in one place and a barrier had to be built around the grass bed to assure they would not get lost.

The next morning the two monks, who had remained in the barn with the birds all night, reported a miracle. During the night several of the swans from the Swannery had responded to the cries of the chicks and descended upon the barn. The monks, awakened by their arrival, sat in awe watching them take over the care of the chicks forcing them to drink water and to eat more of the mash left in another trough. The adult swans seemed to take turns during the night caring for the chicks as there constantly were new swans arriving and some leaving. The monks were simply overcome with joy and spent every moment in prayer thanking God for the miracle.

After two days of care by the monks and the adult swans, all but two of the chicks were fully recovered and the adults simply marched them off to the Swannery and continued to care for them there. The other two cygnets did not survive and the monks buried them in a special grave on a hillside behind the barn.

Team 8 was happy to report back to St. Albans on the success of returning the swans, but only hinted in the message about the miracle witnessed by the monks. Before they returned to Forde Abbey they confirmed that a special watch would be kept over the Swannery the following spring.

The only other enterprise established by Team 8 while at Forde Abbey was to respond to a request from the fisherman engaged in catching and drying fish for additional nets with which to expand their daily catch. To this end the team established another "cottage type" industry enlisting village and farm wives to weave the nets. It took the team several months to get this enterprise fully operational and they spent a lot of time along the coastal areas supervising it.

By the time the team was recalled to St. Albans in April of 1455, the net making and fishing enterprises had grown fairly large. The nets were being sold to other commercial fisheries and the abbey's fishing and drying industry had more than doubled in annual revenues. Part of the market for the dried fish was the Duke of York who had purchased several wagon loads of dried mackerel to be delivered in secret.

Chapter 17—Maritime Country

When Team 9 finally arrived at Netley Abbey in Southamptonshire (now Hampshire) after surviving a close call en route near the London waterfront, it found the structures situated a short distance from the eastern bank of Southampton Water. The Abbey is situated on a gentle mound that rises above the bank of Southampton Water and is surrounded by a nearly square wall with a deep moat on all sides. Two rather large ponds were located close to the buildings and the team could see fish rising to the surfaces. An assortment of tall trees, including oaks, stood with bare limbs completely enclosing three sides of the walled structures. It was an impressive and welcoming sight to the travel weary team members.

After the team identified itself and gained entry to the abbey, it was shown to an expansive guest quarters built into the wall of the abbey facing Southampton Water. Arched windows in the sides of the wall provided a view of the water itself. The abbot greeted each of the team members individually after chapel and gave them a tour of the abbey. The team was impressed especially by the size of the kitchen and the abbot told them it was necessary because of the numbers of visitors who regularly visited the abbey seeking refuge and food.

The abbot continued to tell the team members it was this facet of the abbey's operations that had caused financial problems for the abbey causing it to sell off some of its lands in order to continue to feed and harbor those seeking kindness at its doors. The abbot also said its livestock herds had become quite diminished due to the necessity of feeding the stream of visitors.

When asked by the lead knight of Team 9 why the abbey didn't charge for its visitors, the abbot indicated it was "not the way" of his Order to do so. It took some convincing, but the knight indicated the financial difficulties facing the abbey would immediately be eased if a small fee was charged for lodging and food and the abbot said he would take it under consideration and prayer.

It was three days later when the abbot again met with the team and advised that he had carefully considered the fees in prayer and had dreamed that such action would indeed resolve much of the abbey's financial woes. He gave permission to the team to establish a fee structure, but no one who asked for admittance was to be denied even if they had no money with which to pay.

Team 9 had spent the last three days visiting with the thirty-five or so monks at the abbey and the three lay volunteer's currently in residence and knew they were both charitable and "fed up" with the free loaders and there were many tasks at the abbey that had gone undone due to lack of manpower.

The team sat down and established a fair payment scale based upon charges they had paid at various inns while traveling to the abbey, the cost of food produced and/or purchased by the abbey, and other expenses such as hauling. No consideration was given to a charge for labor as that would have violated the code of the Cistercian Order. The resulting fee schedule was about forty percent less than was being charged commercially for both room and board and there was even a charge for laundry service as required. Provision was also made for those with no money to provide labor services within the abbey in exchange for room and board.

The knight had one of the monks, a skilled wood carver, make a small signboard with the fee scheduled engraved on it and this was posted outside the main gate of the abbey at the entrance to the turnoff from the main road. There was also a notation on the sign about work in exchange. Contrary to what many of the monks—including the abbot—thought, the sign did not drive away visitors to the abbey. Instead, it increased the lodging traffic by two-to-three additional visitors per day. About seventy percent of the guests were "paying guests." The other thirty percent were put to work in various jobs around the abbey. Most of these non-paying types stayed long enough to complete the project to which they were assigned and about one-in-five of them stayed on as permanent lay volunteers at the abbey when they were invited to do so by the supervising monks.

Thus, the new fee schedule brought several favorable economic and labor gains to the abbey and the guest quarters had to be dramatically enlarged after the first few weeks. By this time the abbot had both the money and labor in order to do the job and work proceeded quickly. Local landowners were increasingly aware of the services provided by the abbey and increased their donations in both money and goods since they now had a reliable place to refer "strays" that came knocking on their own doors. And, the resident monks were treating the visitors in a "welcoming" fashion. Two of the monks had musical and vocal talents and often led group sing-a-longs after the evening meal with many of the guests joining in. These sessions quickly became popular and the abbey had many paying guests visiting just for dinner alone. When the abbey bells sounded bringing monks to the evening chapel, dinner guests knew they had about thirty minutes to reach the abbey for the supper session that always followed a chapel service.

When news got out that one of the visitors had seen a ghost, there was an immediate influx of visitors to the dinner sessions and the monks had to employ two separate "sittings" to accommodate all the guests.

An unemployed mariner who was working on an abbey project in the basement of the refectory, in return for his board and room, decided to work late one fall evening since his project was at a critical stage. He was working on a stone doorway leading to an area where the abbey stored its casks of beer and wine, when an apparition appeared and nearly frightened him to death. The apparition was dressed as a pirate and seemed to be blind. The mariner was so horrified that he ran all over the abbey, waking the others, until some of the Green Rose team finally calmed him down enough to tell his tale. What he described was so realistic that no one doubted he had actually seen something. One of the long-time monks at the abbey pretty well confirmed his story when he recalled another had been working in that same area a few years back and had been frightened in the same manner. He died shortly after blurting out his strange story. In both instances it was the evening of Halloween.

Some of the Green Rose team decided to play a joke on the dinner guests the following Halloween evening and dressed one of the squires in a pirate costume, with sword, and he made a cameo appearance in one of the doorways leading to the dining room which was full at the time. About fifty percent of the guests actually saw him, but 100 percent of the guests had a delightful time describing the adventure to their friends in the days to come. The monks, who were not included in the joke, began calling the apparition "Blind Peter," and the legend continued to grow. It is rumored "Blind Peter" made several Halloween appearances at the abbey throughout the following years once the monks were invited into the game. Each time the ghost appeared, dining at the abbey became increasingly popular, so the monks were willing conspirators. Halloween dinner became so popular the monks had to take advanced "reservations" so that all would be assured of a seat at the table. The dinner sittings on Halloween lasted from 6 p.m. until 11 p.m. when the last, and most sought after, seating began for it was at this time of night when an appearance of Blind Peter most often occurred, although he had appeared at some of the earlier sittings over the years.

For the abbey finances, Blind Peter was a bonanza. Revenues gained from Halloween dinners alone, were enough to run the abbey throughout most of the following year. Many of the local nobles, and even Royalty, were abbey dinner guests on Halloween. In some years Blind Peter was spotted flitting through the abbey grounds just at dusk when guests were arriving. For some reason, no one would agree to work in the refectory basement on the evening of Halloween and all the wine and beer for the Halloween dinner sessions would have to be brought up from the cellar on the day before.

The Blind Peter phantom had not yet appeared when the Green Rose team left for St. Albans in April of 1451 for the general conclave, but much progress had been accomplished in getting Netley Abbey back on its feet financially and the team received special recognition for these efforts. In fact, several other teams learned from Team 9 and established fee schedules at their own abbeys when they returned from the conference.

When the team returned to Netley Abbey, much work was accomplished in improving guest quarters and accommodating the increasing numbers permitted to pay for overnight lodging and meals. In just a few short weeks the demands for such services had increased to almost thirty visitors per night and many of the lay volunteers had been converted into inn keepers, cooks, waiters, and dishwashers to keep up with the traffic. An overnight laundry service was also established and the fireplace in the warming chamber at the abbey was often crowded with clothes hanging out to dry so they could be folded and returned to guests early the next morning.

From time to time the Green Rose team was called upon to eject freeloaders who refused to pay or work at the abbey in exchange for services. However, none were sent away without a blanket and a picnic lunch as a gift from the abbey in exchange for leaving quietly. The team also was busy calling on the various nobles in the area gaining donations for the abbey in exchange for military training for the castle or manor troops.

One of the benefits from having so many different types of visitors at the abbey was the information gleaned each evening at the "entertainment" portion of the meal after tongues had been loosened by wine, ale and beer. Many messages were dispatched by Team 9 to St. Albans with news about the wars in France, political liaisons, and even of Royalty after some of these nightly sessions. The news seemed to be coming directly to the abbey from all directions and the Green Rose team was kept busy gleaning the most important fragments and sending them on.

It was August of 1451 when news reached the abbey of the theft of a band of sheep from one of the abbey's granges in the New Forest Area of Southamptonshire. The report was two days old by the time it reached the Green Rose team since the monk bringing the news had to walk clear around the bank of Southampton Water in order to reach the abbey. The

Green Rose team immediately responded, but loaded its horses and gear aboard a ferry craft which took them straight across Southampton Water and landed them on the west shore near Hythe. The monk had told them one of the other shepherds was tracking the stolen flock and he thought they were probably heading towards a well-know smuggling port called Lymington or "Donkey Town" due to the large numbers of these animals growing wild in the area.

Based on this information, Team 9 headed overland towards Lymington hoping to intercept the stolen band of sheep before it could be loaded aboard a ship and smuggled out of the country. On the second day they reached an area called Walhampton on the east bank of the Lymington River where they met up with the monk/shepherd who had been trailing the sheep. He led them to a concealed area adjacent to some salt marshes along the estuary leading from *The Solent* waterway to the port of Lymington on the west bank of the river. They could see the stolen flock grazing peacefully at the edges of the marsh and guarded by about six armed men on foot who seemed to be waiting for a large sailing ship anchored in the river to send boats ashore with which to transport the sheep from the shore to the craft. The ship had just come sailing up the river and dropped anchor after signaling to the men on the shore guarding the sheep.

Since it was nearly dark by this time, the Green Rose team decided it would wait and see what was going to happen. The team saw a boat being lowered from the after deck of the sailing ship and soon it was rowed ashore by four sailors with apparently the captain of the ship in the prow. When it landed, the captain greeted the shore guards. By this time one of the squires had crept forward through the high marsh grass to where he could overhear the conversation which was in French. He reported back a few minutes later that the plan was to wait until daylight to transfer the sheep by boat to the ship. Two men would man each of the two boats from the ship and the shore crew would load the sheep aboard each boat by catching them and hand carrying them to the boats. After the captain had returned to his ship, the men on shore immediately began building a brush enclosure and drove the sheep inside for the night making them easier to capture in the morning. Then they settled down alongside a campfire, cooked their dinner, and seemed to be set for the night.

The Green Rose team leader withdrew his team far enough to begin making plans on how to bring down the smugglers and recapture the sheep. It was decided that the team would quietly overcome the six members of the sheep guard in the middle of the night and then six members of the team would don the clothes and armaments of the guards taking their places in the morning. One of the monk/shepherds, who had military experience, suggested he become one of the replacement guards since he was skilled in the handling of the sheep and could show the other Green Rose members how to do it so as not to bring suspicion down on the team in its disguise. That was quickly agreed to and the four knights and one of the squires were selected to complete the false team. The other three squires and the monk would stand in reserve while the sheep loading was underway in the event the ruse was discovered. When the last sheep were on board the ship then the six would disarm the boat crew, strip their garments, and two of the squires would quickly put them on and serve as the boat crew for the journey to the ship. If a second boat came ashore then the remaining squire and monk would have to deal with it.

It was 3 a.m. the next morning when the Green Rose team went into action. All ten of the men, including the monks, crawled up on the sleeping camp. They immediately covered each sleeping man, put a hand over his mouth and a dagger in his ear and took them all without a struggle. Each man was hauled out of the dim firelight, gagged and bound with his arms behind his back. When that was done each of the bandits was stripped of his outer clothes and then marched back into the protection of the trees while the Green Rose volunteers donned the clothes and returned to the beds in the campsite where they spent the remainder of the night. The camp looked as it had the night before when the first of the two boats rowed ashore a little before daylight. The Green Rose team immediately set to work capturing sheep and carrying them to the boat so as to avoid conversation with the boat crew. The first boat was just loaded and ready to return to the ship when a second boat arrived. This process was repeated nearly all morning until the 120 or so sheep in the band were all loaded. Then the team waited until one of the boats returned before gathering around it and quickly hammering the flat of a sword blade down on the heads of the two oarsmen. The two replacement squires had sneaked up to the brush corral and calmly sauntered over to the boat quickly donning the garments of the crew over their own clothes. The remaining squire and monk quickly dragged the two crewmen over to the brush corral and tied and gagged them leaving them out of sight. The Green Rose team piled into the longboat with the two disguised squires at the oars and they set out towards the ship. The second boat was en route to the beach and the lead knight motioned it on towards the beach where the squire and monk appeared to be waiting.

When the boat approached the ship, some of the ship's crew were waiting to hold the boat to the side while the team members climbed aboard. The last one to leave the flimsy craft was the lead knight who simply kicked two of the crewmen overboard as he climbed up the side. The others, upon reaching the main deck drew their weapons and were engaged in a brief struggle with the vagabond crew. The three squires had brought along their longbows and arrows and were soon making their presence known while the four knights were working as a team driving the crew members toward the stern of the ship.

Meanwhile the monk and squire left on the beach had waited until the second boat came ashore before they jumped the crew members and quickly tied them up. Then they took the boat and rowed out towards the ship. The monk worked the oars while the squire stood in the prow and loosed arrows at the crew aboard the ship. The battle aboard the ship lasted for about twenty minutes before the last of the brigands laid down their arms and surrendered. The captain already had been killed by one of the knights and this took some of the heart out of the defenders. In all, eleven of the gang were captured, including the four on the beach, five were killed in the storming of the ship, and the two kicked overboard by the knight could not swim and drowned.

The squire and monk in the longboat were sent back to the beach to bring the captured thugs on shore back to the boat and the five of the crewmen, including the mate, were released under guard to work the ship. It was sailed on up the river to Lymington where the sheep were offloaded at a dock and sent on their way back to the grange under care of the shepherd/monks. Bodies of the dead pirates and all but the five parolees required to work the ship were turned over to the port authorities where the monks turned evidence against them before returning with the sheep to the abbey grange. They were subsequently hanged for piracy.

The Green Rose team decided to use the parolee crew to sail the ship back to Netley Abbey and that's what it did. Upon return it gave the five crew members a choice of being turned over to the authorities for piracy or become lay volunteers at the abbey where they would be "closely supervised" for a period of five years. If they caused no further trouble they would be released. All five chose the parole offer and agreed they would also sail the newly acquired ship as required. Thus, the abbey profited from the return of its band of sheep, its very own wooden sailing ship, and five years of free labor from the five former bandits. As it turned out, four of the five bandits completed parole and earned freedom. The other was killed in a shipboard accident about two years later when he slipped from one of the upper yards on the ship and fell to his death. Many uses were found for the ship itself.

After some extensive repairs to the ship, a makeshift crew, including the four parolees, sailed the ship down Southampton Water to The Solent and then west a short distance to the mouth of the River Beaulieu and then up the river channel to the docks at Beaulieu Abbey where it was put to use carrying lumber and other cargoes of goods produced from the sister abbeys over to the mainland where they were profitably sold. The ship also was used on occasion when St. Albans wanted to send a quick and private dispatch to the Pope in Rome. It turned out that several of the lay volunteers at each abbey were former mariners so there was no lack of crew for the ship. One of the monks at Beaulieu was a former sea captain and he was placed in charge of the ship.

The Green Rose team in the fall and winter of 1451 was called on for help from the abbot at Beaulieu when one of the king's prisoners, lodged at the abbey, was kidnapped during the night by a party of armed knights all dressed in black. The prisoner had been occupying the King's Hunting Lodge located nearby and was simply "spirited" away leaving two armed guards dead outside of the lodge.

This prisoner, not identified in any of the available records, apparently had royal blood. Some surmised the kidnapping was politically motivated, but no one knows for certain. Apparently, as the Green Rose investigations showed, the prisoner was loaded aboard a small sailing craft which moved swiftly down river to the English Channel and made a rendezvous at sea with a frigate flying a Spanish flag.

While the prisoner was never recovered, the king called for tighter security at the abbey and along the southeastern coast of England. Team 9 sent a suggestion to St. Albans that some of the outlaws taking refuge at Beaulieu Abbey, long noted as a place of sanctuary, receive pardons from the king if they agreed to establish a coast guard network which would include watchers and spies to report on coastal activities. At the time there were some thirty former criminals who were buying sanctuary at the abbey and some of these were former pirates who knew the coast and pirate activities well.

The bishop at St. Albans made a special trip to London with Team 9's suggestion and returned with a blanket king's pardon for any who served five honorable years in the King's Watchers as the new group was to be called. This information and a copy of the King's Decree were sent by dispatch to Netley Abbey and Team 9.

Team 9 immediately went to Beaulieu Abbey and conferred with the abbot who agreed to the scheme mostly because he was embarrassed at losing his prisoner. He agreed to call a meeting of all those in sanctuary at the abbey and from this meeting the King's Watchers was born.

Heading the group was a former admiral in the French navy who had defected to England. He was a master at organization and soon had stations established stretching east from Bournemouth to Dover with the cooperation of other Green Rose teams. Spy stations were established at Bournemouth, Gosport, Portsmouth, Brighton, Eastbourne, Hastings, Folkestone, and Dover and regular information was sent, mostly by sea, back to Beaulieu Abbey where it was evaluated by one of the Green Rose knights and sent on to Netley Abbey where it entered the dispatch circuit to St. Albans and other teams. Much current information about the war with France was forthcoming through this system. There was no lack of volunteers from the various villages along the coast who were tired of being subjected to periodic raids from coastal pirates and the Green Rose team was extremely busy providing arms and training to these men for the next several months.

It is not known how many of those in sanctuary at Beaulieu eventually received royal pardons, but it is known that the King's Watchers became a well-recognized organization and received much acclaim over the years it was operating. It was not long before teams of twenty or more armed and mounted "watchers" were ferreting out pirate lairs all along the coastal areas with many captures to their credit. Particular success was achieved by the King's Watchers in areas known as the "fens," swampy areas that served as natural hideaway spots for those avoiding the law. The Watchers hired locals who knew the shallow paths between the high spots in the fens and could navigate through these territories well. Often the Watchers were able to surprise pirates in their camps thinking they were well protected by the natural habitat.

For a time coastal raids became quite rare and whenever one did occur there was an immediate retaliation usually resulting in the public hanging of those caught.

Things took a turn for the better in the early part of 1452 for Team 9 and it became involved in more of the domestic affairs of Netley Abbey. One of the desires of the abbot was to restore the abbey's prominence in the wool market which had fallen on bad times due to loss of granges, stolen flocks, and economic problems at the abbey. He invited the Green Rose team to accompany him on a trip to the market at Melksham in West Wiltshire, a prosperous wool town. The abbey still owned a substantial grange on the northern part of the Salisbury Plain near Avebury where it had a small flock of sheep and a small, but ageing herd of dairy cattle. Since finances for the Abbey had shown a marked improvement due to the efforts of the Green Rose team, the abbot was determined to increase the abbey's share of the wool markets and milk and cheese.

Melksham was pretty much a forest village but rich pastures surrounding it encourage dairy farming as well as sheep. The town held cattle and sheep markets in the spring and fall each year and these markets were well attended by both buyers and sellers so the abbot managed to deal for some twenty-five dairy cows and a flock of about 250 sheep, including new lambs. These were slowly driven to the grange and left in the care of the herder monks. The abbot wanted to show the Green Rose team two ancient sites en route back to Netley Abbey. The first stop was a short journey to the village of Avebury which is partially surrounded by a large circle of huge stones set upright in the earth. A ditch and bank, forming a henge, surrounds the "outer circle." Two inner circles, North and South, the abbot explained to the team as they inspected the site, are thought to represent female and male. It was an impressive site and members of the Green Rose team were intrigued.

"Wait until I show you another similar site as we travel south," the abbot said. "You will be amazed at the hanging stones."

And, they were!

The monoliths of Stonehenge, just northwest of Salisbury, are impressive. Some of the huge stones weigh as much as fifty tons. "It is believed these stones were erected by Bronze-age Celts in order to make peace with the gods of summer and winter and to assure the darkness of winter would return to the light of summer," the abbot told the group.

The two monuments were the topic of conversation among the Green Rose team as they returned to Netley Abbey. They also spotted three of the five "white horses," carved in the Wiltshire landscape near Avesbury and the abbot explained these probably were made to commemorate victory in various battles fought in earlier times although no one knew for certain. "Many such carvings are located throughout England and not all of them are horses. Some represent giants, some are crosses, and some are figures," the abbot told them.

Ironically enough it was these chalk figures that led to the next effort by the Green Rose team to revive the economic condition of the abbey. It seems the abbey owned a piece of land in Berkshire near Yattendon where, in times past, chalk had been mined to use as a soil conditioner for the abbey fields as well as in conjunction with an old brickworks that had fallen into disuse during the time of the black plague.

Chalk mining in England is nearly as old as the first tribes that occupied the land. The feudal system, with its allocations of land to the various nobles, knights, etc., and made it increasingly important to produce as many agricultural products from allotted plots of land as possible. Heavy soil types often called for some type of "conditioner" in order to make the soils produce more crops. For this, farmers resorted to the chalk and lime formations underlying much of the country. Because boundary lines were closely guarded and violation could cause a local war, farmers resorted to digging vertical shafts through the soil to reach the underground chalk formations. Surface chalk formations were often leached of valuable minerals by exposure to weather and the "unpolluted" chalk was underneath the cover of soil.

These excavations were most often found at the edges of fields so as to preserve as much surface soil as possible for farming. The old chalk mines belonging to the abbey were termed "pits" and later were called "deneholes. A narrow shaft, about three feet in diameter, was dug into the soil until the chalk structures were reached. Footholds were cut into opposite sides of this shaft, sometimes as deep as thirty or more feet, so the miners could climb in and out without a ladder. The shaft was sunk about seven or eight feet into the chalk and then tunnels through the chalk were dug as the chalk was removed. Up to two sets of three tunnels each could be excavated from a single shaft leaving substantial walls of chalk for the ceiling and sides to avoid most dangers of collapse. Most of the miners used a hauling rope and basket as a plumb line for the vertical shaft and to remove the soil. The horizontal tunnels were dug to the extent the hauling rope could be extended without causing too much friction to be hauled up. Usually teams of three miners worked each den hole. One miner worked underground filling the basket at the working face of the mine and the other two worked on the surface hauling up the basket once it was filled with the chalk. Sometimes a small windlass was mounted over the shaft to make this job easier.

While the abbey had used its own monks and lay volunteers to work the chalk mines, most farmers in the area had hired professional miners to work the mines since there was a great deal of skill applied to the digging operations. Besides fertilizer for its fields, the abbey also used the chalk in construction projects, for brick making, and for making mortar with which to cement bricks and stones.

When the Green Rose team inspected the mining property, it had been abandoned for several years, but rather than filling the old shafts, as was the usual custom, the monks had constructed wooden barriers to cover them so it was easy to descend into some of the shafts to inspect them—a job that fell to one of the squires on the team who had some construction experience.

What he reported back was an extensive supply of chalk was still available to be extracted from most of the pits; however, he suggested some modifications should be made to make the mines safer and to provide additional natural light at the bottom of the shaft.

The team rode into the nearby village of Yattendon looking for men to help restore the mines. At first they could not find anyone interested in such back-breaking work until the squire began to explain some of his ideas on how to improve the mining operations. This caught the attention of one of the older peasants living in the village, who had previously been employed in a similar chalk mining operation. He immediately grasped the advantages of what the squire was explaining and volunteered to help. Seeing this example, there were about eight other villagers who signed on to the project with the promise of wages plus a share of the profits from the enterprise.

When the workers assembled the next day at the abbey's mine pits, the squire put them to work enlarging the shaft of one of the mines. He wanted the shaft at least five feet wide at the top and even wider as it descended into the ground. This was to permit more daylight into the bottom of the shaft so that the tunnels could be worked without the aid of artificial light which polluted the air. A square wooden structure was built at the top of the shaft and a windlass was mounted in this structure with turning handles on either side to allow greater lift capacity. The buckets used to haul the mined chalk to the top were constructed of wood and were three feet square and eighteen inches deep with skids attached to the bottom.

A portable frame was constructed and lowered to the bottom of the shaft where it was anchored at the entrance to one of the tunnels. This frame had a slot cut in the underside of its top beam that allowed the rope, attached to the skid box, to be pulled along the floor of the tunnel using the windlass until it reached the center of the shaft when it would be lifted up to the surface, dumped by manpower into a cart, and the skid box lowered back into the shaft to be refilled. After a successful test of the procedure, a second portable frame was built and installed so that the mining team could work two tunnel faces at the same time. It took four men, two on each side of the windlass, to crank up the filled skid boxes and two men down working the mine itself to achieve maximum output. While it would appear the same thing could have been accomplished by utilizing two denehole mines as in the past, the larger skid buckets actually tripled the production using the same number of miners. In fact, production was so great the team had to find markets for the chalk beyond the capacity of use by the abbey.

The first effort was to re-open the brickworks. The drying ovens were still operable after repairs were made and clay was easily obtainable and mixed with chalk slurry to prevent shrinkage in the finished bricks. This was a project that kept the team busy for most of the summer after they found an expert mason among the monks at Netley and recruited him to supervise the brickworks. It turned out that brick production was of a superior quality and quickly became in such demand that the brickworks could not fulfill but about half of demand. This worked to the abbey's advantage in that it could command a higher that usual price for its bricks.

A second effort was the result of an examination of the ruins of some of the old Roman fortifications in the surrounding countryside. The Green Rose team discovered the footings for many of the old walls were made of well preserved chalk blocks. After this discovery, the team opened a second den hole mine and produced chalk blocks. These blocks were a harder sell and the team had to show several of the nobles how well they had worked by giving them tours of some of the older fortifications. Eventually, the team had greater marketing success by using the abbey's captured ship and sending the finished blocks to France where they were quickly purchased for building purposes being easier to handle, but nearly as durable, as stone.

The third benefit came from burning the chalk in simple limekilns to make a dry powder that could be mixed with fine sand and water to make an excellent mortar for cementing bricks and stones during construction.

Within a period of about 18 months, abbey records were indicating profits from the chalk works were exceeding those from other sources of revenue including cheese, wool, and penance.

The Green Rose team was observing the spring wheat harvest at a grange near Winchester primarily as a result of the chalk operations. The team wanted to learn how the chalk was spread on the fields after the harvest in order to develop expanded markets for the chalk. Most fields were "chalked" from pits dug near the borders of the fields and the chalk was broken up and spread by hand using buckets. The team had been told this, but believed there should be some better way of doing the job so it was there to see the operation first hand.

Lay volunteers from the abbey and from Winchester village had just finished harvesting and shocking the wheat and were in the process of hauling the shocks to the grange's barn for winnowing into grain—a process in itself that would last for most of the coming winter as only enough grain was separated as was used up immediately. The wheat stubble was left in the field and wagon loads of chalk from the abbey's mines had begun arriving early in the morning preparatory to "marle" the field. Those not engaged in transporting the wheat began to fill buckets full of chalk and to hand sew it across the field. After a time, the Green Rose team knew this hand spreading process was going to take much too long to accomplish.

By this time there were four wagon loads of powdered chalk waiting to be spread and one of the knights recommended the wagons be lined up across the field with two men to the back of each wagon with shovels to unload the chalk onto the ground as the wagons were pulled slowly across the field. Other men (and women) armed with wooden rakes would follow behind and spread the chalk more evenly along the surface. What developed was a team effort that relatively quickly emptied the four wagons and spread the chalk over a lot more ground than would have been covered by the bucket brigades. As more wagon loads of chalk arrived they were quickly emptied spread by the workers and the entire job was accomplished in one day—a feat that would have taken several days using the old method.

One of the monks, seeing the new operation, suggested a type of wooden auger be installed on the rear of each wagon that could be turned by crank as the wagon proceeded across the field thus more evenly distributing the chalk behind the wagon which would minimize the need for the rakers. A skilled carver was set to work to devise the tool and a prototype was completed in about two weeks. It was installed in the back of one of the freight wagons used to haul the chalk and was an immediate success. Besides the wagon driver, only the two shovelers were required to keep the chalk supplied to the auger apparatus plus another to walk alongside the wagon to crank the auger as the wagon moved across the field. Thus, the labor for each wagon load of chalk was reduced from about twelve people to four and made the process much more efficient as well as a lot faster. Soon three or four fields could be "marled" in one day instead of just one.

The carvers at the chalk works were kept busy making and fitting "augers" to the backs of wagons, carts and anything else that moved on wheels as word spread of the new technique for "marling" the fields.

It was during one of the demonstrations of the new technique to a noble near Winchester that disaster struck. Two of the Green Rose team—one knight and his squire—were demonstrating the "marling" technique with a wagon and crew to the noble and his escort when a band of brigands rode down out of the trees and surrounded the party demanding money. When the two members of the Green Rose team refused a fight immediately broke out and lasted for several minutes.

Although the defenders put up a good fight, there were too many of the brigands and the Green Rose team got the worst of it. The knight was severely injured by a sword wound in his leg, two of the noble's escorts were killed and the other two wounded and the robber band rode off with all the money and trappings of the group, including the horses. The robbers also kidnapped the noble whom they planned to hold for ransom. All that was left was the chalk wagon and horse, the driver and cart workers, and the Green Rose squire along with the three wounded men. The squire had the remaining chalk cleared from the wagon and loaded the wounded men on it. He and the driver left immediately for Winchester and the hospital they knew was there operated by the monks from Hyde Abbey. The cart workers were left behind to notify the noble's manor house of the crime and to dispose of the dead.

It was a fairly quick trip into Winchester for the chalk wagon as the poor horse was hard pressed in order to render aid as quickly as possible to the wounded. It took nearly an hour-and-a-half to reach the hospital grounds and turn the now chalk-covered wounded over to the monks. As it turned out the chalk served to stop the bleeding on most of the wounds, including those of the knight, and hastened their recoveries. One of the hospital monks was so impressed that he ordered a supply of chalk to be used to stop the bleeding for other patients.

The squire commandeered the chalk wagon for a quick return to the chalk mines where he reported in to the rest of the Green Rose team and an extensive search for the bandits was begun. It was to last for three weeks before the searchers found a peasant who had observed the band and knew where it was hiding in the woods. As it turned out the robbers were camped very near the hospital at a place called "Sleepers Hill."

The Green Rose team organized a force, including the guard from the kidnapped noble's manor, and surprised the sleeping bandits who gave up after a brief struggle. The noble was found chained to a wall in a nearby cave and freed. He was very grateful for his rescue, but the records fail to show if he did or did not purchase a chalk auger from the Abbey Chalk Works.

The event did serve as another "wake up call" to the Green Rose team to increase its efforts at military training and it began getting back to its original assignment of increasing the trained military presence in its assigned territories.

However, by October of 1452, another diversion arose to challenge Team 9. By this time it was apparent that the one ship owned by the abbey was not sufficient to meet the combined export needs of both Beaulieu and Netley abbeys. One of the monks at Beaulieu, a former ship fitter, suggested the Order build its own ships and that was the proposition presented to the Green Rose team by the abbot at Netley.

By this time the knight injured earlier had recovered enough to begin returning to normal and he and his squire were sent into the Southampton area, famous for its shipbuilding, to scout out the possibilities asked by the abbot. They left Netley Abbey early one September morning in 1453 along with two of the monks who had shown exceptional fighting abilities during military training. The four traveled on horseback leading two other pack horses traveling south along the banks of Southampton Water through Fareham and Gosport to Portsmouth.

They were gone for more than thirty days before they returned to Netley Abbey to report on their findings.

"We found several shipbuilding yards willing to work with us and plenty of unemployed shipwrights," the knight told the rest of the Green Rose team upon their first meeting after returning. However, our ship fitter monk kept us going until we took ship for the Isle of Wight and we landed at Cowes at the mouth of the River Medina. There we found an old shipbuilding operation manned by two monks from Quarr Abbey at Ryde. Our monk immediately took to his two Cistercian brothers and we were escorted along the coast road to the Abbey where we met with the abbot. He heard our story and immediately offered to work with us to restore and expand the shipbuilding operation although he told us it was pretty much shut down due to a lack of quality shipbuilding oak lumber. When we told him we could ship an ample supply of good quality wood, he was very enthusiastic about the operation and is willing to share in the cost of rebuilding and re-equipping the site on a 50-50 share basis.

When the lead monk heard this story, he immediately invited the abbot and the ship fitter monk into the chapter house at Netley for a formal meeting. The monk was allowed to expand upon what his two Quarr monk friends had told him of the ship building operation and he had brought along a list of needed supplies and tools they had compiled. After a lengthy discussion, the abbot agreed to the plan and said that Netley would share the cost with Quarr on a 50-50 basis, but would provide ample shipping for lease to Beaulieu Abbey and any others that wished to operate their own ships.

With this information, the Green Rose knight, squire, and the two monks again set out for Quarr Abbey with a properly signed "agreement" to complete the deal. They dropped off the ship fitter monk at the old shipyards so he could begin preparations for the shipload of lumber, supplies and tools the rest of the Green Rose team was busy assembling. After the agreement was signed, the abbot at Quarr appointed five of his skilled monks to assist in the rebuilding of the old shipyard and promised immediate payment for his half of the coming load of supplies. He also agreed to the hiring of some of the local skilled craftsmen who were available at the village of Cowes who had been out of work for some time.

The knight and squire returned to Cowes, with the five assigned monks, and began to visit with villagers to find the most skilled ship fitters and craftsmen. They also contacted a local sail maker and signed a contract for him to outfit the new ships with the appropriate sails and cordage. By the time the Netley ship arrived with the basic supplies, work was already underway to improve and extend the size of the operations so that larger vessels could be built. In conjunction with the expert monks and local craftsmen, they decided to build frigate-sized ships capable of hauling a sizeable cargo of goods and also enough armaments to ward off a pirate attack until the ship could reach safer waters. The first keel laid at the refurbished shipyards was of a special design by one of the skilled villagers and, as it turned out, was streamlined enough to move the ship faster in all kinds of winds than currently designed ships. In the twenty or more years the ship was in use, after its commissioning a year later, its crew never had to ward off an attack. It could always hoist enough sail to easily outrun its pursuers.

In the first three years of its operation, the Abbey Shipyards at Cowes turned out five new frigate-sized sailing vessels which were immediately put to use by the three abbeys in shipping products to ports all over Europe as well as Wales and Scotland. It was a profitable venture and yielded much income to the two partner abbeys. In its later years, the shipyards turned out heavily armed frigates for the Royal Navy. But this was after the abbeys turned the operation over to the locals at Cowes and merely collected a share of the revenues from each ship completed and sold as a return on the original investments. The "abbey ships," as they were called by the sailors who manned them, developed a loyal following. Sailors believed the ships were "protected from above" whenever they went into battle. None of the ships was ever captured or sunk while in military service.

Early in 1453 a dispatch came from St. Albans requesting that Team 9 begin developing a pig breeding and raising operation to provide hides for the leather enterprises in operation by other Green Rose teams. After discussion with the abbot at Netley Abbey, the team decided to set up such an operation on the abbey's grange near Avebury where it was raising sheep and dairy cows. The pig operation would go well in harmony with the dairy as any excess milk could be fed to the pigs. While the hides could be shipped to other Green Rose teams, the meat could be turned into smoked bacon, hams, and other products for sale through the various market places.

The monks at the Avebury grange were not pleased to learn they were going to have to raise pigs. That blow was softened somewhat when the Green Rose team explained it had permission from the abbot to bring local villagers into the operation who were experienced in raising the critters. A visit to Avebury yielded six villagers who were willing to work for wages and food. In addition, the team found one farmer who operated a small scale smoke and curing house for hams and bacon and entered into a partnership to expand his operation to take care of that part of the new operation.

Pens and rearing stations were established at the Avebury Grange and the Green Rose took along a knowledgeable villager to begin purchasing breeding stock for the new enterprise. It turned out they didn't have far to go as the local had an uncle who was trying to sell his hogs and retire. The team worked out a deal whereby the abbey would lease his land, buy his hogs, and let him continue to live on his farm. They took half of the pigs to the abbey grange and left the other half where they found them and soon had two operations up and running. Pretty soon they had lots of little piglets rooting around on the two farms and began working on the killing, skinning, and curing operations. It was fall before the first pigs were slaughtered, the hides were shipped to the glove maker in Yeoville at the request of St. Albans, and the carcasses were sent to the local farmer for processing.

The Green Rose team was pretty lucky in its choice of the farmer for processing. He was innovative in his curing process for the hams and used sugar instead of salt to cure them. He also smoked them with apple wood which gave them a unique flavor that quickly became a favorite in the area and even London. The bacon also was sugar-cured and popular. Other cuts of meat were dipped in a coating of honey which was allowed to dry before the now well-preserved meat was sent to various markets to be sold at the abbey-sponsored stalls. One enterprising lay volunteer from the abbey, who was manning a stall, set up a brazier and cooked pork to hand out as free samples. He soon sold all of his meat and had the villagers demanding more. This idea was spread to other marketplaces and the abbey's enterprises sold all the pork, hams, and bacon it could produce. It became to be known as "saintly pork" after the lay volunteer, who originated the "free sample" idea, was called "St. Pork" by the local villagers—a term of endearment.

Interestingly enough, the pork operation and sale enhanced the demand for cheese produced by the dairy operations and the abbey benefited from that, too.

All of the various abbey operations provided for full time supervision by the Green Rose team and it was kept busy all through the rest of the year with little time to devote to military training although there was always some ongoing effort at that. Several troops of men already had been trained and equipped through the coast watching operations and this effort continued to expand. Troops and guards also had been trained for all of the nobles in the area of Netley Abbey who had responded to its earlier calls for help in feeding and housing travelers and the dinners, especially at Halloween, were increasingly popular at the abbey.

Team 9 already had its hands full when a request came from Hyde Abbey at Winchester for woolen cloth to be used primarily in the abbey's hospital operations. The original contact had been made when the abbey monks cared for the injured knight from the Green Rose team. Since the team "owed a debt" to the monks at Hyde Abbey there was no hesitation on its part to help after they received permission from the abbot at Netley.

Netley Abbey already had small wool cloth milling operation at Newbury where there also were monk-run hospitals as well as a leper hostel for female lepers dedicated to Mary Magdalene. The team quickly set out for Newbury to inspect the abbey's operations there. What they found was a small mill along the River Kennet just west of Newbury being used to process a small amount of wool cloth used primarily by the abbey itself.

The production of good-quality woolen cloth had been an expanding industry in most of England helped along by the introduction of water-powered fulling stocks. Fulling was a vital process converting a relatively loosely-woven fabric into a more closely knit one by soaking it in fresh clean water and fuller's earth, and then pounding it by foot (like crushing grapes). Fulling stocks were heavy wooden hammers driven by water wheels which greatly improved efficiency and needed less labor to make the cloth.

Since the abbey's fulling mill was small, there was no way to enlarge it without stopping production for a long period of time. The team decided the best approach was to build a new, larger capacity mill, a few yards upstream from the older mill and this is what it set out to do. It took nearly a year to construct and equip the mill, to build a levee that channeled more water through its turning blades, and to secure enough hand woven wool cloth to fully utilize the capacity of the mill.

When it was at last ready to operate, there were many components besides the pounding. The cloth was first washed with a solution of water and potash to clean the fibers and then it was soaked in fuller's earth (not the pig dung or stale urine used in some operations) to thicken it and give it a firm structure. This was done in a large trough below the heavy oak hammers of the mill which were used to pound and soften the cloth. Each time a hammer struck the cloth bundle, the shape of the hammer rotated the cloth a little for a more uniform action and to prevent damaging the cloth.

After the fulling operation, the cloth was hung on what was known as "tenter frames" used for drying and stretching the fulled cloth. The frames were made of upright wooden posts with a fixed upper and lower rail. The lower rail could be adjusted by the use of pegs or wedges. Both rails were fitted with tenter-hooks (L-shaped double-pointed nails). The wet cloth was hooked by its edges to both rails and the lower rail adjusted to draw the cloth tight and even in width.

It was quite an operation and soon enough cloth was being produced to supply all the hospitals in the area with some left over to sell on the open market. A lot of the finished cloth was exported to England by the abbey's ships. The monks continued to operate the older mill and only were willing to use cloth made from it.

Only one other incident is recorded in the annals of Team 9 and that occurred in November of 1454 at Maydenheth (now Maidenhead), located along the Bath Road from London to Bristol. The town served as a way station for travelers since it was one day's travel from London. The Green Rose team leader and his squire were returning to Netley Abbey after a meeting with the Green Rose leader in St. Albans when they stopped for the night at The Orkney Arms at Maidenhead. They were in the pub part of the inn sitting at a table waiting for their dinner when a party of four came into the pub and sat at an adjoining table. They were dressed for the road and had only stopped their coach en route to Bristol from London so they could have dinner. All wore the emblem of the crown on their cloaks so the Green Rose team was keen to hear any conversation.

What they heard was news that the King had recovered his senses and was about to return to power in time for the Christmas celebrations. The couriers were en route to spread the news to the king's Lancastrian supporters in the various castles and towns throughout the kingdom.

When the four couriers had finished their dinner and re-boarded their coach, the Green Rose listeners immediately rose, paid for their meal, and packed up and left the inn en route back to St. Albans to report the news. This, of course, set off a chain political reaction leading to the recall of Team 9 to St. Albans in April of the following year.

Chapter 18—The Breadbasket

When Team ten approached Hailes Abbey for the first time its members were surprised at the numbers of people along the road leading to the abbey until their Cistercian guide told them they were "pilgrims" on their way to worship at the altar containing the "Precious Blood of Christ" presented to the abbey in 1270 by Edmund of Cornwall, son of Richard of Cornwall the abbey's founder, and guaranteed to be genuine by the patriarch of Jerusalem who later became Pope Urban IV.

The pilgrims were of all ages from young to old and in all stages of health from firm to infirm, but seemed to be a happy lot as they waved and shouted to the team members led by the robed monk which they called a "grey monk" due to the off white color of his robe. Most were very respectful as if they recognized the noble purpose of the party passing by.

The monk told Team ten they were heading for a "lucky abbey" as pilgrims are a main source of revenue for the institution and are induced to visit the relics owned by the abbey. The "Precious Blood of Christ" was indeed a rare relic and attracted many visitors to the abbey, he said.

As it subsequently turned out, the abbot at Hailes Abbey soon explained the institution was not free from financial difficulties which he blamed on the black plague in 1361-1362 which killed many of the monks and lay brothers and put the abbey into financial hardship for nearly the past 100 years. One of the reasons, he said, he agreed to receiving the Green Rose team was to help him restore the abbey to a stronger financial basis. In addition, he said, the abbey was under constant strain by raiding bandits who were making off with sheep, cattle and any other assets they could lay their hands on. He told of one group of raiders who came over the wall and into the abbey grounds proper before they were finally driven off, but only after killing two of the monks.

"We have only a small group left and, if it weren't for our pilgrims, we probably would have to close the abbey," he said.

"Let us have a few days to inspect the grounds and the nearby granges and see what we can do about the bandits and raids. That seems to be our first priority," the team leader told the abbot.

Early one morning, about a week later, the team was inspecting one of the sheep herds when the abbey's bell began sounding in rapid fashion. This was a universal signal that trouble was afoot and the team immediately returned to the abbey where it could see several of the monks surrounded by mounted bandits in one of the inner courtyards. The monks were all putting up a fight, but were sadly outnumbered when the Green Rose team galloped through the main entrance gate to the abbey grounds. The bandits heard and saw them coming and turned to meet the attackers. The lead knight signaled the four squires to stand back and begin shooting arrows while he and the three other knights jumped into the fray. With the accurate arrows fired by the squires, the fierce combat excellence of the Green Rose knights and the monks biting at the rear of the bandits, the contest was soon decided and those bandits, still able, quickly rode off followed by accurate shots from the archers who knocked five of the fleeing men from their horses.

In all two of the monks were injured, but not seriously, the abbot sustained an arm injury, one of the knights received a minor cut on his leg, and three of the visiting pilgrims were killed. There were fifteen of the bandits either killed or seriously wounded. The wounded were treated by the monks and all recovered. The wounded bandits were locked in a room with no windows and one of the monks stood guard outside. The lead Green Rose knight conducted several interrogations of the wounded bandits before finally turning them over to the local authorities. They were subsequently hanged. However, the team benefitted from much valuable information about the bandits which would later be put to good use.

The team continued its inspections of the abbey, it's defenses, and its possibilities for economic gains until it was time to leave for the Green Rose confab at St. Albans. Due to the existing dangers to the abbey, it was decided to leave one knight and one squire behind to continue efforts at protecting the abbey until the return of the rest of the team.

Things were still calm at the abbey when the bulk of the Green Rose team returned from St. Albans, but the knight and squire left behind reported spotting bandits spying on the abbey from various vantage points. The knight and squire had been conducting training classes in sword fighting and had developed "pikes" for some of the monks to use against mounted raiders. He reported about three of the monks were now pretty skilled in the use of arms and that some twelve of the visiting pilgrims had agreed to stay at the abbey for the next few months in order to help protect it. These, too, had been receiving training. The knight indicated he could now call on twenty to twenty-five fighting men, not counting any of the Green Rose team.

This was good news to the Green Rose team leader and he congratulated the knight and squire saying they had made good use of their time while the rest of them were away. He immediately spent the next two hours filling in the left behind team members about the St. Albans conclave and what was to be expected of Team ten in the future.

This done, they met again with the abbot and got personal letters of introduction to the various nobles owning estates in the neighborhood of the abbey and immediately divided into four teams of one knight and one squire each to begin canvassing the manors. It was tedious work and required a great deal of patience, but the efforts ultimately paid off when three of the manors agreed to form a pact to protect themselves and the abbey. This brought about 150 armed and mostly mounted men to the defense of the abbey in time of need and the Green Rose team set about training them. It took six weeks before the men were in shape to fight, and little did they know it would be sooner rather than later that they would be called upon to use their new skills.

A second thing accomplished by the Green Rose team during their visits across the countryside was to offer a reward to anyone who spotted approaching bandits and could warn the abbey or any of the three noble manors in time to sound the alarm.

It was before first light some two weeks later that a rider came pounding for admittance at the abbey gate. When he was admitted, he told of the approach of a mounted force of bandits heading for the abbey via Stancombe woods just outside of the village of Winchcombe. He thought there were more than fifty as he held up all ten of his fingers five times. Riders were immediately dispatched to the manors of the participating nobles with the news of approaching trouble.

The Green Rose team marshaled its forces in the abbey courtyard. It could count on six archers, including the four squires and two skilled pilgrims, ten monk footmen armed with pikes, six knights including two of the visiting pilgrims and some fifteen swordsmen, including monks. The best the defenders could do, the lead knight decided, was to marshal its forces in the orchard south of the abbey. He dismounted the squires and gave their horses to four of the other swordsmen and had each fighter take refuge behind one of the trees in the orchard in a line. The line was fifteen men long at the front backed by another ten slightly to the rear with the six knights at the front. Two of the armed monks were left at the abbey gates to open them in case the defenders had to make a hasty retreat behind the walls of the abbey.

It was about ten o'clock in the morning and the waiting troops were getting restless when the first of the invaders was spotted coming down off the hill from Stancombe wood. The lead knight cautioned his men to stay hidden and counted sixty-five mounted bandits approaching the abbey. At three to one odds, he thought they were pretty evenly matched, but he didn't say it out loud.

When the approaching bandits were about ten yards from the edge of the orchard, he signaled the archers to begin shooting. Each of the first six arrows found a target and put the invaders in a frenzy. Just then the six mounted knights made their charge followed by the pikemen and mounted swordsmen. In the meantime the archers continued losing arrows at the flanks of the bandits with several more hits to their credit.

The element of surprise went a long way towards helping the defenders in the first few minutes of the battle, but the overpowering strength of the enemy was beginning to show when trumpets sounded and two of the forces from the noble manors arrived on the scene and attacked the bandits from the left and right flanks. This turned the tide of battle within a few minutes and the bandits were beginning to withdraw when another set of trumpets sounded and forty more mounted troops from the third manor came pounding full speed down the same slope as had the bandits. They were surrounded and soon began throwing down their arms and surrendering.

The abbot said it was a miracle and spent the next twelve hours in prayer. Not one of the abbey's defenders was wounded in the battle and only three of the troops from the noble's manors were hurt although one received a mortal wound to his stomach and died two days later. Some twenty-six of the raiders had been killed or seriously wounded and ten others had minor wounds. Most of those killed were struck by arrows. The Green Rose team turned all of the bandits over to the houses of the lords who stripped them, beat them, and subsequently hanged all but one. That one had his right hand cut off, bound up, and was sent on his way to warn others not to attack the abbey again or the same fate would befall them.

One week later, the abbot sent out messengers inviting the households of the three nobles to join in a celebration feast at the abbey. The next day the abbey grounds were packed as some 300 people came to celebrate victory over the bandits. Four oxen, six roe, and five sheep were slaughtered and roasted over open fires along with other goodies prepared by the abbey cooks. And, there was plenty of wine and beer available as the feasting lasted for more than eight hours. It was dark by the time the abbey returned to normal, but a good time was had by all and several pledges of aid were given to the abbot as a result.

Looking back, the Green Rose team leader believed this was the turning point in achieving economic success for the abbey although it sure didn't look like it at the time and the abbot almost bankrupted the abbey in providing food and drink for the celebration. In about three days, wagon loads of goods began arriving at the abbey gate from the various nobles around the countryside as news of the victory over the bandits spread. In addition, six more nobles pledged their troops to the defense forces and the Green Rose team was busy melding them into the overall defensive posture for the area. When it was all decided, there was pretty much a twenty to twenty-five mile circle around the abbey that was under constant patrol and protection by the troops and raids became non-existent for the first time in the history of the abbey.

Strangers entering into this protective circle were often challenged by the watchers and whenever they couldn't prove who they were or why they were in the area, they were turned away. Pilgrims headed towards the abbey were welcomed and helped along their way by the understanding troops. The result was no more raids and an actual increase in the numbers of pilgrims visiting the abbey. Since each of the pilgrims was offered a chance to make a donation or purchase a badge proving he/she had visited the site, abbey revenues were increased proportionately.

Several of the monks, with permission of the abbot, performed a play at the evening supper extolling the fight against the bandits and how God had provided the means to defeat them. The play became quite popular and cups were passed at its conclusion for donations and this, too, added to the economic recovery of the abbey.

It was July of 1451 before the Green Rose team finally hit on the idea that eventually was to put Hailes Abbey back into good financial condition and pretty much assure its future. One of the squires, seeing the constant stream of pilgrims visiting the abbey, came up with the idea of asking them what type of skills they had and then asking those who could be put to immediate use to stay on at the abbey for a period of six months or up to a year by assuring them board and room in return for work.

The abbot was reluctant at first since revenues from pilgrims buying badges and donations at the dinners had brought much needed revenues to the abbey and he didn't want to offend any of the pilgrims. When he was reminded how these same pilgrims responded when the abbey was under duress from constant raids, he finally consented to give it a try.

The way it turned out, most of the pilgrims asked to stay on based upon their particular skills, were honored at being asked and about forty percent accepted the opportunity on the spot. Another five percent thought about it overnight before accepting. The other fifty-five percent either had employment waiting for their return from the visitation or simply were not inclined to work for no wages. In any case, the abbey secured more than thirty volunteers in the first week of the program with skills ranging from stonework, carpentry, cooking, blacksmithing, and horse training to leatherworking. All of these skills were much in need at the abbey and the men were put to work immediately on a number of projects. The work was hard—ten hours per day—but three meals were provided as well as clothing and a bed. There was no requirement that these volunteers participate in any religious activities at the abbey, but many of them did by choice. In subsequent weeks the abbey staff swelled by some fifty more volunteers and some of these were assigned to the various granges operated by the abbey.

The sudden influx of volunteer assistance put an immediate strain on the abbey's finances to provide sufficient food and clothing and drink, but a call for help again to the supporting nobles brought immediate assistance. After several months the abbot insisted all of these "loans" be repaid and they were much to the surprise and delight of the nobles. In the meantime, the abbey's sheep and cow herds were allowed to increase for the first time in nearly 100 years since there now was sufficient help to properly care for and watch after the animals.

At one of the neighborhood sheep and wool markets, the abbot met with the abbot from Dore Abbey in Hertfordshire. Dore Abbey was famous for its Relic of the Holy Cross and the Tomb of Lady Matilda de Bohun who represented the power of healing. When the Dore abbot heard of the success using pilgrims at Hailes Abbey, he asked if he could send a couple of monks to spend some time at Hailes to see how the procedure worked. This was done and the experiment was soon expanded to Dore Abbey where it met with similar success only with a slight twist. The Dore abbot only recruited those persons who claimed they had been healed by the power of Lady Matilda. He used those with various skills needed at the abbey to work on local projects, but he also sent those without such skills to accompany monks visiting the various marketplaces in the vicinity of the abbey. The pilgrim's job was to explain the miraculous cure he had received. This program soon paid off as the numbers of those seeking the healing power at the abbey increased by nearly forty percent in just a few short weeks.

Meanwhile, at Hailes Abbey, the nightly entertainment play had evolved into the story of how God had saved the abbey. The result was an even higher percentage rate of pilgrims willing to serve the abbey for a limited time period. The abbot was so impressed that he organized a second performance to be a part of the church services held regularly at the abbey. Only this time instead of saving the Abbey, God was busy saving sinners from such vanities as greed, pride, the devil, evil, etc. In all there were a series of six presentations developed over a period of months. Church services began to increase in attendance at the abbey as word of the performances made the rounds of the market places. It wasn't long until some of the nobles began requesting a performance during feasting festivities in their Great Halls and a traveling troupe was established to help "spread the word and deeds of God," as the abbot proclaimed. These types of morality plays had been presented all over England and Europe for a number of years, but never by a Cistercian Order. Their success for Hailes Abbey was such that two other traveling troupes were organized and sent out by request. Since there was a fee charged for each performance and the actors were allowed to "pass the cup" at the end of each play, the troupes brought in even more revenues to the coffers at the abbey.

It was March of 1452 before Team ten was asked to branch out again and this time the request came directly from St. Albans in the form of a Benedictine Monk sent to Hailes. He was of Italian descent and was skilled at weaving straw into useful craft items. The Green Rose leader at St. Albans, with permission of the bishop, sent him to Hailes to help the economic situation there even though it was a Cistercian Abbey and not a Benedictine one.

Fortunately, he brought a cartload of special wheat (corn) straw along with him because it would have been mostly impossible to find it near Hailes Abbey at this time of year. It was a wheat variety with a hollow stem grown extensively for use as roof thatching. Since all cereal grain crops fell under the common generic term of "corn," most of the finished products were termed "corn dollies" and contained a number of named patterns. It was quite a complicated art and when the Benedictine monk showed some of his work, the monks at Hailes were somewhat in awe that such beautiful things could be made from straw.

Some of them even tried their hand at straw plaiting, but not many were very successful at it. When one of the Green Rose team encouraged the monk to begin teaching a class in the craft to women in the nearby villages, that's when the enterprise just seemed to explode. Soon straw plaited ornaments, leaf shapes, stars, snow flakes, etc., were being sold at the market places as the women learned to make them.

The Green Rose team set out to find the proper straw for the craft. The Benedictine monk told them the best fields were in Worcestershire and gave them a sample to carry with them. There was no problem finding farmers who grew the "thatching" wheat, the problem was finding those who would agree to cut the stalks with a hand sickle close to the ground, cut them when the grain was ripe but the first joint on the stalk was still green, and properly dry them under a roof so the morning dew doesn't continue to make them damp. The small sheaves need to be stood upright for the first two or three days to allow moisture to drain down. They need to be inside at night to avoid the dew. Then the sheaves need to be opened out and the straw turned regularly to dry. After that the straws need to be cleaned and stripped and then graded according to size—small, medium, or large in diameter.

The abbey agreed to pay the farmers based upon the quality of stalks they could provide as well as the quantity. The small stalks brought the higher prices as they were used for the more intricate designs which sold for the best prices. Each fall, the abbey would send wagons to those farmers who had agreed to process the stalks according to specifications and pay them at a base rate equivalent to full price they received for grain for the larger stalks, half the price for medium stalks, and double the price for smaller stalks. Thus each farmer could receive a higher cash return for his crop than it would bring just for grain or for thatching. The straw was brought to the abbey and stored in dry sheds and then sold to individual straw plaiters at the abbey or nearby market places. The abbey not only received a profit from the resale of the specialized straw, but also from the sale of completed pieces at the abbey owned stalls in the marketplaces where the peasant women would bring their completed work.

All of the specialized tools needed for the craft were handmade at the abbey and put together in kits for use by students in the monk's classes. These kits could then be purchased on a share basis using money earned from the sale of finished goods. Included in these kits was a sharp knife for splitting straws, a sharpening stone, strong thread colored the same as the straw, clothes pegs, and a smooth board for pinning the straw along with a supply of sharpened pins. Women could re-supply all these materials and the straw from the marketplace stalls. Some of the more enterprising plaiters bought the straw and used the seeds to plant their own patches of wheat and others used barley or other stems, but most found it easier and still profitable to buy straw from the abbey. The golden color of the wheat straw plaits brought in the higher prices at the market.

It wasn't long before straw-plaiting guilds sprang up over England and the industry grew and prospered for a time. The Benedictine monk returned to St. Albans and eventually laid the groundwork for a straw hat making industry that became quite notable in later years.

In September of 1452, the records show another economic crisis occurred at the Abbey when Southern England had an excellent year for tree crops and the various abbey granges, including the orchards just outside the Hailes Abbey walls, were bursting with fruit. In years past any dropped fruit would be gathered and fed to the hogs and cattle.

There was a small cider making operation at the abbey and this had been expanded as the popularity of the nightly dinners grew, but the monks reported too much crop was going to be produced and would have to go to waste—deemed somewhat sinful by the Cistercians.

Dore Abbey, a few miles north of Hailes, was located in the heart of the apple and pear raising country of England. There were many productive apple and pear orchards in the area and most farm fields even had fruit trees growing in the middle where the farmers would raise their crops around them. Dore, which had adopted the Hailes system of utilizing pilgrims for labor, seemed to the Green Rose team to be an ideal spot in which to begin processing apple and pear juice into cider and Perry, two of the more common drinks of the age. After seeking permission from the Hailes abbot, four members of Team ten rode up to Dore to suggest the enterprise to the abbot there.

Due to the success of copying the pilgrim idea from Hailes, the Dore abbot was eager to begin another enterprise with the Green Rose team and had also been wondering what to do with all the excess fruit. The abbey operated Llyncoed and Llanfair Cilgoed granges, among others, and while they didn't adjoin both had large acreage planted to apple and pear trees. The abbot suggested Llyncoed grange as the most practical site since it was situated along Troddi brook which would supply plenty of fresh water for the operation.

When the Green Rose team reached the grange, it saw the setup as pretty typical with a large oratory, accommodation for the resident lay brethren, and the required barn, stable and animal sheds. One of the monks at the grange pointed out a shed which was already equipped with a cider press. The team immediately got together with some of the lay volunteers at the grange and found two that were skilled carpenters. These men were put to work making two larger presses along with the necessary catch troughs and wooden pipes (barrels which can contain up to 120 gallons of juice) needed to process the crop. Since the same type of press is used for pears as for apples, the team opted to use one new press for apples and the other for pears. One of the other men was a skilled barrel maker and he was put to use making smaller barrels to house the finished products.

The next order of business was to secure the use of carts or wagons and teams to haul the picked fruit to the presses. For this the team visited nearby villages hiring peasants who had suitable teams and carts/wagons to haul the fruit. They were to be paid by the load with the fee dependent upon the size of their cart or wagon. When they had ten carts/wagons lined up for each of the two Dore granges, they sent word back to Hailes for the remainder of the team to do the same so there would be enough transportation to handle the crop on those granges.

Although there are some differences in the cider making versus the Perry making, the processes are quite similar. First the fruit is picked and shipped to the processing area where it is washed and dumped into a crusher, sometimes called a "scratcher." The crushed fruit is known as "pomace" or "pommy" and it is layered into the press where the juice is extracted and runs into the trough below the press. After the first extraction, the layers of pomace are broken up by hand, and a second pressing is done. The packed pomace blocks are then set out in the sun to dry and used to make pectin or for cattle and hog feed. The juice is piped into the large barrels and, with the bung removed, is allowed a natural ferment which begins in about twenty-four hours and lasts for several weeks. The fermenting juice is "topped off" periodically during this period with fresh juice until fermentation ceases. The bung is then replaced and the barrels are moved to huge storage racks inside a protected shed (in this case the large barn) and allowed to age for five or six months although it is sometimes used before that.

In the case of pears made into Perry, the pears are left to "age" for about a week after picking before the processing begins. After the pears are crushed, the pomace is allowed to stand for a period of time before crushing. This allows the pomace to lose tannins and aides in the clearing of the finished drink. After that the fermenting and aging processes are mostly identical. Again, the longer the Perry ages the more mellow and favorable it becomes.

To say that the first year of the operation went off without a hitch would be overstating the case. Records seem to show that several problems occurred during the processing—one of which was that the lay volunteers were found to be "tapping" the fermenting barrels and drinking up the profits. A guard had to be put on the barrels during this period in order to permit the process to fully exploit its natural course. The "tapping" was discovered when one of the monks found that some of the fermenting barrels needed to be "topped up" more frequently than others.

The whole operation was intensely labor driven. During the height of the cider and Perry making period more than forty lay volunteers were working ten-hour days with another two hours spent in cleaning the presses and equipment for the next day's crush. It took nearly three weeks to process all the apples and pears that were shipped to Llyncoed Grange and when the crushing was completed there were fifteen huge barrels of cider and twelve of Perry in the fermentation process. Since each barrel held about 120 gallons of juice this meant the team had 1,800 gallons of cider and 1,400 gallons of Perry for which it had to find markets.

Through conferences with both abbots, it was decided to sell the cider and Perry in one-gallon crock clay jugs so they had to set up a pottery at the grange in order to make the crocks. Since they couldn't identify the product by the name of either abbey, the decided to call it Bishop's Cider and Bishop's Perry which would be fired onto the surface of each of the jugs. It took about two months to get the pottery operation started and the first of the jugs were being produced by the time it came to bottle the cider and Perry. The finished product became an instant hit since it had been aged the full five months and most other cider and Perry never lasted that long before it was consumed.

In subsequent years, one of the more enterprising lay volunteers at the grange made a batch of culled pears into a pear jam and this became quite popular after it was marketed in ceramic jars under the label of Bishop's Pear Jam. For some reason it was the name that seemed to drive purchasing of the jam rather than the jam itself. Apparently no one thought of making apple jelly as there is no record of that ever being marketed.

It was February of 1453 before Team ten received word from St. Albans there was a looming shortage of draft animals to pull the carts and wagons that were being built by other teams. Since the team had been involved in other animal activities and the cattle and sheep herds at Hailes Abbey were increasing under good protection, this was a good choice by St. Albans as the monks were raising cows for meat, dairy products, leather, and as draught animals.

Dore Abbey again seemed the proper choice since the cider making season was over there were plenty of lay volunteers available and they could be used to raise and train the cows since an oxen was nothing much other than an "educated" cow. And, something about the soil, water and climate of Herefordshire had enabled the Abbey to develop some unique qualities in the cattle on one of its granges allowing them to endure heat and cold and still forage sufficiently for food with grass and grass products as their main feed. To be sure the abbey monks fed the main dairy herds the apple and pear pulp left over from cider and Perry making, but the cattle were pretty much on their own when it came to grazing.

The cattle were said to be descended from small red cattle of Roman

Briton and mixed with a large Welsh breed once numerous along the borders of England and Wales, but that was a matter of speculation. Regardless, they were a hardy breed and quite capable of pulling heavy loads.

The Green Rose Team was not familiar with herding cattle so it had to lean on the experience of the current monks and lay volunteer herders to find out all that was involved in handling and training the beasts. It turned out to be a challenging job.

One of the Dore Abbey monks had actually trained several of the animals in the past to pull carts for the abbey and had the rudimentary knowledge required, but had no idea of how to put that training to use on a large scale. After he explained to the team leader what was required, the team developed a plan to expand the monk's ideas so that several animals could be trained at the same time.

Essentially they built two training enclosures along with adjacent holding pens. Carpenters were put to work building training yokes of varying sizes since training the animals is only successful if you start them at a young age. The male cows were generally larger than the females, they could pull heavier loads, and it was these animals that the team decided to use.

Herders were instructed to begin working with male calves as soon as they were weaned from their mothers as part of a "gentling" process. Thus, the males selected for further training were already used to human handling which made the job easier. The team recruited twelve lay brothers from the abbey to serve as trainers and by April they had enough calves to begin. Each of the calves was fitted with a rough leather halter attached to a long line. Trainers would lead the calves around inside the training enclosures teaching them to "go," "stop," "turn left," "turn right," and "back up" in a process that could take days or even weeks. Some of the calves fought every step of the way and some were quite docile and took well to the training.

After the calves began responding to the commands with some regularity, they were attached to training yokes in matched size pairs and learned to work as a team, again at the end of a rope. A third phase of the training came when the yokes were attached to a two-wheeled cart and the young calves were trained to "pull." Larger yokes were used as the calves grew in size as well as heavier carts and finally wagons.

It was a common custom for the driver of an ox team to walk alongside the team while it was working or pulling a cart, but these oxen were trained to respond from commands given while the driver was riding the cart. In this fashion the team eliminated the necessity for the gait of the oxen to match the gait of the ox driver and the carts and wagons could make better and somewhat faster progress during each day's travel although the bad roads often played an important factor in that situation.

It was an interesting sight to see the trainers working with their horned beasts especially when a beast decided it didn't want to be trained. It took patience and a firm hand in order to master the situation. The horns actually held the yokes in place whenever the oxen lowered their heads to back up or slow down or when pulling a cart on a downhill slope.

The latter was the most difficult situation to master since yoked oxen cannot slow a load similar to harnessed horses. The team had to fit all of its training vehicles with wooden blocks pressed up against the front and rear wheels using a lever device mounted alongside the driver's station. Thus, the driver had to learn to handle the ox team with one hand leaving the other hand free to work the brake. Some drivers improvised and used a foot to hold the brake lever.

As soon as the team discovered this reality—the brake—it sent word to St. Albans along with a drawing so that the brake could be built as a part of the wagons and carts being constructed elsewhere.

By the time the training process was well underway, each lay volunteer was working with up to four of the animals each day so there was a maximum of thirty-six animals being trained at one time. Since the training process was a long one, it appeared to the team that more trainers and training enclosures were needed in order to train a sufficient number of the animals. Two more teams of twelve each lay volunteers were sought from the abbey and each trainer was assigned two trainees for a six-week period. After that each trainee was given his own group of four animals to train. This proved to be very successful and the abbey soon had more than 100 oxen in training at one time. Since the whole training process took several months, only one batch of oxen could be trained each year, but it was a good start. In later years, the Dore Abbey trained oxen were greatly sought after and commanded a good price. They were prized for their stamina, their willingness to work, and for the ease of their care and handling.

Just after the training program was initially underway, in May of 1453, Team ten was recalled to Hailes Abbey to discover the source of a problem with the cheese making operations at the abbey. It seems a fresh batch of cheese made at the cheese works had developed a distinct odor and the abbot's first thought was that foul play was the cause of the problem.

When the team arrived back at the abbey and visited the cheese making facility on the adjoining grange they immediately smelled the pungent problem. It took a full two weeks to discover the cause, but by that time the batch of stinking cheese had pretty much become a favorite with those who participated in the dinners each night at the abbey so the search was redirected to see how another batch of cheese could be produced with the same stench.

It seems one of the monks had been sipping at a Perry crock and accidentally washed the curds of the last batch of cheese in Perry instead of the usual milk/water solution. The washed curds were ladled into the moulds before they reacted to the Perry wash and by the time the curing process was completed the entire batch smelled like a pile of dirty socks. However, as the monks and guests found out, the Perry encouraged bacterial activity in the cheese and produced the odor. It also made the cheese soft and creamy with a delicious flavor not as pungent as the odor.

Soon the abbey was producing more of the cheese and making it even more distinctive by washing not only the curds in Perry, but washing the rinds in Perry during the 6-8 weeks in which the cheese is allowed to cure. The nightly diners at the abbey soon began calling the cheese by the name "Bishop's Stinking Cheese," a name which has pretty well stuck ever since. One could not deliver a load of Bishop's Stinking Cheese in secret as anyone within a few feet of a cartload of the cheese could immediately identify what was being carried.

I would like to say that the cheese incident, which smelled to high Heaven, was over and done, but that was not the case. When word got out about the Bishop's Stinking Cheese, a delegation from a few miles south came to Hailes Abbey and asked for the donation of a "round" of the new cheese to use in a traditional "Cheese Rolling" contest held on a hillside near Stroud—since known as Coopers Hill.

When the delegation got a "whiff" of the cheese, they immediately invited the abbot to officiate at the contest and asked him to bring the cheese round with him. Thus, the abbot and the Green Rose team set out in late May for a short journey to Coopers Hill and the Cheese Rolling contest. The cheese followed along a good ways behind in a cart driven by a grumbling monk who kept sipping from a crock of Perry along the way. By the time the group reached a camping area near Coopers Hill, the monk was no longer grumbling and was, in fact, pretty happy about the whole trip and vowing to take part in the contest itself on the next morning.

There was quite a crowd gathered at the top of Coopers Hill just before the cheese rolling was to take place. The abbot was escorted to the top of the hill and was to give the signal to release the 8-pound round of cheese. A peasant woman was chosen from the crowd of onlookers to hold and release the cheese after the abbot refused that particular honor. About 100 or so people drawn from the villages of Gloucester, Cheltenham, and Stroud were eager to take part in the contest for which the cheese itself was the prize for the victor.

As near as Team ten members could recall, the object of the contest was to try and beat the rolling cheese to the bottom of the hill. What happened was pretty close to spectacular. When the abbot gave the signal, the peasant woman started the cheese rolling down the rather steep and rocky hill. The 100 or so contestants surged over the top of the hill in chase of the cheese. Incidentally, the record shows that the monk, suffering from a headache, did participate in the event. He tripped on the bottom of his robe about one-third of the way down the hill and promptly rolled into a large rock breaking his right arm. They had to bathe him in the creek—a job which fell to the abbot—before anyone was willing to set his arm and put it in a sling because he smelled so bad from his association with the cheese.

The other participants—men, women, and children—sustained

numerous bumps, cuts and bruises on the way down the hill after the elusive cheese, but no one was seriously injured. One of the more humorous incidents occurred shortly after the start when one of the race leaders tripped and fell and ten others in the pack behind him "wiped out" as a result.

The eventual winner was a young lass from the village of Stroud who happily accepted the now battered cheese round, which beat her over the finish line, as her prize. She was immediately hoisted upon the shoulders of the other contestants and proudly paraded around after her victory. It is not known whether or not her victory attracted suitors for her hand in marriage, but it would had to have been a pretty brave soul to approach her after she had carried the cheese around for awhile.

For several years after that, the abbot at Hailes was the honorary starter for the annual cheese rolling contest, provided he bring a round of Bishop's Stinking Cheese with him for the event. The Green Rose team, content to stand as observers at the event, marveled at the happenings and talked about it for months afterward. However, it should be noted that two of the Team ten squires participated in the event the following year, but didn't even make it to the bottom of the hill.

Only one other Team ten accomplishment was noted on the abbey records and this took place during the summer of 1454 when one of the lay workers, an artist, took a round slab of wood and painted decorations on it along with a familiar verse often recited by the monks at the nightly dinners at the abbey.

He brought it to the dinner and put it under his trencher. No one took much notice until it came time to recite the verse at the end of the meal and he pulled it out to assist in his recitation. Other monks and guests asked to see the painted slab and admired it greatly. Some asked him to make them one and this resulted in a new industry for the abbey.

The plates, or "roundels" as they became to be called, were quite popular and the abbey soon had some twenty or so lay volunteers working on painting roundels after the lay artist sketched in the design. They were sold at the abbey and business was brisk after each nightly meal when visitors saw many of the monks and guests using them during the meal.

Thus, the Green Rose Team ten spent the rest of its time, before the recall to St. Albans in April of 1455, supervising and improving the various abbey enterprises, military training, and security patrol system. The abbot was sorry to see the team depart and promised each of them safe sanctuary at the abbey should they ever be in need.

Chapter 19—Coming Together

After the Christmas 1454 recovery of his senses, King Henry VI, based upon the counsel of his Queen and advisors, removed Richard—Duke of York early the next year from his role as Protector of England. The Duke, returning to his castle in Northern England, where many of his followers were based, feared arrest and took steps to protect himself. This, in turn, raised the fears of the King's Lancastrian supporters who quickly became convinced that York and his followers intended to seize the throne.

In response, the King issued a summary order for York and his allies to appear before The King's Council to answer the accusations lodged against him regarding his intentions towards the throne. York now feared that if he were to attend such a command performance, the outcome for him personally would be imprisonment and/or death. Instead of obeying the royal summons, York began to gather an army from among his supporters.

The Green Rose spy system first picked up on the probable intention of the King towards the Duke of York sometime in February and immediately sent a special dispatch to all Green Rose teams as well as to the Duke of York. Although no immediate action was to be taken, all Green Rose teams were advised to stand ready for recall to St. Albans should the political landscape deteriorate.

As soon as York made clear his intention to ignore the royal command to appear before the King's Council, the Green Rose leader immediately issued the recall order advising all Green Rose teams to return to St. Albans immediately with "all their possessions." This prompted a series of quick "farewells" from the Cistercian abbeys and the travel across England of all ten of the teams, who by this time, had no need for guides. None of the teams, advised to travel in full armor and with weapons prominently displayed, encountered any difficulties in reaching St. Albans.

That there was no delay in either leaving the host abbeys or arriving at St. Albans was a tribute to the Ancient Templar Rule of Order, still governing the activities of most knights. This order reads, in part:

"In order to carry out their holy duties and gain the glory of the Lord's joy and to escape the fear of hell-fire, it is fitting that all brothers who are professed strictly obey their Master. For nothing is dearer to Jesus Christ than obedience. For as soon as something is commanded by the Master or by him to whom the Master has given the authority, it should be done without delay as though Christ himself had commanded it. For this said Jesus Christ through the mouth of David, and it is true: *Ob auditu auris obedivit mihi*—'He obeyed me as soon as he heard me.'" **(14)**

In a way, it is quite fitting that St. Albans was the headquarters site for the Green Rose Order. Not only was it close to the seat of government in London, but Alban was England's first martyr, dying for his faith around 209 A.D. Alban was a citizen of Verulamium, a Roman city located close to the present-day St. Albans, one of the most important and largest Roman sites in the country. **(15)**

Alban reportedly took in and sheltered a Christian seeking sanctuary from Roman persecution. As the story is told, Alban was so impressed by the prayer and witness of the stranger, that he accepted the Christian faith and disguised the visitor in his own cloak taking his place when the soldiers came. Alban was arrested and brought before the authorities. Despite torture, he would not renounce his new-found faith, and was condemned to die by beheading on a hill outside the city wall. **(15)**

The legendary part of the story is that ***roses*** sprang up under Alban's feet as he walked to his place of execution. Within a few years a shrine was built in his honor and quickly developed a reputation for miracle healings. Later the St. Albans monastery was founded by the Benedictine Order. **(15)**

St. Albans was well suited for defense behind it's thick walls, but several other significant buildings were located outside the walls.

After all the Green Rose teams had assembled, it was decided that only the main walled abbey was defensible in the event of an attack and that's where the efforts were concentrated. By this time the abbey had its own guards and mounted troops and the Bishop assembled these, told them of the possibilities of a coming conflict between the Duke of York and the King. He asked for volunteers to defend the abbey in the event of such a fight and to a man the assembled troops pledged their loyalty to the Bishop. There were fifteen mounted knights and forty-five foot guards among this detachment. These, coupled with the forty knights and forty armed bowmen squires of the Green Rose Order, made a formidable defensive unit for the abbey.

The Green Rose leader assigned his own Team 6, who was most familiar with the abbey, to direct the defense in the event of attack. For the next few days there were a number of preparations including stocking the abbey with food and water, locating defensive positions for the archers as well as foot soldiers, and situating one of the two now finished cannons in the Great Court aimed directly at the Great Gateway which served as the main entrance to the abbey grounds. The other cannon was kept in reserve in the Orchard area for use in the event intruders managed to breach the wall in other spots.

Trumpeters were called on to learn various signals to assemble the troops, to man the walls, to call in reserve squads and so forth and each man had to become familiar with those signals. The knights practiced various maneuvers, including the old Roman Infantry "wedge" formations that could be used to break through invading soldiers.

Some consideration was given to mounted patrols outside the abbey walls and these were finally set up in order to alert the defenders of the approach of any army. All-in-all it was quite a busy time.

There had been several meetings of the Green Rose Team itself to assess where those troops trained by each team were likely to be used. As it turned out most of the Green Rose trained troops joined the army of the Duke of York, but there were a few mounted groups that were likely to be among the King's troops. In reality, the team assessments turned out to be pretty accurate over the duration of the coming conflicts.

One of the meetings was called in the Chapter House at the abbey and involved the Green Rose plans for evacuation from England as soon as possible since the political situation made it no longer possible for it to operate without taking sides.

The Green Rose leader discussed the various options for the team members after first thanking them for their years of exemplary service and pointing out the accomplishments of the Order in the few years it had been operating in England.

Four basic options were offered. These included:

Option 1—Leave England and return to Scotland or the country of choice. For this ships were now "standing by" at ports in Yorkshire (for Scotland) and Hampshire (for Continental Europe).

Option 2—Members of the team, who chose to do so, could stay and fight along with the armies of the Duke of York. The Duke had personally tendered an offer for each Green Rose member to serve with distinction and in a leadership position in his armies. However, the Green Rose leader reminded, that was not the purpose of their work in England and not recommended by His Holiness.

Option 3—Those members who wished could join an established Holy Order either here in England or in another country. He reminded them that both the Cistercian Order and the Benedictine Order had offered sanctuary. St. Albans was the Benedictine site and two Cistercian abbeys—Hailes Abbey and an abbey in Wales—were open for team members.

Option 4—Those who wished could summarily leave the Green Rose Order and take up private citizenship in England with enough money to become landholders although they would not become a part of the nobility unless they rendered some important service to the King in the future.

Of the forty Green Rose knight's members, none chose Option 2. That was not because they were afraid to fight, but because it was contrary to the wishes of His Holiness. It is thought that about thirty of the knights opted to leave England. Of the remaining ten knights, four decided to join the Cistercian Order and seek sanctuary, one opted to remain at St. Albans with the Benedictine Order, and five decided to become landholders with grants provided by the Green Rose Order.

Among the forty Green Rose squires, half opted to leave the country under Option 1. The other half accepted the opportunity to become landholders under Option 4.

With that decided, each member was left to decide his own immediate plans once the defense of St. Albans was accomplished.

Chapter 20—First Battle of St. Albans

The pace of preparations for the defense of the St. Albans Abbey picked up after the 15th of May when it became visibly apparent that the Duke of York was planning to march on London. The Green Rose leader knew that King Richard would raise an opposing force and march north from London to meet his adversary and the likelihood of St. Albans being involved was very high indeed.

Team 6, directing the defense of the abbey, had five major considerations and these involved the four entrance gates to the walled abbey, the mill, and the orchard area which was the largest open space inside those walls. Of primary interest was the Great Gate and the inside courtyard known as Great Court as well as a large open space outside the gate known as Romeland (name derived from *room land*) meaning "open space." The road leading to this area was then known as Hockerhulle (later Romeland Hill). From past experience the abbot knew this was a danger area. Rebels had gathered in this area in 1381 prior to breaking into the Abbot's Prison located inside the Great Gate. **(16)**

Special defenses were allocated for this approach to the Great Gate in order to avoid a congregation of attackers in this area. Among the defenses were pots of oil which could be dumped and set afire, the cannon inside the Great Court in the event of a gate breach, and other defensive measures including storage of a large supply of throwing spears.

The mounted knights were separated into squads of five knights each and taught to operate in a synchronized way in order to protect themselves as much as possible yet deal a heavy blow to any invaders. In any foray outside the walls of the abbey, there would be three such teams sent at one time. These groups also were schooled in operating as teams.

One of the lessons learned by the Green Rose teams in training schools conducted all over the country was that knights were brought up and trained to "fend for themselves." Each fought as an individual under the Laws of Chivalry and it was comparatively easy to engage them in single combat while the bulk of the army surged right on past. The squad or team concept was quite new and the result was a more deadly and formidable attacking force.

Similar tactics were devised for each of the other "entrance areas" to the walled abbey with attention given to Holywell Gate on the far side of the Orchard area and Waxhouse Gate in the front wall. For the most part the archers were to be situated along the various walls with their horses tethered beneath them in the event of a concentrated attack on another part of the wall. The knights were to remain mounted in the center of the Orchard Area, where a stone enclosure was built to protect them and their animals from stray arrows, until they were needed. Their job was to break up any concentrated attacks outside the walls of the abbey using the side gates to launch their attacks on the flanks of the attackers. The archers would be detached to the walls above the fray to hit the attackers with a barrage of arrows.

One extra provision was made by the Green Rose leader and that was a special detachment trained to come to the defense of the oratory and chapel of St. Mary Magdalene located about 600 meters to the east of the abbey in the event troops from one of the invading armies tried to sack the structures. By this time all of the forty-five foot guards were armed with the new "exploding sticks," as they called them and were well schooled on how to use them. Each had a lay brother assistant who helped with the loading and "touching off" of the gun and this more than doubled the rate of fire from these weapons.

All of the abbey's defenders, not in full armor, were equipped with the new armored vests to protect their upper bodies as much as possible.

Although news of the formation of the two armies reached the abbey earlier, things did not become really tense until May 20th when reports were received that the Duke of York was nearing Ware, less than ten miles from St. Albans and the King's forces had left London and intended to camp at Watford on the following night.

Since leaving York, the Duke's forces had been marching down a main Roman road known as Erming street through Royston. When he learned that the King and Somerset were raising an army and advancing north along Watling Street, he moved on south to Ware after crossing the river at a ford just above the village. He encamped at Ware for the night. His forces, including those of Salisbury, Lord Clinton, Lord Grey of Powys, and Sir Robert Ogle, had linked up with those of Warwick and were estimated to be some 5,000 - 7,000 strong. In the meantime the King and his army had been proceeding north out of London along the old Roman road known as Watling street which led directly to St. Albans. The King had not had the time to summon responses from all of his peers and early estimates put the strength of his forces at about 2,000 - 3,000 men, about half the size of the Yorkists.

The King left Watford early on May 22 making for St. Albans. When York received word of the direction the King was marching, he moved his forces west from Ware towards St. Albans. Spies from each camp were keeping constant watch over each other's forces as were the scouts from the abbey at St. Albans. When King Henry VI got word that York had changed direction and was nearing St. Albans, his adviser, Buckingham, urged the king to push on to St. Albans where it would be safer to await reinforcement in the town rather than exposed in the countryside. Buckingham was convinced York would rather negotiate than fight and he also knew York's army was twice the size of his own.

When the Royal army marched into St. Albans on the morning of May 22nd, it found there was little remaining of the old fortifications that once surrounded the village—just a 13th century ditch known as Tonman Ditch. The King immediately ordered his soldiers to occupy the ditch and to build barricades to prevent the Duke's forces from accessing the marketplace. The King established his own camp in the marketplace itself.

Soon after the Royal arrival Buckingham, accompanied by a large contingent of mounted knights, appeared outside the Great Gate of the abbey and demanded to know which side the abbey would be taking in the looming battle. The abbot, accompanied by the Green Rose knight in full battle dress, met him at the gate and delivered the same message that Joshua heard at Jericho—"neither!" With that confirmation, Buckingham returned to the marketplace and supervised the establishment of the barricades.

Townspeople and merchants in St. Albans were soon stripped of anything wooden that could be used to fabricate barricades. In many instances this included the very doors to their homes or businesses, the wooden stalls in the marketplace, and every thing that could be moved to the ditch to form a barrier. Some of the townspeople were even forced into helping. It was a frantic effort.

When the Duke's forces arrived at St. Albans and saw the defensive measures being employed, he ordered his men to establish camp to the east of the village in an area known as Keyfield. He also put his men to work blocking all exits from the town on that side.

St. Peters Street was a wide street leading from the marketplace to the church of St. Peter where it turned into Bowgate. The properties along the east side of St. Peters Street generally extended east to Tonman Ditch. On the other side (western) of St. Peters Street the properties immediately north of the marketplace extended back to Dagnall Street until further north along St. Peters Street they extended back to Tonman Ditch on the west side of the old town.

The Waxhouse Gate to the abbey was the normal pedestrian entrance and it opened onto the south edge of the marketplace. Just outside the gate was the Great Cross which dominated the southern end of the market. It was completed in 1294 to honor the resting places of Queen Eleanor's body on its journey from Lincolnshire to Westminster in 1290. This cross was a focal point of the town and it was here that insurgents in 1381 burnt muniments taken from the abbey. It was also here the "heretical" books of the Lollard Walter Redhed of Barnet were burnt after he recanted in 1426/7. **(16)** This gate was heavily barricaded from inside the abbey and archers were stationed atop the wall overlooking the marketplace. They had a bird's eye view of the 1st battle of St. Albans which opened the Wars of the Roses. It was above this gate where Abbot Whethamstead stationed himself, along with the Green Rose leader, and both saw first hand what transpired.

York drew his army into three divisions which was pretty much the custom of the day. He commanded one division, Salisbury commanded a second division, and Warwick commanded the third division which was kept in reserve.

Similar to the thinking of Buckingham, who thought York would rather negotiate than fight, the battle was delayed for more than three hours while York made every effort to have King Henry listen to his complaints. He sent his messenger, Mowbray Herald, to enter the barrier probably at New Lane, just below the church of St. Peters. Mowbray was promptly challenged and word sent of the messenger to the King. Henry sent Buckingham, brother-in-law to Salisbury, to meet with Mowbray. Mowbray requested the King meet with York, who meant him no harm, but was asking that those in the Royal Court who had wronged him be brought to justice.

This attack on the Royal Court inflamed the King who ordered himself armored and raised his battle standard in the marketplace where he remained during the ensuing battle. The king's knights were expecting a long parley and many of them were not outfitted for battle and did not have time to become fully armored before the first attack came.

When York learned the King refused to accede to his demands, he put on his helmet and ordered his trumpeters to sound the alarm which warned his men the battle was about to begin. He then made a short speech to his men and the battle began.

York and Salisbury opened the attack from the east, leading charges along St. Peters street, Sopwell Street and other streets leading to the marketplace ordering their men to storm the barricades at the end of them. Lord Clifford and other Lancastrian commanders strongly defended the barriers at every entry while more Lancastrian troops rallied to the defense. York and Salisbury found themselves being pushed back. They regrouped and tried again, but still were unable to penetrate the barriers and the stout defense put up by the Lancastrians.

In the meantime, the Green Rose leader dispatched a monk on horseback to make contact with Salisbury leaving the abbey orchard through the Holywell Gate near the old fishponds. Upon receipt of the note, Salisbury led his troops to the south of the marketplace entering the town between the Sign of the Key and the Sign of the Checker in Holywell Street which paralleled the east wall of the abbey. Once inside the marketplace Warwick quickly arrayed his archers, sounded his trumpets, and his men assaulted the barrier defenders in an attack from the rear that sent them reeling.

Within half an hour it was over. Lancastrian defenders rushing to protect Henry were cut down mercilessly by the archers and swordsmen and the south end of the marketplace was red with their blood. The King's army, disliking the sight of blood, broke and withdrew in a stampede to escape knocking down and trampling underfoot the royal standard as they fled. The royal banner was propped up against the side of a house while Henry stood alone watching the fight as his men died and arrows rained down around him.

Warwick had instructed his archers to target those around the King—members of the hated Court Party—and many fell, mortally wounded, near the royal standard. The king himself received a minor wound to his neck when struck by a Yorkist arrow. He reportedly took refuge in the nearby house of a tanner.

Despite the bloodshed, estimates are that only from 60-100 were actually killed. Many nobles on the Lancastrian side, who took the brunt of Salisbury's charge, were killed or wounded.

Somerset had been engaged in a hand-to-hand fight just outside an inn named "The Castle" located on the northern corner at the intersection of Shropshire Lane. It is not known for sure who his adversary was, possibly Warwick, but legend has it Somerset had been warned earlier by a soothsayer to beware of castles. When he saw the name of the inn he apparently faltered leaving an opening for his opponent to make the mortal strike which killed him. He was later buried in St. Albans Abbey.

Buckingham was among those taken prisoner by the Yorkists. Outside the town, the victorious troops were causing havoc by rampaging through the streets looting as they went. Some approached the abbey, but were soon sent on their way when they realized the penalty for launching an attack. By this time the Green Rose Leader had dispatched his special team to the house and chapel of St. Mary Magdalene. The knights left via the Mill Gate crossing the fields to the chapel in time to ward off several troopers who were about to ransack the place. When they saw the Green Rose insignia on the shields, they immediately began to return to the marketplace. Some of them, it seems, had been trained by Green Rose teams and knew immediately the force they were facing.

By this time York had arrived in the marketplace and the King had also been located. York ordered his troops to assemble and get ready to march to London. Abbot Whethamstead requested York's permission to bury the dead and begged him to show mercy in his hour of victory, to which York complied. The Duke also personally acknowledged the help of the Green Rose leader before leaving.

Thus ended the 1st Battle of St. Albans; however, the deep diversions between the English magnates plus the widespread grievances against the government, could now only be settled by future violence.

Chapter 21—Epilogue

With political intrigue and succession to the Crown of England still in much dispute, the Green Rose leader immediately executed the plan of action for demobilizing the Green Rose presence in England as agreed earlier in the chapter house at St. Albans Abbey. Special dispatches were sent to the Pope in Rome sketching the outline of the plan, but no destinations for any of the Green Rose members were included in that plan.

At the final meeting of the Order before the first group departed St. Albans, the Green Rose leader acknowledged the contributions by awarding each member a cash purse designed to assist him in whatever his future plans were. The only exceptions to this were the five knights who had opted to join either the Cistercian or Benedictine Orders; however, each was given a cash gift to donate to the abbey where they were to seek sanctuary.

Many of those who decided to become landowners pooled their gifts and continued to work together. Others took their gifts and went their own way. Of the knights who decided to leave the country, all but two took their squires with them. Some already had landholdings in other countries and were simply returning home until the next occasion when their services were needed. The two squires left out immediately were invited by the Green Rose leader to accompany himself and nine other knights in a return to the abbey in Scotland. This party consisted of ten knights and twelve squires. It was the last to leave St. Albans.

Fortunately, the victory by the Duke of York brought a rather uneasy peace to the land which lasted until 1459 when the two sides renewed fighting. This permitted an uneventful evacuation from England for the Green Rose members and allowed those who chose to stay to become well established before the next conflict. It is reported that none of the former Green Rose members took part in any of the battles fought during the Wars of the Roses; however, each took measures to protect his land and this sometimes led to brief skirmishes.

It was quite a contingent of ten knights and twelve squires that left St. Albans on the 30th of May, 1455, and moved overland along the same Roman roads the Duke of York had used to bring his army to St. Albans. There were still signs along the roadways of the passing army including broken equipment, dead horses, and general trash. Because the group was quite mobile on horseback, including pack horses, it took just two days of hard travel to reach Whitby Abbey at the mouth of the River Esk. The same ship that had carried them from Scotland to England was waiting for them in the harbor below and, much to the surprise of the Green Rose leader, the same legate from the Pope was there to greet them along with the abbot.

"We are honored at our welcome," the Green Rose knight said. He and his men had just dismounted from their horses in the courtyard at the abbey when a contingent of monks led by the abbot and the legate came to meet them. The monks took charge of the others while the Green Rose leader strode forth to greet his friends.

"It is we who are honored to be in your presence," the legate replied.

"Your parents would be proud," responded the abbot.

"Will you be traveling with us to Scotland?" the monk asked the legate?

"It will be my honor. El Papa has asked me to convey his thanks to you and your men for an outstanding job. He has asked me to visit with you on your return journey to get your personal views of what has happened and what is likely to happen throughout Britain in the years to come. I will accompany you to Scotland and then return to Rome aboard the ship below. The captain also sends his greetings and is anxious to renew your acquaintance," the legate said.

"We will have a lot to talk about and I hope it will be informative," the monk replied.

With that they were all ushered into the abbey where a grand feast had been prepared since word had been passed down the line in advance of their arrival. After the dinner it was decided that all of the horses and equipment would be shipped to Scotland aboard the ship. The abbot instructed some of his monks to begin the process of loading the ship and suggested it would be best if the Green Rose team members and the legate all spent the night on board the ship as it was scheduled to leave with the early morning tide.

The monk took a few minutes to visit the grave of his parents on the hillside above the abbey. He found the gravesite lit with a candle lantern and learned the monks had been doing this ever since he had arrived back in England. He said his final goodbyes to his parents with the knowledge that it was not likely he would ever return. He then turned and descended on foot to the abbey where he thanked the abbot for his service and the attention paid to his parents. He then descended the long stairs down to the landing below and boarded the ship.

In just a few hours the ship was untied from the wharf and slowly began its return to Scotland and the Abbey Magdalena Rosa which the Green Rose leader now called home. It was an uneventful trip and the monk and legate spent most of the time together discussing the progress made and the problematic times that were ahead for England. It was interesting to note that the ship's captain ordered the bright yellow banner with the single green rose to be flown from the ship's mast throughout the entire journey.

It was a fairly cold day in early June when the crew reported landfall ahead and the small harbor on the west coast of Scotland came slowly into view with the massive structure of Abbey Magdalena Rosa looming above. As soon as the ship was sighted, a similar Green Rose banner was run up the flagstaff at the abbey. Most of the abbey occupants were at the small landing below when the ship finally docked.

The ship was quickly unloaded after greetings were exchanged with carts carrying the baggage and the Green Rose team mounted on its horses. The horses were pretty skittish after the long boat journey and some of the team had difficulty staying aboard. However, no one was embarrassed by being thrown off and all took that as a good sign. The Green Rose monk said his goodbyes to the ship's captain and the legate and watched while the ship gathered way and left the harbor. The captain dipped the Green Rose banner and then replaced it with the triple gold crown on white flag of the Pope. The abbey's banner was dipped in a return salute.

As it turned out, the legate's report to the Pope was to have some far reaching impacts upon the role of the church in England for the next eighty years or so until the Reformation. Key observations by the Green Rose leader, as reported to the Pope, included:

1. Should the wars between the Lancastrians and Yorkists continue, and that was most likely, it would lead to the eventual destruction of the feudal nobility of England;

2. Thus, the monarchy in England will grow and assume a much larger role in control of the country, providing it learns to:

    a. Prevent invasions from foreign lands;

    b. Keep internal and external foes apart;

    c. Prevent regular English troops from being used against the king; and

    d. Prevent domestic dissent from escalating;

3. The eventual outcome of the current conflict could lead to a more stable economic and political structure for the country, but result in a less powerful, but still important, role for the church;

    a. The Pope should be prepared to turn over monastic properties in a peaceful manner should that occasion arise in the future; and

4. The peasantry in England will become much stronger economically and play a larger political role largely gained through independence from landowners and increased earning power.

These words became almost prophetic as events turned out.

Of the points mentioned above, the last one was almost assured by the efforts of the various Green Rose teams in their establishment of peasant industries albeit mostly through the auspices of the various abbeys. The eventual outcome of these efforts was to teach the peasants they had the means and willpower to build their own futures. This is perhaps the greatest contribution by the Green Rose Order.

In the 1530's, nearly eighty years after the Green Rose efforts in England, King Henry VIII took homage when the Pope refused to grant him a divorce so he could remarry to assure succession to his lineage. This marked the beginning of the Reformation period which led to the dissolution and destruction of nearly all Cistercian monasteries in the country and most of the others. In the north of England, a staunch Catholic area, an uprising occurred demanding restoration of the monasteries, but it was short lived. Spearheading this rebellion were many of the descendants of the Green Rose-trained troops from the various cities and monasteries. The result led to the capture and death of the abbots at some of the monasteries that were most helpful to the Green Rose effort. And, it became apparent it was only a matter of time before such a fate would befall monasteries in other countries of the British Isles, including Scotland.

Shortly after his return to the Abbey Magdalena Rosa, the Green Rose leader had already foreseen the eventual destruction of the abbey and encouraged all to leave. Most took him up on the offer and moved on to other ways of life with many becoming persons of note in Scotland itself. No records exist to show just where the Green Rose knight went although rumors abound that he took ship for a foreign port.

When invaders finally got around to the destruction of Abbey Magdalena Rosa, about 1539, there wasn't much left except some crumbling walls and a few older monks who had stayed behind to serve as caretakers. They quickly surrendered without a struggle. Years later some tourists found an old map in one of the rooms at the abbey showing a rough division of England along with the various abbeys considered "headquarters" or "safe" and a list of assignments for ten separate teams.

That's about all the record that remains of the Green Rose Order at least that's in the public eye, but in some other circles there are notable signs of its existence. Even today in England some stained glass church and chapel windows still have a small green rose included. Roses are embossed on various altars and "small green men" are embedded in others.

All of this has led to some speculation about the Green Rose Order and especially the unnamed monk who headed it.

Some believe the Order was mainly composed of followers of Mary Magdalene and the *Gospel of Mary*. These people also ascribe to the belief that Mary Magdalene was the unidentified "Beloved Disciple" to whom the *Gospel of John* refers. Others believe the monk was an actual descendant of Mary Magdalene.

Another rumor, more persistent, tells of a famous Samarian warrior in the city of Laizhou in China, also known as the *Rose City*, who often worked with children giving those who excelled the gift of a "green rose." This city sports a number of industries of interest including gold mining, quarrying, salt making, beer production, wine making, straw plaiting, carving, leather working, and others traceable back to the industries promoted by the Green Rose efforts in England.

Who knows?

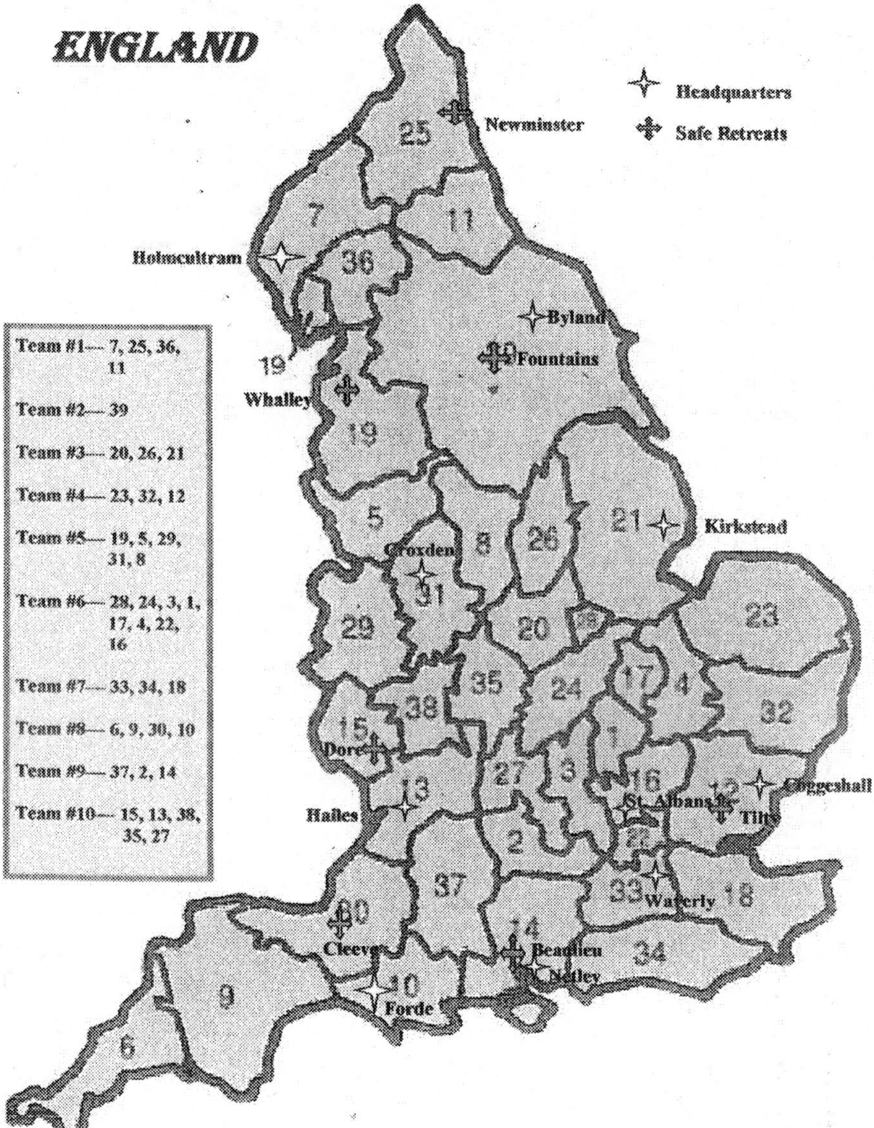

ENGLAND
Headquarters
Safe Retreats
Newminster
Holmcultram
Byland
Fountains
Whalley
Kirkstead
Croxden
Dore
Hailes
St. Albans
Coggeshall
Tilty
Waverly
Cleeve
Beaulieu
Netley
Forde
Team #1— 7, 25, 36, 11
Team #2— 39
Team #3— 20, 26, 21
Team #4— 23, 32, 12
Team #5— 19, 5, 29, 31, 8
Team #6— 28, 24, 3, 1, 17, 4, 22, 16
Team #7— 33, 34, 18
Team #8— 6, 9, 30, 10
Team #9— 37, 2, 14
Team #10— 15, 13, 38, 35, 27

Appendix I

Bibliography

1. Internet: www.newadvent.org, Pope St. Gregory VII.
2. Internet: www.newadvent.org, Papal Diplomatics.
3. Internet: www.newadvent.org, The Pope.
4. Internet: www.newadvent.org, Conflict of Investitures
5. Internet: www.rdrop.com, Rosa chinensis viridiflora.
6. Internet: www.phoenixmasonry.org, Flowers, Plants, Fruits, and Trees.
7. Internet: www.newadvent.org, Pope Nicholas V
8. Internet: www.ehistory.com, Universal History—The Modern World
9. Internet: www.britannia.com, The Benedictines
10. Internet: www.cistercians.shef.ac.uk, The Cistercian Order
11. Internet: www.chivalricorders.org/vatican, The Papal Orders
12. Book: *The Wars of the Roses*, by Alison Weir, Ballantine Books, division of Random House, Inc., NY, August 1995, pages 266-268.
13. Internet: www.hsbourne.co.uk/cheshire_cheese_history.com.
14. Internet: www.ordotempli.org/ancient_templar_rule_of_order.htm.
15. Internet: www.stalbans.anglican.org/history.htm.
16. Internet: www.salbani.co.uk/Med%20Web/dagnall_street.htm.

Printed in the United States
65001LVS00004B/98

9 781424 135066